r

i   - 4

: ١١٠ ،ҫ 9 FE:

A Rather English Marriage

Novels

Love Among the Single Classes
No Talking after Lights

Non-fiction

Unquiet Souls: The Indian Summer of the British Aristocracy
1939: The Last Season of Peace

ANGELA LAMBERT

A Rather English Marriage

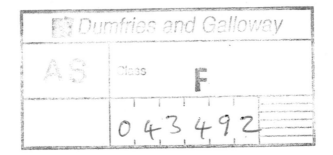

HAMISH HAMILTON • LONDON

HAMISH HAMILTON LTD

Published by the Penguin Group
Penguin Books Ltd, 27 Wrights Lane, London w8 5tz, England
Penguin Books USA Inc., 375 Hudson Street, New York, New York 10014, USA
Penguin Books Australia Ltd, Ringwood, Victoria, Australia
Penguin Books Canada Ltd, 10 Alcorn Avenue, Toronto, Ontario, Canada m4v 3b2
Penguin Books (NZ) Ltd, 182–190 Wairau Road, Auckland 10, New Zealand

Penguin Books Ltd, Registered Offices: Harmondsworth, Middlesex, England

First published 1992

1 3 5 7 9 10 8 6 4 2

The publishers wish to make acknowledgement to the following for permission to
reproduce copyright material: the extract from Hilaire Belloc's 'Lord Finchley',
taken from *Complete Verse* (published by Pimlico, a division of Random Century), is
reprinted with permission of the Peters, Fraser & Dunlop Group Ltd; the words
from the song 'Love and Marriage', by Sammy Cahn and Jimmy Van Heusen,
are reproduced by permission of Warner Chappell Music Ltd and the Sparta
Florida Music Group Ltd; the words from the song 'Smoke Gets In Your Eyes',
by Jerome Kern, are reproduced by permission of Polygram Music Publishing Ltd.

Filmset in 11/13 pt Monophoto Baskerville

Printed in England by Clays Ltd, St Ives plc

A CIP catalogue record for this book is available from the British Library

ISBN 0-241-13164-2

for Tony Price
my love, my love

Acknowledgements

I am grateful (yet again) to the incomparable Peter Scott, of Bertram Rota's antiquarian bookshop, whose knowledge of the first two world wars is unsurpassed and whose creative contribution to this book has been immense; and also to Dennis Sykes, friend and former RAF pilot. Both supplied me with detailed information about the jargon, aeroplanes and fighting tactics of the Royal Air Force during the Second World War. Without their expertise and gentle corrections this book would have been chock-full of howlers. Dennis also kindly lent me half a dozen cherished volumes about the RAF and allowed me to read an unpublished, fictional account of his own wartime experiences. I must also thank my solicitor, Rosalind Sopel of Townsends in Newbury, for her generous advice on the legal niceties of wills and things.

I read a great number of contemporary books about the RAF during the Second World War, in particular Eric Partridge's *Dictionary of RAF Slang* (Pavilion Books, 1990), and relied heavily for facts and dates on the excellent *Chronicle of the Second World War* (Longman, 1990). In the course of my research I learned about the courage of the RAF pilots and the Royal Engineers between 1939 and 1945. The characters in this novel, whatever their fictional shortcomings and attributes, do not reflect in any derogatory way upon those brave young men half a century ago.

It should not need saying that every character depicted in the book is imaginary, even though some of the locations are real and accurate.

Dramatis Personae

The ages given are those in June 1990, when the book opens.

REGINALD VIVIAN CONYNGHAME-JERVIS former RAF Squadron Leader, aged 71, born 1919, married 1942

MARIGOLD (MARY) ELIZABETH his wife, born 1922, died 2 June 1990

VIVIAN GERALD his nephew LORD BLYTHGOWRIE, 3rd Baron; aged 54, born 1937, inherited title 1949

SUSAN Vivian's second wife, aged 43

CELIA aged 26, and FELICITY, aged 26, Vivian's twin daughters from his first marriage, born 1964

ROYSTON WILLIAM SOUTHGATE aged 71, born 1918, married 1939

GRACE EDITH his wife, aged 69, born 1920, died 2 June 1990

ALAN his son, aged 43, born 1948, married 1973

JUNE Alan's wife, aged 39

WILLIAM ALAN *(Billy)* aged 10

JOSEPH ROY *(Joe)* aged 8; Alan's sons, Royston's grandsons

GLORIA June's illegitimate daughter, aged 20

SHEILA Alan's girlfriend, aged 35

VERA aged 45, born 1946; Royston's married daughter, living in Australia with her husband Stan and two teenage sons

MOLLY TUCKER aged 68, friend of Royston and Grace Southgate

ELIZABETH FRANKS aged 51, divorcée, dress shop owner and Reginald's girlfriend

ALICIA *(Lissy)* Liz's daughter, aged 27

MANDY HOPE aged 29, social worker to Reginald and Royston

MRS O'MURPHY Reginald's cleaning woman
MRS 'AGGIE' ODEJAYI another cleaning woman

JAMES TIDMARSH aged 54, a solicitor
CONSTANCE LIDDELL aged 50, a librarian
SABRINA a London prostitute
WHITTINGTON a bank manager

Chapter One

'I am afraid your wife is not at all well.'

Reginald Conynghame-Jervis and Roy Southgate had just been given the same news in the same words, although in separate interviews. Reginald had looked at the doctor and thought, Stupid blighter; I could have told him that. Roy Southgate had understood correctly that his wife was dying. Now both were in the small ante-room that served as a visitors' waiting-room while their wives were being 'tidied up', as Sister had put it with a twinkle.

The view across the lawns that sloped up the side of the Kent & Sussex Hospital showed that there was no money to spare for the garden. The grass was neatly trimmed, but there were no flowers, no borders, no shrubs. Only the black railings of the fire escapes relieved the expanse of incandescent mid-summer green. In a far corner stood a small circular temple crowned with a green dome, like a folly from some rich man's estate. God knows what it's doing there, thought Reggie Conynghame-Jervis. He stubbed his cigarette into an overflowing ashtray and said, 'Ridiculous! Giving them dinner at five-thirty! It's just for the convenience of the nurses. No one seems to think about the *patients* any longer. So much for your ruddy NHS.'

The other person in the room – it was on the late side for afternoon visitors, and too early for the evening batch – was a small, mild bespectacled man whom Reggie had seen several times previously. 'Oh, I don't know. They're wonderful, really. Angels. Just young girls. Some of them aren't yet twenty. They go off at six, you see. Best to get tea over before then.'

'That's what I said. All done to suit the staff. You smoke?'

'Not for me, thanks all the same.'

Reggie snapped open a square silver cigarette-lighter,

inhaled, and coughed irritably. 'Never used to have this trouble with the old Player's Navy Cut. God knows what kind of rubbish they put into them nowadays.' He sat down, and his guttural breathing filled the silence.

Ten minutes later a nurse, older and more senior than the angels, came in, beckoned the smaller man to follow her, and swished away towards Sister's office. She handed him in and closed the door behind him.

'Sit down, Mr Southgate,' Sister said. 'Make yourself comfortable. Now then.'

Roy Southgate looked at her with docile expectancy.

'Your wife isn't eating. We've done our best to tempt her. Special diets. Soft food, but nourishing. She must eat, you know.'

'Why?'

'Well, to keep her strength up.'

'But it tires her to eat, and then she mostly just brings it back up, and that tires her even more.'

'Yes. Well. We could try intravenous. Feeding her through a tube.'

'Why?'

'Because she's got to *eat*. Look, Mr Southgate, your wife isn't getting any better.'

'No.'

'She's receiving very powerful medication.'

'She's not in pain though, is she? Not any more?'

'No, she isn't in any pain.'

'I'd better go and sit by her, then. She knows I'm there. She can tell it's me.'

'I'm sure she can.'

Grace Southgate had shrunk and curled and become almost transparent, like a fallen leaf; and like a leaf, she quivered with each breath. Her lips were the colour of water, but dry and flaky. Her eyebrows jumped and fluttered nervously, as though she were dreaming.

'Let me try and peel a grape for you, dear,' said Roy. 'Then I'll put it between your lips and perhaps you could just suck it. They're nice, these grapes. Very sweet.'

He held the glistening grape against her mouth, but she only turned her head fretfully.

'Not for now, eh? All right then, dear. I'll not force you.'

'I'm going off now, love!' called a cheerful black nurse. 'See you tomorrow, eh?'

'I'll be here,' Roy Southgate said, and turned back to the husk on the bed.

On the other side of the corridor, in a small side ward, Reginald Conynghame-Jervis fidgeted, stood up, sat down, looked at his wife's Patient Record, hooked it back over the end of the bed, and thrust his hands into the pocket of his tweed jacket to touch his cigarettes and scratch his balls covertly.

'Better slip out before the hospital shop closes,' he said. 'Getting a bit low on fags.'

His wife smiled tiredly and murmured something.

'What?' said Reggie, leaning closer. 'Can't hear. What d'ye say?'

'Be some in the pub . . .'

'Dare say you're right. Do with a drink. How's the time?'

Mary Conynghame-Jervis closed her eyes and shifted slightly on the hot pillow. She could feel the hair in scrawny tangles at the back of her head. She opened her eyes again and looked at her husband.

'Reggie,' she whispered. 'Reg . . .'

'What is it? Anything you need? Call a nurse, shall I?'

'Shirts. Still got plenty of clean shirts?'

'Fine, fine.'

'Look after yourself properly . . .'

'Manage till you get back. Won't be long now. You just get better.'

He shifted the vase on the bedside table an inch and then moved it back. The fruit bowl was overflowing with grapes, stout red apples, spotty pears and something exotic the greengrocer had urged on him. Its sweetish, over-ripe smell filled his nostrils. He rummaged for a cigarette again.

'You want the wireless? Shall I put your headphones on? *ITMA? Forces' Favourites?*'

She smiled, with an effort, for an instant, and shook her head.

'Do go now,' she said. 'Bit tired.'

Reginald Conynghame-Jervis and Roy Southgate found themselves walking through the main entrance of the hospital together, just as other visitors were arriving in family groups.

'All well, eh?' said Reggie. 'Things looking up?'

Roy Southgate could not bring himself to nod. 'How is your . . .?' he asked.

'Wife? Oh, fine, fine. Right as rain soon.'

A week later, in the small hours, Tunbridge Wells was in darkness. Only the street lights outlined the tracery of its town plan, the curving roads sloping steeply downhill to the old, cobbled heart of the town; the brighter lights along the railway glinting on the sweep of track as it looped towards the centre and out again. Among the sleeping houses a few illuminated windows showed where, behind drawn curtains, young mothers bent over their infants; lovers enlaced; and workaholics lay awake worrying.

High on the hill above the town a crossword puzzle of lighted windows outlined the hospital buildings. At the central desk in Number 3 Women's Ward a student nurse drooped over her notebook. The sound of groaning, deep-drawn breaths roused her. Her head jerked upright. She stood up, and walked fast to where Mrs Southgate lay in bed 7. She was drawing long, slow, excruciating gasps of air, her face contorted with effort. The young nurse hurried back to the desk and picked up a telephone. 'Doctor! Can you come, please. It's Mrs Southgate in Women's 3. Acute respiratory and cardiac distress. I didn't want to disturb you, but . . .' Her voice trailed away as she realized that the houseman had already put the receiver down.

Minutes later he appeared, still tousled, but purposeful and clear-headed. The nurse led him to where Grace Southgate lay. The harsh jugular wheezing had stopped; instead, she was trying to sing to herself in a tenuous voice, frail as a cobweb:

4

'Sleep, my baby, sleep so softly,
While your Mummy watches o'er you . . .
Dum dum dum de dum and harm you –
Slee-eep, oh sleep, my son.

'Freddy,' she murmured. 'Go to bye-byes, there's a good
baba.' She looked up at the doctor as he stood over her, his
hand cradling her pulse. 'Oh doctor, I'm ever so sorry. I got
you out of bed, didn't I?' she said.

'Shush-sh. Not to worry. Just checking you over,' said the
doctor.'Quick listen to your chest, hmm?'

He bent over her as the nurse swished the curtains shut
around the bed. Mrs Southgate undid her nightdress obediently to reveal the grey and bony bosom that only her husband
and children and a few other doctors had ever seen. The skin
fell away in fine pleats, the breasts were long, almost empty
folds from which pale blue nipples hung limply. Beneath her
skin the tracery of veins ran its gnarled course, and beneath
them curved the skeletal shield of her ribcage.

'Breathe *in* . . . and out,' said the doctor. 'And again for me.
In . . . and out. Once more. *In* . . . and out again. Good. Not
too easy, is it? Would you like some oxygen, or do you think
you could sleep now?' She nodded, and he buttoned up the
front of the nightdress and folded the bedclothes gently back
in place.

'Like another little pill to help you?'

'I'm not –' Mrs Southgate was seized by racking, primeval
gasps which rose to a crescendo of extraordinary noise. Her
eyes were squeezed shut by the violence of her struggle for air.
'Oxygen!' snapped the doctor, and the nurse hurried off, her
shoes squeaking rapidly on the highly polished vinyl floor.
Other patients muttered querulously, half woken from sleep.
With the deep instincts of women who have once been
mothers, they struggled towards consciousness. Somewhere, it
seemed, a child needed seeing to . . . oh not now, not again,
let me sleep, I'm so tired . . . I'll come in a minute, my
poppet. A bell buzzed for attention at the nurses' desk, but

5

they were short-staffed and it was a while before anyone had time to answer it.

By the time its source was traced and the tall Irish nurse had gone to the side ward she found that, quietly, considerately, not wanting to bother people when they had more important things to do, Mary Conynghame-Jervis had died.

Reginald sat in a different waiting-room wearing a plain white shirt and his funeral black tie. He had to see the senior social worker at the hospital ('In your day she would probably still have been called an almoner,' Sister had explained patiently). He also had to collect the overnight case with his wife's last few possessions from the hospital: a flowered pink sponge-bag containing Elizabeth Arden's Blue Grass toilet water, a still-damp face flannel and the soaking solution for her false teeth; a couple of limp nightdresses; and the old lizard-skin handbag from Mappin & Webb that he'd given her for Christmas fifteen years ago.

Sitting in the same waiting-room was the little man who'd been hanging around the ward all week. Reggie snapped open his *Daily Telegraph*, folded it back under itself and stared at it. Index, it said; Appointments; Weather. The words ran together in a nonsense jingle. Indexa pointmen swether. In sex disappointment ever. In depths miss the point forever.

The Irish nurse who had probably been the last person to see Mary alive had passed him no comforting message, no tender last words. She had asked him whether Mary knew someone called Cecil.

'Your wife had been dozing on and off, and in her sleep she seemed to be talking to Cecil Tushing – that's who it sounded like. "Cecil," she was saying. You know who that was, I expect. Family member, would it be?'

'We don't know anyone called Cecil,' Reggie had told her crossly. 'You must've heard wrong.'

'I dare say I did,' the nurse had agreed tiredly. 'Afraid I can't be any more help, then.'

'I'm ever so sorry.'

Reginald looked up. The chap in the corner must have spoken.

'About your wife. So sorry.'

'Ah. Yes. Not at all. Very good of you. Well, well. Comes to us all. Nice weather, eh?'

'My dear wife Grace passed away as well, just a few hours later. I know how you feel. Very sorry.'

'Ah. Really? Rotten show.'

Dear wife Grace, he thought. Bloody silly name. Sounds like that – what was that cat book he used to have to read to his great-nieces? Da-*da*-da and his dear wife Grace. Orlando, that was it. Orlando and his dear wife Grace. The fellow was still looking at him.

'You got any offspring? You know, children?' said Reginald abruptly.

'Our girl's in Australia. Sydney. She's flying home for . . . well, for the funeral . . . We had a little lad, but he . . . well, he . . . How about you?'

'No, no, nothing like that,' said Reginald, and he turned pointedly back to his newspaper.

The door of the social worker's office opened.

'Mr Southgate? Do come in. I'm so sorry to keep you waiting. And you must be . . .?'

'Squadron Leader Conynghame-Jervis.'

'Of course you are. Oh dear. Give me quarter of an hour and I'll be with you' – she paused – '. . . Squadron Leader.'

Roy Southgate sat upright in the hard chair, wearing a shiny suit with wide lapels that could almost have been his demob suit. His shoes were highly polished, the laces securely tied in a double knot. He was attentive and perfectly composed; only his eyes were red, and his face looked as though a tracery of cracks and mould had spread across it, like the glaze on a fine old plate.

'Now then,' the middle-aged woman was saying in a weary voice that struggled to remain kind. It was a well-rehearsed formula. 'I can give you a very useful check-list of things that have to be done. Not just the obvious – you say you've already been in touch with a funeral director – but things like getting your pension book altered; cancelling subscriptions to magazines – those sort of details.'

'Grace liked a good book now and again, but not those women's weekly things,' said Roy Southgate. 'And the post office – well, they'll know straightaway, being so local. They've been ever so kind, asking after her.'

'What about a home help? I dare say you'd like me to arrange for someone to come in temporarily, just to start you off, show you the ropes.'

'There won't be any need for that,' he said. 'I can look after myself. I'm no stranger to dustpan and brush. And I can cook. What with Grace not being well these last months, I looked after the both of us and kept the house spick and span. There's many another must be needing home help more than me.'

The woman smiled. He's not a helpless little old man at all, she thought; how wrong it is to judge by appearances. He'll manage splendidly, if he does his grief-work properly and doesn't try to repress it.

'What about . . . counselling?' she asked.

'I beg your pardon?'

'Grief – bereavement counselling. It can be very helpful, you know. Help to let your feelings out. I could give you some phone numbers. CRUSE, for instance: they're not just for widows. Someone you can talk to.'

His faded eyes filled with tears, which ran out at the corners and made a shining line through the furrows beside his nose.

'Grace and I always talked. I don't think I could get the hang of it with anyone else. There's others maybe, calling for that sort of thing, but not me. Thanks all the same. I appreciate the kind thought.'

He reached into his pocket for a handkerchief and tidily wiped his face.

'You can come back to me any time, any questions, problems, just give me a ring or pop in.'

'I'm much obliged,' said Mr Southgate with dignity. 'If I

could just collect her things, I needn't trouble you any longer.'
He nodded and smiled at her, took the photocopied list which
she extended towards him across the desk, and left the office.

Reggie was on the telephone. 'I'm going to spell that for you,'
he said, with his habitual mixture of pride and exasperating
slowness. 'No, not CUN: it's C-O-N-Y-N-G-H-A-M-E and
then the hyphen and then pronounced Jarvis but spelt J-E-R-
V-I-S. Old family name and all that. Read it back to me,
would you, there's a clever girl, so I can make sure you've got
it right?'

He nodded, tightening his lips at each letter as she read
them out . . .

'*I* don't know how it's supposed to be worded!' he expostulated, frowning into the telephone. 'Not allowed to say "died",
eh? Thought that's what Deaths columns were all about.
Never done one of these things before. Mary took care of all
that kind of nonsense. Conynghame-Jervis, Marigold – no,
she'd tell me off – better make it: Mary, wife of Reginald, and
then the date, I suppose . . .

'*Where* she died? What difference does that make? Oh all
right . . . Flowers? Well of course people will send flowers.
Look here, I'm not paying your chaps any more money. Just
the name and date and place, d'you hear? Oh, and where the
funeral will be. People will want to come and pay their last
respects. Put King Charles the Martyr. It's very well known
in Tunbridge Wells. They'll find it . . .

'*My* address? It's not *me* that's died . . . The bill? Ah yes, of
course; got to make sure you collect your baksheesh.'

The young woman in the classified advertising department
of the *Daily Telegraph* was patient. Deaths were always the
worst. Either people broke down in floods of tears and told
her what a marvellous man he'd been and how much everyone
had loved him; or she got this disoriented, unfocused anger.
Slowly, she repeated the address back to the poor old fogey,
thinking, Fancy still calling himself Squadron Leader! The
war's been over for fifty years or whatever.

'The Cedars, Nevill Park, Tunbridge Wells, Kent. Yes, I've got that, Squadron Leader, thank you. And you don't want "dearly loved" wife or anything? Very well. Please accept my condolences.'

A few days later, Roy Southgate slipped into the church of King Charles the Martyr and chose a seat in the upper gallery where he would be unseen but could look down on the congregation. From that high vantage point he saw that the grey and white marble tiles on the floor of the old church were exactly like the vinyl tiles on the floor of the hospital ward; and this piercing memory – for every detail of Grace's last surroundings stung cruelly – made his eyes fill with tears. He creaked to his knees and bent his forehead on to his knuckles. 'Look after my dear wife Grace, and this woman, Mary,' he prayed, adding 'Of thine everlasting goodness, Amen.'

The church was not crowded. There were barely enough people to fill the first two pews at the front of the church. Above their heads the magnificent plasterwork ceiling was a riot of curving, scrolling tracery. Fruit and flowers, angels and cherubs cavorted joyously around its deep inlaid ovals, like dolphins in a brilliant sea. Above that, from the octagonal tower, the church bell tolled its monotonous single note. At eleven o'clock the coffin entered, borne upon the shoulders of four pall-bearers, followed by the vicar in a white surplice, behind him the minimum complement of the choir, and behind them, straight-backed, eyes fixed rigidly ahead, expressionless, the Squadron Leader. The organ had switched to 'Fight the Good Fight'. The choir sang, the congregation quavering in its wake.

'Let us pray,' said the vicar, and with a soft rustle the people in the front pews sat down.

Roy Southgate sank unseen to his knees, letting the tears pour down his face yet again. The healing words drifted like snowflakes over him: 'Man that is born of woman hath but a short time to live, and is full of misery.' Well, she'd been lucky. She hadn't been full of misery, his Grace, except for that awful time when the baby had died. They'd shared that and come through it, though they'd never understand; but now he was grieving alone. They had loved each other, till death them did part.

He tried to pray for this other woman, glimpsed through the door in the little room off the ward, unknown; but his thoughts would keep stealing back to Grace.

'Stand up! Stand up for Jesus!/Ye soldiers of the Cross!' bellowed Reginald lustily at the front of the church. 'Lift high his royal banner,/It must not suffer loss.' He knew all the words and, conscious of being the centre of attention, he squared his shoulders, threw back his head and roared through his favourite hymn. Jolly good show, he thought to himself, that's what they'll say. Good old Reggie, put on a jolly good show. Taking it well. Still a fine figure of a man. Marry again, I dare say. They'd better not say it to my face – he jutted his chin a fraction higher – or start any of that damned match-making. Women yammering and fussing around. The last words he could remember Mary saying to him had been, surely, 'Are you still all right for clean shirts, dear?' Not much there for a chap to hang on to. He'd taken the last clean white shirt to wear today. He glanced down. Funny to think that her hands had ironed it; well, hers or Mrs Whatsit, Murphy, and now . . . He lifted his chin again. Brace up! he thought sternly, you're on parade!

After the cremation people hung around expectantly for a bit before shaking his hand or clapping him on the back, looking rather harder into his eyes than felt comfortable, and drifting uncertainly away. 'Be in touch, old man,' the men said; and their wives murmured, 'Dear Reggie, now remember, give me a ring *any time* you need cheering up!'

No fear, thought Reginald. Just as I expected, match-making already. Some unmarried sister to foist off on me, some miserable old spinster looking for a husband. Not bloody likely. He stuck out his hand to ward off a peck on the cheek.

'Jolly good turn-out,' he said. 'Mary'd have been pleased. Good of you to come. Long way. Appreciate it, very much.'

11

A few yards away, just out of earshot, the vicar hovered obsequiously at the edge of a family group. 'Er, excuse – if I might – forgive me, Lady Blythgowrie?' he inquired.

Susan turned, icily, and, seeing who it was, bestowed a perfectly modulated smile. 'My dear vicar! What a very moving service. You knew dear Mary well, of course . . . that was obvious from your tribute. Just the right words. We were so fond of her – the girls especially.'

'We *adored* Aunt Mary,' said one of the girls, with real warmth. 'We're going to miss her dreadfully.'

Ah, thought the vicar: good sign. He pressed on.

'I did just *wonder* whether, you know, anything had been *planned*? Next, I mean? People are starting to drift away . . .'

'Oh?' she said, with a sound that encompassed four out of the five vowels. 'You mean, *drinks*?'

'Well, yes, and perhaps something to nibble,' said the vicar.

'*I* haven't organized anything,' said Susan Blythgowrie, thinking, Reginald's an infernal nuisance. Isn't he capable of doing anything right? Little enough to ask, one would have thought. Plenty of local hotels, presumably. All it takes is a quick call to the catering manager. 'I haven't been told of anything. Vivian, darling, why don't you go and ask Reginald what's been laid on next?'

'Wake, you mean?' said Vivian. 'Oh don't look like that, Susan. I was only teasing. Right-ho. Girls! Is one of you going to come along and make this easier for me? Flicky?'

Poor old Uncle Reg was standing by himself, looking, his nephew thought with a pang, more than a little disconsolate. Maybe it *was* up to Susan to have checked that something had been arranged.

Reginald hadn't given the matter a thought. Had he done so, he would have assumed that Vivian or that tiresome second wife of his – never could remember the woman's name, why did he have to marry again and confuse matters? – Susan, that was it: Susan would have organized something afterwards. *He* couldn't be expected to do it – chap on his own. Woman's job, all that – making out lists, ringing round, organizing victuals. Might have given him a tinkle, swung into action, offered to take over.

He looked up civilly as Vivian and his daughter approached, both entirely proper in deepest black. The two girls had blubbed like babies. Never cared that much about Mary while she was alive, surely?

'Uncle Reg,' Vivian began. 'Deepest sympathy. All went off splendidly, I thought – good service, lovely old church. Vicar spoke well, thoroughly decent chap, he seems. What have you got in mind now? Some sort of a gathering? Up at the house, a hotel, anything like that?'

'Hadn't thought about it,' Reginald said, biting back the automatic response: That kind of thing's Mary's department. He frowned at his nephew. No good looking at him like that. Too late now. 'Afraid not.'

'Not to worry,' Vivian reassured him. 'Not a drama. Care to come back to London, join us for dinner tonight? Shouldn't be left on your own, should he, Felicity?'

'I shouldn't have thought so. Come on, Uncle Reggie, we'd really like it if you did,' the girl urged, nicely enough.

'Not this evening, thanks all the same,' Reginald said.

They turned away, duty done. 'Well, we tried,' Vivian told Susan, as the chauffeur pulled away smoothly in the company Rolls. Reginald watched them go with resentment. Bloody cushy number, he thought. All the gubbins. He turned as a tremulous hand was laid on his arm.

'Dear, *dear* Mary . . .' said Mrs Thing, Mary's friend (bloody woman, what *was* her name? one of the Pennys), and the black flowers nodded tremulously in the brim of her hat.

The last of the small group made its way past the tranquil pool and across the crazy-paving that surrounded the crematorium, back to where the cars were parked. Reginald would have liked to say 'Care for a snifter?' to old Harry, whom he hadn't seen for – what? Must be a good ten years, more, probably; but Harry was in a wheelchair, and, after expressing the bare minimum of condolences, Harry's hatchet-faced wife had steered him purposefully away.

'Decent of you to make it, old boy,' Reggie called out after him, and Harry lifted a hand from the metal arm of the chair to parody a feeble salute, but without turning round.

The hushed groan of recorded organ music inside the chapel was switched off and attendants moved about soft-footedly, preparing for the next service and avoiding his eye. Reggie, glancing in, realized there was still someone sitting there. Good God! It was that chap from the hospital – little bloke – what was his name?

'Care for a snifter?' said Reggie Conynghame-Jervis.

'Best wife a chap ever had,' Reginald was saying, for the third or fourth time that evening. This was a new audience.

'Never had a crossword. Cross word.' The barmaid pulled a sentimental face at his companion, a man in a toupée accompanied by a blurred blonde. *Buried today*, she mouthed at them elaborately, not that Reginald would have noticed.

'Marriagizza wonderful instution,' he went on. 'Thoroughly recommend it. Man needs a wife. "Love an marriage love an marriage/Goto getherlika norsan carridge." What was that show? West End. Not long ago. What *was* it called?'

'Dunno love,' said the blonde. 'Never mind. Know the song. "Can't have one wivout the o-o-other." Try telling *him* that.'

'Buy you a drink?' asked Reggie.

'You got any kiddies, mate?' asked the toupéed man, generous over his double Scotch. 'Need a family, time like this, know what I mean?'

'Gotta boy, bigbadboy,' Reggie told him.

'Well, that's nice. Is he a good boy? Looks after 'is old Dad?' the blonde asked cosily.

'Bad lad. Always poking into places he shouldn't go.' Reginald smirked. 'Always after the girls. Pretty girls,' mind you. Doesn't go for trollops.'

The blonde looked uncertain, but the barmaid said, 'Go on. Getaway with you.'

'He does,' Reginald insisted. 'Gets away with it timenagain.

Don't know how he does it. Must be because he's such a big lad.'

'How old is he, then, your boy?' the blonde asked with interest.

'Ooh, now, that'd be telling, wouldn't it?' said Reggie in retreat. 'Not too old for you, I wouldn't say. He likes blondes. You wanta meet him?'

'Time now, gentlemen please,' said the pub manager; and then, seeing Reginald, 'You gonna keep an eye on him?'

'Never seen him before in me life,' said the toupéed man. 'He a regular?'

'No,' said the barmaid. 'Poor old sod. Wife just died. Families today, *I* don't know. Here!' she said, leaning close to Reggie. 'You OK to get home? You live far? Where's your son? Give 'im a ring, should I, get 'im to pick you up?'

'No idea,' said Reggie, leering at her briefly. 'Take me home with you. Call us a cab. Home, James . . . and twice round Hyde Park, if you please.'

'*Time* now, gentlemen, *please!*' called the manager more loudly, and the blonde and her companion drained their glasses.

'Got a pretty decent vehicle outside,' Reggie was telling the barmaid. 'Mercedes. F-reg. Not half bad, not at all, at all, at all.'

'You're not driving anywhere,' said the barmaid. 'Just you leave it to Maggie. Not *her*, pet. Me. I'll look after you. There's a good boy.'

She slipped over to a corner of the room where the landlord was loading a tray with empty glasses smudged with froth. 'He was here at opening time, him and a little bloke. Never seen either of 'em before,' she said, gesturing towards Reggie, who leaned, red-faced, along the bar as though confiding in someone behind it. 'Other bloke went hours ago, and this one's in a shocking state. Not safe on the road.'

The man sighed. 'Get him a taxi. Let's hope he remembers his address.'

'I don't like to let him go home alone. He's been telling everyone it was his wife's funeral today.'

'Don't be daft, Maggie. You'd be wasting your time. That one'll never make you a rich widow. And the glasses need fetching. Taxi'll be here any minute now, squire,' he said, raising his voice, and then looked away as he saw that Reginald was crying.

He was crying for his youth, and Mary's. For the exciting days when life had been worth living and death worth dying. He couldn't remember the names of his wife's best friends, but he remembered every detail of those days.

It was the winter of 1940/41, when Reginald was flying Spits over Europe. The officers' mess was a fug of masculine noise and laughter, redolent of hot sweaty uniforms, beer, pipe smoke and Capstans. Pearls of perspiration crept down the mirror behind the bar, the stuffy emanations of several rowdy young airmen. The barman was shiny with effort as he pulled pints of beer or pushed up the nozzles of inverted bottles to squirt large whiskies or gins. Young men in Air Force blue crowded along the bar's puddled length, while others lounged in deep leather chairs or shouted across low tables. At one end of the room hung a large portrait of the King and below that, scattered over a long table, were several magazines, including *Country Life*, *Illustrated London News*, *Lilliput's* and *Picture Post*. Dog-eared copies of *Men Only* were all in use. On the opposite wall were arranged a number of proficient caricatures of Air Force types, several formal group photographs of the squadron (some joker thumbing his nose and grinning from the right-hand end of the back row) and a number of aerial shots of aeroplanes: a formation of Spitfires flying just above the cloud level, a row of aircraft on the ground, each flanked by its crew, and a single Hurricane in flight photographed from above, a grid pattern of fields and coastline just visible thousands of feet below. These pictures, like the mirror, were fogged behind a beading of moisture.

From one table rose the deep sound of singing:

> 'My bomber came down in the ocean,
> My bomber was lost in the sea,

Where it lies I just haven't a notion:
Oh bring back my bomber to me . . .'

More voices joined in, roaring:

'Bring back, bring back,
Oh bring back my bomber to me, to me . . .'

The voices were those of a bomber crew holding their own among the fighter boys after having made an emergency landing. They were now being treated to the hospitality, and general mockery, of a very different variety of Air Force types. The mess steward wove between tables collecting empty glasses and passing a damp rag across their glass-covered surfaces.

'Bring us another round, there's a good chap,' called one of the young men, and, looking up at the new arrival, he added, 'What's yours, old man?'

'Pint of booze-wine'll do to start with,' said Reggie Conynghame-Jervis.

'Sir,' said the mess steward.

'Tiger piss,' said the man who was buying. 'What kept you?'

'Better be the late arrived than the dear departed,' said Reginald. 'Been going over the Met reports with Tuppy. Tomorrow's rained off. Official.'

'Close the hangar door, C-J,' one of the others ordered cheerfully as Reggie settled his narrow blue-trousered buttocks on to the wide leather arm of his chair. 'What's the bogle outlook for Saturday night?'

From the next table came snatches of conversation: 'I gave him a squirt and he broke up. Straight in the drink.' And from the other side, the end of a story: 'So I said, "Built for comfort, lady, not for speed, but if it's speed you're after . . ." And then by crikey I speeded her up, tinkered with the top hamper and ground her down carbobloodyrundum!'

A shout of laughter surrounded the mess steward as he bent over the table to set down fresh glasses. They lifted their drinks.

'Bung ho all,' said Reginald.

'Here's to yours, Reggie, old boy,' said Lionel 'Long Gone' Manners. 'May it never grow shorter.'

She rang her parents without fail on the first Sunday of every month, but even so, Roy Southgate was surprised all over again by his daughter's Australian accent. Vera (after Dame Vera Lynn) looked older than when they had visited her in Sydney three years ago; but it was her strong, twangy voice, louder than either his or Grace's, and unfamiliar vowel sounds that came as a shock.

He had waited for her in the eager crowd of people craning across the barrier of Terminal Three at Heathrow Airport. Strangers flung themselves at one another, laughing and hugging; small children in their best clothes were picked up, exclaimed over, kissed and put down again; and suddenly his daughter was there: a small, tanned woman in a flowered sundress with a smart little jacket. He was glad she hadn't worn black.

'Vera, dear,' he said, but she didn't hear him amid the hubbub, and he left his place at the barrier and walked round to where the channel disgorged a stream of passengers with laden trolleys. She was looking above his head and didn't see him until he stood directly in her path.

'Oh Dad!' she said. 'Oh Mum!'

In the thirty-six hours before the funeral, Vera took over arrangements for the party, buying food and baking cakes and pies until exhaustion drove her to sleep. She had sorted through Grace's linen cupboard, exclaiming at the fresh piles of sheets and tablecloths interleaved with muslin bags of lavender. 'She learned that from her Mum,' Roy explained, although Vera had heard the history before. 'When Mrs Reynolds – that's your Gran that was – was in service, before she was married, it was always done like that. Lovely linen, they used to have.'

On the day of the funeral they set out the front room,

pushing the dining and kitchen tables together to make one long table and putting chairs around the edge of the room. Grace's seldom-used starched table napkins were unfolded, shaken out and refolded. Roy went up to the allotment and stripped it of flowers to set around the house in great banks of midsummer colour.

'Dad, that's marvellous!' said Vera admiringly. 'It looks more like a wedding than a wake! Mum'd be proud of us. I wish the kids could see it. Never mind, I'll take some piccies.'

They smiled at each other.

'Hey, that's an idea. Where's your wedding photo? And the one of Mum with me when I was little? And her and me and Alan when he was a schoolboy?'

'She put them away in her memory box. I'll have to sort it out, now. It seems wrong, somehow. Those were her private things. I think she kept my letters from the war, and all your school reports, and Alan's.'

'Well, you go and fetch them, Dad, and we'll put some pictures of her on the table. Wouldn't that be nice? Here, where's your hanky? Sit down now, you've done wonders. That's enough for the time being. Look for them later. I'll make us a nice cup of tea.'

She got a lovely turn-out, people were saying to each other in soft voices as they left St John's Church, and so she should, poor soul. Several of her ladies from Meals on Wheels came, and the three with whom she'd done the hospital's mobile shop rota for years; all her friends from the bowling club, besides people she and Roy had known way back when they were young marrieds just before the war. Vera recognized some of her former schoolfriends' mothers, and one or two schoolfriends themselves, now middle-aged women older than their parents had been when they were all little girls together. There was no one from Alan's school, nor any of his former friends. They thought it more tactful to stay away, she supposed, though it would have been good to have them there: evidence that Mum had also had a son. Oh Alan, she thought for an instant, oh my wicked, worshipped brother, Alan!

A few old men came along as well, men who'd worked with him at the Unigate, right back to the old days when it was still called John Brown's Dairy. They came to show solidarity and to personify the times they had shared, to clasp her Dad's shoulder wordlessly outside the church, gripping it with gnarled, arthritic fists.

'How's your missus?' Vera would ask; and sometimes they'd bring their heads close to hers and, with proper respect, confide in a whisper, '*She died,*' so that Vera breathed, 'So sorry,' and smiled a crooked smile.

'See you down at the Social?' they asked Roy, who nodded and said, 'I'll be there. I hope you're coming back for a cuppa tea after? You're all welcome. Everyone's very welcome.'

At the side of the grave he had wept, and Vera, her arm tightly round his shaking back, wept too. The gleaming spades shovelled in giant clods of dark earth, which fell with dull thumps on to the pristine coffin until it disappeared. Goodbye, love, God bless. You're with Him now, Roy thought numbly, my dear wife Grace.

The young vicar smiled a sad smile, shook him by the hand, and turned with practised expertise to lead the mourners away from the graveside. As they walked side by side at the head of the procession along the neatly raked path of the cemetery, Vera nudged her father.

'You all right, Dad? You going to be all right, later on, back home? You could go and lie down. They'd understand.'

'I'm all right, pet. I'll see it through. Everyone's been so good, turning out for her.'

'There were people I've never seen before. Like, who was that man, tall chap, who stood at the back? Kind of military-looking geezer.'

'I don't know who you mean. Don't point, dear, it's rude.'

They had nearly reached the sleek black funeral cars, whose uniformed drivers stood with eyes professionally downcast outside the cemetery gates. Vera turned and looked back up the gravelled path along which mourners walked in low-voiced groups of two and three.

'Can you see the very last feller?' she asked. 'Him.'

Her father shook his head. 'Can't make him out from here,' he said. 'Should have brought my glasses.'

'They'd only have got all misted up,' said Vera. 'There you go, Dad, sit in.'

They sat on the wide back seat of the huge car. It smelled sickeningly of leather and a synthetic flower air-freshener.

'Well done, Dad. You OK? Reminds me of my wedding, this car,' whispered Vera, squeezing his hand. Those whom God hath joined together let no man put asunder, Roy remembered. No man ever had. Death had them parted. And Death shall have no dominion, the funeral words came back to mind. In the midst of life we are in death. He rooted in his pocket for a handkerchief, and the driver, whose ears had been expecting those very rustlings, said deferentially, 'We have some organ music . . . I could play the tape, sir, madam, if that might be a comfort.'

'No, thank you', 'Thanks, no', said Roy and his daughter simultaneously.

By seven o'clock the last aunt and neighbour had left, and by nine the washing-up was finished, and the kitchen shipshape again. Let him help me move the furniture back, Vera thought; it'll tire him out and then maybe he'll sleep. Together they carried the table into the kitchen and replaced its flowered plastic cover; then they arranged the dining table in its usual place down the centre of the front room and replaced the lace doilies that decorated its shining surface. Kitchen chairs were carried through to the kitchen; bedroom chairs upstairs to bedrooms, and the garden seat returned to the garden shed. Two plastic bags of rubbish were stacked against the side of the house ready for the dustmen. Roy Southgate locked the shed and the back door, and put the chain on the front door.

Vera was sitting at the kitchen table, her palms swishing

across the plastic tablecloth. She's a good girl, he thought, always been a good daughter to us both, and I don't know what to say to her.

'Well,' said her father, 'I think I'll turn in. Been a long day.'

'Cup of tea before you go upstairs?' said Vera, thinking, This is it; this is the worst moment. The first of all those lonely nights.

'Bless you, pet, no thanks.'

'Think I'll watch the telly for a bit. Won't keep you awake, will it?'

'No, no, you go ahead. You've been a big help. She'd have been proud of you.'

'And you, Dad, and you. Night-night, sleep tight.'

Awkwardly he bent over and pecked a kiss at her forehead. They'd never gone in for hugging and kissing as a family – apart from him and Grace, of course, in private, never when the children could see – and he felt ill at ease alone with his grown-up daughter. But she'd been a good girl, a comfort to him today, as far as anyone could.

'You've been ever so good to me, love. Don't be too long going to bed, will you? It's been a long day.'

After he had cleaned his teeth and combed his hair, Roy Southgate put on his pyjamas and pulled the cord into a bow round his waist. He dropped his vest and socks and underpants and white shirt into the laundry bag that hung on the back of the door and put a set of neatly folded clean clothes across his chair, ready for the morning. Thank God for the Army. Taught you discipline. Kept you going. He took one of his wife's sleeping pills from the tiny plastic bottle in her bedside drawer. He got into bed, folded his glasses on the bedside table, lens side uppermost so as not to scratch them, and buried his face in her last pillow. He'd have to change it soon, but not yet . . . not just yet. He still fancied he could catch the scent of her face-cream and the dry, brittle smell of her hair. It could comfort him a while longer. His young wife, his best girl, his little lady. *O for the touch of a vanish'd hand/And the sound of a voice that is still!*

'Sleep well, lovey,' he whispered into the darkness, feeling the drowsiness roll in like fog. Sorry, Gracie, but I think the pill's taking over. You don't need me to cry. You know it all.

An hour later, Vera lay awake in her narrow schoolgirl bed. And now it's me, she thought. I'm the older generation now. Wonder if he wants to come and live with us? Not that he'd ever say. He'd think it was too much trouble. Long way to uproot him at his age, away from here and the allotment and everything. What would the boys say? Stan wouldn't care for it, but then he never does care for much except his beer.

Weighing up the possibilities, Vera fell asleep.

Chapter Two

How *small* the working classes are, reflected Reginald Conynghame-Jervis as he lay drowsily next morning on Mary's side of the bed. Those two, absurd pair, side by side in the back of the funeral director's Daimler. *He* can hardly be five foot six: size of your average prep school prefect, and as for that skinny daughter with her strident Ozzie voice, I doubt if she's as much as five foot. Couldn't tell with the wife, by the time I saw her she'd shrunk, anyway. Beastly thing this cancer. Even Mary was half her normal self by the end. Poor old girl. Miss her. House is too damn quiet. He snivelled to himself and then stopped at the sound of a key in the front door.

'Squadron Leader . . .? You still here?' called Mary's cleaning lady.

'Be with you in two shakes of a duck's tail!' he said, and struggled into his striped towelling dressing-gown.

'What's that?'

'I *said*, I won't be a tick!' And, wrapping the cord round his paunch, Reginald went to the top of the carpeted stairs and looked down into the hall. Elsie O'Murphy stood looking up at him.

'I'm ever so sorry, sir. I didn't realize you was still in bed. Shall I bring you up a nice cuppa char?'

'You do that.' And he walked into the bathroom, yawned into the mirror, scratched his stubble, scratched his belly, and flexed his knees once or twice. They creaked. He pissed into the basin, then swirled cold water round after it. Mary hated him doing that.

Back in the bedroom he looked in his chest of drawers: no luck. Just in case, he swung open the wardrobe, but there were no clean shirts except for a couple of checked Viyella jobs, or short-sleeved ones for holidays.

'Where are all my clean shirts, Elsie?' he shouted down the stairs.

She emerged from the basement kitchen and craned her head up to see him through the banisters. 'You what?'

'I can't find any clean shirts.'

'Where did you put them after the wash? I didn't iron none, not last week.'

'Wash? What wash? Mary does that – no, you do . . .'

'I ain't done none, not since Mrs C-J, God rest her soul, went into hospital.'

'Where's the washing machine? Go and have a look. Perhaps there are some in there.'

Elsie O'Murphy walked out of his sight and went down the stairs into the kitchen, then into the back scullery where the washing machine stood, and opened its fish-eyed door. Inside were several shirts, mould creeping over their dampness, turning the edges a pale, lichened green. She tightened her lips in exasperation, pulled the shirts out – they smelled rotten – and ran cold water and bleach into the sink.

She knocked at the bedroom door with his cup of tea on a tray.

'Come in!' he called out irritably, and, as she entered the acrid, musty room, he turned towards her helplessly, belly straining against his vest and spilling over his fawn trousers.

'I can't wear *these*.' He pointed indignantly at some Viyella shirts.

'And why not?' she asked.

'But, good heavens, woman, it's a *Monday* not a *weekend*,' he expostulated.

'Well, sir, they're all you've got clean, so put one on and drink your tea, and when you're ready I'll show you how to work the washing machine,' she said. 'If you strip the bed and bring those sheets down we can start with those. I've already done Madam's room.'

Bugger that for a lark, he fumed to himself. Strip the *bed*, work the *washing* machine?! Who does the woman think I am? What's more, I don't like her tone. Insolent. Now Mary's

25

gone, she thinks she can talk to me like that? Bloody nerve. But he shrugged into the clean checked shirt, twitched the faintly greasy sheets from the bed and carried them and the pillowcases downstairs.

Before Mrs O'Murphy left three hours later, the beds aired and freshly made, the house sweet-smelling, the sheets blowing on the line, she stopped and looked into the study, where Reginald sat replying to letters of condolence.

There was a very good turn-out for the funeral, he wrote, *old Watters was there, and 'Bullfrog' Hamilton* . . .

He looked up.

'Yes, Elsie? Off now, are you? When will we see you again?'

'Wednesday,' she said. 'As usual. Mondays, Wednesdays, and Fridays I've done for the last three years.' And hardly a day off sick. Not that *he'd* notice.

'Begging your pardon,' she said, 'and I know things haven't been easy, and I couldn't be more upset for poor Madam, such a lovely lady she was, ever so kind, and always regular . . .'

'Wednesday, then,' said Reginald, and turned pointedly back to his letter.

'. . . but I haven't been paid these last two weeks,' Elsie concluded.

'Ah.' He looked up. 'Haven't you? I see. And do you normally get paid monthly, or what?'

'Weekly, in cash.'

'Cash, eh? How much would you want?'

'I do two hours, three mornings a week – I done nearly four hours today, but that was on account of all the washing having to be done again and I won't charge you nothing for that, though I'll have to if it happens again – but in a normal week that's six hours. Madam paid me four pounds an hour, six fours is twenty-four and she give me one for luck, that makes twenty-five pounds a week, cash, on time, and a week's bonus at Christmas, sir.'

'You mean I already owe you *fifty pounds*?' said Reginald, thinking, And I'm supposed to make my own bed and do my own washing for that? Woman's grossly overpaid.

'When it's convenient.'

'Well, it's not convenient now, Elsie. Have to go to the bank. Friday suit you?'

'Seventy-five pounds on Friday will suit quite nicely, thank you, Squadron Leader. I'll iron those shirts Wednesday, those that come up all right, some'll be spoilt, bound to be. If you'd be sure to bring them in off the line. And the sheets. They go in the airing cupboard. *If* you know where that is. I've made your bed up fresh. And Madam's sickbed as well. Silly, isn't it? Well, must be getting along.'

'Yes. All right. Very well,' he said in a series of irritable bursts, but as she stood in the doorway elbowing her arms into the sleeves of her coat, he suddenly thought, Fine figure of a woman, and felt the big bad boy stirring in his trousers.

It would be Wednesday afternoon before he could see his solicitor, or the bank manager, since he could hardly turn up in a fraying soft shirt good only for fishing holidays in Scotland. It switched on in his mind like a light: Roxburghshire, those last unclouded days when Nanny and Mother kept the world safe for good boys. Reggie sat at his desk overwhelmed by images from the past.

Fishing was something he and his older brother, Gerald, had both been good at. He remembered the pair of them, very serious and frightfully knowledgeable, under the eye of a ghillie with red hair and mutton-chop whiskers (who used to get drunk once a year at Hogmanay and utter the most appalling obscenities). They had both started off with a second-hand greenheart fly rod, with which they had practised casting until they could feel the whip at the moment of the turn, and only when they had mastered that were they allowed to stand at the river's edge and try to catch a fish. The skill and delicacy, the patience, required for the mysterious grown-up art of fishing had enthralled them both. In those days it had been their own river they fished; but death duties had put an end to all that. Poor old Gerald had died first, even before the war started, in a flying accident in 1939. But Gerald and Julia had bred early and there'd been a little son, Vivian, to secure the line.

Their father, laconic and grim, having survived four years of the First World War – not that 'survived' gave any clue to the lifelong damage those years had wreaked – died in 1949 aged fifty-seven; still a comparatively young man (thought Reginald, from the perspective of seventy-one). His death left Reggie, as the second son, with few responsibilities but a decent sum of money. Along with Mary's legacy, they could afford to buy The Cedars, a substantial Georgian house set in three acres of grounds and commanding a green view across the valley. It was nothing compared to his childhood home, but it was a very handsome residence in the most sought-after private road in Tunbridge Wells. Mary had fallen for it at first sight. 'The perfect house in which to bring up children,' she had enthused. 'Lovely big garden, no noise, and miles away from the traffic.' Some hope! Reggie thought to himself.

His nephew, Vivian, the old man's grandson, had been just thirteen and newly arrived at Eton when he inherited the title. *Lord* Blythgowrie, 3rd Baron, he'd become: *there* was a name to catch the eye on the school list! Might as well have something to make up for the tangle of debts and estate problems he'd inherit in due course. Reggie, as his nearest male relative, had been the boy's official guardian. Time enough to worry about that when his education was over, he had thought and scarcely saw the boy: a neglect of duty he now bitterly regretted. Vivian had sailed through Eton, whose following wind had swept him effortlessly on to Christ Church. There, to everyone's surprise – for it was a couple of generations since the family had been noted for possessing any brains – he turned out to be a brilliant scholar and a prominent figure among the young bloods of the House. He got a First in PPE just as he reached his majority, and by then it was too late for Reggie to exert any influence.

Family business (Jervis & Co., Importers) going to pot, had been for years, said young Vivian. Get rid of the dead wood, doddery old men who've lunched and fallen asleep in their clubs after looking in at the office for a couple of hours; put in some capable new managers who know what they're doing, understand trends and know how to read a balance sheet. Don't worry, Uncle Reginald, we'll write you in for a sinecure. Your name on the firm's letterhead shows continuity, reassures people, all that. Just keep on doing as you always did: up to the City a couple of times a week, seat on the main board, appear on the platform for the shareholder's AGM; no loss of face, Uncle, wouldn't do that to you.

Twenty thousand a year and face saved. Thanks for nothing! thought Reginald, the old bitterness welling up again. He'd wanted the sort of respect he'd earned as a pilot. Instead he'd been, to all intents and purposes, retired by the time he was forty.

Then there was the house in Roxburghshire: Finepoint, a pink and grey and many-turreted Victorian Gothic mansion that was built in the days when importing meat from Australia could make a man's fortune. Invest ten years' worth of profits in South American railways, and you could make the fortune of the next three generations as well. Flog the place, young Vivian had said: it would cost thousands to make it comfortable, and *he* didn't want to live there. Reggie was appalled. The trustees had tried to hold things up till Vivian was twenty-five, better still thirty, but the young whippersnapper wouldn't hear of it. The title was his, and he'd finally acquired the authority that went with it. He ignored their protests.

Having sold off the estate and got control of the business, Vivian and his new young wife (pretty in that bold, black-eyed modern fashion) got down to breeding. Two little girls arrived, twins: Celia and Felicity. Poor, childless Mary would have loved to see them running around the empty lawns of The Cedars, but her eager invitations suggesting that Geraldine might bring them down for a weekend were never accepted. Half the time they didn't even have the grace to invent a decent excuse. In 1976, when the girls were twelve, their parents had divorced. Vivian wanted an heir and could hardly be expected to like the idea that the title might pass to some remote Canadian cousin. He'd married, shortly afterwards, a leggily glamorous London model – Susan – but she hadn't produced a son, either.

29

On other fronts, Vivian had done pretty well for himself. Board of this, chairman of that, and just enough money lobbed in the direction of his uncle to keep him quiet. Reginald and Mary had had to manage on a fixed income and, although still affluent, were not able to live in the style to which they had been accustomed. His father had left him a piddling trust fund, growing ever smaller due to blasted inflation. *Not* what he'd been brought up to expect. But then, nothing was.

Life had been simpler back in those happy fishing days. He had managed on the whole to be a good boy; and he and Nanny and Mother and his teachers and everyone else had taken for granted that he would grow up to be a good man. Reggie wondered if Nanny would think him a good man now, and whether she would speak his name in the respectful voice she'd always used about his father: that scarred, stiff-legged, terrifying figure.

Reginald stared at Mary's worn blue leather address book. People had to be thanked for notes of condolence, flowers, letters with postmarks from abroad. She'd always done all that. He was no good at letters, though he liked to dominate a conversation and hated silences. But since he'd left Oxford abruptly in the summer of 1939 to become one of the RAF's 'long-haired boys' he had seldom opened a book and even more rarely written anything. He would do scarcely more than add 'and Reggie' on holiday postcards or Christmas cards, and half the time Mary did this too, filling in the space with her looping schoolgirl hand.

Suddenly, piercingly, he missed the sight of her handwriting. Her fountain pen was put away neatly in its pigeonhole in her desk. He took it out – it was the green mottled Conway-Stewart he'd given her one Christmas – and unscrewed the cap. On the underside of the cardboard box that held their embossed blue writing paper he wrote 'from Mary and Reggie', in a loose, flowing script that was not like hers but not properly his own, either. The nib of her pen slanted the wrong way, softened by two decades of her hand.

For the first time since her death, Reginald wept genuine

tears in memory of his wife. He felt self-conscious, snivelling away all by himself, and embarrassed at the clumsy, gulping sounds he made. Blubbing. Not allowed. Could do with a drink, he thought. He sniffed loudly to himself, and went through the double doors into the drawing-room. Good crystal glasses stood in glittering ranks on the top shelf of the drinks cupboard; decanters were displayed below. Gin and whisky were arranged on top, with a half-finished bottle of sherry – Mary's. He hated the stuff. Port was in cases up in the attic. His father had sent him a case every year at Christmas till he died. Not a tradition his nephew had followed, stingy blighter. All his muttering about death duties was nothing but an excuse.

Finally he ate a dozen peanuts, some less than crisp Twiglets and, because he still felt hungry, a bowl of cornflakes, accompanied by three stiff gins. Cradling a mug of Nescafé, he returned to the drawing-room and contemplated ringing the bank manager. It was three o'clock. Bit late. Time for a nap. Better to give him a call in the morning, when he was fresh. Make an appointment. Feel better after a zizz.

He climbed the stairs heavily, his right hand clutching the banister rail. There was an open-sided corridor at the top with several rooms leading off it. Just before Mary went into hospital for the last time, she had had a bedroom to herself, so as not to disturb him at night. She often couldn't sleep, and liked to be able to switch the light on and read. He threw back the apple-green satin cover from their double bed, noted with pleasure the clean sheets and eased his feet out of his shoes. He closed the curtains to screen out the sharp afternoon sunlight streaming through the huge windows, lay down on his side of the bed and slept. The empty house resounded to his snores.

Roy Southgate was in the public library, changing his books and returning Grace's last selections. She had liked historical novels: Margaret Irwin, Georgette Heyer, or Daphne du Maurier's tales set along the Cornish coast that they knew from their caravanning holidays. As he placed the books on the counter, he saw that his favourite librarian was on duty, so he pushed across Grace's library tickets and said, 'She won't be needing these any more.'

Constance Liddell, senior librarian at Tunbridge Wells Central Library, glanced at his collapsed grey face and said, 'Oh, Mr Southgate, oh dear. Not bad news, I hope?'

Roy dropped his voice and leaned forward across the counter. 'My dear wife passed away two weeks ago.'

'I am so sorry. I am dreadfully sorry. Is there anything I can do? Any help you need? Social Services or anything?'

'Bearing up, thanks all the same for the offer. She's gone to a better place, that's the main thing. All the pain is over.'

'I remember now: she hadn't been very well for, oh, months, had she?'

'Not since Christmas last, not really. They were wonderful up at the hospital; nothing was too much trouble.' He raised his voice again and said brightly, 'Well, mustn't keep you. There's others waiting.'

'Just ask if there's *anything* you need. Would you like to keep her tickets, or shall I . . .?'

'I'll go and see if I can find something for myself.' He walked away, leaving three dog-eared library tickets on the counter: 'Mrs G. Southgate, 4 Thomas Street, expires June 1990.'

Reginald woke to the sound of the door bell shrilling and the knocker banging. He looked at his watch. Just gone five. He sat up and rubbed his face. His mouth tasted foul. Lurching upright, he corkscrewed his feet into his shoes. The bell pealed again and he heard the letter-box being lifted as though someone were peering through. He went to the top of the stairs.

'I'm *coming*!' he shouted. His bladder was full. Had to piss. 'Wait a minute! Be down in a tick.'

The rattling stopped, and a strange woman's voice called out, 'No hurry. Take your time. I'll wait.'

Shirt-tails thrust inadequately into his trousers, hair roughly slicked back, Reginald Conynghame-Jervis did not look like a coping widower, Mandy Hope noted professionally when the door was eventually opened. But the red-rimmed eyes were probably caused by weeping rather than alcohol, so she smiled warmly at him and thrust out a friendly hand.

'Hello . . . Mr Conynghame-Jervis? My name's Mandy Hope. I work for Social Services. I hope you got my letter? — I wrote to you last week. Your doctor asked us to visit you.' Reggie stared at her blankly. 'Didn't you get my note?'

'No, I didn't. Well, I might have done. Been a lot of letters.' Good-looking girl, he thought; a honey. But what the blazes does old Duncan think he's up to, putting Social Services on to me?

She stood on the top step beneath the portico, unperturbed by his scrutiny. 'Would you like to see my identification? Or may I come in?'

'I suppose so,' he said, inwardly thanking his luck. Good thing Elsie had been in today. Place wasn't in too much of a mess. 'Duncan should have given me a tinkle. Well, now you're here. This way to the drawing-room. Do sit down. Would you care for a drink?'

'I won't, thanks, Mr Conynghame-Jervis,' she said, pronouncing his name correctly.

She glanced around the plumply furnished, sunlit room, its heavy curtains looped back into hooks on either side of the French windows and soft Devis watercolours arranged in formal groups on the pastel walls. He expected some approving comment — this was surely not her usual territory — but she only said, 'Now, how've you been getting on?'

Reggie sensed danger, and seized the initiative.

'Most people address me as Squadron Leader. And what do I need a social worker for? Nothing personal, of course — in fact, my dear, I'm delighted to see you, pretty girl's always welcome — but why should some pen-pusher at the town hall decide I need you?'

'Well, perhaps you don't. But, as I say, your doctor suggested someone might look in, *Squadron* Leader. I dropped you a note, asking if this would be a convenient time. I tried to ring you once or twice as well, but kept missing you, so I thought I'd chance it.'

Fine time to pester a chap, he thought mutinously. Pretty little thing, though. Not the sort you'd expect to be a social worker.

'I believe you're living on your own, now that your wife has died? You must miss her a great deal. It isn't easy to adjust,' Mandy Hope said.

'Yes. No.' Blunt sort of girl.

'Perhaps I could just ask you one or two questions. I don't want to intrude.'

'Fire away.'

'I assume you have some sort of help, domestic help?'

'My wife's little woman comes in and does three times a week. Got a part-time gardener. I don't need anyone from the council.'

'Oh good. That's nice. Does the cleaner cook for you? Do any shopping?'

'Haven't needed that. Freezer was well stocked up,' said Reginald, thinking. Not for much longer. Blast! Haven't de-frosted anything for tonight.

'Would you like a cup of tea?' he asked more civilly. 'Or a drink?'

'Tea would be lovely,' she said. 'Let me come and give you a hand.' They walked down the stone stairs to the basement kitchen.

As the fridge swung open, she observed that it contained eight pints of milk, some bottles of soda and tonic water, and not apparently a great deal else. But there were only a couple of unwashed side-plates and a bowl on the draining board. He must be coping better than his doctor had feared.

'Forgive me, I know it must sound nosy,' she said, 'but are you eating properly? It's very important to maintain a bal-anced diet, you know, Squadron Leader – regular, nourishing food, not just bits and bobs.' Reginald took a Pyrex casserole dish out of the freezer and put it on the kitchen windowsill in

34

the sun. A label stuck on top of the frost-rimed foil cover said, 'Shepherd's Pie. 3 Feb 1989. Enough for 3–4,' and his eyes smarted again at the sight of Mary's schoolgirlish writing.

'There you are. See for yourself.'

'Who cooked that? You?'

Not stupid, was she? he thought, trying to work out the consequences of saying no.

'This one's my wife's,' he said cautiously. 'Did you say sugar? Shall we go back to the drawing-room?'

She sat on the shiny chintz sofa with her knees decorously together and placed some pamphlets on the nest of tables beside her. Reggie learned that he could eat five lunches a week in the community centre for 75p a time; three courses. He could join a bridge club or a bowls club. He could meet in the church hall for socials every second Saturday, and ballroom dancing on Thursday afternoons, tea and a biscuit included for 50p.

'Are you friendly with the, um, vicar?' she asked. 'Does he ever drop in?'

Preserve me from the church parade, thought Reginald, but he nodded vaguely. Then there were the voluntary organizations . . .

'Help the Aged are very good.'

Who does she think I am? thought Reggie, resentfully. Some poor, lonely old fellow with no friends or relations?

'There's one and a half acres here, you know. Hence the gardener. Used to be more, but we sold part of it. And I'm not yet a complete cripple,' he finally said, stung to indignation. 'Furthermore, I'm now going to have a drink. I usually do at about this time. You are welcome to join me, or not, as your professional etiquette dictates, but I shall have a Scotch.'

'So would my father, at about this time,' she said, and smiled her glorious, disarming smile. 'I'd like to join you, but I have another appointment at six. I must go. I'm sorry if I have offended you. You seem to be getting on very well. All the same, I'd like to call round again, if I may – say, in a couple of weeks' time, Squadron Leader?'

'Call me Reginald. You could meet me for a drink tomorrow evening,' he said, feeling his heart jumping and the bad boy fidgeting.

'Unfortunately that *is* something the guidelines don't allow. But I would like to come and see you again.'

She took a large appointments diary from her handbag and laid it across her lap. He was surprised to see how full it was. 'How about today fortnight?' she asked. 'That'll be July fourth. Same time?' He couldn't bring himself to say no. It had been refreshing to see her, and she meant well.

'Right you are,' he said.

'Should you write it down?' she asked. 'Or will you remember?'

He walked through to the little study and bent over Mary's desk. His week-at-a-glance pocket diary was empty, but Mandy Hope was too far away to be able to see that.

'July the fourth. Independence Day. Yes, I can fit you in at five,' he said as he walked her towards the front door. 'Jolly good show.'

She drove round the corner and parked the car beside the road while she scribbled down first impressions in her case-book. *Conynghame-Jervis, Reginald,* she wrote. *Aged 71. Likes to be called Squadron Leader, otherwise friendly and sociable. Health apparently good; no complaints. Financially secure. Large house in good order due paid help and p/t gardener; fridge emptying; drinks cupboard full. Client appears in good spirits with few signs of grief or depression; cd become lonely in near future and physically neglected very soon. Needs (a) company & friends (ch. this next time) and (b) stimulus (ch. hobbies, interests, clubs etc.). Look out for alcohol abuse. Visit booked 2/52 July 4 at 5 pm.*

After she had gone, Reginald turned the oven full on and put the Pyrex dish into it. He went back to the drawing-room and poured himself a stiff whisky. He stared out of the window. There were foxgloves and delphiniums climbing up the red brick wall at the end of the garden, and the pleached apple trees that linked arms along its length were ripening nicely. The edges of the lawn were looking a bit whiskery, but then old Fred was pretty whiskery himself, soon be too stiff to straddle the motor-mower. Straddle, eh? The bad boy twitched again, just slightly. Reggie sat himself down at Mary's desk and tried to concentrate on a letter.

Dear Betty and Pongo, he wrote, *thank you for your very kind note about poor Mary. Her death came as a great shock, though she had been ill for some time, the last few weeks in hospital, but not in any pain. She passed away peacefully in the middle of the night, unfortunately I got there too late to be with her during the final moments.*

His last words that evening had been, 'Stop fussing, Mary.' Not much of a farewell. What else could he have said? They'd never been the sentimental sort, once the baby language of their early marriage had petered out in self-consciousness. In the very early days he'd called her 'Nanny' and she'd called him 'Rumble-Tum' or 'Rumbly' for short; and in the secret darkness of their bed they'd called his penis the 'naughty boy', the 'big boy', or (deep, gruff voice) 'the big bad boy'. Mary was virginal and shy so they'd called her breasts 'the bunnies', her private parts 'the warren'. This nursery vocabulary had enabled them to grow quite bold under cover of its innocence. 'Does that *naughty* boy want to poke about in the warren again, and romp with the bunnies?' she might ask – Mary: the most sexually shy girl he had ever known – and at the thought he thrust his hand into his pocket and rolled his penis to and fro between his fingertips. Back to the letter.

If ever you find yourself in this part of the world I do hope you'll look in for a natter about old times. Thank you again for your kind message, yours ever, Reggie.

He looked up their address: Commander and Mrs R. S. G. Fiennes-Hampton, The Old Watchtower, Ardnahein, Near Carrick, Scotland. Dammit, why did people have to go to the ends of the earth when they retired? A few drinks with old Pongo would set him up nicely; Mary and Betty pottering about in the kitchen doing their women's chat. Well, not Mary of course.

37

Time for another drink. Gin this time. Whisky getting a bit low. Save it for later. Nightcap. He shook three drops of Angostura Bitters into the glass and watched the oily gin flowing thickly over it, shinier and more transparent than water, diffusing the pink into the faintest gleam. He whooshed in some tonic and took a deep gulp, relishing its acid clarity. Right-ho, Reggie, concentrate now.

He detached a crisp dark blue sheet of paper from the unanswered pile of letters of condolence. Wendy and Chaggers Fortescue. Never liked the woman. Sharp-nosed and sharp-tongued. God knows why Chaggers had tied the knot. She used to patronize poor Mary, telling her to go out and find herself some charity work. 'That would take you mind off, you know, *things* . . .' she always said, and Mary would nod and give her sad smile.

Chaggers was a good sort; excellent man in a crisis. The steadiness of his voice over the RT, cutting through the hiss and crackle, calm and measured as all hell broke loose. Reginald gazed out of the window, lost in a reverie that owed much to memory, something to Kenneth More, Richard Todd and the cinema, and not a little to wishful thinking.

He and Chaggers had been pilots together when the squadron, at that time eight-strong, attacked a tight, defensive circle of twenty yellow-nosed ME 109s, the hardest formation to break up. The usual tactic – risky – was to form up into a line astern, encouraging them to attack, and then at the last moment to haul hard back on the control stick and do a steep climbing turn. In seconds, you'd have the advantage. Reggie's eyes blazed as he relived it. Another second, then I'd fired, saw Chaggers fire his own four-second burst, and·we were both safely away. My Messerschmitt hung motionless; time was suspended; had I got him? Yes! A jet of red flame shot out and upwards and he spiralled away down, out of sight. Moments later another 109, bent on revenge, flashed across my bows, followed by a Spit, chasing him with the same motive. I gave him a quickie – his number was up! 'That's for Eric Johnson, you swine!' I shouted. No doubt about this one! and heard Chaggers across the RT: 'Yours, Reggie!' The skies blazed in a chaos of flame, smoke, gunpowder and sudden death.

An hour later we'd be tucking into ham and eggs back at the mess. That was the life! thought Reginald. Nothing in the next fifty years had ever equalled the glory and the recklessness of those times. Life? Death? You didn't stop to think about it. And your victim: married or single? Husband to a fat Frau with two fat blonde German children? Or a lean, ascetic young bachelor, not keen to tie himself down? Fighting men were better off without a young bride to worry about. Only hamper your freedom of action – or so he'd thought, till he met tender, gentle, trusting Mary. Until you were married, you didn't care. The Germans weren't individuals, hardly even rivals; they were just targets, the object of the day's exercise.

Am I still the same person, Reginald wondered, as that daredevil boy? How they praised us, the women and the old men; they talked of our bravery, courage, valour, gallantry, envying us our clouds of glory. But among ourselves *we* knew we were competitive young daredevils, superbly tuned to physical and mental health, who had been given a wonderful fighter plane with which to play aerial games. We were playing God, dicing with life, giving or taking death. That shrunken old woman who died in hospital three weeks ago: was *she* the same person as my slender, clinging girl?

When the gin bottle was empty, Reggie steered past the walls and through the doors towards the kitchen. An acrid smell stung his nostrils. He reached for the oven glove, but it wasn't in its usual place, so he opened a random drawer and found a couple of neatly folded tea-towels. He crouched down awkwardly, opened the oven and manoeuvred the Pyrex dish on to the worktop beside the cooker. The shepherd's pie was blackened at the edges and dark brown on top, but he could always scrape that off. He dug a spoon in, blew on it several times, and began his supper.

Chapter Three

Roy Southgate woke early, disturbed by some distant clamour in his mind that would not be harmonized into his dream. He opened his eyes, looked at the alarm clock beside the bed, and remembered that Grace was dead. 'O Lord, look after my dear wife Grace, who is now with Thee in paradise,' he prayed, as he had done each morning since her death. He remembered the little dead bird chucked into a rubbish bin up by the allotments, flies busy in its eye sockets, its scrawny bunch of feathers an empty rag, the innards eaten away; remembered above all how bad it had smelt, and squeezed his eyes tightly shut to banish the vision and all that it implied . . . maggots . . . change and decay . . . crawling and rotting . . . He had seen enough dead bodies to know what disgusting changes happened within days of breath ceasing.

He'd spent the war with an assault unit of the Royal Engineers, petarding houses and road blocks, launching assault bridges, ferrying powered rafts and, after going through France and Belgium in the wake of Jerry, he knew all too well what death looked like, not only in its immediate aftermath but weeks later. Charred bodies were more bearable; their blackened flesh and bloodless corpses hardly seemed as though they could ever have been alive. It was the sight of flesh decomposing, caving in on itself, returning to compost and anonymous matter that was hardest to reconcile with his belief that the living were merely at one stage of their path towards eternity.

He'd been such an eager lad before it all began. Joined the local Territorial Army after Munich, when he was just eighteen. Always wanted to be an engineer; he'd loved working things out, could imagine weights and stresses in his head. First he'd been a sapper, then in 1941 they made him a lance corporal, and by the end of the war he'd been promoted to sergeant. How proud Grace had been when he came home with a third stripe to sew on to his khaki uniform. No matter how much he protested that it was automatic, she had disagreed. She knew better, she said, as she stitched it to his sleeve. She'd been right, too; he'd distinguished himself at the D-Day landing.

Right, he thought, that'll do for now. Cup of tea and then I can get in a quick two hours up at the allotment before anyone else arrives. He liked the silence of the dawn: the earth still damp and the scent of the flowers strong and clear, clearer than it ever was later on in the day, as though they withdrew from the competition of pipe tobacco and clothes saturated with smoke. The birds sang fearlessly first thing in the morning, and the usual robin would come and perch on his spade or watch him from a nearby bush, turning its head from side to side, its black eyes checking for worms.

He liked doing housework because it made him feel like Grace. She had always taken a pride in her shining kitchen, put together item by item as they began to discard the bits and pieces they'd started out with when they got married. Nobody in their two families had money to spare, but people had given what they could; and what they hadn't got and couldn't afford, Roy had made.

'Royston Southgate, you're a wonder, you are!' Grace would say after he had showed her how he had sawed and planed and fitted joints together, working in the evenings up at his old school on the workbench where he had learned his carpentry. He'd built their table, and two benches with nice firm legs splayed to take the weight; he'd built a wardrobe for their bedroom and, while they waited for the first baby, an old-fashioned cradle which Grace had trimmed by cutting up her wedding dress.

'I'm not likely to need it again,' she'd joked. 'Might as well put it to good use.'

Their child lay like a little prince in a bower of yellowing satin with lace ruffles encircling the sides. The pair of them had leaned over him at night, straining to hear him breathe – their boy, their precious boy, their son and heir – smiling at each other in relief when the infant face crumpled in a petulant frown.

'What can he be dreaming?' he would wonder. 'He doesn't know anything to dream yet.'

'He's dreaming of before he was born, wishing he was still inside me,' Grace would answer; and Roy would say, 'So do I,' and they would smile at one another and go back to bed.

He washed his teacup, rinsed the pot, poured milk from the jug back into the bottle and put the bottle back into the fridge. Painstakingly he scoured the sink and work surfaces till they shone.

Moving through the familiar chores, he felt as though he inhabited Grace's body, yet stood outside it too, watching as her sinewy wrists wrung out the cloth and draped it limply over the taps. Her physical shape was so familiar to him that his mind was slow to believe that she no longer existed. He kept walking into rooms and mistaking an arrangement of colour and shape for her, so strong was his continuing expectation of seeing her. The eyes, he discovered, have their habits too, and the habit of seeing his wife was hard to relinquish. *O for the touch of a vanish'd hand/And the sound of a voice that is still!*

He had never ceased to find her attractive. It made no difference to him when she aged or became gaunt and stringy from the illness that chewed away her vital substance. She was always his girl, the only woman he'd ever known. Physical love was identified with her body. In their darkened bedroom, the street lamp shining through the bobble-edged slit between the curtains, what did lines and folds matter so long as the dear flesh still accommodated his?

They had made love for the last time only a few days before she went into hospital.

'No, love, you don't have to,' he had said. 'I'm afraid of hurting you.'

'But I want to. I may be a bit slow – you'll have to be careful – but I want to, really I do,' she had assured him.

Gently he had gathered up her nervy body, feeling the bones like knife handles in his grasp, and she had stood docile and childlike as he undressed her. He folded her clothes on the chair and eased the eiderdown over her, for being so thin she felt cold and shivered, even in this warm weather. He undressed himself and slipped in beside her.

Her noises had never changed; the quick intakes of breath that accelerated and held and shuddered a little . . . and then relaxed in a long smiling sigh.

He looked at the clock on the wall. Seven. Five regular pips, and one longer one. Time for the news, and then he'd go up to the allotment. Must keep busy. Tomorrow he'd wear her apron, to bring her closer. He'd wear all her clothes if he could, if it weren't that someone might catch him at it and think he was going a bit gaga. He could wear her nighties in bed, that was the answer. Not the hospital ones, but the brushed nylon ones in soft, pretty colours. No one would see, and it would feel as though he still had her next to him. Time to bring some fresh flowers down from the allotment for her shrine.

The bell chimed its double note, like a church bell in counter-tenor, and Roy Southgate flicked the switch on the kettle before going to the front door. It was the social worker whom Grace and Roy had met earlier, when Billy and little Joe had come and spent a few weeks with them over Christmas, about the time their Dad was sent away. She had visited him a couple of times since Grace's death; not, Roy believed, out of necessity let alone to check up on him, but out of friendship. Charity he could never have accepted; kindness was different.

'Afternoon, Roy! Oh, I've had such a day of disasters, you'll have to cheer me up. How are you?'

'Come in Miss Hope –'

'Come *on* – Mandy, *please*.'

'Tea's on and I'm warming some scones in the oven.'

'Music to my ears. Where are you taking me? Not the front room? Why bother, when it's much cosier in the kitchen?'

She glanced in at the door of the spotless room and ex-claimed, 'Oh *look*! How lovely. What is it?'

'Well, up at the cemetery, you see, there's been a lot of vandalism. It's those lads with nothing to do with themselves, they spray paint all over the place, and take flowers out of vases.'

'Roy – do they really? I didn't know about that. I'll mention it. How awful for you.'

'Well, you know . . . the devil finds work . . . Anyhow, I thought to myself, the answer is to *plant* things on her grave, that way they're less likely to be nicked, and I can put in some lovely bulbs for the next spring, but till then I've made her this – well, I call it her shrine.'

The dining-room table was polished to a high gloss; not the plastic gleam of aerosol sprays dizzy with chemical scent, but the deep, loving shine that comes from hard work and elbow grease. Arranged along its length were a number of lace mats, on each of which stood a vase spilling over, brimming, jubilant with fresh flowers. The centre one held rosebuds, drowsy with their enclosed perfume; soon the petals would open out and release it into the still air of the room. On either side were tall delphiniums, foxgloves and sweet williams. A whole cottage garden was assembled in the cramped front room.

In front of the flowers stood a collection of family photo-graphs, including one silver-framed snapshot of Grace South-gate taken in the Forties. She was remarkably pretty, even in makeshift wartime clothes. The nipped-in waist and elaborate hat of the time suited her well; the laced platform-soled shoes had a kind of stoic chic. Her shoulder-length hair was rolled back from her forehead in a shining curve, her mouth was juicy with dark lipstick and her expression was one of the utmost relief and joy.

'How smart she looks!' said Mandy Hope.

'There's my little sweetheart,' said Roy proudly. 'That was taken on VE Day. May, you know, the eighth of May, 1945. I wasn't there, of course: still in Germany, but Grace was up in London waiting to hear Mr Churchill make the announcement on the wireless, and afterwards she went and stood in the crowd outside Buckingham Palace, to see him on the balcony with the King and Queen. She paid half a crown to a street photographer to get this picture taken for me. She was ever so glad the war was over, and me coming back safe and sound. We both were, of course.'

Next to the black-and-white photograph stood a printed card with the Order of Service from her funeral, and, neatly cut out and framed, the notice of her death that he had inserted in the local paper.

'Can I read that?' she asked.

Enclosed within a black border, it recorded that Grace Edith Southgate, dearly beloved wife of Royston Southgate and mother of Frederick, Vera and Alan, had passed away on 2 June 1990 at the Kent & Sussex Hospital. It thanked the nursing staff for their devoted care. Below were four lines of verse:

> All you good people that now stand by
> As you are now, so once was I.
> As I am now, so shall you be.
> Remember death and pray for me.

Mandy Hope was surprised. She looked up.

'We saw that on a tombstone in Ireland once,' said Roy. 'We were on holiday there with the children, hired a caravan, went all over the place. She copied it down from some old abbey churchyard. She liked it. Said it made you stop and think.'

'And you wanted people to stop and think about *her* death?'

'Yes I did. Right – ready for that cup of tea?' he asked, and let her precede him through the door, closing it gently behind them.

'Roy, forgive me,' said Mandy Hope, after she had praised the warm scones and Grace's homemade jam; 'but you know, of course, that I have access to your Social Services records?'

His face seemed to cave in on itself and grow shadowy, like a room in which the curtains have just been drawn.

'Yes,' he said.

45

'From which I understand that – well, perhaps you'd like to tell me about your son, Alan?'

'Why?' he said.

'He couldn't be at the funeral?'

'No.'

'And did his . . . wife come?'

'No.'

'Not the boys, either?'

'No point in upsetting them. They're too young.'

'It isn't anything you'd care to discuss with me? There might be something I could help with.'

'Some other time, perhaps,' said Roy Southgate, his tone flat and weary.

'Some other time, then,' she agreed.

The telephone rang, and he walked out to the hall to answer it. Vera, his daughter, was ringing from Australia, and Mandy, professionally responsive to tone and body language, noted the gallant lift in his voice. Instantly he was cheerful, inquiring about the grandchildren, laughing at some anecdote.

'What about you, pet?' she heard him ask. 'Bearing up? . . . Good . . . Grand. Don't you worry about me. I'm like the electric message about King George the Fifth.'

The what? thought Mandy; and Vera evidently did so too, for her father explained, 'When the old king was dying – you must know the poem? "Along the electric wire the message came:/He is not better – he is much the same."'

Mandy Hope looked around his kitchen. Modest, orderly, functional, it looked just as it had done when his wife was alive, with a pot of parsley on the kitchen windowsill and the dish-mop stuck into a little vase hand-painted with the words 'A Souvenir from St Agnes'. He'd be all right; habit and self-respect would keep him going – which was not to deny the pain. It was too soon to try and find out about his son. One thing at a time. She drained her cup of tea.

At the other end of Tunbridge Wells pools of sunlight basked

46

in the desert shades of old rugs. Reginald was upstairs, peering at his bared teeth in the bathroom mirror. Like an old horse, he thought, yellow and crumbling. At least they're my own. He swung open the mirrored door of the cabinet above the basin. Inside was an ancient bottle of A Gentleman's Cologne. Trumpers: that'll do. It stung his newly shaved skin, but he patted it bravely on to his jowls. Funny old pong; still, women liked that sort of thing. He twitched the cravat in his shirt collar. Come off it, Beau bloody Brummell, what you need is a nip before take-off.

Minutes later the door bell rang and the heavy thud of the lion's-head knocker resounded through the house. Reginald threw the door open with a grandiose gesture.

'Ah!' he said. 'My guardian angel. Come in, come along in, just in time for a char and a wad.'

'A what?' Mandy Hope asked, smiling. 'Mmm, you smell just like my father!'

Bad start, thought Reginald.

'Char and a wad. Cuppa tea and a piece of cake. RAF lingo. Or can I tempt you to a proper drink?'

'Certainly not,' said Mandy. 'It's only five o'clock.'

'Just trying it out for size,' said Reginald. 'Come on, then.' He led the way down to the kitchen.

Mandy assumed he had tidied up, since there was little to suggest neglect apart from a grubby milk bottle full of dead flowers. But when, unable to find a teaspoon in the drawer, he swung open the front of the dishwasher, a sour smell of rotting food emanated from it and she saw that it was full of dirty dishes. She made no comment. From the cold pantry Reginald brought out the remains of a cake, crumbling drily at the edges but evidently homemade.

'Mrs Thing made this,' he said. 'Try a slice?' Carrying the tea-tray, he led the way upstairs to the drawing-room.

Reginald was bluff and cheery, spreading enough *bonhomie* to fuel a party. His way of making her acquaintance was to boast about himself, so she had already gathered – as though anyone living in this house needed to labour the point – that he was well-connected, his wife had been well-connected, his nephew was titled, and his wealth would have been beyond most of her clients' dreams of avarice. He then disarmed her by saying, 'I'm shooting a line but pretty girls always bring out the worst in me, and you're the prettiest I've seen for a long time.'

Plenty of her old boys took her through a blow-by-blow account of every twinge and ailment, every detail of diet and bowels, feeding on sympathy, looking for pity, interested only in the gloomy catalogue of their own physical decrepitude. I'll say this for him, she thought, he doesn't complain. He's got a lot of spirit, still works hard to be good company; you have to admire that. He doesn't talk about his wife, but he's not the domesticated type and coping without her can't be easy.

Her social-work training had alerted her to the danger signals in the initial case report. These old men were much harder to deal with once they'd got into the habit of neglecting themselves. Either they were self-reliant from the start, or they went into a pretty rapid decline. Finding herself visiting another case on the council estate where his cleaner, Mrs O'Murphy, lived, Mandy had gone to see her.

Elsie began by saying loyally that Reginald was managing fine. She ended by admitting that he was driving her mad. 'Now that he's emptied the freezer and eaten up all Mrs C-J's lovely stews and puddings, when he's not round at his local – you know the one, Broker's Arms – he's living off cornflakes and TV dinners, judging by what I find in his waste-bin; *and* more gin and whisky than's good for him. It's not my job to cook for him, whatever he may think. I've got my hands full as it is, running round picking up his shirts and worse, dropped on the floor or anywhere else he happens to undress. My seven-year-old's better trained than him! Mrs C-J would turn in her grave, God rest her soul, if she could see the state of that bedroom.'

'You're doing a marvellous job, Mrs O'Murphy,' Mandy had soothed. 'I'm sure he's very grateful. I don't know where we'd be without you. I don't suppose TV dinners will do him any harm. But he needs a bit of showing how. You know what widowers are like.'

'Useless. He can no more look after himself than a toddler. He was that rude to my poor lady while she was alive, always making fun of her, even in front of me. He told me once she didn't know how to change a toilet roll! Was I supposed to believe she was that stupid? A *loony* can change a bloody toilet-roll, pardon my French. She were that mortified, poor Mrs C-J, but she never contradicted him. Let him say whatever he pleased, she'd just smile and say nothing. Now she's gone, God rest her soul, he's like a baby what needs its nappy changing.'

'Mrs O'Murphy, you've been very patient.' Mandy had interrupted the indignant flow. 'It's just while he gets used to being on his own . . .'

'I'll give him another month,' Elsie had concluded through lips pursed with self-righteousness. 'After that, if he can't pull himself together – *and* keep his hands where they belong – I'll be giving my notice. If my husband knew what he tries on, he'd be round there with a horse-whip, not but what it isn't what he deserves. I don't know how she stood for it all those years.'

At the team meeting Mandy had suggested that she should visit Reginald once or twice more before leaving him to his own devices. Discreet questioning had revealed him to have remarkably few friends. He had relatives living in London, but they had not been down to see him since his wife's death. It was the usual story: wives organized the social life and had close friendships with other women while their husbands tagged along. She hoped the vicar might drop in. He could take a firmer line; perhaps even put other members of his congregation in touch with Reginald. Give it another month, they'd said; they were short-staffed in the Social Services Department, and even fortnightly visits to check out the Squadron Leader put an unnecessary strain on resources. It was hard to justify devoting much more time to his self-inflicted problems.

Mandy Hope sat forward in the plump chintz sofa, crossed

her legs deliberately and looked across at Reginald to signal that it was her turn to speak.

'How's the cake?' he inquired bluffly. 'Not bad, eh? Better than that Kipling rubbish.'

'I've been thinking, and there's a suggestion I'd like to put to you . . .'

'More tea? Help yourself.'

She laughed. 'Don't worry, I'm not about to tick you off. You're doing pretty well. But there's something I want you to think over. I'd just like you to *consider* having a chat with your vicar.'

He sighed deeply, and composed himself like a naughty boy to be rebuked. When she had finished he said, 'I'll do a deal. I've never been much of a one for God-botherers, but I'll think it over if you'll come out one evening and have a drink with me; better still, dinner. No, you don't have to answer straightaway. I'd just like you to *consider* it.'

She laughed at his parody of her own careful phrases, and at her laugh he beamed complicitly, so that for a moment she glimpsed the charmer he must have been.

Then he said, 'Have a snifter? Sun's over the yard-arm, as they say in the senior service. Sherry? Or will you join me in a pink gin?'

'Yes,' Mandy Hope replied. 'A gin, please. But don't tell the director of Social Services!'

Half an hour later she had gone, after just one pink gin and without agreeing to have dinner with him. No joy. Bloody difficult these modern girls, Reggie reflected, as he poked around in the rustling paper of the chocolates he had bought for her. Milk Tray, according to the advertisements, would make any girl swoon into your arms. Precious little swooning he'd got from Mandy Hope. Wouldn't even take the chocs.

'I've broken enough rules as it is,' she had said. 'Drinking with a client! Whatever would my team leader say?'

'Same as my old station commander I dare say – station master, we used to call him. Go for the bluebird. Make the most of it. Enjoy yourself.'

50

'You belong in one of those black-and-white Forties films, you know, or at any rate your language does!' she had said, and then, seeing his hurt expression, 'I don't mean to be rude. I'm sure an evening with you would be terrific fun. It's just that the guidelines are fairly strict. Positively *no* socializing with clients. And no accepting gifts, either.'

'So that's what I am, eh? A client? One of your poor old boys who can't cope on his own.'

Mandy had patted his arm and given him one of her glorious smiles. 'Don't you worry, Squadron Leader, I'm scheming and plotting. Now, you think about my idea and we'll discuss it next time. I've really *got* to go. I'll see you in two weeks. Five o'clock as usual suit you?'

Reggie munched his way through the box of sweet, sticky chocolates until only his least favourite ones were left. Toffee-covered nougat was hard on the teeth. Those things with the violet centres were revolting and he'd always hated coconut. Never mind, they'd all taste the same washed down with a stiff gin.

He never used to buy Mary chocolates, but then it was a long time since he'd had to woo her. Nearly fifty years: half a century, over half a lifetime. No wonder he was brassed off living on his own. She had moved in and out of the rooms and mealtimes of his life, her pleated Gor-ray skirts swishing round her trim calves, smiling gently, saying less and less as time went on but always *there*, modest and serviceable in pastel twin sets, until she had seemed as inevitable as his reflection. She had always been the quiet type and that had appealed to him at the beginning. The raucous, laughing girls – nattercans, they'd called them behind their backs – whose chatter chatter would soon turn to nag nag were all very well at a party, but a chap didn't want to wake up to it for the rest of his life. Mary's shyness had seemed touching after the Waafs, with their defiantly bad language and hard, knowing eyes. He preferred innocence in a girl. He could teach her all she needed to know. Virginity had suddenly become old hat in the war, but not to him. A fellow wanted to be the first, was only natural.

Reggie eased himself down into the armchair to give his belly room to expand comfortably and thought of the time when they'd met. It had been in 1940, when he was going through Operational Training Unit. He'd pranged the Spit in a stupidly daredevil manoeuvre and pranged himself too – no bones broken, but bad enough to put him in hospital for a week.

Mary had been a Red Cross nurse, more of an orderly, really; very earnest about doing her bit. She used to stand meekly to one side of his bed while the old termagant of a Sister – Sister Girdlestone, that was her name, funny how things came back to you after all these years – Sister Girdlestone had ordered the nurses and patients about.

'Come along now, Nurse Bagnal! Hold the bowl steady! Don't know what some of you girls think you're doing here. Never be any use if you can't stand the sight of blood.'

Mary's hand trembled as she held the enamel bowl into which his soiled and bloody dressings were deposited. Reginald had winked at her to show he was on her side, and as she caught his eye a deep blush suffused her transparent skin.

'Sorry, Sister,' she'd whispered, hardly audible.

After that he had made a point of looking out for her. She seemed too frail for the long hours she worked, and her paleness took on the pearly quality of complete exhaustion. She moved with the robotic steps of a sleepwalker, but she always came on duty punctually and often left late. On his last day before being discharged he had called her over.

'Would you mind drawing the curtains round my bed Nurse Bagnal, please?'

She looked startled. 'Is there anything wrong? Shall I get a doctor? Are you in pain?'

'If you'd just draw the curtains for a moment . . .?'

Trained to obedience, she had done so.

As soon as they were alone in brief, swaying privacy, he had said urgently, 'I know you're off duty tomorrow night,

I've looked at the roster. Will you meet me in the Star and Garter at eight?'

'Oh, I couldn't,' she said immediately. 'I'm sorry, I couldn't possibly.'

'Why not? Already fixed up with another chap?'

'*No!*'

'Well, then. I'll be there, waiting for you. Eight o'clock. I won't leave till you come.'

She drew the curtains back so quickly that he thought he'd offended her. Shouldn't have tried to rush her into it. Tea would have been better. Blast!

Nevertheless, the following evening she arrived. Not at eight: he'd been waiting for nearly an hour, watching the door, when suddenly he spotted her slight, apprehensive figure. She was wearing the sort of frock girls wore then: wide, flat shoulders, cut in a fashion that somehow made the rest of her look shapeless. Reggie didn't mind that. He always looked first at a girl's legs, and knew already that Mary's were lean and finely muscled. Her mouth was shiny with fuchsia lipstick. He took her elbow and guided her through the crowded pub to a secluded corner.

'I had to stay for dinner at home,' she said. 'Mummy and Daddy would never have let me get away otherwise.'

'Couldn't matter less,' he reassured her. 'I'd wait for you till the cows came home. Now then, what'll it be?'

'Lemonade, please.'

'Drop of gin to cheer it up?'

'Oh, honestly, no, thank you, just plain lemonade. I'm not used to drinking, it makes my head go all funny.'

When he brought back their drinks, she said, 'I don't know why I'm here. I told a fib and said I had to fetch something from the hospital that I'd forgotten. Daddy would be furious if he knew I was meeting a strange man in a public house.'

'I am *not* a strange man. I am Pilot Officer Conynghame-Jervis, known to his friends as Reggie, one of the long-haired boys. Now tell me *your* name, Nurse Bagnal.'

'Mary. Mary Elizabeth.'

'Like the Royal Family.'

'Well, not really. I mean, I'm named after my mother. To tell you the truth, she's called Marigold and I am too, but I make everyone call me Mary. The other name comes from Granny Bagnal, Daddy's mother.'

'Mine's Reginald.'

'Yes, I know,' she admitted, and he thought, So she looked me up, did she? Promising.

'Reginald Vivian, I'm afraid. That's a family name as well. They're a bind, aren't they?' he added, but she didn't follow it up.

Instead she asked, 'What are the long-haired boys?'

'Chaps training for the RAF who were at university. In my case Oxford.'

'Gosh!' she said. 'You don't look old enough to have a degree.'

'Quite right. I'm not. I was sent down, Nurse Bagnal, another code word meaning that the authorities in their wisdom required me to vacate my ancient college before I had completed my studies. Not, I may say, a decision greatly regretted by yours truly.'

'Does it mean you did something wrong?'

'I made a thorough nuisance of myself. Tormented the proctors and bulldogs mercilessly.'

'They set *dogs* on you?'

He roared a young man's laugh, and she looked disconcerted and blushed again.

'The "bulldogs", in the coded language of the university, were burly fellows whose job it was to overpower objectionable young men like me who were determined to disobey the rules and all those set in authority over them.'

'Oh!' she said, and he could see he'd assumed heroic stature in her eyes. It was too easy.

Her London Season had taught Mary how to make polite small talk, and when she found they had acquaintances in common she relaxed and became quite giggly. He got the barman to put a dash of gin into her second glass of lemonade and, when she didn't notice, a larger amount into the third. Soon her cheeks were bright with colour and her eyes shining. She was a good listener, laughing at his jokes and concentrating when he told her about his training with the University Air Squadron.

He wanted her to trust him, so after an hour he said, 'Your parents will be worrying about you. I'll run you home – I get a petrol ration: we count as operational pilots at OTU – but first . . .'

'What?' she said, wide-eyed.

'First you promise to see me again.'

'I . . . it isn't that simple . . . I'm supposed to be on nights soon.' Her mother had instructed her that young men didn't like girls who were too easy; she must make them think she had other commitments if she didn't want to be thought 'fast'. This was difficult for Mary, who had fallen in love with Reginald already, for the first time, and for ever. Luckily Reginald was not easily discouraged.

'Then you can meet me for tea, like a good girl. We'll have sandwiches and buttered scones at the Cadena, and a nice pot of Earl Grey.'

'You are funny,' she said. 'I can't imagine you in the Cadena.'

'You don't have to. You'll soon be able to see the real thing. How about next Thursday at four?'

'Well, all right, then, I will if I can. How do I get in touch with you, if I can't get the time off?'

'You can leave a message for me at the OTU. But it's an order, Nurse Bagnal. Tea with the patient, Cadena, sharp at four.' To soften it he added, 'Don't let me down, Mary. I very much want to see you again.' That blush, that schoolgirl's blush . . .

Three weeks later she invited him home to meet her parents. Acre Lodge was exactly what its name suggested: a small Georgian house that had once stood at the entrance to a large estate but was now surrounded by an acre of carefully tended garden. 'Do praise the roses,' she'd said. 'They're Mummy's pride and joy.' So he had noticed the roses.

'Caroline Testout!' he said. 'Lovely old-fashioned rose. You don't often see those nowadays.' As her mother glowed, he caught the resemblance between them.

Her parents had questioned him discreetly about his background, but Reginald knew better than to be specific at this early stage. He'd been modestly evasive, knowing they would read between the lines. There was a *Debrett* on the bookshelf; they would look him up and put two and two together. Place in Roxburghshire; father's old school: must be Blythgowrie's younger boy. They'd be more than satisfied. Such a *suitable* young man for dear Mary. He would make up for the disappointment of her Season, when they'd spent money lavishly on her coming-out dance in the hope that she'd be married before war broke out. If only . . . But the sentence would be left unfinished. It was bad form to mention death.

The Southgate home in Thomas Street was a semi-detached house of the kind built in the first decade of the century and again between the wars on ribbon developments stretching from south London to the coast. An arch of bricks surmounted the porch, and the front door – set back by a yard of red-tiled doorstep – was inset with a small window decorated with stained glass in a design of indeterminate petals and leaves. A bay window reflected in one of its five black glass facets whoever was ringing the door chimes. Entering the house, a flight of stairs led directly up to three bedrooms and a small bathroom, in which Roy had lately installed a kingfisher-blue basin and bath. Next to it was a separate toilet, still white.

The entrance hall was hardly more than a corridor; there was just enough room for a coatstand, a mirror with a wavy bevelled edge, and a small table for the telephone. Two doors opened off to the left: the first into the dining-room, now Grace's shrine; the second into the lounge. A triangular sloping cupboard under the stairs held Roy's workbench, his tools neatly arranged on battens fixed to the wall above it, while under the bench were stacked tins of paint, tubes and bottles of white spirit, Araldite, wood fixative and the DIY paraphernalia with which he kept the house in good repair. A glazed door at the end of the hallway opened into the kitchen. When it was closed, the bubbles in its ornamental glass reduced anyone moving around the kitchen to a pattern of brightly coloured changing shapes, suggestive yet imprecise, as if seen through a kaleidoscope.

In this small house, bought with pride after the war with Roy's demob pay and a great-aunt's legacy, they had watched their children turn over from their backs on to their tummies, then lever themselves into a sitting position, from which, next, they dropped forward on to all fours. When crawling became too slow and cumbersome for their burgeoning energy, they had turned into toddlers, lurched forward and walked. Being securely upright freed concentration from the limbs and focused it upon the urgent problem of communication. 'Da-da,' Grace had instructed. 'Look, there he is. Say it. Da-da. *Hel-lo,* Dada.' Roy had beamed into the infant faces and enunciated clearly through rolled-in lips, 'Ma-ma. *Ma*-ma.' The first few words came slowly, weeks apart, but, once mastered, they were followed by a lava flow of speech, as words multiplied and joined up into sentences. The process was infinitely gratifying. 'Say ta' became, 'Say, thank you, God, for my good dinner. May I get down?'

Grace was gentle, orderly, spotlessly clean. The children wore fresh clothes every day, lovingly hand-washed in the evenings before yesterday's batch was ironed, folded and tidied away, everything in its proper place. The house ran like clockwork to their mutual satisfaction, and their rosy children promised nothing less. This, Roy used to think, was why people were born: to bring up children and teach them to be good; to cherish and protect one another; to work hard and honestly; and to retreat at the end of each day into their snug and individual paradise. He was perfectly content; he asked for nothing more.

The kitchen had been Grace's domain. The two of them were happiest when Roy was working away in his cubby-hole under the stairs and Grace was baking, the wireless loud enough for them both to hear it, concentrating on their separate tasks while sharing laughs or enjoying the music together. They preferred the wireless because it didn't force them to sit passively. They had delayed getting a television for as long as possible, but as Vera and Alan grew into teenagers, they had bullied them into it.

'It's hopeless if you don't know what's happening on *Coronation Street*,' Vera had complained. 'Everyone at school talks about it next day, and *What's My Line?* and *Six Five Special* and all those . . .'

'It's a terrific laugh, Dad!' Alan had pleaded. 'I've seen lots of things at Stan's and they're ever so funny. You and Mum would love it. There's loads of plays and sort of concerts and things.'

Grace had interceded for them, so Roy had given in. From then on Alan sprawled in front of the television every evening, his grey-trousered legs and big feet stuck out in front of him, his eyes glued to the black-and-white screen. It was a battle to make him do his homework. They'd had to compromise and let him work while it was on, but it wasn't the same with the manic laughter of strangers filling the house. Vera had always been more conscientious, but then girls were like that.

Roy Southgate sat at his kitchen table, staring at a plate of sardines and a cup of tea. He'd been to visit Alan. The place always depressed him and upset his stomach. Not even the tantalizing smell of fried sardines on toast could restore his appetite.

It had taken him several weeks since Grace's death to pluck up the courage to go and see his son, and the visit had not gone well. He had hoped that June, Alan's wife, might be there, but she'd left him to cope on his own. Alan was unpredictable; he might weep and be maudlin with self-reproach or he might launch on one of his tirades, grinding round like a treadmill, rehearsing all the old grievances. Roy had learned that there was no point in trying to disagree or even interrupt; it was best to let him have his say.

'How are things, son?' Roy had asked placatingly as he sat down.

'How do you *think* things are? Not much choice, is there? You can have it like a steak in a French café: bloody or fucking bloody. Too much time to think, that's my problem. Too much time to work out where it all started to go wrong. Remember my tenth birthday? Oh no, you wouldn't, would you? But *I* do. There was the cake, "made with *real eggs*, Allie darling", there were the candles, there were all the *nice* little boys and girls from school.'

What's wrong with that? Roy thought silently; and for a moment Alan's imitation of her voice conjured up Grace with unbearable vividness.

'And what about Stan? He was my best friend, but Mum wouldn't have him in the house, oh no, because he was a nasty rough boy, his Dad kept a barrow in the market. Never mind that he always saw we got the best vegetables; *Stan* wasn't good enough for my precious birthday party. It all had to be perfect, see, everyone polite and nicely mannered.'

If we've got as far as Stan, it'll be Chrissie next, thought Roy, knowing better than to point out that, with the allotment, they didn't need Stan's father's vegetables.

'And then finally I got myself a girlfriend. About a year later than everyone else, because *I* had to be back straight after school to do my homework, *I* mustn't lead my sister into bad company or distract her from her brainy bloody exams. The only kids Mum approved of were the prim-and-proper goody-goodies at *Sunday* school. But at last I plucked up courage – and, believe me, it took some doing – to ask a bird out. Chrissie. God, I remember Chrissie. She was funny and she was pretty and she was about as different from my constipated family as chalk and cheese. But *I* picked her, right? Me. Myself. Aged sixteen.'

Yes, Roy remembered Chrissie, too. Bold eyes thickly rimmed with smudgy black paint, short skirts fluffed up with grubby nylon petticoats, bruises on her neck and thighs and a guttural laugh to go with her hoarse, breathy voice. Vera had seen the two of them together after school, and eventually Grace had persuaded Alan to bring her home for tea one Saturday. Roy winced as he recalled the girl's sharp mockery. 'Oh Mrs Southgate what a *delicious* cake! What a *wonderful* cook you must be! Oh yes *please*, I'd *love* another cup of tea . . .' – shooting sly glances at young Alan in a conspiracy that excluded his parents and his sister and made fun of their home. Grace had been bewildered, hearing the polite words and sensing the sarcasm behind them.

Stung to retort, Roy said, 'She was a hussy. She was rude and ungrateful to your mother, after she'd put herself out to do you proud.'

'Do me proud!' Alan snapped back. '*Proud?* I cringed with shame every time I walked through the front door!'

'No need for that. Mum and I did our best for you both, gave you a secure home, plenty of love.'

'You never loved me. *You* never loved anyone except each other . . .'

Oh my dear wife Grace, let me hold my tongue and remember dear you, worrying about their schoolwork and their vaccinations, having their teeth and eyes seen to regularly, giving them the right sort of food so they'd grow up fine and strong. Roy looked across at his son. It had worked, too. Alan looked remarkably fit, considering: a well-built man with a pasty complexion, features set in an angry scowl but splendid white teeth. Grace's years of devotion had paid off handsomely. Their son was a handsome man.

Alan's tirade had got as far as June. He had been twenty-three when he met her, not living at home any more, but somehow June was their fault as well.

When eventually Alan fell silent, Roy felt he could not leave without having described Grace's funeral. He told his sullen son about the hymns they had sung, the people there, the gathering afterwards.

'Junie couldn't come, but, then, I didn't really expect that, the boys would have been upset, and it's not a thing for children. She'd have been ever so welcome, of course. She and your Mum, well, it may not always have been easy, but by the end they'd a real understanding.'

'And Sheila? Would Sheila have been,' he mimicked, '*ever so welcome*?'

'Now Alan, Sheila's different, you know that.'

'No she isn't. She's the same. Just, exactly, the same.'

Roy lowered his eyes and looked at his empty teacup. Nearly time to go.

Alan was talking about Sheila, and for the first time his words were tender rather than vicious. He was saying things his father had never heard before. 'You've never met her, Dad. You and Mum refused to meet her, and I don't suppose I ever thought you would. It flies in the face of everything you stand for. But if you had, you'd know what I mean. Sheila's different. She was born for me, and I was born for her. What we had, we knew right away, was something special. It was magic. It was – well, it was like you and Mum. We was meant for each other. *That's* why I'm here.'

Roy was moved. He reached across the table, but Alan snatched his hand back and busied himself lighting another cigarette.

'Never forget,' Roy had said finally, 'your mother loved you. Nothing changed her feelings for you. You were her son and she loved you, till the day she died.'

Alan sucked viciously on his Dunhill. He made a whistling sound as he inhaled, lighting each cigarette from the butt of the last before crushing the filter convulsively into a saucer.

'OK, Dad, I tried – do you hear me? *I tried*, and you wouldn't listen. And here's another thing. These sodding fags. Don't bring me tips next time, you hear? *Every* time I tell him, every *single* time, but does he listen? No. He brings these lousy filter tips. I need a good hard smoke, right? Got that? Untipped.'

'These are the most expensive, son. I thought they'd be a treat.'

'Don't need a *treat*; I need a proper smoke. Not these yuppie fags.'

In the last five minutes Alan had talked fast, urgently, purging his venom, as Roy's greatest source of joy turned into the stuff of accusation and bitterness.

'You and Mum,' Alan had said, 'the perfect couple. So devoted. Just like newly-weds, weren't you? All your lives. Everything to each other. And me? What about *me*? What about Vera, for that matter? Never occurred to you there might be anything wrong with *her*, did it? There she was at whiter-than-white bloody Twigs, one of the *nice* girls at Tunbridge Wells Grammar School. Oh what a thing to be proud of! Come off it, Dad! She was fucking *loony*. "I wonder why your sister's so lovely and slim when you're such a *big* boy, Allie?" Shall I tell you why . . .?'

Roy stood up abruptly and took his plate across to the kitchen sink. He scraped congealed sardines and cold toast into the swing-top rubbish bin, rinsed his plate under the hot tap, sniffing to make sure that no trace of sardines remained, and stacked it in the double-decker wooden plate-rack. The knife and fork could go straight back into the cutlery drawer. He'd make a fresh cup of tea. Looking out of the kitchen window into the back garden, he noted that, already, the flowers were past their best. The roses needed dead-heading. That had always been Grace's job. Not now, thought Roy Southgate and, as the picture of her dear, stooping figure carefully wielding the secateurs filled his mind, he said out loud, 'Grace, my Grace, my dear old darling Grace, how shall I carry on without you?' It was too late now to go up to the allotment, but tomorrow he would choose fresh flowers for the shrine.

Dusk had fallen, and the hedge cast long shadows across the close-cropped lawn. A few steps from the back door stood the clothes-line, strung like a giant cobweb, throwing its angular webbed shadow. How many vests and underpants had she pegged out over the years; how many socks suspended in pairs by their toes; how many grey school uniforms and blue milkman's shirts? She'd never cared for drip-dry, said they smelt funny and she'd rather see everything starched and crisply ironed. 'If a job's worth doing, it's worth doing well' was

Gracie's motto. Her flowered dresses, aprons and blouses had flapped in the breeze, and Vera's pretty teenage skirts had danced on the line as, later, Vera herself ought to have run and danced in them. Now the clothes-line sagged, motionless and empty in the sharp evening light.

In an effort to distract himself he went into the lounge and sat in his armchair. He turned on the wireless at his elbow and searched through the airwaves for a comforting voice, but found only high-pitched drama or laughter or the howl and thump of pop music. He switched it off and settled down to think instead about Miss Hope's visit.

She had dwelt on the plight of the Squadron Leader, apparently much worse off than himself, a man shipwrecked on an island of desolation, not even eating or looking after himself properly. To Roy, trained by the Army to a lifetime's discipline, it was hard to imagine. The poor old fellow must be desperate, quite frantic with grief. He felt he ought to do something, perhaps offer to cook him a meal or visit from time to time – they had, after all, the shared experience of those last days to bind them – yet he could not bear the thought of leaving his house and abandoning the images of Grace waiting in every room just out of the corner of his eye. He knew, though, what the man must be feeling: poor widower – the emptiness. Roy, pondering, sighed, and slept.

The clock was chiming eleven as he woke to the telephone's shrill summons. It had been ringing in his sleep, incorporated into the dislocated events of some urgent dream landscape. He stood up, hearing his knees creak, and went out to the hall.

'Hallo?' he said, thinking, Must be Vera.

'Mr Southgate? Willatts here, governor, Ashford Prison. Bit late to disturb you.'

'No, no – I wasn't . . . What is it? What's happened?'

'Your son, I'm afraid, Alan Southgate. He's all right. Found in time. He's in the hospital wing. Doctor says he'll pull through.'

'What happened to – what did he do, sir, please?'

'There'll be an official inquiry. Its findings will be conveyed to you in due course. The matter will be properly investigated.'

'I thought he was sharing his cell.'

'He was troublesome late this afternoon, after visiting time. My men had to put him in isolation. Checked regularly, of course. Just as well. If you wanted to visit tomorrow, I think we could make an exception. In the circumstances.'

I've only just been, thought Roy. Tomorrow's Sunday. What about Grace's flowers?

'Could I make it after lunch?'

'After lunch will be fine. Tell my men on the gate. I'll leave a message there in the morning.'

'Please tell me: you're not . . . Is he really all right?'

'Doctor says so, Mr Southgate.'

'Can he talk? Is he asking for me, or anyone? Has his wife been told?'

'He's under heavy sedation for the time being. I have spoken to Mrs Southgate, Mrs June Southgate. And, as I say, there'll be a full inquiry in due course.'

'When he wakes, I'd be obliged if someone could tell him I'm on my way.'

I will *not* say thank you, Roy Southgate told himself fiercely.

'Anything else?'

'No, no, that's all,' said Roy. 'Thank you. I mean, goodbye.'

'Sorry about this. Bad time. His mother died recently, I believe?'

Seven weeks and three days ago.

'Yes,' said Roy. 'I have just lost my wife. Goodbye, Mr Willatts.'

Chapter Four

'Hello? Hello, that you, Southgate?'

'This is Tunbridge Wells 45829. Who's speaking, please?'

'Jolly good. Thought we ought to have a word. Vicar's idea, you know. Something to do with Mandy Hope. Gather she's talked to you as well.'

'Oh, yes, Mr Conynghame-Jervis —'

'Squadron Leader, don't you think?'

'Look, I'm ever so sorry, I've only just got back. Been visiting my son. He's not, you see, been very well.'

'Bad show. Never mind. No time like the present. Don't know what to make of it, really. What's your view, Southgate? Think it's worth having a chin-wag? Care to come round for a snifter? Give you the address, might as well nip round now.'

With his other hand Roy Southgate pushed open the dining-room door. The scent from Grace's freshly cut flowers drifted towards him. He had grouped three vases together in the middle of the table and they formed a fountain of leafy stems erupting into colour, rearing up straight and triumphant, vibrant with life. You never got that sort of vigour from florists' blooms. One rose nestled its head against the top of the photograph frame and her face laughed out at him below its soft petals.

In his ear the bluff voice chuntered on.

'. . . carry on past the hospital, past the cricket ground, and it's on your left, first turning off Bishops Down and then first right. If you get to High Rocks, you've gone too far. The Cedars. Can't miss it. Easy. Park in the drive. See you in, what, half an hour? ETA twenty hundred hours, eh? Eight o'clock?'

'Not tonight,' Roy said. 'Not feeling quite up to it.'

'But good heavens, man, it's *Sunday*.'

Roy understood that nothing he might say would be listened to. He had to get the man off the phone. 'Kettle's boiling,' he said. 'Have to go. There's a tea shop in the Pantiles. First one on the right. I could be there tomorrow morning, round about eleven.'

Surprised and cross, the Squadron Leader assented.

Roy Southgate put the telephone down very carefully. With equal precision, he walked into the kitchen, unhooked Grace's apron, wrapped it round his head, put his hands up to his face and wept. Behind him the kettle whistled, emitting clouds of steam through the little black bowler hat that crowned its spout. Under cover of the noise and the apron, Roy howled his pain. Gentle images of laughing Grace were overwhelmed by the memory of Alan, his throat encircled with soft white bandages, a striated purple bruise showing over the edge and running up past his ear to disappear into the springy thickets of his hair. Roy's head rocked from side to side. 'Gracie,' he moaned, 'I can't bear it alone, I can't, I can't, I can't.'

Fellow's damned impertinent, said Reggie to himself. Good mind to tell him to forget the whole idea. Who does he think I am? Frigging tea in the frigging Pantiles? Make myself a laughing stock. Suppose someone saw me? Think I'd become a poofter. He strode over to the drinks cabinet and poured himself a tumbler of whisky. It splashed on to the polished mahogany top, and he wiped it away with his sleeve before taking a deep swig.

'Haaaa . . .' he sighed aloud, thinking, That's better. Too good to waste on that miserable little pongo. Don't know what gave the vicar the idea that he'd make himself useful about the place. Sounds damned uppity to me. Ought to have shot the idea down in flames straightaway.

He opened and slammed shut a couple of silver cigarette boxes lined with cedar wood and imbued with the sweet lingering smell of decades of tobacco. Empty. He rooted around in his trouser pockets, rummaged in his jacket: no good.

'Have to go down to the pub,' he said out loud. 'Just pick up a packet of fags. Nothing else. Nanny's good boy.'

*

Reggie leaned on the bar, a large double whisky tucked cosily inside the curve of his sleeve, a cigarette smouldering in the glass ashtray on the other side. He was rehearsing an old and much-loved controversy.

'Say what you like, and I've heard all the arguments, I still think stunting's essential. You've got to know everything your kite can do, and how else are you going to find out? Risky, I grant you. Put myself in hospital during OT, messing about in a Spit, but it teaches you what you're both capable of.'

'Couldn't agree more, squire,' said the barman absent-mindedly. He was in his thirties, a weary figure revolving the puddles of beer on the bar with a sodden rag, and he had no idea what Reggie was talking about, but he knew better than to disagree with a drunk.

'Then, when it comes to a scrap, when it counts, you've got the experience,' Reggie went on happily. He was back in the Nissen-hut crew room, sitting round a coke stove waiting for the weather to clear up so that they could fly, going over the old arguments. Long Gone Manners would disagree with him on principle, and the two of them would bicker knowledge-ably, without the least hope of either being converted. After a while the others would say, 'Knock it off you two, for Pete's sake!' and Reggie would appeal for somebody to back his point of view . . . The barman would have to do for now.

'Let's face it,' he went on, 'the tighter your turn the better your chance of escape in a dog fight. Round you go, couple of boxers in the ring, you're feinting' – his head ducked from side to side, his jowls wobbling – 'you're on guard. Suddenly you put the Spit into a stall-turn. Bingo! You're ready to attack! Difference between life and death, that sort of practice. Take my instructor: now *he* was a pretty handy stunter. Get him on your tail and you'd never shake him off. Practice – all good practice. Never enough time, of course. We're talking about the days of Dunkirk, now: not your University Air Squadron messing about.'

'It's all in the lap of the gods, I say. Taking your life in your hands, aren't you, every time you fly?' said the bored barman.

67

'Trouble was,' Reggie continued, his mind perfectly sharp as long as he stabilized it around the age of twenty-one, 'trouble was, their tactics changed all the time. Fight from height – that's one thing that never changed; come at them straight out of the sun: that's another. Get your Messerschmitt from behind – that's where he's vulnerable. All very well with the 109s, but when the 262s came along, rules changed again. *If* you could catch them.'

'That's what it's all about, isn't it?' said the barman.

Reginald looked up as he moved to serve a strikingly dressed woman who had come in by herself. She wore a lime-green car coat and a narrow skirt slit some way up the side to show off good legs. She placed her handbag on the bar and levered herself on to a stool with a flash of thigh. The barman winked at Reggie.

'Spot of sympathy required, Jim,' she said. 'I've had a hell of a day! I could really do with a Scotch.'

'Glenmorangie for the lady,' said Reginald. 'Make it a double?'

She looked across. 'I don't know who you are, but the way I'm feeling at this moment, all I can say is that sounds like a lifesaver! Yes, a double would be lovely.'

'Two double Glenmorangies, Jim,' said Reginald. 'Mind if I join you?' She swept the edge of her coat aside to show that he was welcome.

'Smoke?' said Reggie.

'Oh dear, I know I shouldn't. Yes, all right, go on, lead me astray.' As he snapped open his silver lighter, she said, 'I'm Elizabeth Franks but everyone calls me Liz.'

'And I'm Reginald Conynghame-Jervis but everyone calls me Reggie. How do you do, Liz?'

'Cheers, Reggie!'

'Give you lift?' he asked a couple of doubles later, and the big boy shifted hopefully.

'You are a sweetie,' she said. 'Bless you, but no, thanks – I've got my own car outside. Only meant to pop in for a pick-me-up. Never meant to stay so long, you wicked man!'

The big boy twitched.

'Be popping in tomorrow?'

'I might – after I've closed the shop, but it's not a promise . . . Look, really, I must be off.'

'Shop?' said Reggie, grasping at the last fragment of conversation, but with a final smile she swept out.

He turned back to the barman.

'Who's she when she's at home?'

'Our Liz? Quite a looker, isn't she? Well stacked – in both senses. Keeps one of those posh dress shops – down near the Pantiles, I think. Never checked out the goods myself. Too pricey for me.' He laughed uproariously.

It was long after eleven when Reggie got home, but he telephoned Roy Southgate immediately. When after several rings a dazed voice answered, he said abruptly, 'Squadron Leader here. About that confab tomorrow, Southgate. No can do. Some other time. Give me a tinkle. Or not. Suit yourself. Cheer-oh.'

He hung up without waiting for a reply.

Roy lay in bed, the softness of Grace's brushed cotton nightie against his skin. He knew he would not get to sleep for hours. Mentally he called off the whole idea – the Squadron Leader would obviously drive him round the bend in a week – and, to make the night pass, settled down to play an old game of Grace's.

'Ro-oy?' she would ask, 'how many times do you think we've made love *now*?' They would do the familiar arithmetic together, an excuse to remember their happy youth. During the last glorious summer of peace they'd bicycled off into the country and picnicked in fields, curling up to fall asleep afterwards in each other's arms, or gazing up into the green branches flickering brilliantly against a sky of palest blue. They had married in May that year, just after he'd finished training to be a sapper with the Territorials (Royal Engineer Field Company). They'd decided on one of those hurried last-minute weddings, never knowing how long these halcyon pre-war days might last, and never mind that she had to buy rather than make her wedding dress. He'd wangled a week's leave after that . . .

'Twice a night ánd then some: call it fifteen, *minimum . . .*'

And then odd weekends' home leave, if you could call her parents' cramped terraced house in Purley *home*. They had felt self-conscious about slipping away too obviously; all the same . . .

'Probably three or four times per weekend . . .'

'Call it four . . .'

They hadn't made love often once they knew she was expecting. Roy had been afraid of hurting her. Not that he minded the swelling pregnancy: her slight figure, back curved to take the weight of the great mound that strained forward from below her rib cage, filled him with pride and joy. The pale skin of her belly seemed almost transparent, so that he felt he should have been able to see the child curled inside. He could certainly see her flesh twitch when it kicked, and would lay his hand against her bare skin as they lay in bed and murmur, 'Feel him, Gracie! That's our boy. Isn't he strong?' But the district midwife had told Grace that it wasn't advisable to permit relations in the last three months and, precious as their weekends together were, they had, not without difficulty, abstained.

So it had taken about sixty tries before they had got it right, they had decided. 'Yes, and wasn't the practising fun?' Roy would whisper. They both took it for granted that they would make love until the end of their lives.

He was born in 1940, during the Blitz; desperate times. What sort of a world are we bringing him into? Grace used to ask. What if Hitler *wins*? And Roy would sáy, Now now, girl, you know that can't happen.

After his birth – and he *was* a big baby: nine pounds, three ounces – Grace had to have a few stitches, and stayed in hospital for three weeks. They named their son Frederick, after her father, knowing it would please him, and Albert, after his.

'Frederick Albert Southgate,' Grace said, gazing at the child rolled up tightly in a shawl and lying on her bed. 'He'd better be prime minister when he grows up, with a name like that!'

Outside feeding and visiting times their child took his place in a room with all the other babies, two· rows of them in identical cots. No matter how much they yelled, feeding was strictly regulated. No point in tiring yourself out, feeding him all hours of the day, the starched sister told Grace. You feed him every four hours and he'll soon learn what's what. He did too. By the time she came out he was feeding at six, ten, two, six, ten: regular as a mathematical progression.

Roy was back with his Company by then. They wrote to each other as often as possible, and she would describe the baby, how he smiled and waggled his arms about, how greedily he fed. Roy would imagine him sucking at her breast and wondered whether it was wrong to find this idea exciting. Then, when little Freddie was just over three months old, came the news. Grace had slept late one morning, exhausted by broken nights, and woken up to find him dead in his cot beside her. They gave Roy forty-eight hours' compassionate leave, and he and Grace and her parents had buried the baby and wept together.

'I should have taken him to the country!' she said, over and over again. 'It was the raids that killed him, I'm sure of it! Night after night, having to get him out of his warm cot and go underground to a stuffy air-raid shelter – that can't have been good for a tiny baby.'

'And where else could you have gone?' Roy had said, wearily, guiltily. 'To my Mum in Folkestone? That'd been just as bad.'

After that they had decided: no more babies till the war was over. Hitler had taken one child from them: he wasn't going to have any more. Grace spent the war in Purley, grieving over her one small death in the midst of so many others, and never forgot Frederick Albert.

Where was I? thought Roy drowsily. Oh yes, sixty ... But instead of counting further, he fell asleep thinking of his little lost son, rather than of the grown-up man who was also his son, and whom he had also nearly lost. The thought of Frederick and Grace together brought some hint of comfort; the thought of Alan was no comfort at all.

A couple of weeks later, Reginald was preparing to go up to London to see the family solicitor. Mary's will was to be read and her estate distributed – what there was of it. In the afternoon he had an appointment with his trustees to discuss new ways of investing his money and her bits and bobs – the odd shares, if she had any left. High time he had a chat about how his affairs were to be looked after from now on. Might even – he censored the thought, which persisted – might even pay a visit to Sabrina. Reginald dressed carefully. He chose one of his best Harvie and Hudson shirts, white with a faint blue stripe, a dark red patterned silk tie, a Christmas present from Mary, and dark red socks.

It was ten years since he'd travelled regularly to London, and his best business suit – navy blue, pin-striped, double-breasted – was tighter than he remembered. Despite the warmth of the August day he wore a waistcoat to obscure the ample curve of his belly. He chose a good pair of black shoes, dusted them with a corner of the blanket, and slipped them on to his elegant small feet. Then he stood up and examined himself in the mirror. He looked distinguished, no doubt about it. Still a fine figure of a man, he said to himself; credit to any woman.

Matters were moving more slowly than he had hoped with Liz Franks. She had turned up in the pub again, rewarding several days of hopeful vigil. She had recognized him, accepted a drink; then two more. Reginald learned that she was divorced with two grown-up children, and did indeed, as the barman had informed him, own a dress shop in the centre of town. Reggie couldn't guess her age but reckoned 'a woman is as old as she looks, and a man's old when he stops looking'. Liz, in his eyes, was a highly desirable woman with a shapely figure, well-preserved, amusing and evidently unattached. He did not care to ask himself what she was doing alone in a pub.

The answer – that, like himself, she was lonely, looking for male company, and fond of a drink – would not have occurred to him. It occurred to Liz almost immediately, on the other hand, that Reginald was a rich widower at a loose end who would fall like a ripe plum into the arms of a younger wife. If she wanted him, he could be hers. But did she want him?

When she appeared in the pub a second time, he asked her to have dinner with him. Not dinner, she said, smiling; not just yet. But she'd love to have lunch. They had met for lunch, therefore, in a chic little restaurant in the High Street. She had told him that the shop did well, and did not reveal the problems created by high interest rates, with a mortgage on her house as well as business debts; instead, she asked about his own professional life. (Here Reginald exaggerated a little his seniority and indispensability to the firm of Jervis & Co, Importers.) Delicately, she had offered sympathy upon the recent death of his wife. Reginald's brusqueness warned her off the subject.

Liz told him about her children. Her son, Hugo, had dropped out of university in his final year and was now travelling. She did not enlarge on the reasons that lay behind this, the nightmare that she had lived with ever since discovering that he used drugs. Her daughter, Alicia – she displayed the photograph of a lovely young girl – had been a model for a time, given that up, and was now, said Liz, 'learning the catering business'. What this actually meant was that Alicia had worked as a waitress in a number of modish London brasseries; but Reginald would not have been interested. It was the mother he was after. Lunch had gone well but she wouldn't be tied down to a definite date for dinner. Pity she couldn't see him like this, he thought, looking approvingly at his best business-suited reflection. He would suggest an evening in London soon, perhaps dinner and a show. Maybe that would do the trick.

He opened a drawer and selecting a pale blue handkerchief, just the colour to go with his shirt, tucked it into his top pocket. Using two hairbrushes, he smoothed back the thinning grey strands, now with only the slightest kink to indicate what a fine head of thick, wavy hair he had once possessed. It still tended to curl upwards at the back of his neck and he smoothed on some Brylcreem to plaster it down. No time for a haircut: had to be in the Temple by eleven and it was well past nine already.

Elsie looked up from her hoovering as Reggie descended the stairs.

'You look ever so smart!' she exclaimed admiringly.

'Must dash,' said Reginald. 'All right if I pay you on Monday?'

'No,' she answered firmly. 'I've got to shop for the kiddies tomorrow. All that running about in the summer has made their feet grow and their trainers is full of holes. I'd be obliged if I could have my money now.'

He riffled through his wallet and extracted two twenty-pound notes and a tenner. 'There you are,' he said grandly. 'That's two weeks. Don't spend it all at once.'

'All the best, sir,' she said as he left.

The streets round the Temple were choked with cars and it took Reginald so long to find a parking place that he arrived at Tidmarsh, Spencer, Tidmarsh over ten minutes late. The receptionist welcomed him coolly and Reggie smoothed his hair nervously as she rang through to say he'd arrived. She was black, a fact which astonished Reggie, as did her immaculate voice and composed manner.

'Would you come this way, please, Mr Conynghame-Jervis?' she said, and he followed her through to Tidmarsh's spacious office, whose tall windows overlooked the green square in the centre of the Temple buildings.

They were all there waiting for him: his nephew, Vivian, and Susan, his thin-faced, angular second wife. Also the twins from his first marriage, Thingy and Thingummy. Good-looking girls they'd both grown into, he noted again with pleasure.

'Morning Vivian,' he said. 'Susan. Hello, girls. My how you've grown! Parking's appalling round here, Tidmarsh.'

'*Do* take a seat Squadron Leader,' said James Tidmarsh silkily, subsiding back into his own. 'Now that you're here . . .'

Reginald sat down, the buttons on his waistcoat straining. This is it, he thought. Now we have lift-off.

When they married in 1942, just before he was posted to North Africa, Mary's parents had settled quite a generous sum upon her. She had the income from a trust of £25,000 and quite a nice little parcel of shares. Their generosity had surprised him, for he'd never thought them well off. But then, she was their only child. Reginald, never seriously short of money himself, had left her to play with her shares or not, just as she liked. He was amused sometimes to see her pore over his *Financial Times* or *Standard* at home in the evenings, watching prices move up and down. He regarded it as a little hobby for her, and as long as the money paid for her clothes and hair dos, Christmas presents and trips to town to see old school-friends or whoever it was she did see, he found no reason to interfere. She didn't consult him, and – not that he told her this – he wouldn't have known how to advise her. His view was that they paid accountants and stockbrokers to look after that sort of thing. Reggie grumbled at their fees and let them get on with it.

Old Tidmarsh, lugubriously conscious of his role as the family solicitor, began by fastening his eyes on them all in turn. 'It is not usual,' he started sonorously, 'to call the benefici-aries together in order that they may hear a will being read. Indeed, in this day and age, it is commonplace for most wills to be sent through the post. However, in the circumstances, I suggested, to the late Mrs Conynghame-Jervis, that it might, *in this instance*, be correct. Preferable, even. And to this the late Mrs Conynghame-Jervis assented.'

Get on with it, man! Reggie thought irritably, just as Tid-marsh, after droning through the formalities, finally came to the point.

'The value of the stocks and shares on the day of the de-ceased's death, 2 June 1990, amounted to £621,043. In addi-tion she held unit-trust funds amounting to £141,756. The late Mrs Conynghame-Jervis owned a half share in the matrimonial home, currently valued at approximately £475,000. She left no personal debts.'

Reginald struggled to take in the implications of these figures. Mary had somehow increased her parents' money to over three-quarters of a million pounds. Mary was *rich*. She had played her cards close to her chest, never told him any of this – true, she never *asked* for anything – but all the time she was rolling in it. Well, now his worries were over. He fixed his eyes on James Tidmarsh's grey, impassive face as he began to read out the will.

'This will is made by Marigold Elizabeth, wife of Reginald Vivian Conynghame-Jervis, on the sixteenth day of March, 1989. I hereby revoke all former wills and codicils made by me . . .'

Let's get to the point, thought Reginald again, more irritably. He stared intently at his own plump crossed legs. Shoes could be cleaner.

'I desire that my husband, the afore mentioned Reginald Vivian Conynghame-Jervis, if I should pre-decease him . . .'

Reginald looked up.

'. . . be permitted to continue living in the jointly owned matrimonial home, The Cedars, Nevill Park, Tunbridge Wells, Kent, but that after his death, my share of its then value should go to the British Association for Adoption and Fostering, to aid those who are childless. Its furniture and all contents, with the exception of specific bequests mentioned hereinunder, shall remain for his use during his lifetime.'

Up to her, though Reggie. Won't make any difference to me. Funny, though. She never talked about adopting a child. Would have been easy, back in the Fifties. Never knew she wanted to. Taboo subject, of course. Never mentioned. Still . . . his concentration snapped back into focus.

'I bequeath to my husband, Reginald Vivian, five thousand pounds a year, and release him from the obligation to repay such sums of money as I may have lent to him in the course of our married life and which may still be owing.'

Reggie flinched. The odd bill paid now and again – can't have amounted to more than a thousand a year, two at the most. Why was she making him sound like a sponger, in front of everyone? Man and wife are one flesh. Those didn't count as *loans*. He'd have done the same for her, if she'd asked. Funny, come to think of it, that she never did. He hadn't noticed till this moment. She paid Mrs Thing, O'Murphy, but that was her department. And the wine-merchant. Quite a number of bills, if you began to tot them up. No wonder the bank manager had been binding away these last few weeks.

'I give the remainder of my property, after all taxes, duties, costs and any debts have been paid, to my beloved nieces, the twin daughters of Lord Blythgowrie, Celia and Felicity Conynghame-Jervis, to be divided between them in equal shares and held in trust for them until they shall marry or until they shall have attained the age of thirty, whichever is the sooner; these monies to be payable directly and only to the said Celia and Felicity, for their enjoyment and disposal, in token of my loving thanks for their affection and support.'

James Tidmarsh looked up. 'As far as I am able to ascertain at this stage, that clause means that you, Celia, and you, Felicity, should receive approximately £250,000 each, after payment of estate duty.'

He smiled thinly at their astonished young faces. The two girls had clasped each other's hands, and it was evident that the bequest was completely unexpected. Their father smiled, too.

'*Well,*' he said. '*That*'s awfully good of her. Dear Mary . . .'

Nobody looked at Reginald, who was staring intently at his feet, one of which shook slightly. He uncrossed his legs. His face began to burn. He glanced covertly across at the two young women, sitting tidily in their neat black jackets and short skirts, legs tucked under their chairs, eyes demurely downcast. They, too, were high-coloured with emotion. Yet his first reaction was not indignation but, rather, sheer surprise. *But*, he stuttered mentally, but, but . . . *Mary*? He'd known that she dabbled now and again on the stock market, but had had no idea that she was so successful at it; no idea that she had been so fond of his nieces. How could she be? She hardly ever saw them! He began to feel indignant, as though he had just learned that his wife had cheated him. Nanny, Nanny, it's not fair. Tell her it's not fair to keep secrets from me. It's *mean*.

Tidmarsh's assistant was whispering something to him. Tidmarsh nodded, and looked up.

'Before I go on to the remainder of Mrs Conynghame-Jervis's bequests,' he said to Reggie, 'I should give you this letter, which she left with me the last time she redrew her will, with instructions that I should personally see that it was handed to you.' The whey-faced assistant crossed the room smoothly to hand over the letter. Reginald tucked the envelope into his inside jacket pocket. Could do with a cigarette, he thought. No one else was smoking.

'Would you bring me an ashtray?' he asked, and the deferential figure checked his glide and looked at Tidmarsh. An ashtray was found in some bottom drawer and placed on the floor beside him. Reggie expelled a long vee of smoke.

'Right ho,' he said. 'Cleared for take-off. Carry on.'

When the formalities were over, he declined the offer of a glass of sherry, shook hands with Vivian and smiled at the girls.

'You'll forgive me if I leave you. Lunch appointment, you know. Business calls.'

'We'd love to come down and see you, Uncle Reggie,' said Celia.

'You've got my number. Give me a tinkle,' said Reginald. 'Treat you to lunch . . .' biting back the words Or rather, you can treat me. They both kissed him on the cheek, their young skins petal-soft, a faint breath of scent wafting around him. Susan leaned her immaculate face beside his for an instant; Vivian shook his hand in a manly grip.

'Be in touch, everyone,' said Reginald as he left the room. 'Keep me informed, won't you, Tidmarsh? There's a good fellow. Toodle-pip.'

*

He waited till he was sitting in his car before taking the letter from his jacket and ripping open the envelope. The sight of his wife's handwriting gave him a pang which dispelled his rising sense of outrage. The letter was dated 16 March 1989.

Darling Reginald, she wrote:

I am afraid this will may come as a bit of a shock to you. Of course you had no idea what I did with my money. Most of the time I didn't do very much. But gradually I got interested in the City, learned to read the financial pages and began to get the hang of how the stock exchange works. About 15 years ago, roundabout the early 70s, I had a bit of luck. I sold those old brewery shares and invested in different ones, and after that things sort of began to go quite well for me. I don't know when I'll die or how much money I shall leave, but I'm pretty sure it'll be more than you expect, which is why I'm writing this. I've worked out how much you've been borrowing in recent years, and tried to make sure you'll get roughly double that. I hope this means you won't be any worse off than before, in fact probably a bit better. By making over £5,000 a year to you, you shouldn't need to draw in your horns in case I die before you – though with luck I hope that won't happen!

Here followed a tidy list of her annual loans to him, beginning in 1975. From £678 in the first year it rose steadily, and the last figure, for 1988, was nearly £3,000. Can't be right, thought Reggie, she's wildly over the top; but he knew that from time to time, perhaps almost from week to week, he'd asked for 'the odd' hundred pounds. He wondered now why he'd never been surprised that she was always willing to write him a cheque from her own account. He turned back to the letter.

Now about the girls. You remember that about the time of the divorce, they gave Vivian and Susan a bit of trouble? It can't have been easy for them to lose their mother. Well, anyway, that's when I started seeing a good deal of them. I used to slip up to London during their school holidays to give them lunch and take them to a matinée, and sometimes we'd go clothes-shopping together which was tremendously good fun for me. In time they started to confide in me. Susan's a darling of course but it must have been jolly intimidating for teenagers, having such a glamorous step-Mama! Anyhow I began to get very close to them.

You mustn't feel indignant about all this, Reggie dear. I would have told you, if you'd seemed interested, but although in the beginning I used to mention that I was seeing the girls you only said, Jolly good, give them my love – which I always did, by the way – and never asked questions. I suppose I felt you didn't really care about them. To tell you the truth, I sometimes wondered if you heard what I said.

I know I haven't been a very exciting wife to you. But I have loved you and writing this now brings the tears to my eyes. I wish I had been able to say it more often. A couple of weeks ago I took you out to dinner for your 70th birthday at Luigi's – I expect you remember? I asked you then whether you were happy and you looked at me in sort of surprise and said, perfectly. I thought to myself, well that's something, if he can say he's perfectly happy. I can't have made too much of a hash of things.

Perhaps if we'd had a child, or more than one, it might have brought us closer. Oh Reggie. I did so long for children! But we were never very good at talking about all that. I know you'll understand why I made over my half of the house to BAAF.

BAAF? thought Reginald. What the hell's . . . oh yes, that adoption thing.

If I do go first, I want you to know that I hope you'll marry again. I don't think you're very suited to living by yourself. Marriage is a funny thing, it isn't easy, it hasn't been what we expected, has it? We've had a rather English sort of marriage.

Well Reggie dear, I'm getting sentimental, so I'd better stop. It's hard to imagine you reading this, and I hope you'll never have to. But I'm nearly 70 too, and I get the odd ache and pain and had to pop along to Dr Duncan last week, so I suppose it could be me that goes first.

Well, if you ever have to read this, my famous last words!! are, look after yourself, try not to drink too much and also you ought to lose a bit of weight, dear, or your health will suffer. Be kind to the girls and don't think they sucked up to me because I promise you it isn't true.

They had no idea I was becoming fairly well off, either. *They just treated me like a sort of second mother which was wonderful for me, just what I've always wanted. They're a grand pair.*

Oh heck, I don't think I could bring myself to end this if I ever actually thought you were going to read it, but I don't so I'll just say, lots of love from your wife

Mary

P.S. And 'the bunnies'!!

It was the 'Oh heck' that finished him. It had been one of her favourite expressions, long after everyone else had stopped saying it, and Reggie could hear the mock-cockney tone in which she would say it: 'Oh 'eck!' Her strongest terms of criticism would be 'I'm a bit browned off about ...' or, 'Oh really, that's *too* bad!' She hated to make a fuss. Pleased by something, she would exclaim like a schoolgirl, 'Good-*oh*!' Gentle Mary, meek and mild. She was so innocent that it amounted to foolishness sometimes, but always on the look-out for the best in everyone and always stoical. He saw now the gallantry in her patient stoicism. She hadn't nagged him or found fault, but gone on putting up with things, even at the very worst of times.

Reggie put his head down on to the steering wheel of his car and wept. One hand clutched the letter tightly in his lap and the other was laid across the top of his head. *I sometimes wondered if you heard what I said.* He hadn't heard; he had never listened, never heard, and now it was too late.

After a while, two passers-by noticed the stout, elderly man heaving convulsively, and, wondering if he was having a heart attack, went in search of authority. First a meter maid rapped on the windscreen.

'Everything all right, sir?' she mouthed through the shatter-proof glass.

Reggie looked up, shook his head, waved her away and went on sobbing. In due course she returned, bringing with her a policeman, who signalled to him to wind down the window.

'You feeling all right, sir?' he asked. 'Need any help?'

'Thank you, officer. No. I'm fine now. Be on my way in a tick. Cleared for take-off?'

The policeman looked at him in puzzlement, but Reggie's accent and his opulent car and evident sobriety reassured him. 'Very good, sir,' he said. 'Mind how you go.'

Reginald folded the letter in two, replaced it in his pocket and drove to Simpson's in the Strand for lunch. He'd definitely give Sabrina a miss. That was the least he could do. But he badly needed a double Scotch.

Chapter Five

'I do appreciate your coming, what with you being so busy, but I don't think you should keep on,' said Roy to Mandy Hope. 'We've sorted out the forms and the money. I just have to get on with whatever life's left.'

It was a dank and gloomy afternoon in early October. By half past five it was already almost dark. Rain dripped with tiny audible blips from the roof overhanging the kitchen, and Mandy's umbrella stood in a pool of water by the front door. Despite the warmth of the coal stove and the steaming cups of tea in front of them, Roy Southgate wore a knitted Fair Isle waistcoat to keep the cold off his chest, and a tweed jacket with leather elbow patches. Nowadays he never left the house without a woollen muffler up to his ears, a flat cap and warm gloves. The earth felt cold and heavy when he visited the cemetery or dug in the allotment; its clamminess weighed down the spade and clung to the soles of his shoes.

Mandy was concerned about him. Grace's death and the drama of his son's acute depression had left their mark. Roy was no longer a gallant, chirpy figure. He looked old, frailer and greyer than when she had seen him for the first time, his slight frame more stooped. She smiled vigorously to reassure him.

'But I love coming – and, anyway, it's important if you *do* decide to give it a try up at The Cedars, that you and the Squadron Leader should get off on the right footing. For a start I don't see why you shouldn't call him Reginald.'

Roy Southgate looked appalled. 'I don't think that would be right. He'd not like it, not one bit. And I don't think I could get my tongue round it.'

'You may be staying in his house, but you'll be there on equal terms. There's no question of him paying you. He won't be your employer. He calls you Roy, doesn't he?'

Reggie in fact called him 'Southgate', but Roy thought it would only make matters worse if he admitted this, so he ignored the question.

'We've met twice now for what he calls a chin-wag. I still don't think he's really keen on the vicar's idea.'

'That's just his manner. I notice it's got worse since his cleaner left. The hospital came up with a nice woman who works as a ward orderly there on a part-time basis, but Elsie was a link with his wife and that was important. Someone who remembered her and could talk about her.'

'Why did she leave?'

Mandy remembered Elsie O'Murphy's outraged Catholic propriety and searched for an excuse that was reasonably true but would not scandalize Roy Southgate. 'I think,' she said eventually, 'she felt it wasn't proper for her, a married woman, to be alone in the house with him quite so much.'

Roy sighed. It was true that he craved company, the presence of another human being to eke out the long lonely evenings now that winter was coming. He had felt that he and the Squadron Leader must have so much in common, that the coincidence of their wives' deaths in the same ward, on the same night, made a palpable link between them. The other man showed little sign of recognizing this or of wanting to discuss his wife. That much Roy could understand: some things were too deep to be talked about with a stranger. But he had hoped for some gesture of comradeship. However, though the War might have ended forty-five years ago, the difference in rank between them yawned almost as wide and deep as ever. Mandy and the vicar, he thought, were being over-optimistic. Still, it was hard to reject the idea entirely.

'It's a big house,' he said cautiously.

'Yes, I know. You wouldn't get on top of one another.'

'I'd have my own quarters.'

'You'd have your own bedroom and bathroom, and you could have a sitting room downstairs if you wanted one. It's the old servants' sitting room, to be honest, but don't read anything into that. You would be there as an equal. You would *not* be his servant – I've made that quite clear to him – and nobody expects you to wait on him.'

'I know it would take my mind off things. I sometimes, tell you the truth, often, howl my eyes out here on my own. It's just that if I leave here, it feels like, well, abandoning Grace.'

'Roy, the decision's entirely up to you. But as I say, *he's* keen to give it a try. And it *would* be on a trial basis at first.'

'Tell him . . . tell him, I'll move in the beginning of November, up until after Christmas. Then we'll both see how we like it. That gives me a few weeks to sort myself out.'

'I'll talk to him. I'll make sure he understands that at this stage it's not a permanent arrangement.'

She smiled at Roy's worried face. He did so want to do the right thing. She also knew that it was realistic for him to be worried. The Squadron Leader could be maddening, yet he was surprisingly open to suggestion, and keener than Roy to give this idea a try.

'I'm seeing him for the last time next week. I'll warn him he's got to be on good behaviour!'

She would, Mandy told Roy, always be on the end of a telephone. Any problems, any difficulty settling in, and he had only to ring; but he should not expect her to visit them regularly.

After she had gone, Roy looked out some things for mending. There was a smashed cup and saucer that needed Aralditing – just the sort of meticulous job he liked – and his pyjama trousers wanted threading with new elastic: tasks on which his fingers had to concentrate, leaving his mind free. He assembled everything he needed and picked up the cup.

What was the alternative to the vicar's idea? He was lonely here by himself, true enough, and while the Squadron Leader wouldn't have been his first choice of companion, who else was there? He didn't know any other widowers – most of them went into those old people's dumps after their wives had died, and anything was better than *that*. He'd visited once or twice, with Grace. The smell hit you first – mouldy vegetables, mouldy bodies, and stained linen: suit yourself as to which you noticed most. Then the listlessness. They sat about in collapsing armchairs, usually in a circle round the television, any old rubbish blaring from the screen *and* far too loud, on account of the ones who were deaf. He didn't think he'd deteriorate in the same way, but once you were institutionalized you weren't in control any more. Look at Alan . . . He banished the thought. Blokes from the dairy who had been cracking a joke in the Kelsey Arms not a year before went into a home and were suddenly fit for nothing but the compost heap. By comparison with that, the Squadron Leader and his posh house sounded like paradise.

No one was suggesting *he* should go into a home, but somehow women seemed to manage better on their own. Grace had several friends whose husbands had gone first. 'Free she is now, after a lifetime of drudgery, bad language and worse than that when he'd got drink in him!' Grace had said more than once. These old women became brisk and bright-eyed, skipped off on their Old Person's Railcard to visit grandchildren all over the country, even went off abroad on coachtrips sometimes, if the money allowed. Old Jack Simmonds, the milkman who'd turned to lashing his wife when they got rid of horses and brought in milk floats – now there was a vicious man! He'd had a heart attack soon after he retired from the Unigate, and Edith Simmonds had been a happier woman without him, no doubt about it. But he could hardly turn up on *her* doorstep and say, Hello, are you lonely too?

Then there was Molly Tucker, who'd kept her improbable mop of blonde curls all her life. 'It wasn't me own when I was twenty and it ain't me own at sixty,' she would say. 'So where's the difference, may I ask?' Molly and Ted had been happily married, too, till Ted got cancer in his chest and it carried him off in three months. That was when Grace had persuaded Roy to give up smoking. It hadn't been easy – he'd smoked all his life – but she said, 'You always promised me we'd grow old together, Royston Southgate, and after what I seen of Ted's last weeks I don't want to have to nurse you down the same road.' He sighed, and the delicate fingertips pressing two fragments of china together shook so that he had to start that section again.

Sometimes the one left would move in with married children. That was the best solution, if it worked. But Roy didn't want to up sticks and go out to Australia, though it wasn't for want of asking on Vera's part. He didn't feel old, not often; but he felt too old for *that*. Fly thousands of miles to arrive at a strange place on the other side of the world, different weather, different ways of doing things? Too much of a risk. Besides, he'd never got on with Vera's husband, Stan. Roy suspected that Stan was a bully, dreaded lest he was violent to her and their sons, although Vera was loyal and never so much as hinted at any such thing. None the less, he wouldn't care to put himself under Stan's roof or at Stan's mercy.

And then there was Alan's wife, June.

'The less said about *her* the better!' he'd commented to Grace, after Alan brought her home for the first time; but Grace had said, 'Now Royston: give her a chance. Nobody gets condemned out of hand in *this* household. All right, she's got a child with no father to give it his name, but what would you rather? Should she have done away with it, poor innocent mite? That would have been tidier, I grant you, but would it have been right?'

He had done his best to be open-minded about June, but Alan hadn't given them the opportunity to get to know her. They'd married in a register office, had a party above a pub afterwards, and from then on he and Grace were lucky to see their son and his wife once a year.

It was five years before the first of the little lads came along, William Alan, and two years after him came Joe – Joseph Roy. Grace would sometimes take the train to south London to see June, whose own mother lived in Dublin and could seldom visit her; she would spend all day minding the boys, washing and baking. June was defensive at first. '*My* standards aren't good enough for you, I suppose?' But Grace would answer, 'Now don't be silly, lovey: it's to give you a break from babies and toddlers. Go and get your hair done, see a film, better still, go off with Alan somewhere, just the two of you.'

Grace would return from these outings pale and overtired, but she always said it was worth the trouble. 'How else do you get to know a kiddie except by changing its nappy or wiping its little nose? If you wait till they can talk to you, it's too late! You've lost 'em by then.'

But he, Roy, had never changed the nappies, hardly even wiped the noses, of his own children – that had been Grace's side of things. He wouldn't know how to begin with his grand-sons. Then came the shock of Alan's news, right after Gracie's diagnosis had been confirmed. Grace had had to endure an interminable series of visits to the hospital for tests and more tests, and then the operation. But the cancer had spread too far. The surgeon could not remove it all. Thank God Roy had been able to keep from her the news of Alan's trial and Alan's prison sentence. Eighteen months he'd got: longer than normal because he refused to express regret. I am not brave enough to think about that yet, Roy said to himself deliberately. I will put it out of my mind. He tidied away the work basket and left the cup and saucer beside the stove to harden.

Time for supper. He fancied rissoles and baked beans, but there didn't seem much point in going to all the trouble of making a rissole for one, so he'd bought a frozen hamburger at Tesco's. Give that a try, with some of Gracie's potted plums to follow with custard. Vera kept telling him in her letters how important it was to eat properly.

An hour later, the taste of artificial fat still circling gluti-nously around his false teeth in spite of a cup of strong tea, Roy sat at the kitchen table and prepared to write to his daughter. She'd have to have his new address, he supposed, or at any rate the telephone number in case of emergencies, and perhaps if he explained to her on paper why he was moving it would all come clear in his own mind, the pros and cons, and he would feel less bad about leaving Grace behind. *Grace*, he asked again, *oh Grace – why did you have to leave me?*

*

Roy was awake before the alarm went off at its usual six o'clock. His working day had begun at five for so long that six seemed a late indulgence. The November dawn was still distant and the first bird had not yet begun its tentative song as he got out of bed and, with Grace's soft nightie brushing against his legs, started his bath running before going downstairs to the kitchen to make a cup of tea. He'd finished packing last night and his suitcase stood by the hall table. While the kettle boiled, he went in to Grace's shrine. A vase of late chrysanthemums blazed in the centre of the table, surrounded by her photographs and a birthday card he'd bought her last week. She would have been seventy.

'Oh my dear wife,' he thought, 'it feels like another parting. I don't like having to leave you alone here. But I'll look in often. He's lonely, that poor old chap, and he doesn't look after himself. He needs company. And I do, too. I'll soon be back. I'll always be with you.'

He picked up a photograph of Grace, put it down again and went through to the kitchen to make his cup of tea.

After he had finished bathing and shaving, Roy dressed and put fresh sheets on the bed. He pulled them tightly over the mattress, Army-fashion ('If I can't bounce a sixpence off your beds when they're done,' the sergeant used to say, 'I'll make you lazy blighters do 'em again until that bloody sixpence bounces like a barmaid's tits!'), and smoothed the candlewick bedspread over its hospital corners. He decided not to risk packing the nightie, but took it downstairs and washed it through by hand in Lux Flakes while the last sheets and pillowcase spun in the machine.

He checked the kitchen cupboards once again, opening and shutting each to look at the saucepans and mixing bowls in their serried ranks. The cups hung in a still row from their hooks above the sink, the mended one back in its proper place. On the shelves above, plates and saucers were stacked in sixes, with the good bone china placed carefully at the back. If Grace were to walk in now, it would look exactly as she'd left it five months ago. He'd emptied the fridge, apart from a last half-pint of milk. Two hours to go before the vicar collected him in his car for the short drive across Tunbridge Wells to Nevill Park. Roy sat down at the kitchen table and leafed through the *Mirror*.

Had he . . .? Yes, of course he'd stopped the papers.

'Going away, are you, dear? That's nice. Do with a bit of a break, help you get over . . .' And the voice of the Indian lady in the newsagent's had dropped to a reedy, tactful diminuendo so that the name of death should remain unspoken. The *Mirror* was making a great hoo-ha about the poll tax but it left him unmoved. People should set aside money to cover the necessities before they started buying luxuries. He had no sympathy with anyone who complained yet had a houseful of TV gadgetry. He turned to the Letters page, which could sometimes make him smile, and stared at the blur of print before him. He could see himself at this same table, reading it aloud while Grace in her apron dished up supper for them all.

'Eat up your nice shepherd's pie, Vera,' she would encourage. 'It's bananas and custard for afters!' Vera in her teens had become a fussy eater, endlessly picking at her food. 'Don't you want yours?' Alan would say. 'Give it here, I'm starving.' He grew before their eyes, until he towered above his mother and, by the time he was fourteen, his father as well. Grace was proud of her strong, vigorous son, his body seeming to burst through his school jumpers, his legs ever longer below the grey uniform trousers. He was a tribute to her good cooking and the fresh vegetables that Roy brought down from the allotment. He would eat until there was nothing left on the table, and then call out for plates of bread and butter to sustain him while, reluctantly, he did his homework. When Alan was around, the cake tin was always empty, the rice-pudding bowl always scraped clean. 'Let him have mine,' Vera would say. 'He's hungry, and I haven't got much of an appetite tonight.'

So Alan grew into a muscular lad with big feet and a deepening voice, and Vera's slenderness was a source of pride to her mother. Dress-making patterns had to be adapted specially for her narrow ribcage and eighteen-inch waist ('Same as Scarlett O'Hara and no need for laced corsets, either!'), and she swayed like a reed above the bouncy petticoats and short skirts that suited her so well. Only her teeth had been a problem, and – though none of them ever used the shameful words – bad breath. Well, it certainly wasn't down to poor diet.

Roy unloaded the washing machine and spread the heavy wet sheets across the lines in the airing cupboard. Time to get into his suit. He took it from the wardrobe and hung it up to give it a good brush. Best shirt . . . good suit . . . black shoes . . . If it weren't for the regimental tie, he might be going to a funeral. He went downstairs to sit in the dining room for the remaining half hour while he waited for the vicar.

Up at The Cedars, Reggie's new cleaning lady was reproaching him. She was a stout, ebullient black woman. There had been no answers to his advertisement ('Widower wants dependable char for large house three times a week, £2.50 an hour'), so his doctor, to whom he had complained about the impossibility of finding servants these days, had suggested Mrs Odejayi. She worked as a ward orderly for the Kent & Sussex Hospital five half days a week, and was more than able, reflected Dr Duncan, to hold her own with difficult old men.

'You should shame yourself, Mr Squadron Leader!' she scolded. 'A guest arriving today, and I find you still in your bed at half past nine. Come on, up with you and into that bathroom while I fix your bed. Pooh, this room needs a good airing. Out you get, or we'll never be done in time. You been down to the laundry to pick up those sheets?'

'Yes, I have,' said Reggie crossly. 'They're put away in the usual place.'

'"Usual place," he says. I ain't been with him above two weeks and he expects me to know usual place. You get yourself out of that bed and bring 'em up here to me while I air this room. You could do with a good bath, I'm telling you.'

Yes, Nanny. No, Nanny. Sorry, Nanny. I'll be a good boy

today. His Nanny had been just as stout and bossy, and if this one hadn't been black he would have found her bustling commands reassuring, a sign that his life was taken care of and everything was going to be ordered and all he had to do was obey.

'If you wouldn't mind, Mrs Owsyerfather, I'll get up by myself,' he said, adding firmly, 'When you leave the room.'

She laughed. 'Leave the room, he says! Leave the room! If you'd seen as many gentlemen in their pyjamas as I've seen, not to mention out of them, you wouldn't have no worries about me leaving the room. But if that'll get you up, out I goes.'

Her magnificent black bum swayed from side to side as she bustled out and Reggie took his erection into the bathroom to let it subside before having a long pee.

He'd never had a coloured girl in the house before – nigger, not to mince words, though you weren't allowed to say 'nigger' these days, not even 'girl' if you listened to some of those crazy harpies.

As he lay in the bath pleasurably soaping his cock and balls, he tried to imagine fucking her huge black body. Back in Cairo, when he got a weekend's leave from the hell of the Desert Airforce, he'd visited an officer's brothel in the side streets behind the Sharia Kasr-el-Nil, although the risk of VD always made him uneasy. The Arab tarts, with their smoothly oiled, coppery bodies and flying fingers, had been skilful and exciting, but the ululating songs that they played on a wind-up gramophone stimulated them to lashing, writhing movements that made him come too fast. By the time a 78 record was over and done with, he was too. Hardly worth it, not unless you were desperate and supercharged. Then he'd been injured, and the pale-skinned, faintly perspiring English nurses in the Cairo hospital had restored his desires to their proper place. He'd always had a thing about nurses. Those crisp uniforms . . . Reggie rubbed harder.

'Mr Jervis!' shouted Agnes Odejayi, banging on the bath-room door. 'You hurry up in there now! Nearly ten and you not even dressed, what sort of a welcome is that?'

'Coming!' yelled Reggie, thinking, Silly old Nanny, silly old Mrs Black Mambo. But the sight of his clean shirts arranged in tidy rectangles on the shelf in his wardrobe restored his good humour. He slicked some brilliantine on to his hair and combed it back – such as it was – in neat wavy lines across his scalp.

Before going downstairs he looked in to the second spare bedroom. The single bed was made up and she'd put flowers on top of the chest of drawers. The room, long unused, looked tranquil and welcoming, ready for its new occupant. Reggie himself didn't feel particularly tranquil or welcoming. He felt that he'd been talked into this daft idea by the vicar against his better judgement. With Mrs Owsyerfather getting the hang of things the house was back to normal and he didn't need a soldier-servant – if that's what the little bloke had in mind. Now a stranger would be sleeping here, barging down the corridor in the middle of the night for a slash – damn fool idea, damn fool whole ruddy business. He scowled into the spotted silvering of the toilet mirror on top of the chest of drawers, and saw over his shoulder the laughing face of Mary, young Mary, his new bride.

'Isn't it a darling?' she said. 'It's been in my room ever since I was little. My godmother gave it to me. She said, "Mirror, mirror on the wall, Marigold's the fairest of them all."' She had blushed. 'Only joking. I'm not vain really. It must be – oh, I don't know – walnut, do you think? The number of times I have peered into that glass to look for pimples, or see if it was true that if you told a fib you got spots on your tongue. Oh Reggie, we're going to be so happy! I just know it! Look at us. Look at us both smiling. Oh, I *love* being married!'

Mary, he thought, Mary, Mary, quite contrary. Why did you have to go?

He closed the door and went downstairs.

'Can we get one thing straight?' he said to his new cleaner. 'You may call me Squadron Leader, or you may call me by my name, which is Mr Conynghame-Jervis, or – which would be easiest for you – you may call me "sir". But you will *not* address me as Mr Squadron Leader, or Mr Jervis. Is that clear?'

She turned to look at him.

'That's better,' she beamed. 'Very smart. And my name is Agnes Odejayi and you may call me Aggie like everyone else does since none of 'em can manage to hold on to a name like Odejayi and you're no exception. But you may *not* call me Mrs Owsyerfather. Is that clear? Now hurry up and drink your tea.'

Reggie smiled because he couldn't help it and lit a cigarette to calm his nerves.

As the vicar's car entered Nevill Park past the sign saying PRIVATE ROAD, Roy's apprehension almost overwhelmed him. Sitting upright and gazing straight ahead, he could hear the thudding of his heart beneath the vicar's cheery banalities. Grace, Grace, Grace, Grace . . .

'Have a look at that view over there, to your left,' the Reverend Morris was saying. 'Marvellous, isn't it?' Roy turned politely to have a look.

The road was bordered with lichened walls beyond which a field sloped away steeply into the valley. On its far side in the distance stood white Victorian houses and behind them the boxy rows of a post-war housing development. The big houses to his right were set well back behind tall hedges and even taller trees. Massive, solemn, separate, their symmetrical sandstone façades could be glimpsed through the branches of pines and cedars. The car bumped along the road, past a nursing home, past a letter-box set into a wooden gatepost, and slowed to turn up a narrow drive leading to a porticoed entrance.

It stopped, and the vicar turned to Roy.

'Here we are!' he said. 'Can you manage that seat-belt? Fiddly things. Let me get your case out of the boot.'

Before the vicar could reach the bell the door was flung open and a beaming black woman stood at the top of the steps. 'Well here you are!' she boomed, as though they had been the first arrivals at a weekend house party. 'Come on in. Good morning, Reverend and welcome to you Mr . . .?'

'Southgate,' said Roy.

'Southgate! Southgate? Why of course – *I* know who you are – you must be Grace's husband.' Before she could explain, Reggie emerged from behind her.

'Take his case upstairs, Aggie! – Morning, vicar, Southgate. Coffee? Yes? – and then bring us all some coffee.'

As Reggie and the vicar exchanged small talk, Roy looked around the drawing room. Everything gleamed with age and polish; even the fabric covering the sofas and chairs had a faint sheen. A fire danced in the wide grate, and the pictures on the walls reflected its points of light. Roy looked for a portrait of the Squadron Leader's wife, but there wasn't one. He understood. The memories evoked by wedding photographs were too painful to have constantly before one's eyes. It was that pain which had brought them together and, however intimidating this great house, however unfamiliar this huge room, he'd be all right as long as he remembered that.

'Right. Jolly good. Now then. I'd better take you upstairs,' began Reggie, just as the vicar started to say, 'Well, time I was making tracks . . .' They both stopped and looked at Roy.

'I'm much obliged to you both,' he said. 'I'll do my best.' The coffee tasted bitter in his mouth. 'I know it's hard. We all know that . . .' and his voice trailed away.

'Good man!' said Reginald. 'That's the spirit! Another cup, vicar? No peace for the wicked! Look in any time, see how the new boy's settling down, won't you?'

'Righty-ho,' said the vicar, wondering what he'd let them in for and what on earth they would say once they were left alone together.

'All the best. God bless you both.' Roy and Reggie stood up and he shook their hands before Reggie escorted him to the front door.

When he came back, Roy who had sat down again, said, 'It's five months to the day, and next weekend's Remembrance Sunday. Will you be going to church?'

95

'Since they died?' said Reginald. 'Yes. Hadn't clocked that, but you're right. Well, I don't usually. Like the hymns, though. Jolly good tunes. What about you?'

'Brings it all back. The war. Don't really like to think about it.'

'Well then,' said Reggie with relief. 'We'll agree to give it a miss. Now. Your room . . .'

Before he could turn away, Roy said formally, 'I'm willing to give this a try. I know how you feel, because I'm feeling it myself. We've got that in common. The loneliness, missing them . . .'

The door opened and Aggie came in, wearing her coat and a red hat. 'Still sitting here?' she said. 'What sort of a welcome is that? Come on Squadron Leader, you and me'll show Mr Southgate his room. It's all ready for you; just needs your bits and pieces to make it nice and homely. Got time to take you upstairs and then I must be off to the hospital. My shift starts at twelve-thirty.'

She works at the hospital, thought Roy. So that's how she knows Grace. Well, there was something to talk about next time. A new person, with new memories. He could look forward to that.

'When will you be coming again?' he asked.

'Monday,' said Aggie. 'Mondays, Wednesdays and Fridays I do. Not that it's enough, great big house like this. And now there'll be two of you.'

'Oh, I look after myself. I won't give you any trouble.'

'It's not you I worry about,' she said meaningfully.

'Off you go, Mrs Owsyerfather,' Reginald interrupted.

'What did I tell you? Odejayi. Your manners needs attending to, Squadron Leader. My name's no more hard to remember than yours. And *you* can show your guest his room.' After a pause she added, 'Working for free, then, am I, this week?'

'Ah. Yes. Your money. How much did we . . .?'

'Twenty-five pounds,' stated Aggie firmly. 'Thank you, Mr Conynghame-Jervis.' She winked at Roy and left the room.

96

Reggie waited until he heard the front door close behind her and then he said, 'Doesn't do to be too familiar with them. "It is the duty of the wealthy man/To give employment to the artisan," I say. She's paid to work, let her get on with it. She'll do your room, laundry, all that sort of thing. You can chip in to her wages.'

'If it's all the same to you, I'd rather look after my own things,' said Roy. It hadn't occurred to him that living with the Squadron Leader could prove expensive, and he only had his pension, plus a bit extra from Unigate.

Reggie was about to expostulate, but Roy's set face looked surprisingly determined. Little chap could become tiresome, he thought, and muttered, 'Let's not argue about it now. Want a wash and brush up?' He indicated the way upstairs.

'. . . and you've got your own bathroom, of course – down the corridor, last door on the left. Right. Time for a snifter. I'll be downstairs, and when you're ready we'll talk about lunch.'

Left to himself, Roy drew a deep breath and looked around. He didn't think he'd ever in all his life slept in such a large bedroom, let alone *alone*. The single bed was covered with a faded sprigged cover which matched the faded flowered trellis on the wallpaper. A bedside lampshade was covered in the same material. On the walls were pastel portraits of two smiling girls, so alike that they must be sisters. He peered closer. They were signed John Ward and dated 1979. The beige carpet was recently hoovered, and his footsteps left imprints in its deep pile. A white-painted bookcase held a few books and an assortment of glass animals. He crossed the room and lifted one side of the heavy lace curtain draped diagonally across the sash window. It faced west and, Roy thought, must get the afternoon sun.

His room was the last of three in a side wing of the house. The window overlooked a high brick wall covered with climbing roses – darkened stems by now, bearing a few rosehips and faded blooms. Beyond the wall lay the spacious grounds of the neighbouring property. He raised the sash window to let some fresh air into the stuffy centrally heated room, and found it stiff from long disuse. He wondered who had last slept in the bed: one of the smiling girls, perhaps?

His suitcase stood beside the tall dark chest of drawers, and he lifted it on to the bed and with a heavy heart began to unpack.

'Everything hunky-dory?' inquired Reggie bluffly as Roy entered the drawing room. 'Found the bathroom all right?' Beside him on the table stood a large tumbler of whisky, and the warm room was filled with cigarette smoke. 'Drinks on the side. Help yourself.'

'Thanks ever so much, but I'm not allowed. The doctor prescribed a glass of Guinness sometimes to keep my strength up, and when I'm at home I have a pint at the local some nights, but that's all.'

Reginald looked at the little man, an incongruous figure amid the lordly proportions of the room and its ample furniture. Sooner he buckles down to his duties the better, he thought.

'Righto, then, how about a spot of lunch . . .?' he began, at the same time as Roy turned towards the French windows and said, 'Lovely garden you've got. Must keep you busy.'

'Got a chap who comes in for one and a half days a week . . .' Reggie started to say, just as Roy asked, 'Which way is the kitchen?'

'Look here, Southgate,' said Reginald in his I-give-the-orders voice. 'I'll show you the layout and you can get cracking. Mrs Thing's sorted out the kitchen, I've filled the fridge, far as I'm concerned from now on that's your department. If I've got other plans, I'll let you know. Been eating at the local mostly, Broker's Arms, sick of it. You can cook, you said? Good plain food's all I ask.'

'Very good, sir,' said Roy, and the sarcasm went unnoticed. Reggie nodded.

'Good man,' he said. 'This way.'

*

Mr Dear Vera, Roy wrote:

How are you all, Stan and the children, keeping well I hope? As you can see from the new address I'm now moved in with the Squadron Leader. It's been a week so far, too early to tell, but it seems to be going OK. You remember the big houses up past the cricket ground I expect, well if you turn down the road opposite the Spa Hotel that's where I am now. Never thought to see your dad so posh did you ha ha. The Squadron Leader is a decent bloke, lonely like me though he doesn't talk about his wife so I don't talk about Mum but I expect we'll get round to it, after all that's why I'm here. A very nice black lady comes in to do three times a week and being as she knew Mum at the hospital we have some good chats. I miss your Mum a lot she was everything to me RIP. Next week I'm visiting Alan, I'll send him your love. Well no more for now, must get back to my duties!

Ever your loving Dad.

He hadn't told Vera the truth. No point in upsetting her. Things might be going OK as far as the Squadron Leader was concerned, but he, Roy, felt lonelier than ever. It was easy enough to get the hang of the kitchen, though he still couldn't see the use of a dishwasher when there was just the two of them. Less bother to do it by hand. But he missed the sense of Grace's dear shadow that lingered in every corner of their home and hated being in a place she'd never entered. She was slipping from his grasp, leaving him behind. Like Tinkerbell, her voice was fading and her light grew dimmer. He struggled to believe that she must be somewhere, not just boxed in under the tidy plot in the cemetery but waiting for him in corporeal glory. His imagination tried to give her continuing life, but already it was harder and harder to make-believe that she was beside him in everything he did.

Sometimes, especially at night, he still felt her watching him, and although he couldn't imagine making love to her in that chaste, single bed, he could picture her in his bedroom, exclaiming at the drawings of the two girls, sitting on the bed to make sure that it was comfortable for him, opening and shutting the chest of drawers, running a businesslike finger along the bookshelves to check for dust. During the day the solid, rumbustious figure of the Squadron Leader seemed to crowd out her frail presence, and when he tried to talk to her there was so much explaining to do.

He addressed the airletter and stuck down its three sides. Time to get back to his duties.

'There you are, Southgate!' boomed Reggie, as he came in to the drawing room. 'Everything under control? Jolly good. I'm out for dinner tonight. Don't wait up.'

Roy knew already that he couldn't say, 'I wasn't going to,' so he merely answered, 'Very good, *sir*,' but once again the sarcasm was lost on Reginald.

It had been strange for them at first: two men sharing the house, emitting masculine noises and smells, after half a lifetime of living beside a woman. Reginald had been briefly uncertain about the etiquette of this odd new relationship foisted upon them both. Should he say 'Good morning' and 'Good night'? Should he inquire, as with an acquaintance, after Roy's health, or his family? Chap obviously expected to commiserate about Mary and wanted to talk about his own wife, but Reggie knew that wasn't on: two blokes blubbing away together.

The answer, he discovered, was simple. He reverted to the status and authority of the war, which put Roy firmly in the category of 'other ranks'. Once he'd seen it that way, there was no more problem. Didn't do to get too pally with other ranks, just as his mother had told him it only confused the servants if he tried to be friendly. 'They know their place, Reggie, dear,' she had said gently, after Nanny had reported that he was spending too much time watching Cook in the kitchen. 'It's up to you to know yours. They prefer it that way, and I think you'll soon find you do too.' From then on Reggie, aged eight but already at prep school, had been banished from the warm exciting smells of the kitchen, the roaring range, the bowls to be licked and sauces to be tasted, and sent firmly back up to the schoolroom, where Gerald, his clever older brother who had gone to Eton and left Reginald far behind, ragged him for not being able to read Greek or remember his Latin verbs. Then they would settle down to a game of L'Attaque! and he would realize how wise Mother was – this sort of soldierly activity was far more fun for chaps.

Roy had hoped Mandy was right when she said their shared plight made them equals; but he soon discovered that Reginald took for granted a master/servant relationship from which it was already hard to extricate himself. 'Don't you take no nonsense from him,' Aggie said. 'It's all talk. Stand up to him and he won't give you no trouble. He paying you a wage?' 'No,' Roy had replied, wondering for the first time why not. And Aggie said triumphantly, 'There you are, then! You're as good as he is – better. I see you polishing his boots this morning, well, he's too big for them as it is.' She looked at Roy sternly and waggled her finger. 'He's got no call to order you about, so don't you stand for no nonsense. The way he eyes *me* up and down – I've thrown water over cats for less.'

But it wasn't exactly nonsense that Reggie gave him; rather the feeling that a gulf existed between them which could never be breached. The one thing they had in common, the thing that had brought him here, was never mentioned. On the occasions when Roy had ventured to say, 'You must miss your wife . . .' the Squadron Leader had looked at him as though he had made a remark in very poor taste.

'I'll cook myself a bit of tea –'

'You mean *dinner*, I suppose, not tea?' said Reggie. 'Or to be exact, more probably *supper*? Tea is sandwiches and cake and things: char and a wad, we used to call it in the crew room . . . Doesn't matter, I suppose. Sorry. You were saying?'

'And then nip in to the local for my Guinness. Have a look at the house, see if there's any letters for me. My son might have written.'

'Where did you say he was?' asked Reginald.

'I ought to go over and see him next week. It's not far, only over by Ashford. There are trains from here, though it means changing.'

'You could take the car, if I don't need it,' said Reginald unexpectedly. 'What day were you thinking of going?'

'Has to be a Wednesday.'

Roy felt anxious at the idea of handling the big Mercedes, so much more powerful than any vehicle he'd driven since the war, but he wasn't going to rebuff Reginald's first attempt at kindness.

'That's all right, then. Have to go to London on Tuesday, see my accountant, stockbroker, that sort of thing. Wednesday's free. Just fill her up with petrol for me. Be back in time for dinner?'

'Bound to be,' said Roy, witholding the 'sir', but Reggie's mind supplied it.

He was thinking ahead to his evening with Liz. Fellow would have gone to beddy-byes by eleven. If he gave her dinner at the Chandelier Restaurant, just up the road at the Spa Hotel, it would sound perfectly natural to suggest she come in for a nightcap. She hadn't yet seen the house. Bound to be impressed. Might work wonders. 'Don't wait up,' he said again.

Mary had been quite a good sport about his little flings. He'd get himself into a stew over some girl, some pretty thing he'd seen in the typing pool or at the Motor Show, bit of fluff with good legs or a cracking figure. He was a man, after all, with a man's needs. Then it would all become too much. The girl would start expecting proper presents, want to know why she couldn't ring him up in the office, then at home – in no time at all it would be 'Oh Reggie darling, if only we could be together *always* . . .' At that point he'd confess. He'd sit on the floor, head on Mary's knees, blub a bit, she'd go quiet for a few days, he'd promise to turn over a new leaf and after that the girl's name would never be mentioned again.

Mary had been a sensible woman who didn't get things out of proportion, and a good wife to him – which made this business about the money, her making a mystery of it, such a blow. If she'd *told* him it might have brought them closer. They could have done with something to talk about during the difficult years – besides the dogs, of course. Huntley and Palmer, a pair of bouncy, stupid Dalmatians, had taken the place of children for Mary and had monopolized their morning and evening conversations. The dogs had nicknames ('Dandy' and 'Beano'), personalities, preferences, and were talked about in special silly voices. They generated a series of jokes and anecdotes without which the pair of them would have had little but their bridge evenings to fall back on for conversation. If only she'd told him about the money, Reggie thought, he and Mary could have played the stock market together. He reflected, not for the first time, that he'd never understand women. Who was that fellow who said, 'Why can't a woman be more like a man?' Song from some musical or other. Never spoke a truer word.

'Well, time for a snifter,' he said. 'Fetch me some ice, there's a good chap. Don't suppose you'll join me?'

'No,' answered Roy.

'. . . sir,' Reginald muttered as the little man left the room. Teaching him his place was taking longer than he'd expected, but the fellow could cook, no doubt about that, and meals appeared on time. The vicar was right, Reginald reflected: he did prefer knowing there was someone in the house apart from himself.

The Equestrian Bar at the Spa Hotel was crowded by seven o'clock. Reggie greeted the barman, who responded by saying, 'Your usual, Squadron Leader?', and seated himself on one of the white wicker chairs with scrolled arms, from which he could keep an eye on the door. The bar lived up to its name with sporting prints and a prancing bronze horse displayed against one wall. The carpet was turf green. All around him men were putting off going home, rattling the change in their pockets with guttural sounds and coughs of laughter. 'Yah, yah,' they agreed, or 'Christ's *sake*, man,' they objected. They were relaxed, expansive, conspiratorial. The atmosphere was layered with cigarette smoke and snatches of conversation.

'He has a personality problem, old Graham . . .' was strung above the insistent bass throb of sporting talk. 'He's been the best defender I've seen for a long long time . . .' From the next table a woman's voice, shrill and fast in the attempt to make herself heard, asked, 'Is he going to be a pain?' and then reassured, 'Oh no, Robert – you'll be *great*! Just don't take any crap from him.' 'Nothing but a bullshitter. Arsehole, really. Don't know why I bother,' came from over to his left. Reginald kept an ear on the cacophony and an eye on the door. He stretched his legs comfortably. Pity there was no one here he knew. Liz was a humdinger and he would have liked to show her off. He pulled on his cigarette and cradled the Glenmorangie. Pace yourself, Reggie, he thought, pace yourself. Don't want any disasters tonight. The bad boy twitched obediently.

Liz Franks stood in the doorway and surveyed the room. She wore a brilliant-green silk dress, sharply angled at shoulders and waist, over which was draped a flimsy matching jacket. Her good legs were elongated by high heels; her hair a confection of gold and bronze highlights. Her face, not young, was burnished to a gloss so that her cheekbones and eyelids caught the light. More brilliance was refracted from the chunky jewellery she wore. Liz had made an effort. Reggie, oblivious to the details, knew only that she was the best-looking woman in the place, and she was waiting for him. He stood up, twitched his waistcoat and strode forward to claim her.

The damask tablecloth was littered with the debris of their meal. Reggie cradled a brandy and Liz held a tiny coffee cup between both hands as she leaned forward, her breasts pressed together into a cleavage, looking promisingly into his eyes. They had shared two bottles of wine, and Liz, at the wine-waiter's suggestion, had accepted a glass of Beaumes-de-Venise with her pudding. Her eyes were glittering; her half-open lips gleamed. Reggie knew the signals. 'How about . . .?' he began, just as a hovering waiter stepped forward. Without glancing at the bill, Reggie slapped a gold credit card on top of it. 'How about a nightcap? I'm only round the corner.'

'You're very sweet, but I've got my car here.'

Reggie closed his hand over hers. 'You're very sweet too, Liz.'

'Bless you. I'd love to, but –'

'I've been very lonely, you know, in the last six months. Haven't had an evening like this in a long time. Meeting you has been the best thing that's happened to me since . . .'

The waiter, with practised timing, laid the plate bearing Reggie's credit-card slip in front of him. Liz watched as he added 10 per cent to the unnoticed $12\frac{1}{2}$ per cent service he had already been charged, scrawled his signature and tucked the card back into his wallet. As the waiter sketched a bow, raised an eyebrow to indicate coffee and wheeled smoothly away, Reggie looked across at her and pleaded: 'Say yes. Say you'll say yes. Or haven't you enjoyed this evening?'

'Of course I have. You *know* I have,' said Liz, thinking, Oh Gawd, what am I letting myself in for? 'All right, Reggie dear. Yes. But only on condition we go there in *my* car.'

'Absolutely. Jolly good idea. Ready to scramble. Chocks away.'

The low-slung red sports car crackled to a halt on the gravel and Reggie levered himself out and climbed the stone steps to the front door, lit from above by a five-sided brass lantern. Liz took a step backwards and surveyed the balustraded portico flanked by tall sash windows against a looming façade. He wasn't kidding, she thought.

Inside, under the glare of artificial light, he looked rumpled, red-faced and much older. I dare say I could do with a spot of Polyfilla myself, she thought, and was relieved when Reggie asked, 'Shall I show you the geography?' By the time she returned, he had softened the light in the drawing-room and tried clumsily to put his arms around her as she entered, a move which Liz sidestepped. She ignored his pat on the sofa and sat down in a winged armchair beside the fire, so that it would be awkward for him to sidle close to her.

'What's your poison?' he asked. 'Scotch? Or there's some rather decent brandy.'

'A small brandy – and I do mean small. I've got to drive home. Lovely house. I love this room. Are you all by yourself here?'

'More or less – for the time being,' said Reginald evasively.

'Stop me if I'm being too curious, but do tell me about your wife. How long ago did she die?'

As he chuntered on, boastful and maudlin, Liz reflected that this indeed was a house worth marrying. Reggie would drop into her lap like ripe fruit, if that was what she wanted. Divorce had left her with a small house, a flashy car and two grown-up, but still troublesome, offspring who lived away from home. It was hard work running the dress shop, and she was sick of flattering the overweight middle-aged women with too much money and too few distractions who were her customers. Marriage to Reggie would be leisurely and secure, and she had no doubt that she could cope with him. To give him credit, he had not moaned about his health, but he looked dangerously flushed and had a smoker's cough. High blood pressure, bad lungs: she calculated that he'd be lucky to last another five years. By then she'd still be comfortably this side of sixty, and could afford to go off and be a rich widow in the sun. Mellowed by drink and this train of thought, she allowed Reggie to take her hands and lift her to her feet; allowed herself to be kissed.

The kiss was better than she had expected. Reginald took his time, didn't paw at her dress, kissed her gently, then not so gently. He smelled clean and expensive. He reached behind him and switched off the table lamp, so that the room danced in firelight.

'Come and sit down,' Reginald murmured. He led her to one of the sofas and laid his hand against her cheek with disarming gentleness. 'You're a very, very lovely girl.'

They kissed again, and she leaned back against the sofa and

allowed him to stroke her breasts through the green silk of her dress. She could smell her own perfume, higher and sweeter than his. Reginald's breathing quickened.

'Liz,' he murmured. 'Oh darling, you're so exciting . . .'

'Dear Reggie,' she said. 'Oh don't. I never meant . . .'

He sat away from her. 'I want to make love to you,' he said. 'I do, very badly, want to make love to you.' A wisp of hair stood up at the side of his head and his tie was crooked. He was perspiring slightly, and she could see flecks of gum at the corners of his bloodshot eyes.

'Oh Reggie, I don't know, it's much too soon. We hardly know each other.'

His shoulders slumped, and she felt a gust of pity.

'Kiss me again,' she said, closing her eyes.

She allowed herself to be led into the marble-floored hallway and was just turning towards the stairs when from above she heard the sound of a lavatory flushing. She stiffened against his guiding hand. 'Who's that?' she whispered. 'I thought you said you lived alone.'

Reginald cursed, but silently, Roy Southgate: his timing, his bladder, his all-too-intrusive presence. 'Don't worry about him, darling. It's only Southgate, my manservant. Come along . . . let's go upstairs.'

She heard a door open and close, footsteps, then another door. 'No. No, I can't. Sorry, Reggie, but really not. I shouldn't have come back, it wasn't fair on you.' She glanced at the long-case clock. 'Do you realize it's after one? I have an early start tomorrow. No, Reggie dear, let me go.'

What could he do but let her go? He stood silhouetted in the open doorway, framed by two stone pillars, the stairway she had still not climbed curving upwards behind him, and waved.

'Phone me!' she called, as she swung the car around. 'Promise?'

Reggie nodded and gave her the thumbs-up. His shoulders collapsed the moment she was out of sight and he turned and slammed the front door. 'Fuck him!' he said. 'Fuck the

miserable bleeder! Home and dry and he went and fucked it!'
For a moment he was tempted to charge into Roy's room, but
instead he extinguished the lights and hauled himself up the
stairs.

Chapter Six

Roy Southgate walked through his house opening the windows to let cold December air blow through the lifeless rooms. He looked into the wardrobe where Grace's clothes still hung and buried his face in the folds of dresses and blouses, inhaling deeply. Her presence was ever more elusive. On the dressing table stood a bottle of the perfume she had used once or twice a year. He unscrewed the stopper, but its contents smelled sharp and rancid. He sat on their bed, shoulders sagging, and stroked his own cheek, as she used to do when he was what she called 'glum'. 'Now, now, Royston Southgate,' she would say. 'There's no room in *this* house for faint hearts! We've always got each other, and that's all that matters.' 'Always' rang hollow now.

She had been so strong; much stronger than he, but then, women were. She had squared her shoulders and smiled radiantly when Alan announced that he was to marry the disastrous June. 'So long as you love each other, that's all I care about!' she'd told the sullen young woman, and, crouching down to the child beside her, she'd said, 'Well, Gloria, now you've got a new Daddy – and a new Nana as well! Aren't you a lucky girl? Will you give your new Nana a kiss?' The child had turned her head away and leaned into her mother's skirt. 'Poor little lamb . . . she's shy. Never mind. We'll soon win her round,' Grace had said.

She had, too. Snotty-faced Gloria, in her absurd infant jeans, the over-long blonde hair trailing raggedly across her slight shoulders, had warmed to Grace's loving kindness. Soon she was trotting round the kitchen after her, proudly helping to lay the tea-table and reluctant to leave with her mother when the time came. 'Wanna stay wiv noo nana!' she had whined. After that Grace would sing her little nursery rhymes, the first time the child seemed to have heard any songs apart from advertising jingles, and tell her fairy stories. 'Shut it, Mum,' Alan had said, 'You'll only spoil her,' but Grace had understood that he was on the defensive against any suggestion that June might have neglected the forlorn little girl.

Alan and June had lived together openly for nearly two years before eventually getting married in a register office. Grace had found it easier than Roy to come to terms with their living in sin. 'It's not like when we were young,' she'd said. 'Look at Ted and Molly Tucker's girl – five months gone, *she* was – and Bill's daughter, been living with that young fellow from the pop group nearly five years now. It's no shame to share the same bed nowadays while you make up your mind. People don't see it like they used to. Main thing is, Allie's not leaving her and that poor little kiddie in the lurch.'

'Don't know why,' Roy had muttered. 'What with this blessed Pill, there's no need to have a baby out of wedlock. *We* managed it, even without the Pill.'

'Wasn't easy, though, was it?' Grace had answered fondly.

Roy curled up on the bed and thought back to their wedding night. They had married in 1939 and, although it meant taking precious pennies out of their savings, they were both determined not to spend their first nights together in her parents' front room. So they had caught a train to Tunbridge Wells (thus deciding, although they did not realize it at the time, where they were to live and bring up their family in years to come) and walked from the station, Roy in his uniform, carrying their suitcases, to a friendly boarding house. The landlady had taken one look at Grace's smart suit and new hat and given them her best bedroom. 'Bathroom's first on the right; toilet next door. I do breakfast downstairs at eight, though I don't suppose you'll be wanting any . . .' And she had left them alone.

Together they had stood looking at the double bed with its curved mahogany bedhead and two plumply rounded pillows. Grace had folded the counterpane tidily and checked the sheets for damp. Then – oh, and then she had taken out the hat-pin and removed her hat and come into his arms.

Later that night, despite their shyness and her modesty, despite her long embroidered nightdress, despite their consciousness of the landlady across the corridor, despite his awkward fumblings with the French letter and his gentleness and her brave, uncontainable tears, they had finally, in pride and triumph, consummated their marriage. It was May, in the springtime, the last glorious spring before the war. And now ... how long is it now, thought Roy, since anyone touched me? He stumbled over to the chest of drawers and rummaged for Grace's winceyette nightie. Rolling it into a ball, he pressed it to his face, so that the soft material muffled his cries. What is life to me without you, what is life without my love?

He sat at the kitchen table over his elevenses and looked through a pile of early Christmas cards. One or two were inscribed 'To Dear Grace and Roy', but most bore the message that people would be thinking of him specially this Christmastide. A card from June and Gloria, Billy and little Joe stung him to remorse by its invitation to spend Christmas with them in Balham. He picked up the telephone in the hall and dialled their number.

'Hello – June? Roy here. How're you keeping? Oh, bearing up, bearing up. I've moved. No, just temporary. It's ever so nice of you to ask me for Christmas. Well, if I can make myself scarce. How's the boys?' It was all prevarication, to put off the moment when they would have to talk about Alan. June had lost her job; money was tight; the boys were playing up, what with Alan away and Gloria having left home; nobody knew how hard life was for her ...

Eventually he said, 'You been to see him lately? Since his ... trouble? Thing is, see, I've got the use of a car now. I could come and pick you up, we'd go down there together. Bring him his Christmas presents. Cheer him up. He's not been in good spirits lately.'

If he wanted visiting, June spat furiously, that Sheila could go and see him. Roy sympathized and soothed and ended by persuading her to come with him the following Wednesday. By then he'd be able to let her know for definite about Christmas.

He was just about to hang up when June said, 'You must be that lonely without Grace. I often think about it. You were like Darby and Joan, you two. I always envied you. Alan was ever so jealous.'

'June, June . . . I don't know how I get through the days. I think about her all the time. But she slips away from me.'

He wept.

'A trouble shared,' said June, her voice more tender than he had ever heard it. 'I miss Alan, too, rotten sod. I never thought I would, but there it is, sometimes you surprise yourself. Never mind, Dad. We'll have time for a chat when I see you next Wednesday. Do us both good, remembering the good old days. Chin up.'

Roy put the phone down, thinking, First time in twenty years she'd talked like that. Funny what it takes before you see people as they really are. He set off for the allotment with his chin up to see if there were any late flowers for Grace.

Roy bent over the dahlias he had lifted and stored in his potting shed, checking them for signs of rotting around the tubers. On the plot of earth that had supplied them all with vegetables and flowers for over thirty years, he scratched away with a trowel round plants that would flower another year, clearing some of fallen leaves, discarding others and turning over the soil. There was still a good harvest of sprouts, broccoli and parsnips, and he wondered what to do with these. He could always take them back to Nevill Park, but the memory of being called Reginald's manservant rankled. It was not the actual *word*, but the fact – Roy now understood – that this was all his presence in Reginald's house amounted to: he was there to be a manservant. Not an equal, not a friend in need, just an unpaid, peacetime batman. Maybe he should have a word with the vicar, see if he could sort it out. But that would be cowardly – fight your own battles, his mother had always told him when he came back from the playground bruised and bloodied by older, bigger boys – and anyway, what was the use? The deed was done. Well, he'd undertaken to stay until the end of December, and he would keep his word. After that he'd be off, back to his own house. He should never have left it. Meanwhile there was a lovely crop of parsnips that needed eating up.

He decided to go and visit Grace's friend Molly Tucker, who lived alone and might be glad of them. They could reminisce together over a cup of tea. He'd go up to the cemetery first, then walk into town from there. Picking the very last of the late chrysanthemums, a bit droopy and ragged now, he crammed the fresh, earthy vegetables into two plastic bags and set off.

Molly brewed a pot of tea and settled back, smoothing the apron across her lap with arthritic, purple-red hands. 'You missing her then?' she said briskly. 'Got to pull yourself together. You're all the same, you bloody men, hopeless without a woman to chivvy round after you. Took her for granted while she was there, let her worry about that great boy, never stood up to him yourself, did you? And as for poor skinny little Vera . . .'

This wasn't what Roy had come for at all, and he drained the cup of tea and prepared to take his leave.

'Oh no, don't you be off yet,' she said. 'You sit and hear me out now I'm started. You're not a bad bloke, Roy Southgate, don't get me wrong. I'm just telling you, now's the time when you've got to do for yourself what she used to do, find yer own backbone. She were a strong woman, my friend Gracie, though she never made it to five foot, and I'll not see you fold up and collapse without her. Where you living, did you say?'

He tried to explain about the Squadron Leader, how lonely the man had been without his wife, how sorry the vicar had felt for him, but she wasn't prepared to accept that. '*You're* the one that's lonely! Vicar was trying to give *you* something to do with yourself. It's six months she's been gone; how much longer you going on like this? Where's he live, this posh fellow?' When Roy told her, she made a great parody of falling about impressed, squawking in a la-di-da accent, roaring with cracked gusts of laughter. 'Up there! Well I never did! I wish

Gracie was here – how she'd have laughed. "My Roy," she'd a said, "up there with the nobs! He'll never be able to enjoy it, though. He'll be blacking their boots in no time."'

This was uncomfortably close to the truth, so Roy said, 'Don't you be so sure. I'm taking his car – one of those big German jobs, a Mercedes – over to June's next week, then driving her down with the boys to visit Alan.'

Molly's eyes streamed with fresh laughter. 'Turning up at prison in one of them gangster's cars! Ooh, I don't believe it! Well, it'll give the boys a thrill, anyway. *And* June: she always liked a bit of swank. She weren't a bad lass underneath those trashy looks. Grace was never too hard on her. She knew what a difficult bugger young Alan could be.'

Roy found himself angered by this glimpse into a side of his wife that he'd scarcely known. 'It's all very well for you,' he muttered, 'your old man went years ago. You might show a bit more respect for her memory.'

'*I* respect her memory,' said Molly, '*I* respect her, but look at yourself. You look like a wet week. She were a fighter, your Grace, so don't you make her into some goody-two-shoes. She were flesh and blood, tough and bright and ready for a laugh, and she'd be mad if she could see you now.'

'I thought you'd listen to me,' Roy grumbled. Thought you'd cheer me up, make me feel a bit better. Thought we could chat about the good old days.'

Molly leaned forward and patted his arm. 'And so we will, lovey, next time. My knee's playing me up rotten today, that's why you got the sharp edge of my tongue. Give me some warning next time, time to do me hair and paint a smile on me face. There you are, off you go – I'm ever so pleased with them fresh vegetables. Course you miss her. Life goes on, though, and you got to trudge along with it.'

Reginald sat in the drawing-room wondering what to do with himself. Southgate had been here for no more than a month, yet already he'd grown used to his presence about the house. It wasn't Aggie's day, it wasn't the gardener's day, and Southgate had taken himself off soon after breakfast to poke about in his allotment. Reggie poured a stiff drink at eleven to fortify him before ringing Liz. But when he dialled her number in the shop, she said briskly, 'Sorry, love, can't talk – I'm snowed under with customers. Give me a buzz at home sometime.' That deflated him. Two empty hours suddenly yawned, instead of a flurry of action. He'd pictured himself sweeping her off for a drink, better still lunch . . . Why did she have to *work*?

He would have liked to go upstairs and peer into Roy's room, see how the little bloke had arranged it, take a look at his things, but the voice of Nanny, still the voice of his conscience, wouldn't allow it. 'Don't you meddle with what's not yours, barging into other people's business without a by your leave. Everyone's entitled to their privacy and what you don't know can't hurt you.'

They were the cadences, it was the morality of the nursery, and it had served him well enough. Christianity had never sunk in so deep. Pity the nursery didn't have rules for dealing with women. That's where Nanny had let him down. From her he had learned that all comfort, all warmth, all order and well-being came from women. From his mother he had learned that women of his own class, *ladies*, were soft-voiced, precious, unfathomable. He could hardly think of them as having bodies at all, and it was other boys who had initiated him into the astonishing pleasure of ejaculation. Later on came the realization that some women – not his own kind, but fast, Bohemian types – could be cajoled, mastered and enjoyed. Waafs had taught him the ordinariness of women; that, as well as sobbing or giggling, they could be coarse or, in a crisis, strong, but above all that they too wanted *sex*, which meant they were not as different from himself as he had been brought up to believe.

The end result and main beneficiary of this education had been Mary: timid, yielding, biddable and, after nearly fifty years of marriage, no less mysterious than his mother. As instructed by Nanny long ago, he hadn't pried into her business, never opened her letters, and look what had happened. She'd let him down, betrayed his trust. Mary had led a secret life, amassed secret money, and instead of saying, *There* Reggie, *look* what I've done for you as a surprise, she had gone behind his back and given it away, leaving him looking like a fool.

She might not have made him richer, but she hadn't left him poor. The solicitor had assured him that Mary's will was perfectly legal and he shouldn't waste money fighting it. Reggie poured himself a third gin. The accountant had pointed out that, with all his debts paid and an extra five thousand a year under the terms of the will, he was now more comfortably off than before. Provided he didn't go mad ('No wild, wild women, Squadron Leader,' he had said drily), Reggie would be able to afford a good standard of living: top rate of BUPA, a new car every two or three years, decent booze and wine, the odd luxury or trip abroad. Reggie wondered what luxuries he was supposed to covet at his age – besides, of course, wild, wild women.

Age was the problem. Not that he was ill, thank God; mind and body still in pretty good shape, but he lacked *energy*, get-up-and-go. A course in monkey-glands like Noel Coward and Somerset Maugham and the old Aga Khan was another luxury he could do with. He'd been hard as nails when he kissed Liz, but whether he'd stay that way if he got her in between the sheets was the question that nagged at him. It was years since he and Mary had made love; years since he'd made love regularly to anyone. The occasional tart on his evenings in London didn't really count. They were paid to make sure that it worked. For the last couple of years (made circumspect for fear of Aids), he had confined his visits to just one: the sensual and costly Sabrina. Never had any problems with her. Sabrina was *very* understanding.

Reggie settled deeper into his armchair and fidgeted with the bad boy. Reassuringly, he grew big and bad almost immediately – yes, master, here I am, master, where can I do your bidding? Getting an erection was no problem. Keeping it and using it – that he couldn't be certain about. He remembered Liz's heavy breasts, the firm weight of one cupped in the palm of his hand, its soft resistance to his fingers, unique and unlike any other resistance: not like melons, whatever people said, smoother and more give than a peach, firm nipples like berries ... His hands flexed and unfolded as the bad boy became harder still.

Time for a trip to London, Reggie, my lad, to check out the equipment, make sure it's all in good working order. Not likely that any of his former popsies would deliver the goods, but there was always Sabrina, in her overheated, perfumed top-floor flat up behind Marble Arch. Reginald ran his finger down the alphabetical index in his diary as far as the Ps (she was listed prudently under 'plumber'), and dialled the number in London. Her maid answered.

'Who shall I tell her is calling, please?'

'It's the Squadron Leader here. C-J.'

'Oooh, is it now?' she teased, and he heard the click of the phone as she put him on hold to give her mistress time to check him out before he was put through.

Sabrina punched in her electronic Psion organizer *search* S-Q-U-A-D-R-O-N L, and the information flashed up:

Pompous buffer, late sixties?? married, clean, breasts = Charlies, penis = big bad boy. No kinks exc. Nanny, erection no prob. £250. Visits 12.9.89, 20.12.89, 09.03.90.

She sighed. Well, at least it wasn't a sabre or a scimitar, a greasy piston or a hot rod, an elephant's tool or a rhino horn. 'Big bad boy' meant he'd be the naughty schoolboy type, not a fantasy merchant, nor a trouble-maker.

'It's my beautiful, big, *bad* boy!' Sabrina's playful and alluring voice came down the line. 'Where have you *been*, you bad lad? And *when* are you coming to see me?'

Straightaway Reggie wanted to cry into the telephone, blubber about Mary, and the money, and the infernal nieces, burrow his head between Sabrina's springy breasts and ask her to make it better; but he only said, 'How about one day next week?'

'That'll be a treat – for both of us, hmm? I'll hand you back to Leontine. She'll fix you up with a nice *long* rendezvous. Afternoon, my darling, or can you stay with me for an evening? Well, you talk to Leontine. Till then, *bad* boy – oh, we're going to have such fun.' Another click, another pause while he waited.

Wednesday was arranged, from two o'clock onwards. Evenings were more expensive and, anyway, he didn't want to drive home too late.

'Ms Sabrina says not to forget about inflation, Squadron Leader!' giggled Leontine. Presumably that meant her price had gone up. Well, why not? Everyone else's did. Feeling pleasantly shamefaced with anticipation, Reggie built up the fire, poured another drink and lit a cigarette. He unfolded the *Daily Telegraph*, which Roy had left on the side-table next to his chair, and turned to the letters page.

Reginald was asleep when Roy got back, mid-afternoon, carrying a W. H. Smith bag full of Christmas cards. He went down to the kitchen to brew a cup of tea, deduced from the debris on the table that the Squadron Leader's lunch had been a makeshift affair, and took a chicken out of the fridge to reach room temperature so that it would roast evenly.

They ate dinner together at one end of the dining table, over whose polished surface Roy had thrown a backing cloth of green felt and then one of Mary's damask tablecloths. Reginald carved the bird and served the vegetables and roast potatoes from the sideboard; Roy cleared the dishes and brought in the bread-and-butter pudding. Only Reginald drank wine. They didn't say a word until, over the crumbs of Jacob's cream crackers and farmhouse cheddar, Roy said, 'About next Wednesday . . .'

'Ah,' said Reggie. 'Yes, good thing you mentioned it. Wednesday I'll be in town.'

'If it's all the same to you, I'll be off quite early so as I can fetch June, that's Alan's wife, and the boys. They're ever so excited about going in the Merc.'

'Oh, that's off. Operation scrubbed. Wash-out. I'll be needing the car myself to get to London.'

Roy stared at him for a moment. Then he said, 'Begging your pardon Squadron Leader but you can't do that. You promised, and I've made all the arrangements.'

'Well, you'll just have to cancel them, won't you? Tell them to make it the following week instead.'

'You can't do that,' Roy said doggedly. 'The week after's Christmas and I've already let Alan know we'll all be coming Wednesday. I can't let him down – June, and the boys too – I can't.'

Reginald looked across the table at him. The little man's hands were shaking, like his voice, and although he kept blinking he met Reggie's eyes with desperate resolution.

'Look here, Southgate, it's bad luck about this, but you'll just have to do your visiting some other day. The car belongs to me. I said quite clearly that you might use it occasionally if I didn't need it. Next Wednesday I need it. Finito. End of story.'

Roy interlaced his fingers and clasped his two hands together. He cracked them to and fro, flexing his hands from an arch into a fist. He breathed deeply. His heart was pounding. He looked across the table. 'In that case, Squadron Leader, you must give me enough money so I can hire a Mercedes.' (He pronounced it to rhyme with Hercules, and Reggie smirked at the fellow's ignorance.) 'For the whole day. That I'll accept. Either that, or you'll have to change your appointment. We made an arrangement and there's four people is depending on me to keep it. Cost you about a hundred pounds, at a guess. Lucky mine's a clean driving licence.'

Reginald was thunderstruck. 'Never heard such infernal cheek in all my life,' he said, and took a deep swig from his wine glass. 'I wouldn't dream of doing any such thing. You want a car, *you* pay for it.'

Roy pushed his chair back and stood up. 'You call yourself a gent. Think yourself a class above me. All you've got is more money and a bigger house – and a big car that you promised to *me* next Wednesday. Where I come from, a gentleman keeps his word. Far as I'm concerned, you've broken yours, time and again. I thought I was moving in here to keep you company, help you over a bad time, the worst of times it's been for me. I thought we had that in common, we'd help one another. Now it seems all you want is a servant – unpaid at that. You think I'm here to cook your dinner and clean up after you for the privilege of living in your big house? I tell you, I'd a thousand times rather be back in my own. Thousand times.'

He paced up and down the length of the dining table, staring at the carpet. Then he raised his head. Looking directly at Reginald, he said, 'Either I has that car next Wednesday – and I mean a Merc, not just any car – or I go upstairs and do my packing now.'

'Sit down, man, keep your hair on. Don't get so excited. You can have the ruddy car. I'll go by train, pick up a taxi at the station. Suit me better, come to think of it. Parking in London's a nightmare these days. Nothing to get steamed up about. Sit down.'

Roy's shoulders sagged, and he shook himself and snorted a couple of times. 'Very well,' he said. 'Very good. That's done, then. Want a coffee, Squadron Leader? I'll put the kettle on.'

'Sit down, I said. That was a good meal, good as the cooking at my club. Have a glass of wine. Jolly decent claret. '83. You can call me Reginald.'

Roy sat down. 'Thanks all the same, but I don't think I could do that. Doesn't come natural now. I'd rather keep with Squadron Leader. I get vexed calling you sir but I couldn't get my tongue round . . . your Christian name. And your other name's a bit of a tongue-twister. Nobody ever call you C-J?'

'Not if I can help it. Tell me, Southgate, man to man, what do you do for *women*?'

*

All four of them were very quiet in the car as it glided through the rainy, glittering streets of south London. The two boys had begun the journey sitting bolt upright in the back seat, hoping to be seen by people they knew, overawed by the size and leather-armchair comfort of the big Mercedes. June too had been quiet, less because of the car than because, as Roy understood, she was nervous at the prospect of seeing Alan, uncertain what to say, unsure how he would look.

Once they left behind the crowded shopping streets and the car could unfold some of its reined-in power along the M20 towards Ashford, the boys became over-excited and noisy, bouncing up and down, pretending to superior mechanical knowledge, swapping jargon about torque and engine-power picked up from the motor-racing they had watched on television. As they approached the prison they fell silent again, and it was June who kept some kind of conversation going, reminding them of the Christmas presents they had brought for Alan, anticipating his surprise and pleasure. 'No point in making Dad wait till Christmas Day. Much better if he opens them now and we can all watch.'

The sight of Alan shocked them back into silence. Roy tried to break the tension but none of them listened. Their eyes were fastened on Alan's throat, only partly obscured by a high-necked sweater. Above its thick ribbing, pale bruises coiled around his neck, faded now to a greenish-yellow but still clearly visible. Roy pitied June, who would have to try and explain them away to the boys.

Alan's face was bloated by tranquillizers, and his tongue seemed thick in his mouth, so that his speech was slow and slurred. 'You shouldn't have let them come,' were his first words to June, adding to Roy: 'What you doing, bringing them here, Dad?'

The explanations – Christmas, wanted to watch him open his presents, chance for the boys to ride in the car – drew a glance of sluggish contempt.

'Grandpa's got a Merc, Dad!' said Billy.

'Like hell he has,' muttered Alan.

'Honest, Dad, no kidding: it's ace. It smells just like them stalls down the market for leather jackets and bikers' gear. Cor, what a lovely motor!'

Half an hour of this seemed interminable: forty minutes was unbearable.

'Shall I take the boys back to the car now?' asked Roy. 'Leave you two on your own for a bit?'

June grimaced. 'I'm OK,' she said. 'What about you, Dad? There must be things you need to tell Alan – about Mum and all that.'

'Why don't you just push off, the lot of you?' sneered Alan.

They had stuck it out for the full hour in the end, the boys trailing glumly after Roy and June as visitors were escorted off the premises by warders with jangling, heavy key rings bumping at their belts.

In the car the two boys had said nothing, asked no questions; they fell asleep almost at once.

'It's a disgrace!' June had muttered angrily. 'Making them see their Dad like that. What am I supposed to tell them about those bloody great marks on his neck? Poor bloody Alan: Christ, he must have been desperate. Those bruises are serious. He meant it. And why can't they provide a decent lounge where people can come and talk in a bit of peace, bit of dignity? You're treated like a criminal from the minute you cross the door. X-raying his presents. What do they expect? Three files and a wire-cutter?'

'Drugs more likely,' Roy had said.

'They make a pretty good job of that without needing no help from us,' June spat. 'Did you see his eyes? The pupils? All black. God knows what those bastards pump into him. Poor old Al.' She lowered her voice to a hissing whisper, though the boys slept on in the wide back seat. 'I hate Billy and Joe having to see their Dad like that. How are they supposed to keep their respect? Christ, they punish the bloody innocent . . .'

Suddenly she turned to him. 'Does *she* visit him? That other one?'

'I've no idea,' said Roy.

It wasn't true. He did know. Yes, Sheila visited Alan, and Alan had written to him warning that once he was out of prison, he would divorce June so as to be free to marry Sheila legally. Roy couldn't bring himself to tell June that, not just before Christmas. To his relief she fell asleep as well.

The plush grey car rolled smoothly along the middle lane, content to be overtaken by frantic smaller cars whose drivers sneered as they shot past. I did her an injustice, Roy thought. She does care for Alan, she really cares. I never knew that before. She's not a bad girl, and *he* thought she was the bees' knees, once. Why did it all go wrong?

It was nearly seven o'clock when Reggie came home in high good humour.

'Jolly good show!' he said. 'Jolly good show! Join me in a snifter? Good day out?'

'Car went like a bird,' said Roy. 'Thanks for letting me have it.'

'Any time, old chap. Just let me know. Any time.'

Chapter Seven

Christmas was over, and both men had been given boxes of crisp cotton handkerchiefs shaped into triangles with vicious hidden pins, soft pairs of chevron-patterned socks, and ties, sludge-coloured for Roy, and fat silk for Reggie. Christmas was over, and the tree had started to drop greyish needles in a circle around itself. Christmas was over, and the dry, curling remnants of turkey were finally discarded. Without waiting for Twelfth Night, the decorations had been taken down and put away in carrier bags under the stairs. And with Christmas over, life returned to normal. Only New Year's Eve was still to come.

Reggie still thought of New Year's Eve as Hogmanay, harking back to the boisterous times of his childhood, family and servants whirling together, drunk together, on just this one night of the year. He had cajoled Liz into agreeing to have dinner with him that evening, though he was forced to accept her proviso – rum idea, he thought – that they would separate before midnight. He was cheesed off at the prospect, but it was that or nothing and with a bit of luck and a following wind he could manoeuvre her back to his place, or himself into hers. He had not yet seen her house, except from the outside on the one occasion he had dropped her off.

After some research he'd decided to take her to eat at a restaurant called Thackeray's House. Not too big to provide a nice cosy atmosphere for the turn of the year, but without vulgar hilarity. He wanted no sashaying round the tables in a conga to destroy the romantic mood he hoped to create. The place offered good English food, nothing on the menu he wouldn't be able to translate, and the owner, Bruce, was a nodding acquaintance from occasional visits to the Conservative Club next door. Most important of all, it was his end of town not hers, and he'd rather operate in his own airspace.

*

Liz had spent the day in the shop behind drawn blinds, marking down prices for the sale. A lot of stock was hanging about on the rails – city suits with long shorts had been a non-starter: she didn't see how she was ever going to shift those, or the gauzy Renaissance-style evening dresses that were too advanced for the tastes of Tunbridge Wells, however rapturously they were acclaimed in Milan. Sometimes you had to stay ahead of the trend, and sometimes you had to dawdle behind it; the problem was knowing which. The recession everyone talked about seemed to have arrived, and, as she slashed prices, she knew she was shaving her own profit margins uncomfortably fine. But with Christmas over, none of this stuff was going to sell at full price; she depended on people picking up a bargain with their gift cheques from indulgent husbands or daddies. After that it was cruisewear until the spring. Cruisewear! I should be so lucky, she thought, and was reminded of the advantages to be gained by succumbing to Reggie's increasingly ardent hints. He'd given her a piece of expensive costume jewellery for Christmas, with the clear implication that next year it could be for real.

Liz selected a dark blue Jean Muir evening dress, cut on the bias from silk crepe that slithered round her breasts and over her hips to toss and flicker just above her ankles. She needed a piece of good gold to complete the look. On an impulse she had slipped down the road to her friend Colin Thurlwell, who designed and made real jewellery in clever modern shapes. His face lit up with conspiratorial glee when she explained why she needed to borrow a piece just for the evening. Together they sorted through the necklaces that lay coiled in their separate chamois-leather pouches, deciding on a rose-gold chain of interlinking Paisley shapes that lifted and slid and caught the light as her head turned and her collarbone moved.

'Colin, you're an angel! Bless you,' she said.

'Just make sure you bring it back, OK? No, I won't charge you anything; but it's £1,500 if you lose it, so don't leave it on the bedside table, or in his pocket. And get him in here when the time comes for the ring, darling, or I'll have your guts for garters.'

She had refused a drink at Reginald's house; refused even to let him pick her up; she wanted to make an entrance on her own terms. She let him wait ten minutes at the restaurant while she sat with crossed ankles on her own sofa at home, weighing the odds as she downed half a pint of milk to keep her head clear. She had not yet been to bed with him, though she knew she would have to before it came to a proposal. Did she want the proposal? That was the point.

Liz stood up and examined herself in the long mirror in her hall. She looked good; indeed, she might never look this good again. The dark blue dress was as chaste as a nun's habit until she moved, when the long shallow undulation from throat to waist and waist to knee was outlined as though by a Greek breeze upon Greek drapery. The necklace was the only piece of jewellery she wore; she had decided against his brooch and even taken off her watch. Her hair was rolled into an old-fashioned French pleat. Her make-up had taken three-quarters of an hour, yet its final effect was smooth, almost invisible.

She walked into the restaurant unsmiling and saw the bluff, anxious expression drain from his face and his jaw drop.

'I am dining with Mr Conynghame-Jervis,' she said to the head waiter.

Roy and Molly Tucker sat facing one another in her front parlour. She had cooked a joint: rolled breast of lamb with onion-and-sage stuffing, accompanied by parsnips and potatoes from the allotment and followed by a fluffy treacle pudding. Roy had brought a six-pack of Guinness ('And you'll be taking five back with you!' Molly said), and now, replete, they sat in front of the popping, honeycombed gas fire that gave out a faint odour of singed dust. She had been good company, sentimental but not maudlin, jolly without being raucous and Roy had made an effort to be cheerful rather than (as he would have preferred and thought proper on New Year's Eve) reminiscent.

She listened sympathetically when he told her about the prison visit, and Christmas with June and the boys. With a heavy heart he had concealed from them Alan's plan to move in with Sheila.

'Hope you've given him a piece of your mind!' she said indignantly.

'Don't like to go poking my nose into what's not my business. He's a grown man now.'

'*Course* it's your business!' Molly said, eyes flashing, fists clenching unconsciously. 'Your *grand*sons are your business. Now they're got no Nana to stick up for them, you have to do it! Give him a good old dressing-down, your next visit. Time to think – that's what he's got plenty of. You give him something to think about!'

'If he wants to go off with this other one, I can't stop him. Not if he doesn't want to be married to June.'

'*She* hasn't got no children, has she? The new one – what's her name? Sheila? Well then. That's what makes the difference. He'll be brooding about his boys, wondering what's going to happen to them, whether they'll end up in the nick like him. You got to harp on that. A man wants his family, deep down. June's given him family and this other missus hasn't. Grace would have told him, fair and square.'

'Grace never knew, and thank God she didn't.'

'Well, let's hope she didn't.'

'Molly! What're you saying?'

'She was no fool. For all I know, she may have thought she was protecting you, just like you think you protected her. No, we didn't never discuss it. But *I* knew, and there's plenty of wagging tongues ... Well, too late now. You worry about those lads. Now then, Roy Southgate, I hope you don't think *I'm* sitting up to see the New Year in. Time I showed you the door, or the neighbours'll talk.' She cackled with laughter, teasing and suggestive despite her seventy-odd years. Roy looked at her, thinking, She'd still be game for a bit on the side; and censored the thought that followed.

*

The long-case clock in the marble hall was chiming eleven as Roy entered. He had been tempted to go back to his own home, but in the end the melancholy thought of spending his first New Year's Eve without Grace alone in the house they had shared drove him reluctantly to Reggie's. Here at least the lights burned in the hall, a fire in the grate, and his bedroom was warm. He went down to the kitchen to put the remaining cans of beer in the fridge, and made himself a cup of tea. He'd see the new year in on the television, since Reginald didn't seem to be back.

The drawing-room glittered softly, pristine and plump. Roy stirred the fire, which hissed and flared as he settled a couple more logs. He switched on the television, sat down in front of it and almost immediately fell asleep.

Slack-shouldered with weariness and disappointment, Reginald climbed the steps to the front door, turned the key in the square brass lock and shut the door behind him. Damnation take the woman! He folded his fist around the small box in his coat pocket for a moment. He could hear the television next door, blaring bloody jollity. He took off his navy blue coat and slung it over a chair. The little man must be sitting up, waiting for him, blast it.

As he looked into the drawing-room, Roy started awake. 'Must've closed my eyes for a minute,' he mumbled. 'Whatsa time?'

Reginald shot his cuff. 'Quarter to,' he said. 'Midnight.'

He crossed the room towards the squawking kaleidoscope on the screen and turned it off. The silence was abrupt and shocking.

'Music,' he said. 'Anything but that rubbish. "Put another nickel in, in the nickelodeon. All I want is loving you and –"'

'"Music, music, music."'

'I need a stiff drink,' said Reginald. 'How about you? Break a rule?'

'I don't mind if I do,' Roy said. 'Seeing as it's –'

'Scotch? Cognac?'

'I'll have a brandy. Shall I pour it myself? I like soda in it.'

'Soda? You're not wrecking my Remy Martin with soda.

Here you are. One for you and one for me. Down the hatch!'

Roy cradled the big brandy balloon, inhaling its potent, fiery fumes, while Reginald bent unsteadily over the record cabinet discarding various classical symphonies and opera selections. That was Mary's stuff. Never been his taste. But they must have had music for parties, long ago and far away. They'd given parties in their time, when they were young. Must have done. Of course – there was that fancy-dress party they'd had once. He'd dressed as a goat, with horns on an elastic band round his temples; little goatee beard stuck on; and – the crowning touch – a small bunch of grapes tied to a string, dragging behind him. 'What's that for?' Mary had puzzled. 'Goat's, turds,' he had said and she shrieked with delighted laughter. 'Oh Reggie, you are a hoot!' she'd said. 'You really are a scream!' *Had* he really been a scream?

Where the blazes . . . ah! *The Music of Jerome Kern.* He picked out the dog-eared record sleeve, the sleek Forties face of a bandleader smiling invitingly beside a list of favourite tunes, and slipped the record on to the turntable. Sweet, nostalgic rhythms filled the room.

'That's better,' Reggie said. He snapped his fingers in time to the beat, tapped his foot and began swaying to the familiar sound of 'A Fine Romance'. Roy's feet, too, were tapping, his shoulders lifting alternately. The tune changed to 'Smoke Gets in Your Eyes'. Reginald began to move forward, his arms extended, hands cupping the air in front of him. '"They said, someday you'll find,"' he crooned '"all true love is blind . . ."'

Roy stood up. '"I at first replied, when a loving flame dies, smoke gets in your eyes."' His gruff voice was uncertain but he knew the words and joined in with the yearning tremolo on the record. He shut his eyes.

Reginald stepped forward and gripped Roy's hand, putting the other around his waist. 'No, you fool, here: on my shoulder,' he muttered, and Roy reached up hesitantly. 'Right.'

The chap was about the same height as Mary, but Reginald was not thinking of his wife as he glided forward with closed eyes, much less of Liz (sitting on her own sofa with her shoes off, downing a double whisky and grinning more at herself than at the inanities on the screen in front of her); he was thinking of dancing classes in the gymnasium at school, steering pliant younger boys around its springy floor; or in the village hall, where local girls had giggled at his clumsiness over the Scottish reels he would be required to perform at their Christmas parties. He thought of all those supple young bodies, innocent and available, of opportunities grasped and many more opportunities missed. If he'd had a son, he'd have told him, Fuck while you can; there'll be plenty of times when you can't. Never mind the scruples, get your fucking done, son!

Roy thought of the Orchid Ballroom in Purley, where he used to take Grace dancing occasionally to the big-band sound of Harry Roy and other orchestras who came from the London clubs and hotels for the evening, the polished floor crowded with young men in uniform, girls in their best frocks, dancing to these same tunes. He couldn't remember ever having danced with anyone but Grace, though he must have done. It was Grace who had manoeuvred his clumsy feet into some sort of rhythm and taught him to indicate by the pressure of his hands and the angle of his body which way they were going to move; just as they had learned together the silky friction of each others' nakedness. Roy felt an erection imminent and moved slightly back from Reginald's forward step, man and girl at once, urgent and yearning.

Together, eyes closed, the two men swayed in unison. Midnight passed, the clock chimed, the long-playing record played on. They hummed to the familiar music, dancing a few inches apart, smiling at memory. When at last the needle ground to a circular hiss, Reggie dropped his arms and walked away from Roy without a word. He lifted the stylus arm from the turntable, swung it to rest and turned the radiogram off. Roy placed the guard in front of the fire and switched off the standard lamp that had softly illuminated the room. The dying fire flickered in a momentary draught as the door closed behind them.

At the top of the stairs they turned towards their separate bedrooms at opposite ends of the landing corridor.

'Happy New Year,' said Roy.

'Auld lang syne,' said Reginald.

Chapter Eight

When Alan was sixteen, a strapping lad with a couple of O levels and not much else to his credit, Roy had managed to get him a job in a local men's outfitters. The time was the early Sixties, and Alan had been reluctant to give up wearing the tight trousers and winkle-pickers that got him noticed by girls, but the old-fashioned shop insisted on dark grey flannel trousers, a white shirt, tie (not kipper, not floral), and round-toed black lace-up shoes.

'Might as well be back in school uniform,' Alan grumbled.

Grace said, 'They didn't pay you eight pound ten a week to go to school, though, did they, Allie?'

'Shut up calling me Allie, Mum,' he muttered. 'Anyway it's not eight pound ten. After what I've got to give you and Dad and National Insurance and tax on top of that, I'll be lucky to have a fiver. Costs almost that for an evening up in London.'

'You don't have to go to London, Alan,' Roy pointed out mildly. 'There's plenty to do here at home. Meet your mates, go to the flicks . . .'

'*Flicks!*' Alan said, witheringly.

A friend of Roy's from the depot had wangled Alan the job. His brother-in-law was chief salesman at the shop, a dull, deferential man who combed his hair from a parting just above the ear on one side to sweep across the top of his balding pate. The man had taken one look at Alan's defiant young figure, vigorously male from his Beatle fringe to his elongated shoes, and determined to break his spirit. Roy understood now, as he had not then, that he had picked the wrong job for Alan. It had been a chance, perhaps his one and only chance, to introduce his son to a grown-up world of work and wages where he might have felt valued and found his feet. He had been wrong to challenge Alan's emergent sense of self by forcing him to wear clothes he despised in order to conform to the humiliations imposed by an ageing poof. The dreary salesman's attire and the dreary goods he offered from behind the old-fashioned, glass-topped counter, made Alan a figure of fun among his contemporaries. Worst of all, the shop was the sole supplier of the local school's uniform, so that Alan found himself forced to serve kids over whom he had been lording it just a term or two earlier. He had to display socks and shirts for their mothers' appraisal, advise on the buying of blazers and trousers – 'Would one size bigger be an economy or will the cuffs have frayed by the time he grows into it?' – as the lads sneered openly, knowing that Alan was powerless to retaliate.

The wonder was that Alan had stayed in the job so long – six months, maybe eight. Roy looked in once or twice, peering sideways through the shop window to catch a glimpse of his son. Alan resembled a wild bird in a cage, his movements cramped and humbled, only his eyes darting furiously at his captors.

'Leave him be,' Grace urged. 'He'll settle down in time, and the money's good. Another year and he can move on, maybe get a job in one of those modern shops, Michael Somebody, selling the smart young men's clothes *he* likes. It's a start. It's got prospects, no shift work and half days Saturdays. He might even end up in one of the big London stores, Barkers or D. H. Evans; buyer, floor manager, anything. It gives him a real future.'

Grace's vision of Alan's horizons had been wrong, and their son never forgave his parents those months of enforced humiliation. He lost faith in their judgement, even in their love for him. Silently he beseeched them to release him from the trap; silently they waited for him to get used to it. In the end he broke out without their permission.

'Sodding poofter kept touching me up!' he exploded on the Friday he came home with his cards. 'Nothing obvious – wouldn't bloody dare – but *squeezing* past me behind the counter or using me to guess the right trouser lengths. "Would your son be about *this* size, Madam?" *Spastic!*'

'Allie, darling, that's unkind . . .' Grace had pleaded, but Alan said, 'I'm not *your* Allie darling any more, Mum, so forget it. My name's *Alan* and you might as well know I'm getting married.'

'*Married!*'

'Getting *what?*'

That had been the wrong response as well.

Vera, silent, spindly Vera, had spoken up for once.

'Is it Chrissie?' she asked.

'*Course* it's Chrissie,' Alan said. 'Any reason why not?'

'I'll give you one good reason why not,' Grace put in unexpectedly. 'She's under age.'

'No she's not,' said Alan.

'How do you know that?' asked Roy in the same moment.

'I know what I know,' Grace answered. 'You go and ask her Mum and Dad how old she is. She can't marry without their permission. There's other things she shouldn't be doing, either, permission or no permission, and the less said about *that* the better.'

'She's left school,' Alan said, defiant and sullen. 'She's earning her living. We both are. And we're going to get married.'

'Not till your Dad and I have discussed it, *and* talked to her parents as well,' Grace told him firmly. 'Is he, Royston?'

'How did you know?' Roy had asked Grace afterwards. And she had said, 'I guessed she might have had her tonsils out, or her appendix – even chance she'd be in the hospital records somewhere. I've got influence. I had someone look her up. And I was right. She can't have been fifteen when Alan first brought her home. And she's not sixteen yet. It's just a phase. It'll pass.'

It had passed, all right. Chrissie's parents, furious, had forbidden them to see each other till Chrissie was past her sixteenth birthday and by then Alan had found a new job and a new girlfriend.

Roy still saw Chrissie in Tunbridge Wells sometimes: a stout young matron in fancy sweaters pushing a laden trolley round Tesco's. She always looked right through him, pretended not to recognize him. She'd turned out all right in the end. Married one of the porters at the station; station manager he was now, cocky in his BR uniform.

Had they been wrong there, too? How could they have known? Chrissie had looked like a tart, behaved like a tart, been brash and cheeky. How were they supposed to see behind that fifteen-year-old's bad language and lack of respect a suitable wife for their beloved only son? They'd done their best for Alan, then and always. And look where he'd ended up.

'Your son's in jug, isn't he?' Reginald asked Roy one evening during dinner. They were eating late and Reggie had drunk several double whiskies.

'What makes you say that?'

'Instinct. Got a nose for these things. He's in Ashford Prison, am I right?'

Steak-and-kidney pudding congealed to tepid on Roy's plate. He'd cooked it himself, spent hours in the kitchen making proper suet pastry, cutting fat off the beef, peeling skin from the kidneys and washing them under running water.

'Yes,' he murmured, just audible.

'Not your fault. Can't be responsible for him all your life. How old is he? Forty something? Fifty?'

'He's forty-three.'

'Well then. What is he in for? Theft? Embezzling? Drunken driving? What? Not a nasty sex crime, I hope. Sorry, old man. Don't have to tell me if you don't want to. You can ask me questions, too. Ought to know each other better. No secrets.'

Roy said, 'He's in for bigamy. He married two wives. Bigamy. He got eighteen months. It's more than what you normally get for bigamy, but he wouldn't express remorse, the judge said, so he gave him the extra.'

'Did he, by Jove?' said Reginald. 'Well I'll be damned. Bigamy, eh? Didn't think it still existed. Wouldn't have thought there was any need. You just get a divorce. Easy nowadays. No one minds any more. Even the Royal Family does it. Wonder what stopped your son?'

'It isn't as though we didn't set him a good example,' Roy said after a silence. 'His Mum and me, we was always happily married. Me and my wife, Grace. We had a wonderful marriage. Darby and Joan, people used to call us.'

'So you say,' said Reginald. 'Don't think I ever got the hang of it.'

'More steak-and-kidney?'

'Yes all right, give us some more. Jolly good pud.'

'You never talk about . . . your wife. Don't mind me if you'd rather not. I can mind my own business.'

'Mary? Not much to say. Ordinary sort of Englishwoman, good legs, not bad-looking. Just your usual sort of marriage. Quiet. No fireworks.'

'How long were you married?'

'Forty years. Forty something, must be, at least. Let's see, 1942 . . . No, by Jove: almost fifty! Would have been our fiftieth next year. Hadn't realized that till now. Give us another Scotch, there's a good fellow.'

Roy refilled the glass, adding more than half water. By this stage of the evening it wouldn't be noticed. He cleared the plates and set them on the sideboard, not wanting to break the mood by going downstairs to the kitchen. He placed the cheeseboard in front of Reginald, flanked by a tall jug of celery and a bowl of bright red apples, and watched him cut wedges from the fruit and cheese.

'I'm not a marrying man, not in the sense that women mean. That lovey-dovey, sentimental guff isn't my line. I was *fond* of Mary when we met, of course, but *love* . . . at the same time as *flying Spitfires*? What could compare with that? Main reason I married her was to please her. She'd have felt let down otherwise; couldn't have faced her parents. Don't suppose I ever really wanted a wife; more a matter of someone to look after me. You − or Mary − or even Mrs Owsyerfather: doesn't make much difference. Miss her, though. I'm surprised how I miss her. Keep seeing her about the place. Funny thing, that: walk into the bathroom and there she is, cleaning her teeth or wiping cream off her face. She looks up at me, always that sort of guilty look – and then she's gone. Or I look out of the window and she's on the lawn with the dogs. We haven't had dogs for years. She used to love Labradors, sloppy sort of dogs, or Dalmatians. Spots the size of a half-crown, no bigger. At one time she even walked young greyhounds. Two or three at a time. Kept her fit, she said, the excercise. She'd go on long walks with them, up over there, at High Rocks. Know the place?'

'Yes,' said Roy.

'Ever been to the Dordogne? In France? No, you wouldn't. Well, she used to say High Rocks was like that. Great grey rocks like elephants. She liked wandering about there with the dogs. Then one of them got run over and killed, and that was that. That put a stop to it, of course. She said we were cursed.'

Roy was surprised. 'Cursed? Because a dog got run over? It's hard when you've got fond of them, but it happens all the time.'

'Affected her very badly. She took the other one – Palmer, that's it; Huntley was the one that got killed, Palmer was pining for him, so was she. Took Palmer to the RSPCA and asked them to find him a new home. Couldn't bear to take him to the vet, have him put to sleep. Lovely young dog he was.'

'Dalmatian?' asked Roy, since Reggie seemed to be winding down, and he wanted to hear more.'

'Yes. Huntley and Palmer: they both were. Hope he found a good home, poor old chap. Never knew a dog could grieve.'

'Just like a human being,' prompted Roy.

'Better than a human being,' Reggie answered. He pushed his chair back and stood up. 'Leave all this. Do it in the morning. Let's go next door. Coffee done?'

'All present and correct.'

During dinner the pattering of rain against the windows had worked itself up into a storm. The wind was howling and shaking the tall cedars and pines in the front garden, making

137

the top branches of the spreading cedar beside the road rattle and creak. The five-sided brass lantern hanging in the front porch squeaked as it was whipped back and forth by the gale.

Reginald wasn't thinking about Mary, but about himself – himself when young, unencumbered by bulk or drink or the bulbous accretions of age that covered him like scar-tissue. He often escaped from the weight of his present self by thinking back to his airborne youth. Was it the same for Harry, that unrecognizably elderly Harry who had sagged in a wheel-chair at the funeral, pushed around like a giant baby by his wife? He and Harry had been pilots together in many a scrap.

One, he recalled, had been an utter balls-up. Overconfi-dence, he thought now, reliving it with the benefit of hindsight. We hadn't had any losses for days but this time we got too near Abbeville, home of Adolf Galland's boys, the best in the whole bloody Luftwaffe. We were bounced good and proper. Sud-denly the sky was full of yellow-nosed 109Gs, tracer everywhere. Two kites went down straightaway and after that it was every man for himself – throttle right through the gate, full left rudder, stick hard forward and across, then right back into a tight turn. Blacking out for a second, then something flashing across your front – hoping to God it wasn't a Spit – hearing the cannon hammering before you even knew you'd fired.

It had seemed to go on like this for ages (must've been all of twenty seconds) and then it was over. Not a thing in the sky. But he didn't trust his luck, and had dived right down to the deck and flown home like that, practically dodging houses and trees and scaring the hell out of Jerry's cows.

He landed to find more than thirty holes in the tail, and himself dripping, *drenched* with sweat. He hurried to the flight hut to find out about Harry and the others. Harry had come through it, too. And now look at him.

Reginald looked up to see Roy still fussing over the coffee as though mere seconds had passed. His heart was thudding with the intensity of what he had just relived. Roy, having poked the slumbering fire into brief activity, tried next to rekindle the embers of their conversation.

'Was *she* happy, your wife?'

'Mary? No reason not to be. We didn't go in for bickering or shouting. I never would have struck her; never anything like that. No need.'

'How about – you know, women like . . . well, flowers, surprises?'

'I didn't fart around telling her how wonderful she was, if that's what you mean.'

'Uh-huh,' said Roy.

'Get used to each other, for Christ's sake. Can't be expected to get a stand like a schoolboy every time you see your wife without her clothes on. Same sort of thing. Eh?'

'Gracie and me always spoke to each other *kindly* – politely.'

'Polite? To your wife? Can't keep that up for a lifetime!'

Roy pushed the spectacles back up the bridge of his nose. 'She used to say, if people are polite to strangers they can be polite to their nearest and dearest. If people are kind to stray dogs and old ladies, they can be kind to their better half. And we was.'

Reginald couldn't be sure if he'd been polite to Mary; on the whole he thought probably not. 'What time's dinner?', 'Finished with that paper yet?' or 'My blue shirt being washed?' had been his normal tone. She hadn't seemed to mind. She usually seemed to be smiling. Her smile rose up now before his eyes. It was a smile of stoicism rather than enjoyment. It indicated that she hoped to please, rather than to be pleased. Above it rose her neatly waved hair, pale blonde at the beginning, pale grey by the end, and below it curved her grandmother's single string of pearls resting on a softly coloured twin set. In between was Mary's smile. So it was, and so it ever shall be . . . The wind roared higher and harder through the trees.

'Of course I was *kind* to her!' he said truculently. 'For God's sake, man, what are you trying to suggest? She was my ruddy *wife*, wasn't she?' Reggie felt under attack, not only from Roy but still, in his imagination, from the Germans whom he had so narrowly evaded over Abbeville. Time to redress the balance; remember one of the times when *he* had come out on top.

Suppose you spotted some Nazi swine in a 109 squirting one of your pals. You see red. You throttle back, turn up and over. The bastard can't pull up in time. He's in front of you, less than fifty yards ahead. Your thumb's on the tit – gun button – seems to have been there all your life, and bullets are pouring out of you. You can see them smashing all along his fuselage – he's just a few yards ahead of you by this time – piercing the engine, shattering his hood. Thick clouds of black smoke are pouring out. He rolls over, chockful of bullets, and down he goes, vertically, at 400 m.p.h. Do you feel pity? Remorse? Not bloody likely! Tit for tat, eye for an eye. Next minute you could find a couple of them on *your* tail trying to kill you.

Those were the days, Reginald thought, nostalgic for their simplicity. That was the kind of morality I could understand. Wives, marriage – always a mystery. Life and death I could cope with.

As the pause in conversation extended and deepened, Roy broke it. 'Love is ever such a private thing,' he said.

Reggie lifted his head and looked across at him. 'No,' he said. 'That's where you're wrong. Love is such a *public* thing. You parade yourself in front of everybody as a couple, you have to look happy and united for the benefit of her parents, fool your pals, look what I've done, chaps: gone and got myself a wife. It's not "good old Reggie" any more; it's "love from Reggie and Mary" or "Reggie and I would love it if . . ." Like getting an extra double-barrelled name: "Reggie-an-Mary", "Mary-an-Reggie". I never felt the Mary bit was real.'

'But you miss her?'

'It would seem more natural if she were sitting there instead of you, granted. Not otherwise. We never talked much. Hardly ever had a conversation as long as this.' Except, he added to himself, when I had a confession to make.

It's the first time. Roy thought, that *we've* had a

140

conversation as long as this in nearly five months. He thought of evenings with Grace, how impatiently they'd wait for Vera and Alan to go up to bed so that the two of them could settle down to mull over their day; she at his feet, her head resting on his knee, or curled up on the settee in the crook of his arm. Talk would lead to murmuring and stroking, and as often as not to bed, to love. He'd never dreamed that a man of seventy could still want to make love so badly. To take his mind off it he asked. 'What about the war? What did she do? Have a hard time of it?'

'She was a nurse,' Reginald answered. 'That's how we met. I'd pranged the Spit, got myself grounded for a few days, stuck in a hospital bed. She was a trainee VAD. Always used to say I met her in bed.'

'Gracie had a bad war,' Roy said. 'I never knew how bad till afterwards. She told me a story once, about sleeping down the tube station. You know how in the Blitz everyone went down the Underground?'

'Yes. Seen the drawings,' Reggie replied. He lit another cigarette.

The rain slewed against the windowpanes.

'Gracie and her Mum were settling down for the night, you had to get there early, you see, to bag the best places, and this woman came down, she was up from the country, visiting, and she'd brought a goose with her. Don't ask me why. Maybe she was going to kill it and give it to her daughter – everyone was going short, what with rationing. Maybe she just didn't want to leave it alone. Don't know. She was a plump, rosy little woman and it was a nice, round white goose – a real breath of the country, Grace said. Anyhow, she pushed it all the way down the steps in a pram, bump bump bump, while the goose sat there, all happy and relaxed, watching all the people with its black beady eyes, not bothered. And all the people looked at it.'

'Go on,' said Reginald.

'She pushed the pram along the platform, found herself a place, gave the goose a stroke, and then other people, kids at first, came up and started stroking it, making a fuss of it, see? Then their Mums crowded round and started stroking it too, feeling it, nice and plump and soft it must have been. Till suddenly one of the women, she had a load of kids with her, took hold of it and wrung its neck, all of a moment. She wrung its neck, and it hadn't got a chance. Must've known the right way to do it.'

'Good God! And then what happened?' asked Reginald.

'Then they all fell upon it, Grace said; fell on it like wild animals, ripping and tearing at it. The poor woman was crying and moaning, "Don't do that! Leave her alone!", trying to protect it, putting her arms around it, but they took no notice. They just screwed it apart, into pieces. Screwed its wings off, but the legs wouldn't come, so they took out pen-knives and hacked it to pieces. Blood and feathers everywhere, flying about in the air. Tore it to bits.'

'Bloody hell . . .'

'People were hungry, and their nerves were all to pieces, and Grace said it must've been sort of crowd madness. One started, they all went for it. Way she described it, they were like cannibals. Shocking. Horrible . . . It wasn't cosy, the Blitz, cosy and well-behaved, all pulling together, like they try and make out. It was savage. It was its own kind of war.'

'Did Grace get a piece of the goose?' Reggie had to know.

'I never could bring myself to ask. I don't think I wanted to know the answer to that one.'

'Pity,' said Reginald. 'Not that it would have made any difference, I don't suppose?'

'Nothing would have made any difference. And war's a terrible thing. But I didn't want to think of her little hands covered with hot blood and feathers.'

'Extraordinary story,' said Reggie.

Such an evening increased their intimacy and taught them more about one another, but afterwards Reginald was no more inclined than before to treat Roy as an equal, or even as an individual. He was merely the latest in a long line of people who had ministered to his wants, of whom Nanny had been the first and most significant, and Mary had lasted longest. His father's ghillie, his own scout at Oxford, any batman or cleaning woman – or Roy – all served the same function: they enabled him to be idle, affable, and bored. Reginald, like most people used to being waited on hand and foot, was profoundly lazy. On the rare occasions when he had to look after himself he was appalled to find how much effort it required. Yet he could not attribute the same degree of effort when others did it for him. His gratitude, like the payment he offered, was the minimum necessary to ensure the continuation of the service.

Reggie's upper-class behaviour, a mixture of condescension and charm, had been drummed into him since childhood. It was often attractive, chiefly when he wanted something done, but any appearance of consideration for others was deceptive. He faithfully observed his parents' precepts. His mother had told him, 'Don't get too friendly with the servants, darling, it only confuses them.' And his father had said, 'Give the orders, keep it simple. Reprimand for the first mistake, warn 'em for the second, sack 'em for the third. Never give you any trouble once that's understood.' Reginald believed that it was the mark of a gentleman that he knew how to give orders without being overfamiliar or apologetic. He would no more have thanked the washing machine for spinning his shirts than Mrs Odejayi for ironing them.

Reginald soon abandoned even the pretence that Roy would drink with him, or was on any sort of equal terms. Mrs Odejayi was quick to notice. 'Don't you stand for none of his cheekiness!' she told Roy. 'I wouldn't let no grown man talk to me like that. Good manners cost nothing.'

'He doesn't mean anything by it. He doesn't think of it as rude,' Roy soothed. 'It's the way he was brought up. I came across it enough times in the Army. "It is the duty of the gentleman/To give employment to the working man." They believe that.'

'In which case he ain't employing *you!*' she said

triumphantly. 'He don't pay you nothing, you don't owe him nothing. You could walk out tomorrow, no sins on your conscience, and if you want my opinion, you should.'

'It gets him down, being on his own. He wouldn't admit it, but he's lonely. He needs me,' said Roy, and added, stating a truth he hadn't hitherto recognized, 'and I need to be needed.'

On days when Mrs Odejayi didn't come in, Reginald treated Roy like his valet. 'Fetch me a clean shirt,' he would say, after Roy had brought his early-morning tea and the *Telegraph*, or perhaps, 'These trousers could do with pressing.' Soon it became, 'Which tie am I going to wear today?' or at weekends, 'Which cravat?' Before long Roy had got into the habit of selecting Reginald's clothes, drawing his bath, and even standing beside the bed with a striped towelling dressing gown held ready for him to slip his arms backwards into the sleeves. He did not feel demeaned by these services. He had become used to dressing Grace and, by the end, helping her on to the lavatory or bedpan. Acting as manservant to Reggie helped to pass the time, gave some structure and purpose to his day, leaving fewer patches of solitude in which to brood.

She still came to him at night. Less and less often did he dream of her alive. Instead, he would be in a strange, many-chambered palace which he assumed to be the kingdom of heaven, climbing sheer stone staircases or dwarfed by high-vaulted rooms with scowling statues and gargoyles, pursuing the diaphanous figure of his wife. He swayed and undulated through sometimes subterranean, sometimes underwater, sometimes arid lunar landscapes which grew stranger as she became more elusive. The familiar background to their life together hardly ever reassembled itself. Instead, she drifted through alien territory just out of his reach, beckoning him to hurry. He seldom managed to catch up and it was weeks since he had dreamed about making love to her.

After these nights, Roy would wake early and unsettled at four-thirty, five o'clock – a milkman's hours, a milkman's dark winter mornings – and spend all day oppressed, worrying.

He wondered if she was waiting for him, as the vicar and the Bible and the funeral service promised. He would have liked to share these thoughts with Reginald but, fearing ridicule, he preferred not to risk it. Aggie, with her powerful evangelical faith, was a comfort; but Aggie believed the dead could be reached and talked to with the aid of a medium, and Roy preferred not to risk that, either. He was forced to mourn alone.

He went back to his own house in search of her small and kindly figure and stayed to dust, to collect his post, and spruce up the neglected shrine. He stared at her photographs one by one. She seemed more real to him as a young woman. It was increasingly hard to visualize her at the end of her life, for there had been no pictures taken of her since Vera's wedding, getting on for twenty years ago. That spring Roy would have to buy flowers to place around the shrine, for he visited the allotment less and less often.

When he bumped into Molly Tucker in the library, he started guiltily, but she only said, 'Well I'm blowed, Roy Southgate, I'd hardly have known you! My, but you're look-ing better! Anyone'd think you'd had a holiday. Carry my library books home for me, and I'll give you a cup of tea and a nice bit of homemade cake.'

Constance Liddell, the librarian who used to recommend books for Grace to while away the bedridden hours, watched as Roy carefully held the swing door open for Molly. Well, she thought, my mother married again at seventy-three: no reason why those two shouldn't get it together. No reason why I shouldn't, in theory. Hope springs eternal – she smiled wryly – even in Tunbridge Wells.

'How's life treating you, then?' asked Molly across the kitchen table. The teapot nestled under a quilted cosy. Beside it on a flowered plate with a doily stood a home-baked cake made with fresh butter and eggs. The milk jug, sugar bowl, side-plates and teacups were of matching china, the tablecloth and napkins hand-embroidered. In ten minutes she'd done him proud. She poured the tea, cut them each a slice of cake and sat back.

'You look as though you'd got yourself a new girlfriend. Thought you might have had a vacancy for me, a few months ago. There's no call to look so shocked, Roy Southgate. Grace wouldn't have minded. Well, go on. Bakes a nice Victoria sponge, does she? Good as mine?'

'There's only ever going to be one girl for me, you know that. I look in at the Kelsey Arms once in a while to see my old mates from the dairy – fewer of them there each time I go – but aside from that I haven't been out since we had our New Year's Eve,' said Roy.

'What you up against? Money tight?'

'No, not that. Been keeping myself busy, looking after him and cooking for the both of us, bit of shopping sometimes – like today.'

'And here was me thinking you a gentleman of leisure, living up at Nevill Park all posh, real la-di-da you'd become, no time for old friends. He look after you all right, all found?'

'He doesn't pay me.'

'What, no wages? Nothing is for nothing, sonny, nothing is for free.'

'He buys food and everything. I've just got my rates to pay –'

'Poll tax.'

'Whatever they call it – on my house; and the insurance for, you know, funeral and all that. I been sending Junie a bit of money now and again, for the boys. Nothing else.'

'If you're so rich you can take me to the pictures. Do you good to get out. That Woody Allen's ever so funny. Nearly as good as Charlie Chaplin. Make you laugh.'

'I'll ask the Squadron Leader.'

'Mind he lets you go. Long time since I had a date. That's that, then. Time you was heading off home. Been good to see you and have a chat.'

Reginald and Roy ate in the dining-room, usually in near silence. Roy put the food on the table; Reginald dished it out. Sometimes, if the meal had been particularly good, he said so.

Afterwards, smoking a cigarette in the drawing room, he watched the Gulf War on the *Nine O'Clock News*, and then, as often as not, again on *News at Ten* and again on *Newsnight*. He was both thrilled and dismissive about the pictures of aerial bombardment. The technology enthralled him; but as far as the pilots were concerned, he said, there was nothing to it. 'All done by numbers now – or robots. Where's the skill, what's left for your rear-gunner to do? Ruddy computers taken over.'

When Roy had finished the chores and made coffee, he would join him, and they would watch whatever programme Reggie had chosen. He liked old films best, and police serials: *LA Law* or *Inspector Morse*. Once or twice a week he went out for the evening. If he put his sheepskin jacket on, Roy knew he was 'going for my constitutional', which meant down to the Broker's Arms. If he changed from his tweed jacket and corduroys into a suit, it meant he was seeing his lady-friend. Roy had spoken to her on the telephone once or twice, when she had asked peremptorily for 'the Squadron Leader', and he knew her name was Liz something or other, but Reggie had revealed nothing else.

Occasionally, if they had spent an evening talking about the war and had felt, briefly, some sense of camaraderie, of shared experience, Reginald would invite Roy to come with him to the pub. It was half-timbered and horse-brassy, with aged wooden settles and wheelback chairs. Confident, loud-voiced young people stood around saying 'Yah, yah,' and when he was there, Reggie said 'Yah' as well, instead of his usual 'Roger' or 'Okey-doke' or 'Yup'. The barman would pour a double Glenmorangie without being asked, and after a cursory glance at Roy, would listen to one of Reggie's flying stories. Roy and Reginald would buy each other a token round of drinks and as often as not go home separately. Roy knew that they might live under the same roof but the social divide was always and for ever unbridgeable. He did not mind; he was even relieved that it should be so. His best jacket and sharply pressed trousers looked all wrong among the ribbed sweaters and kitten-soft jackets of the Grahams and Joyces in the Broker's Arms. Their bad language shocked him, though no one else seemed to mind, not even the girls.

If ever Reginald happened to come to the basement kitchen at eleven o'clock when Roy and Aggie were having their mid-morning coffee together, the position was reversed. Last time, Aggie had been telling some tale of hospital life. 'What she's done she ain't admitting,' she concluded. 'But she's knitting!' As Roy shook with laughter, he saw the Squadron Leader appear briefly in the doorway. He looked discomfited, apologized and withdrew. Aggie had called after him, 'Come on, join in the fun!' But Reginald's feet on the stone steps did not even falter.

Chapter Nine

The house in Nevill Park now ran like clockwork, to Reginald's complete satisfaction. He was so delighted with the outcome of the vicar's plan that he invited him round for a drink just after Easter. The vicar was slightly perturbed to find that Roy served the drinks and did not join them. But Reggie's vigorous defence of American air support during the Gulf War provided such a beguiling subject for agreement that he soon forgot about Roy, who had slipped away down to the kitchen. Reginald had lost his neglected, dishevelled look and was as sleek as a seal. The vicar stifled his doubts; he congratulated Reggie on looking so well, and they toasted the success of General Schwarzkopf and the modern RAF.

From time to time Reginald wondered briefly if he ought to be paying Southgate. He was a good cook; meals were on time, plentiful, and tasty. Of late he had also acted as an efficient and tactful valet, looking after Reginald's suits, brushing and pressing them, and taking them to be dry-cleaned. What with him and the big black mammy laundering, ironing and folding away, his clothes were more efficiently organized than even Mary had managed. Then Reginald would reflect that Roy was living free, a permanent house guest, in surroundings he could not possibly have afforded for himself; that he contributed nothing towards the household and little enough for the car, beyond an occasional tank of petrol. Honours, he would conclude, were pretty even. His conscience was clear.

Reginald's pursuit of Liz was no longer motivated by practical necessity. It became tactical, a game of conquest marked by small erotic concessions on her side, little local advances that might be denied at their next encounter, or consolidated and even improved upon. She had not yet permitted him to make love to her, although he had once got as far as her bedroom, where they had wrestled on the billowy satin bedspread, the bad boy painfully stiff and impatient. He was not importunate enough to force her, and not only because he doubted whether he had the physical strength and agility to overcome any real resistance. After seeing her for nearly six months he had, in the language of his adolescence, done 'everything but'. The 'but' impaled him with a young man's baffled desire. Love, he believed, had nothing to do with it; but Reginald, a few weeks after his seventy-second birthday, found himself obsessed with lust.

Despite a lifetime of trivial infidelities, he had never been a man of ungovernable or even urgent sexual appetite. He had taken his opportunities where he found them – be it a compliant typist or another man's inebriated wife after an evening of dinner or bridge. Just occasionally chance proximity on a commuter train had allowed his free hand to wander and, even more occasionally, it had encountered no defence. Then he and a stranger, their averted faces inches apart, would engage in furtive pleasure, all the more acute for taking place in public, marked only by a few seconds of quickened breathing. Those impassive, covert encounters had ended with his commuting days. Thereafter, Reginald visited Sabrina in London, because otherwise he might as well be dead. Cock gone, all gone.

It had been a very long time, however – probably not since his courtship of Mary – since Reginald had enjoyed the tantalizing suspense of an evening, let alone many evenings, in the company of a woman without knowing whether he would end up in her bed. Mary, of course, had kept her virginity until their wedding night. But Liz was a divorcée aged, what? – forty-five, forty-six, mid-forties, surely? Sometimes, displaying her body to its best advantage for his benefit, she would seem to signal that tonight was the night, and the big bad boy would be rigid with happy anticipation. At other times she would be so preoccupied and distant that he took an early leave of her. Then she might clasp him with quite unexpected passion and guide his head down to her breast, his hand to her thigh. 'Reggie,' she would breathe, 'Oh Reggie, I mustn't. Oh darling, no!'

He did not at first acknowledge in so many words that these games of advance and retreat were campaign tactics, conducted with skill and deliberation on Liz's part; yet he knew it to be so, and thought none the worse of her for that. This was the sort of encounter that he understood. There could be no victory without opposition; no satisfaction in a too easy conquest. Women had always bartered their bodies in return for male protection; or their parents had done it for them – what else was the London Season for? He knew that Nanny, let alone his mother, would not have judged Liz to be quite a lady, but as far as he was concerned she was near enough; and when did he get a chance to meet *ladies* nowadays? Long-dead Nanny and Mamma would never know; and they certainly wouldn't have wanted him to be lonely.

Reginald, when finally invited to dinner in Liz's swagged and striped, tarted-up but cramped Georgian terraced house, knew very well that she was wagering her body against his status and worldly goods. The knowledge did nothing to diminish his lust or his enjoyment of the chase.

Liz found the game, not the man, erotic. She did not dislike Reginald – far from it; she often found herself moved by his gallantry and naïvety, the simple way he could be relied upon to play the rules. He had evidently been handsome once. But he had let himself go to seed; food and drink and cigarettes had taken their toll, so that, however smartly he dressed for her benefit, he wheezed and he smelled. His distended belly, coarsened features and stiffened limbs could hold no possible sexual attraction. It was her own body that excited her.

She enjoyed the narcissism of dressing for Reggie; selecting from her new spring stock an artfully cut evening suit which looked perfectly correct, even formal, yet revealed more of her breasts than – surely? – she could have intended. She enjoyed lying in a scented bath with pads soaked in eye lotion placed coolly against her closed lids, nail varnish drying on splayed fingers; enjoyed standing naked in front of her long mirror, admiring the taut result of thrice-weekly aerobic classes while she blow-dried her hair to a soft halo. She enjoyed the skilful application of expensive cosmetics. Preparations completed, she enjoyed sallying forth – sometimes without a bra, sometimes with only the skimpiest silk pants – to meet this rich, spoiled, rubicund old man who could, if she played her cards right, solve all her financial problems. Above all, she enjoyed watching him reduced to childlike, pawing desire.

She took care to amuse him. She would pick up gossip and jokes like a magpie, cocking an ear to her customers' conversation for sparkling titbits that would make him chortle. She read the *Daily Mail*, watched the news on television. She did not bore him. Yet sometimes, as he held forth on Saddam Hussein or the prime minister or Japanese imports, Reginald would find himself thinking of the long, cold mornings when they waited for the mist to lift and the order to scramble: a dozen young men sitting around not knowing which of them, in a few hours' time, might be alive, and which dead or maimed or burned or limbless.

Sometimes Liz would remember her mother telling her the story of how, as a little girl, she had pointed skywards out of a train window and said 'Spitfires!' – correctly, as chance would have it – which made the other passengers admire her precocity. Might he have been flying one of those? It was not impossible. They did not reveal these thoughts to one another. Liz could not because to do so would have given away her age, something she was careful to conceal from him; Reggie could not because they might have come under the category Nanny had called 'moaning and groaning', which was taboo in conversation. So she sparkled and he chuckled, or he pontificated and she concurred, and this staved off silence well enough while he wondered what his chances might be later on, whether in car, or sofa, or bedroom.

Afterwards she would close her own front door behind her in a fever of excitement, sure that her goal of a trouble-free, luxurious life was perceptibly closer. She would go up to her bedroom, undo her jacket and skirt and let them slide softly down her body, watching herself in the full-length mirror as her scented nakedness was gradually revealed. Satisfied, she would drop her underclothes fastidiously into the laundry basket and walk into the bathroom to cleanse her body of Reggie's bloodshot eyes and liver-spotted hands. Finally she would wipe the subtle colours and textures from her face until the pale lashless eyes and wrinkled mouth of an ageing woman looked back at her. Then she would wink at herself, for this image was a secret known only to Liz and her mirror. Usually she slept very well indeed.

Business in the shop was bad, and getting worse. Her newly rich customers came in not to buy, but to perch on the sofa and drink coffee, lamenting over husbands who were on edge with the fear of redundancy, or had already been made redundant. Some would complain at length, and bitterly, about dress allowances cut by half; holidays cancelled; weddings at which last year's outfit had to be worn again. The old rich kept their own counsel in rambling russet houses set behind high walls or hedges in quiet villages skirted by the main roads, but even they were staying at home. Liz offered free alterations, free delivery – even, if she was sufficiently desperate to secure a sale, a week's free trial of some sumptuously extravagant garment; and still the stock stayed on the hangers.

She knew better than to bring these tales to Reggie, let alone to ask him for a loan to tide her over. Instead, she visited her friend and ally, Colin Thurlwell. Leaning on the highly polished glass counter in his tiny shop, she gazed hungrily at glowing lumps of gold displayed against black velvet, twisted into molten shapes and sprinkled with diamonds.

'Believe you me, my darling,' she told him, flashing her eyes and crinkling here long fingers at him, 'once that fish is hooked I'll be in here once a month asking you to make me another bracelet, with earrings and brooch to match!'

'If wishes were horses then beggars should ride,' he told her.

'Don't be too sure. How do you know there aren't ill-begotten sons or rapacious little nieces tucked away?'

'There aren't, I'm pretty sure. I've looked him up in the reference books and there's only a nephew, who's got the title and assets coming out of his ears. He's got a couple of daughters – clever you, how did you know? – but they're not short of the odd bob. And if they were, the old boy would have been invited to spend Christmas with them instead of having it on his own, poor darling. Wish I'd known! There was an opportunity missed. I'd have got him to take me to Paris or Florence; it never occurred to me he'd be by himself. He'll leave it to Battersea Dogs' Home, that's who. Lucky he met me first. Don't you worry, Colin: our Reginald is up for grabs. Trouble is, *he*'s got to do the grabbing; and if he doesn't hurry up, I shall be in Carey Street.'

'Business stinks?'

'Oh Colin . . . never worse! I haven't shifted a thousand quids' worth of stock in a single week since Christmas! If I had any sense, I'd fold my tent and steal away. But I *can't*.'

'Because of him? Or because of cash-flow problems?'

'Both.'

'If it's him you're worrying about, best thing you could do is remove yourself for a while. Let him stew. Nip off to the Mediterranean for an early summer holiday, send him some nice colourful postcards of big hotels, blue seas and pine trees saying "Wish you were here" . . .'

'If only I *could*.'

'Postcards are simple. It's getting you there that's the tricky bit. Haven't you got any rich friends you could go and stay with?'

'They're all so *boring*.'

'What makes you think *he*'s interesting? Sounds catatonic to me. You're going to need the practice. Go on, think . . . Former customers? Schoolfriends? Early retirements? Doesn't matter who they are, and you can go by train, so it won't cost you. What you need is a little absence to make the heart grow fonder and a premature suntan to make everyone else look wishy-washy.'

'Colin,' she said, 'you're a genius, a scheming bloody genius!

You're right. I'll do it. I'll find someone who'll have me to stay whether they like it or not. I'll come back with a load of cheap baubles from the market: call them "new summer accessories from the resorts", sell 'em at a 200 per cent mark-up and finance my trip!'

'That's the spirit. Now then, what did you come in to ask me for?'

'Can you lend me five thousand at $12\frac{1}{2}$ per cent?'

'No,' he said, 'I cannot. That's bank-manager time. But what I will do is ring up pretending to be your accountant, give him a bit of flim-flam, say you've been a silly girl and got behind on your VAT or something, make it easy for you. OK?'

'OK,' she said.

She telephoned Reggie a few days later.

'Well,' he said flirtatiously, pleased that she had taken the initiative. 'Well, and to what do I owe the pleasure?'

'Reggie, darling, I can't bear this cool English weather a day longer. I'm fed up. I'm going away to look for a proper spring.'

'When?' he asked, a little boy bereft. 'Where? Who with?'

'Oh darling, you're so sweet,' cooed Liz. 'I've got some dear friends I'm going to stay with. They're always pestering me to go. They live in the hills behind Genoa. Heavenly view, all sea and sky . . . and then there's another, known him donkey's years, who lives in Rome – I might go down there for a few days as well.'

'Who are these chaps? How long will you be gone?'

'Not *chaps*, Reggie, just friends. Old mates. I'll be away, oh, two weeks – three – depends.'

'When are you going?'

'As soon as I can get a flight. Tomorrow, if there's a seat on BA to Genoa.'

'*Tomorrow?* Well, you'd better have dinner with me tonight.'

'Reggie, my pet, you're so impractical. I've got to pack, get myself organized.'

'Pick you up at nine, then. Nine-thirty, if you like.'

Big sigh. 'Oh all *right*. Nine-thirty. By-ee!'

This time he took her to dinner at a soft pink and blue pin-cushion of a restaurant where the food was delicious and the cook round and pretty and shining with health – a wonderful advertisement for her own cooking and no competition for Liz.

'If you'd *told* me you wanted to go away,' Reggie was grumbling, '*I*'d have taken you. No need to be all underhand about it. What will I do with myself while you're away?'

'When you and I travel together, my poppet,' said Liz with a reckless toss of the head, 'it'll be in grand style and for a very special reason. All right?'

'Is that a promise?' he said, poor old heffalump, straight into the trap.

'It's a promise. You can make plans while I'm away.'

'I warn you,' he said, 'I'm bored to tears in museums.'

'How about casinos?' she asked.

'Gambling? I've never gambled, not more than a shilling a hundred at bridge or a fiver on a horse. You mean roulette?'

'Oh Reggie, my darling, how have you got through life without ever playing roulette? Never mind: I'm going to have lots of fun teaching you!'

Next morning at crack of dawn Liz caught the early train from Tunbridge Wells that connected with the boat-train from Dover. She was dressed in jeans and sandals and a big white sweater, carrying a roll-bag full of unsold resort wear. She had left behind a notice in the shop window that said : 'Closed for collections and spring-buying trip. Re-opening end of May with new Continental stock.' This, when reported back by his wife, did not amuse Whittington, her parsimonious bank man-ager.

Roy found it easier to remember Grace as she had been when young, rather than as she had looked towards the end. He wondered if it were because of the intensity with which he had missed her during the wartime years when they were separated. Then his longing gaze had burned up the curling black-and-white or brownish snapshots with deckled edges that he carried with him everywhere. He had them still, tucked away carefully in an envelope at the back of a drawer in his own house, to be looked at again when (if ever) he could do so without tears. Their wedding photographs had been taken out for the funeral and put away again; but not the youthful pictures of Grace leaning against a bicycle, laughing, or Grace lying in a meadow, propped on one elbow beside a picnic cloth. People said the past grew clearer as you got older, while more recent events were forgotten. It must also be because the past was so sweet, the days of idyll.

He thought of their early marriage in the little house they had rented. They had discussed endlessly whether – since they could only afford a carpet for one room and would have to make do, for the time being, with lino in all the rest – they should put the carpet in the lounge or the bedroom. 'We're going to spend most of our time in the bedroom,' he had pointed out. Grace, not disagreeing nor falsely prudish, had said, 'Yes, but it's the lounge people will see.' 'What *people*?' he said. '*We're* the ones who matter.'

In the end, so that they could make love on the floor as well as in bed, they'd bought a carpet for the bedroom. 'In any case,' she reasoned, 'it's not as though we often sit in the lounge. Mostly people chat in the kitchen, and nobody would expect a carpet there.'

Their first home. The rent had been twenty-six shillings a week. He had made a lot of the furniture himself. He'd been good at carpentry at school, so he went back to his old wood-work master and asked if, outside term-time, he could borrow the workbench and tools. The man had been touched that Roy remembered his lessons. He advised him on the best wood to buy, which pieces to make and which were too much trouble. 'Don't bother trying to build a chest of drawers,' he had said. 'It's not worth doing unless you do it well, and doing it well means dovetail joints, and those aren't easy. So buy your chest of drawers – second-hand is better than new; better made.'

Grace had bought lengths of sheeting cotton which she had hemmed to make their sheets, and stitched pillowcases with their initials embroidered across one corner – intertwined curl-icues, skating swoops of Rs and Gs looping around an S. She had hemmed table napkins and tray-cloths and later, when she was pregnant for the first time, she had knitted and sewed a beautiful layette: white, as befitted a first child. When she wasn't stitching, she wrote him yearning letters into which she poured her hopes for their baby, her fears about the war, and her dreams of the life they would have together at the end of it.

They had missed each other so powerfully, so painfully, that the image of his young bride was the one that had burned itself into his memory, despite fifty years of married life. Grace as she had been in their last years together, a stooped, greying, methodical figure polishing and hoovering from room to room, *that* Grace was slipping away from him. He murmured his talisman again: '*O for the touch of a vanish'd hand/And the sound of a voice that is still!*' But although the tears pricked in his eyes and he had to swallow the lump in his throat, he was no longer battling against an arching, drowning crest of pain that, six months ago, would have thumped him in the solar plexus and doubled him up with grief.

He did not confess this to Vera, when he wrote his monthly letter to her in Australia; nor to Alan, when he visited him in prison. Alan looked pasty-faced and sullen, but the bruises had gone from his throat. Roy had never asked his son why he had not applied to the authorities for permission to attend his mother's funeral. Such permission was nearly always given; the fact that Alan did not go suggested he had not wanted to be there. Was it guilt, or shame at being seen, prison-pale and under escort, by his parents' friends and neighbours? Losing face would be more than he could stand; worse than not paying his last respects to his mother.

Roy would have been comforted by reminiscing with Alan about their family life – the outings they'd been taken on as children; days by the seaside; visits to the circus – but he knew this would unleash a flood of accusation.

One day Alan seemed mellower than usual, less inclined to go through his litany of history and grievance. After Roy had been there for ten minutes, drinking thick prison tea out of thick prison cups under the averted but wary gaze of prison warders, Alan poked his head across the table, the only privacy their circumstances allowed, and said, 'It's like this, you see. You and Mum had, like, a really good marriage, OK? You never stopped wanting to be together. You wasn't tempted by anyone else. Well, me and Sheila have got the same. And it could be better. Much better. Perfect. For ever. I know that. She does, too. We're both sure. I've made up my mind. I'm going to get a divorce from June and me and Sheila'll marry again, I mean properly.' Roy kept quiet as Alan drew deeply on his cigarette. He stuck his head forward again, confidingly, and beckoned Roy towards him.

'All we need now – when I get out – is a kid; a little girl to sit on my lap. She might look like Mum, be nice and dainty like her. I'd be a better Dad with a daughter. I was too rough on the boys; used to hit them; couldn't seem to not. Dad, you've got to do something for me. I want you to talk to June. You and she are close these days, aren't you? You never used to like her; well, you was wrong.'

Roy closed his eyes and hung his head in acknowledgement of this.

Alan went on: 'My trouble was, I never got on with that Gloria. Cheeky, snotty little kid, always acting like I was the one who'd butted in. If June hadn't had Gloria it might have been different, we might have got off to a better start. But she was always there, clinging to her mum, giving me funny looks. No need to tell June that, but make her see – explain for me. It's never going to come right with us, not now. She's young still, she ain't bad-looking: she'll find a bloke. I want a divorce.'

He frowned, and lit a new cigarette from the butt of the old one, inhaling ferociously, avoiding his father's eye. 'Junie's still a good-looking bird,' he repeated. 'Kept her figure. Plenty of blokes could go for her. She'll get married again, find someone to set an example to the boys, keep them out of trouble.'

'What if he feels about them the way you felt about Gloria?'

'He won't, though, will he? They're good kids. Look, I'm telling you, Dad, she'll be better off without me. And then Sheila and me'll be free to be properly married, by law, and have what you and Mum had.'

'And what was that, son?'

'A good *marriage*. Like everyone wants. No fights, no hard words, no fucking around with anyone else and walking out. You two was always lovey-dovey, I never remember you shouting at Mum. Me and Sheila can be the same. We're like that, too: even with all the lies I had to tell, keeping June and Sheila secret from each other, not letting on where I was half the time – even then, Sheila trusted me. She's a really good kid and she loves me, and I love her.'

'You loved June, too.'

'That was different. I might never have married her if you and Mum hadn't been dead against it. Listen, you owe it to me, Dad, fucking *life* owes me another chance. I made one mistake, OK, that's why I'm here, I know that. But I've paid for it, bloody hell I have. Now it's my turn for a new start.'

He leaned across the table and clapped his father on the shoulder. That's the first time my son has touched me in years, Roy thought, and his flesh tingled from the contact. First time anyone's touched me, except by mistake, since – the funeral? No, can't be as long ago as that. Since New Year's Eve, when the Squadron Leader danced with me. He must've been lonely that night, poor bloke, and so was I. I'm lonely now. I'll always be lonely with Gracie gone.

Recognizing his own loneliness, he acknowledged that Alan was suffering the same pain. He too, in prison, surrounded by men, was lonely for a woman: not any woman, but one particular one, the wrong one. Not the mother of his sons, but the woman he had married against the laws of the land and of God and nature. But nothing I can say will change his mind, thought Roy. He stretched his hand across the table and laid it beside Alan's, but Alan looked away.

'I'll go and see June,' said Roy.

Chapter Ten

Reginald decided that while Liz was away he'd take some soundings; test the water. Trip to London to talk to his lawyer and accountant; maybe see how the girls were getting along. Might even tell them about Liz; fix up for them to meet her, perhaps, to see how she looked in their company, whether she could hold her own. No: bit soon for all that. Better to bide his time. Mary hadn't been dead a year yet: spot of respect would be in order. While Southgate and Mrs Big Black Mammy were jabbering away in the kitchen one morning, she ironing and he fiddling about at the stove, Reggie sat down at Mary's desk in the study, consulted her address book and his own, almost empty 1991 dairy, and began dialling.

Tucked away in the pigeonholes of the desk were several leather pocket dairies that had belonged to Mary over the years, and, as he waited for a secretary to connect him, Reginald pulled one out and began to flick through it. It held no secrets; Mary's life was just what it had seemed. 'Coffee, Sue & Betty, 11' or 'Penny, Primrose and J, Tea here, 4' were the social highlights of her week.

'I'm sorry, Mr Conynghame-Jervis, I'm afraid he's in a meeting,' sang the brisk female voice down the telephone. 'Can I ask him to call you back, or will you try again later?'

'Get him to ring me as soon as he's free, there's a good girl.' ordered Reggie.

'Has he got your number?' she said icily.

'Of course he's got my sodding number,' muttered Reggie, but when she called out, 'Sorry . . .?' he answered audibly, 'Yes.'

He returned to his scrutiny of Mary's diaries, jabbed by the blameless life they revealed, and by the sight of her rounded schoolgirl handwriting. Gradually it dawned upon him that she had seen the girls regularly, nearly always on the first Thursday of every month, but at other times as well. 'Usual lunch, C & F' would be followed by 'Meet Harrods 12.30' or 'Meet Liberty's, 12.30,' and then, as often as not, 'Matinée, 2.15' or 'Film starts 2.55'. She had always made arrangements that would enable her to be back home by the time he arrived, even if sometimes – Reginald thought – she must have caught one commuter train ahead of his own. Why had she not talked about these meetings? he wondered, and knew the answer for himself. She had never told him because he had never asked; and if he *had* asked, he would not have waited for or listened to her reply.

Yet his wife was much loved, if her circle of friends was anything to go by. Penny, Primrose, Madge, Lisa, Penelope (who was different from Penny: Penny being fussy and henlike while Penelope was grand and contralto), Rosemary and Beth . . . women whose husbands he had glimpsed on his commuter train, back in the days when he still commuted, and towards whom he used to sketch a gesture of recognition. Women were better at friendships than men, he reflected; but then, women had the *time*.

Each diary had a list of birthdays carefully copied in from year to year; of which, Reggie noticed with a foolish surge of emotion, only his own merited capital letters. Against 2 March she wrote every year 'REGGIE!!' while in the 1989 dairy – he checked – yes, she had written 'REGGIE 70!' She had insisted on paying for dinner that night, up in London, at Luigi's (an old favourite and handy for the station afterwards). That evening, before they settled down to choose from the menu, she had taken from her bag a small gift-wrapped box and offered it to him tentatively, imploringly.

'What's this, then?' Reginald had trumpeted. 'What is all this nonsense, eh?'

A waiter had approached and popped a champagne bottle open just as Reggie snapped the spring of the jeweller's box. Inside lay a pair of heavy gold cufflinks engraved with his monogram, a baroque RCJ. Hadn't it occurred to him *then* to wonder how she could pay for all this? He was about to stand up and go to his bedroom to look at them – had he ever *worn* them? he wondered guiltily. Surely she had had something engraved on the back: what the hell was it?

At that moment Southgate entered the room with a tray of coffee and biscuits, while at the same instant the telephone rang. Reginald waved the tray down and lifted the receiver.

'Yes, yes, yes of course I'm here now . . . Well, put him through, then. Hello – MacNamee? Pat? . . . Excellent . . . Oh, tootling along, and you? Good, good. Thought I should look in for a chat. No, nothing's wrong. Lunch? Yes, suit me very well. Thursday? Friday? RAF Club as usual? Jolly good. Be there at half-twelve. Cheer-oh.'

Cufflinks forgotten, he turned to the back of the diary, where he was sure he would find an alphabetical list giving the girls' telephone numbers. He would arrange to meet them for tea at Fortnum's or the Ritz on the same day as his lunch with Patrick. The pages headed 'Cash' and 'Accounts' were meticulously filled in with dates and amounts – '3.01.89 sold 600 RB&K . . . £4,675' was a typical entry – and on the last page she had calculated the profit and loss for the whole year. He was staggered by the amounts she had been dealing with. Tens of thousands of pounds had passed through his wife's hands, unknown to him, right up until the last year of her life.

Reginald lit a cigarette and drank his cooling coffee. Resentment and guilt in equal parts disturbed his racing heart. (Shouldn't drink coffee, doctor says; shouldn't smoke; shouldn't do sweet FA: bloody doctors.) He knew she couldn't be accused of keeping secrets from him, yet he could not help feeling that at some point – when her dealings reached five thousand a year, say, or ten – she should have come clean. Yet . . . she had never asked him for money; had, on the contrary, willingly lent him quite large sums of her own. Perhaps she felt it was up to him to have noticed that her parents' initial twenty-five thousand pounds seemed to be stretching an awful long way. The diaries had always been here – not that he would have looked into them, of course, Reggie told himself virtuously.

The truth was, his wife had lived out her days unnoticed beside him. He had taken for granted her presence and her services, had dispensed with her sexually when she no longer welcomed him (the curtain had fallen sometime in the late forties or early fifties), but continued to find her useful domestically and socially. Mary had been responsible for every aspect of his life except his barber, his *Telegraph* crossword and his other women – such as they were: he always confessed eventually, and she used to blush when he told her and hang her head, as though the fault were hers. He found these episodes healing. He felt better afterwards and, feeling better, felt new desire for his wife. He would embrace her, and she would seem to nestle against him. Yet he was never sure that she really wanted his touch.

In due course they had stopped touching altogether, except the formal gestures – his hand under her elbow when they crossed the road or into church, a palm cupped ready to hand her out of a car or up from a sofa. I do not know, he thought, when I last kissed my wife. Was it months before she died, or years? He had not touched her, kissed her, listened to her, worn her gifts, met her eyes ... and, by ignoring her, had diminished her to a creature who asked nothing of him. She had continued to give what she could – food and shirts appeared in the expected times and places – but their provider was a cipher, might as well have been a robot. Yet ... isn't that what we all secretly want, Reggie wondered, once the first fine frenzy is over? He had more or less assumed that all husbands were like him, all wives like Mary, all marriages like theirs: a smooth-running service arrangement, give and take – men giving women status and taking home and comfort, organization, *order*. He had given Mary his name, made her his wife and helped her surpass the expectations of her parents and schoolfriends ('Mary *Bagnal*? Marrying an RAF pilot? How *very* unexpected!'). Thinking of Southgate, he knew there should have been more to his marriage than that.

Mrs Odejayi stuck her head round the door and waved at him energetically. A strong female odour filled the room.

'I'll be off, then!' she bellowed. Reginald looked up at her with swimming eyes.

'Now now now, what's going on here?' she asked. 'What's up? You been blubbing? Wash it all out of your heart, don't be shamed. God's good tears wash all man's sorrows away.'

She crouched down beside him and laid a huge arm across his shoulders. Her shiny black face was very close to his own and the smell of her hot, hard-working body was overwhelming. She smelled like Nanny, of starch and sweat. Her voice was tender.

'There, there, poor soul,' she cooed. 'Is it your dear missus as has passed away? You and Roy should get together. He's the same. Many's the weep he's had down in the kitchen with me. Sorrows should be shared, Squadron Leader, and then they're halved. Not hidden away in secret. Crying's a fine thing when you've got good cause.'

'I was so horrible to her,' Reginald said indistinctly.

'Horrible? Well there you are. All the same. Men treats their wives like dirt when they're alive and regrets them when they're dead. It's the law of nature and the way of the world. Women should live with women, and men stick to men. There'd be less trouble and no babies.'

She laughed, and stood up. 'And what do you want for your other two wishes?' she said.

Reginald smiled glassily at her.'Have I paid you?' he asked.

'Bless my soul, if that ain't the first time he's ever suggested it!' she said, throwing her arms wide as if appealing to an audience of thousands to witness. 'No, you haven't – but this is Monday and it ain't due till Friday. But if you've got it, I'll take it, in case it ain't here the next time!'

'If it's not due yet, I ain't payin' it!' said Reginald in imitation, and she grinned at him.

'There you are – that's better now! Like I was saying, I'm off, or my poor old men up at the hospital won't get their lunch.'

She patted his shoulder. 'You be all right now? Safe to leave you? God bless and keep you, then.'

Reginald would not have been surprised if she'd concluded

by saying, 'And you promise to stay Nanny's good boy now.' He was almost more surprised that she did not, so vividly had her brisk, God-fearing kindness evoked the tears and consolations of the nursery. He watched her leave through the study window, squared his shoulders and walked through to the drawing room to pour himself a stiff whisky.

He swirled its jewel-clear liquid round the glass, thinking, If I marry again I won't neglect her. It won't be like poor Mary. I'll – imperceptibly the hypothetical became the definite – I'll be good to Liz. I'll look after her and pay attention to her. I won't visit Sabrina. Treacherously, the big boy twitched. Reggie scratched his balls crossly through his trouser pocket. The pocket had a hole in it. He poked his fingers through, and scratched again. I'll *try* not to visit Sabrina any more, he amended.

Later that week Reginald sat in the theatrical, ivory-and-gold foyer of the Ritz, awaiting his nieces with a mixture of apprehension and pleasure. Pleasure because they were good-looking girls and it would do him credit to be seen with them in such a place. Apprehension because he had come from an excellent lunch at the RAF Club, after which Pat, his accountant, had urged him to pay a surprise call on his father, Reggie's wartime flying contemporary.

'He's always at the Reform in the afternoons,' Pat told him, 'fast asleep in an armchair. Do him good to see you.'

Reggie had caught a cab to Pall Mall, and there he and Douglas MacNamee had reminisced happily over more than one balloon of the club's excellent brandy. Both slipped unconsciously into the tones and attitudes of their youth. Dangerous days; simpler times; a world of grey-blue uniforms and black-and-white certainties.

'You heard Emily's boy got shot of his wife?' Douglas asked him.

'Yes, Chaggers mentioned something, but not the pukka gen.'

'Well, he married this model girl. Very odd type, always

dressed like a Swiss milkmaid. Mind you, she was a terrific looker. Great pair of lungs on her. Been a bit younger, wouldn't have minded taking down her particulars and filling in her little pink form myself.'

'I say,' said Reggie, alarmed as Duggie's high colour deepened to choleric purple, 'I say, steady down old chap.'

'Sorry. Anyway, I wasn't the only one who took a shine to her, it seems. Boy got back early one day and found her being rogered by the farm manager's son. Turned out they'd been at it like knives for months. What's more, this lad wasn't the only one. She'd been doing bumps and circuits with the local gentry for ages.'

'Station bike, in fact.'

'Absolutely. Poor show, very. Don't suppose it would have mattered so much if it had been the farm manager. Sort of a perk, really. Boy was such a twerp.'

They roared with laughter and summoned a hovering club servant to bring another brandy. It was after half past three by the time Reggie tottered unsteadily down the Reform Club's marble steps, clinging to the railing for dear life. A walk to the Ritz would sober him up. Poor show to meet the girls in this state. It was a warm, late spring day and garish purple and yellow bulbs billowed from window boxes on the pompous Piccadilly façades. Gradually Reggie's step grew steadier, and by the time he rounded the corner of St James's Street he flattered himself no one could tell he'd had a noggin or two.

It was the first time he would have seen his nieces – great-nieces they were really, but he'd have no truck with being called great-uncle and made to feel 105 – since that morning at Tidmarsh's. He was not certain how, or even whether, he should introduce the topic of Liz. Safest just to stick to Mary, and how he missed her. Plenty of time for Liz later.

He had booked the best table in the place, the one called the Loose Box because – so it was said – King Edward used to bring his little fillies here. Not bloody likely, thought Reggie, he would parade his popsies in public; why would the King want to advertise his misdemeanours in the Ritz? Discreet private brothel more likely, in Paris, so I've heard, with a specially adapted chair. That'd be the stuff. The big boy thickened, and Reggie thought, Down boy! Wrong moment. Don't be awkward. He signalled to the head waiter.

'I've booked a table for four o'clock. Conynghame-Jervis's the name.'

'Certainly, sir. Would you like to come this way?'

He led Reginald up and to the right, giving him a commanding view across the ornate room. From there he could survey the chattering tables of brightly dressed people, most with shiny carrier bags parked on the floor beside them. Loose Box, eh? Just a story to draw the tourists. Works, too, judging by the skinny bowing little Nips and flashy American women with quacky voices, Yankee men as usual talking too loud and line-shooting . . .

Reggie felt himself becoming irritable, and glanced at his watch. Ten past four – where the blazes? He looked up to see the head waiter escorting Celia and Felicity across to his table. One was dressed in pink, one in yellow, both with modest flat shoes and open smiling faces. He stood up, and they converged on him from two sides, both kissing him at once. It was most agreeable. They sat down amid a small landslide of handbags and carrier bags, and Reggie said to the waiter, 'Three large teas. Super de luxe. The works.'

'Indian or China, sir?'

'China,' said Reggie. 'Lapsang. With milk *and* lemon. And cucumber sandwiches and toasted scones and cream cakes. The whole flapdoodle.'

'Oh Uncle *Reggie*,' said Felicity, 'you mustn't treat us like *school*girls!'

'No fear of that,' said Reginald indulgently. 'You've grown up into very lovely young ladies.'

'*Women*,' said Celia. 'You're supposed to call us women nowadays, not ladies. Or girls.'

'In my young day you'd have been called bogle, or frippet, or the target for tonight, *and* liked it,' said Reginald. 'Lot of nonsense. Your women's lib gives you all these ideas, I suppose?'

'Tell him about your new job, Celia,' said Felicity soothingly. 'Wait till you hear what Celia's pulled off!'

'I've got a job working at Sotheby's,' said Celia.

'Not just *working at*. She's been made assistant to one of the directors. She'll travel all over the place with him, abroad too, looking at people's stuff that they might auction at Sotheby's. Meeting rich widows and all that.'

'Rich widower's more up your street,' said Reggie, before remembering that, what with his wife's bequest and her father's wealth, Celia was amply well off in her own right. 'Jolly good show,' he added. 'What about you, Flicky?'

Felicity blushed slightly. The tea arrived on a trolley escorted by two waiters. Swiftly they set the table and retreated.

'Shall I be mother?' said Celia. 'Go on, Flick, tell him.'

'It's not official yet. It hasn't been announced,' mumbled Felicity.

'Aha! Engaged!' said Reginald. 'Congratulations in order and all that?'

'Well, as I say, it's still not sort of official, but, yes, we're going to be married. It's all thanks to Aunt Mary, really. She made it possible.'

'Mary did?'

'Well, Gavin and I've been living together for ages —'

'*Living* together?' trumpeted Reginald. A couple of Americans looked round, and he went on more quietly, 'What do you mean, living together? Does your father know? Did Mary?'

'Actually Aunt Mary *didn't* ever know, because I thought it would upset her – oh, Uncle Reggie, don't look like that. Everyone does it nowadays, you know. It's perfectly normal. We've been together for nearly three years now, and I moved in with Gavin, oh, well over a year ago, must be nearly two. My parents have known all along and they don't mind.'

'Don't they? Well they damn well should!' he blustered.

'Uncle Reginald, drink you tea and let her tell you,' said Celia.

'We've been sharing his flat in Kentish Town since then.'

'Where?'

'Kentish Town. Just north of Camden Town. Oh darling, I'd forgotten, you haven't lived in London for ages, have you? It's not all Mayfair and South Kensington and Regent's Park any longer, you know. People live all over the place. Kentish Town is sort of north of St John's Wood.'

'St John's *Wood*?' snorted Reggie, and saw that they were teasing him. 'Go on, then . . .' he subsided.

'Gavin had this flat in Kentish Town, which he rented with a couple of other men while they were all students. Eventually they moved out, and I moved in. It's on the first floor and actually it's lovely. He's stripped and sanded all the floors, and polished them, and painted all the walls white, and Susan and Papa let us have some odds and ends of furniture and rugs and things, and it looks really nice. But we wouldn't have wanted to marry into it, there's nowhere near enough room for babies and nannies and things. Well, anyway, because of Gavin training to be a barrister . . .'

'Thank God for that, at least,' muttered Reggie, 'chap might have been anything.'

'. . . it was going to be simply ages before we could afford to buy anywhere decent, even if Gavin had been prepared to let Papa help, which he wasn't keen on. And then along came this wonderfully generous thing from Aunt Mary, and it's just about to come through, if you remember, I get it once I'm married or thirty, whichever is the sooner. So we've been house-hunting. When we've found something we like, then we'll put the announcement in the papers.'

'*Times*, *Independent* – probably not the *Telegraph*,' said Celia, and Reggie, looking up, saw that she was teasing him again. She laughed and laid a hand on his arm. 'Course it'll be in the *Telegraph*,' she said.

'Anyhow, we'll let you know in advance. The wedding will probably be late summer. Quite soon, now.'

Yes, Reginald thought, it's the end of May, and summer is almost here. My wife died last June, not very long ago, yet already almost a whole year, and here is this girl, this child, ready to become a wife in turn. How time flies! Will he treat her well, this Gavin? Barrister, she said. Sounds a tough sort of chappie.

'What's he like, this fellow? Decent school, family, all that?' he asked Felicity.

'Oh Uncle Reginald, you'll adore him. Everyone does.'

'I can see that you do.'

'Well of course *I* do, but, honestly, everyone does. He's big and sort of woofly, wears dreadfully baggy clothes, all over the place; got a beard –'

'Never seen a barrister with a beard.'

'But he's frightfully kind and capable and practical, as well as having a brilliant mind. He's wonderful. Mother and Papa and Susan think so, and so does Ceel. Tell him: you do, don't you?'

'No worries, Uncle. He's great. They'll get married and have loads of babies and he'll be a famous barrister and stinking rich and they'll all live happily ever after. Don't waste your worries on her. What about *me*, poor old me, lost in the vast green wastes of Sotheby's, endlessly climbing staircases looking for masterpieces?'

'More to the point,' interrupted Felicity, 'gosh, we are awful, we haven't asked, how are *you*? What's your news, Uncle Reginald?'

'Well, since you ask, I might be getting married, too,' said Reginald.

Immediately he cursed himself. It was pique that had made him blurt it out; that, and those last two brandies with Douglas. Shock at Felicity living in sin with some fellow; shock at how the young – not just that model girl, Thingy's wife, but even his own properly brought-up nieces – rogered whomever they wanted, married or not; shock, then, at how the world was changing and, on top of all that, yes, he was a bit peeved that they had spilled out the news about themselves, their busy and engrossing young lives, without first making sure they'd heard his. But now he'd given the game away. He hadn't mentioned Mary, said nothing about missing her, paid her no tribute; instead he'd barged straight in about Liz without preparing them. Now he'd blown it.

Imperceptibly they had retreated: from crowding impulsively over the table to interrupt and amplify, they leaned back to crumble scones and nibble at sandwiches. But their manners rescued the situation, as good manners do, and after the briefest space Celia said, 'Go on, then, Uncle Reginald, tell us about her.'

'Name's Liz, Elizabeth Franks. Known her about, oh, six months, bit more. Met her before Christmas.'

'How?' interpolated Celia.

Better not say in a pub, thought Reggie, and he improvised quickly. 'Friend's place; drinks one evening. Usual thing.'

'OK. So then . . .?'

'Good-looking popsy – *woman*,' he corrected himself meaningfully.

'Aged?'

How shrewd they were.

'Haven't asked. Not on, you know, to ask a lady's age. Younger than me, good bit, I should say. Fortyish.'

'Has she been married?' asked Felicity. And then. 'Listen to us! Gosh, we are awful! Go on, you tell us and we'll shut up.'

'Yes, she's been married; couple of children, I think.'

'Have you met them?' Celia began, but Felicity kicked her in the shin.

'No, I haven't met them,' he said, realizing for the first time that this might be thought odd. Here he was thinking of marrying a woman, and he didn't know what her children were like. Didn't even know their names. 'They're grown up. Live away from home.'

'Are you, well, you know, are you, I mean, in love with her?' asked Felicity.

Am I? thought Reginald for the first time, or am I just enjoying the chase? The question was too complicated to be dealt with there and then, so he set it aside and said, 'Nothing's fixed yet, nothing's definite. She's away at the moment, travelling, visiting friends in Rome, that sort of thing. Spring holiday, you know. Search for the sun.'

'So she's quite well off?' asked Celia.

'No problems in that department,' reassured Reggie. Being far from certain about that, either, he changed the subject.

'How're your parents? Seen your mother recently? Vivian keeping well?' On the calm waters of platitudes they wound down their meeting and gathered up their possessions. Reginald paid the bill and they parted under the colonnade of the Ritz and went their separate ways.

Roy unlocked the door of his own house to find a pile of letters on the doormat. Circulars in brightly coloured envelopes with jagged comic-strip stars screaming YES!!, a couple of brown bills, and a blue-and-red bordered envelope from Vera. He went through to the kitchen, which smelled stale and airless, and threw open the windows, then ran water into the kettle. While it warmed up, he scanned the circulars before dropping them into the swing-bin. He set aside the bills for later and slit open Vera's letter.

Dear Dad, it said:

Hoping this letter finds you well and to let you know how things are here. Summer's pretty well over and it's autumn so not as much time spent on the beach nowadays, much to the boys' regret. But they're working hard at school and Brian came top in his latest French test. Not bad, eh? He says he wants to hitch-hike round Europe for his next vacation and come and visit you.

However, as I'm sure you guessed a long time ago . . .

Guessed what? He hadn't guessed anything! Roy's heart began to race and he pressed a hand to his chest. Mustn't get excited; bad for him.

. . . things aren't too good with me and the old eating problems are back. I've gone down to six stone and don't look or feel right, so in the end I had to go and see a doctor about it the other week.

Stan would be OK if it wasn't for the drink. He meets his mates in the evenings and has too many beers and then he gets rough. I don't know why that should make me stop eating, but you might remember that worrying always had that effect on me. It's daft really because Stan says he prefers big women and here I am going the opposite way! I even thought about coming back to you and maybe living at home for a bit so I could look after you, but I'd be miserable without the boys in no time. So I'll stay here for the moment and see how things work out. The doctor recommended Stan and me to go for counselling, but Stan wasn't too keen on that idea.

Hope the Squadron Leader's treating you all right and that you're bearing up and missing Mum bit by bit less as time goes on. I think of you both a lot and the good old days when we were kids.

Well I guess that's all there's room for, so lots of love from me and the boys.

Ever your loving Vera.

Roy stared out of the window, his hands folding and unfolding the letter, smoothing it out with flat-iron gestures and then refolding it and running his fingernail along the creases. He didn't know what to think. Whatever happened to marriage, to kindness and gentleness, mutual support one to the other till death us do part? It was Vera's duty to stay with her husband, but it was Stan's duty to treat her well, not to harry her so that she couldn't eat properly. He'd never understood all that; he thought she had a slimming craze like so many young girls. But now she was down to – he checked the letter – *six stone*? Counselling wasn't going to put weight on her.

It was easier to think of her childhood (unconsciously his face softened): his little darling, his tiny, pretty daughter nestling on his lap or dancing round holding out her skirt. How had that little girl come to this? Grace, oh my Gracie, where did it go wrong? What happened to the carefree future we planned for our children, with no war, no bombs, no separations, and a decent house of our own? We built up healthy young bodies full of good, fresh food, sent them to good schools, gave them the step up, so where is the *happiness* we planned for them? No consoling ghost rose before his eyes; and where her soothing voice had always been, a roar pounded in his ears like the sea.

His need to talk to Grace was overwhelming, but Roy couldn't face going through to the dining-room to the shrine. He feared that the unwatered flowers would have dried to withered shells, the shiny frames of the photographs be dulled by dust. Instead, he walked stiffly into the hall and picked up the telephone.

'Molly!' he said with relief as she answered. 'It's Roy. How're you keeping?'

Despite his struggle for self-control, he could not prevent his voice from breaking. 'I'm ever so sorry,' he wept, 'I didn't mean to burden you . . . It's nearly a year since she died, my darling Gracie . . .'

'I knew her too,' Molly's voice reminded him. 'She weren't your possession, Roy Southgate, you remember that.' As he choked his sobs down the telephone, she relented. 'There, there,' she soothed, 'there there.'

'I know,' he gulped, 'she weren't just mine – *our* Grace, our dear Grace, but I *miss* her so – and now Vera . . . Vera and Stan.'

Although there were a few flowers in the back garden, and one or two early roses blooming delicately on their unpruned stems, he neither picked them nor looked in to the dining-room to water the flowers there before setting out. He wished for the thousandth time that he could stride, as he used to in the old days, but any attempt to hurry was bad for his heart. Stiff-legged, aching in every part, he made his way down the hill for tea at Molly's.

Chapter Eleven

Liz bent over a table in the front of the shop, admiring her long fingers and coral nail varnish as she arranged a group of trinkets. She wore a white cotton shirt to show off her early tan, sleeves pushed up to display her slender, sinewy brown arms and the double bangle on her right wrist. She had tipped a basket on to its side so that a jumble of covetable small objects spilled invitingly towards each customer entering the shop. Few had cost her more than five pounds in the street markets of Genoa, Portofino and Rome; none, now, was priced under fifteen pounds. Shift half these, she thought, and my trip's paid for; shift them all and I've made a decent profit.

The brilliantly choreographed windows of Italian boutiques; the apricot-skinned women whose social and love lives were conducted with such *élan* under the discerning eyes of sleek, well-tailored men in restaurants and cafés; the laughing, flirtatious, casual young with their loose hair and fresh faces – the spectacle of Italy's exuberant pavement life had given Liz new impetus. She herself had attracted many admiring glances and comments. In Italy, a middle-aged woman was still desirable. Here in England, she thought tartly, you were – what were the expressions? – a wrinkly; a crumbly; almost a pariah, unless you had the time and money to stop the clock. Yet in Italy, had she wished, she could have had a number of erotic adventures in darkened hotel rooms during the long, warm afternoons. Only the fear of Aids had stopped her.

She spent the morning dressing the shop window in subtle colour combinations that made everyone else's look dull. Customers were soon drifting in, exclaiming, embracing, envying, demurring, deciding and finally, thank God, buying.

Five minutes after she got home that evening, the telephone rang. She knew it would be Reggie and was tempted not to answer. She needed a bath and a drink or two before dealing with that problem; but in case it was her troubled daughter, Alicia, she picked up the phone.

'Darling!' she cooed, soft and low. 'How lovely to hear your voice! How *are* you?'

'Long time no see,' said Reggie gruffly.

'I know, sweetheart. Hold on, let me just reach for my drink.'

She went through to the kitchen, opened the fridge, took out a bottle of Muscadet, found a corkscrew, opened the bottle and poured a pale glass of wine. Taking a packet of cashews from the cupboard, she walked leisurely back to the telephone.

'Hello? Hello? Are you still there? Liz? *Hello!*' Reggie's querulous voice rose to a panicky crescendo. Silly old fool, she thought, calm down, of course I'm bloody here.

'Sweetheart? Sorry . . . couldn't find my cigarettes. Now tell me how you've been? Have you been good without me?'

Reggie, mollified, told her about his accountant, at which point she sipped her wine and began to pay attention, and his nieces, at which she listened very carefully indeed.

'They're curious to meet you,' Reggie was saying, and she thought, I bet they are!

'They sound sweet girls,' she said neutrally.

'I said they must come down one day, one Sunday perhaps, for lunch, spend the afternoon . . . maybe with their father and stepmother.'

'Hang on!' she laughed. 'Not all at once. Why don't I just meet the girls first? Maybe we could have a drink with them in town one evening? Then if that goes all right, the rest of your family.'

'Jolly good idea,' said Reginald. 'Oh, and by the way, if we're doing the social hoo-ha, what about your children? Isn't it time I met them?'

'Sweetie. Certainly, if you'd like to. Are you sure? Hugo's out of the country, of course – he's in Malaya at the moment, or maybe it's Australia by now. But Alicia's around. I'm sure she'd be thrilled to meet you.'

'Have dinner with me tonight,' Reggie said impatiently. 'Then we can discuss it.'

'Not tonight, darling, I'm knackered. Flying's so exhausting. Need my beauty sleep. How about next Thursday?'

'*Next* Thursday?' he grumbled. 'Why wait till then?'

I've got him in the palm of my hand, thought Liz. What am I getting myself into? I need to sit down and work it all out. Suppose things at the shop suddenly got better? Do I want to tie myself down like this and be patronized by his snobby relatives? It's been great, my freedom. Travelling light was good fun. Absence may have made his heart grow fonder, but it hasn't done wonders for mine.

'Don't bully me, sweetie,' she cooed. 'I'm dying to see you, too, absolutely dying to . . . but Thursday's really the first free evening. Possess your soul in patience, hmm? Now, where shall we meet?'

They agreed. Eight o'clock. He'd book a table. He mumbled and grumbled a bit, but eventually let her go. He's just a silly old buffer, she thought from her new perspective. This house is fine: bit small, but fine for me on my own. I've been over-pessimistic about the shop – all it needed was a fresh eye and some different merchandise. The whole world is full of interesting people and half of them are male. I'm fifty-two and I look ten years younger. What on earth was I thinking of? Marry *Reggie*? I must have been mad.

Roy caught the train to London and got off at Clapham Junction. He had timed his visit so as to be able to talk to June by herself, before the boys got home from school. She had a pot of tea brewing up for him, and offered a plate of biscuits.

She smoked unceasingly, lighting one cheap cigarette from the butt of the previous one. He was amazed at how scrawny and scruffy she had become . . . June, who had always taken care of her looks. She had given up the usual heavy make-up, and her hair, normally bright orange, had returned to its natural mousey brown. Only the ends betrayed a once vivid tint. She had lost weight. Her arms were criss-crossed with fine scars: as though, he thought, she'd been dragged through a hedge backwards – which, come to think of it, was what her hair looked like, too. Her black tights were full of holes and her shoes were down-at-heel.

'Junie!' he said, stung to pity. 'You don't look well. You been neglecting yourself?'

'Course I have,' she retorted. 'Ain't much choice. Money's down to next to nothing, the Social don't give you a penny more than's enough to scrape by on. I can smoke or eat, one or the other, and I can't do without the fags so I don't eat. But don't you worry about Joe and Billy: they get fed all right. Not that modern muck; good nourishing stews I cook them, breast of lamb, split peas, all the stuff me Mam taught me. Thank God she did, or it'd be five nights from the fish 'n' chip shop and two nights you goes without. Plenty round here live like that; those mean Paki shops don't give you tick, not if you're on Social.'

He kept quiet and let her get it off her chest before asking, 'Heard from Alan lately?'

'Billy had a card for his birthday and he sent us all an Easter card, and that's been our lot. When I rang the prison and said I'd visit, I got a message back that he'd said not to come. Tell you the truth, I thought he might have tried to do himself in again, and I couldn't face seeing that a second time, so I didn't go. You been down?'

'Ten days ago,' said Roy, and drew a deep breath.

'From the look of you you needs another cuppa first,' said June.

If he had thought the news might come as a relief to her, finally putting an end to the uncertainty, he was wrong. She broke down, heaving tears from some subterranean well of misery. Her wan face became raw and corrugated with weeping. As soon as she had regained control of her shaking hands, she pulled hard on a cigarette. Roy watched her with horror and sympathy, his own grief rekindled by the sight of hers. Alan's marriage might not have meant much to him, but to his wife it was real, and, in spite of everything, she was racked at the prospect of its ending.

Finally he got up and walked round to where she sat. She stretched out her raw, skinny arms and wrapped them round his waist, leaned her head against him and shuddered into silence. He patted her hair and stroked her shoulder. Touch is what we all need, me as much as her, he thought. Touching her comforts me, makes me flesh and blood.

'I'm still the lawful wedded wife, aren't I, though?' she asked him finally, as they sat facing one another once more across the plastic-covered table. 'He hasn't got two wives, just because he went through a form of marriage with this other one. I'm his real wife?'

'You are, love,' said Roy. 'But he seems dead set on going ahead and getting this divorce. I don't know the rules nowadays, but far as I remember, you can't stop him. Or only for a time.'

'I can *try*,' she said fiercely. 'I don't have to let him go without a fight. I'm the lawful wedded wife and I'm the one's got his children. Never mind Gloria, even though she's been putting her wages towards helping me and the boys – but he can't deny Billy and Joe.'

'When are they back?' asked Roy.

'Any minute now – that's if they don't stop on to play football in the playground, or with a detention more likely.'

'They good boys, good at their lessons?'

'Not bad, considering. Little Joe ain't half bright. Nothing's hard for him.'

'Alan could have been a clever lad,' said Roy, 'if he hadn't been lazy.'

'Yeah – and look where it's got him!' she said bitterly. 'And me. I could have done my As, got a decent job. My teachers wanted me to stay on. Then I went and fell pregnant with Gloria, fucked it all up, pardon my French. Now listen, Dad: you've to go down to the prison with the boys – they'll come if you promise them that posh car again; they liked that – and let Alan see them. He can't say no to them visiting, and maybe if he sees them – not me, them – maybe *then* . . .' Her hopes trailed away into silence.

'I'm not holding out any promises,' said Roy. 'But I'll give it a try. Chin up, lovey. Tell me what you need for their tea and I'll nip down to the shops.'

It was early evening by the time he got back to The Cedars to find Reginald sitting on the terrace behind the house, a whisky bottle and ashtray on the table before him. The contrast between this lush, flower-filled garden and the barrenness he had just left overwhelmed Roy. All his life he had been a staunch Conservative. It was his personal tribute to Mr Churchill. But at moments like this he understood what those Labour types were on about. Reginald had so much – and God only knew how he'd earned it, if at all – while poor Junie had so pitifully little.

'Ha!' barked Reggie when he saw him. 'Southgate! Back are you? Bit bloody late. Getting peckish.' He must have seen something of Roy's desolation in his face, for he added in a gentler voice, 'Fetch yourself a glass and have a snifter first.'

A balustrade ran around the edge of the terrace and from it stone steps led down into an extensive back garden. A line of pleached apple trees made a decorative frieze along the end wall, in front of which was the vegetable patch. Paving stones led through the lawn from the terrace. Birds sang. The low sun cast slanting shadows.

Roy put a glass on the wrought-iron table and sat down heavily. His legs hurt. He took his glasses off and wiped his eyes.

'Stiff whisky's what you need,' said Reggie. 'Don't bother about cooking tonight. I'll go to the pub, get something there.'

In the pause, the unspoken question 'Anything wrong?' hovered between them. Roy needed to hear it, although Reginald was unable to say it.

'Oh sir,' said Roy, 'I wish my Grace was still alive. I'm ever so worried about my grandsons, I don't know which way to turn. She would have known what to do. She always did.'

'Don't have to talk about it unless you want to,' said Reginald, who would have preferred not to get in too deep. Roy didn't notice.

'There's two of them here in England,' he explained. 'Two more in Australia – Vera's two. The ones I've just been to see, I told you about them, that's William Alan and Joseph Roy. Billy's eleven and Joe's nine. They get enough to eat, they don't go hungry, but where they live, Balham, that's south London, it's a bad area for lads with no father. Their Mum's ever so worried they're getting into trouble. The little one isn't, not yet, anyway; but Billy, well, she thinks he's fallen into bad company . . .'

'Discipline. That's what they need at their age. A firm hand,' said Reginald, thinking of the flogging he'd got from his father for letting his gun go off accidentally; or prep school, where he'd been beaten for years by masters and prefects, for trivial offences against the school's unwritten code. 'Did me no harm. Taught me respect.'

He poured himself a stiff drink, then held up the bottle at an angle towards Roy. This'll do my heart no good, thought Roy, but it does warm the cockles. He leaned back and gazed at the garden.

'They taught us discipline in the Air Force, too, by Jove they did!' Reginald was getting into his stride. 'Wouldn't have lasted a day without it. Glorious days, those were. Blue English skies and always the chance of seeing a Hun. You didn't stop to think that your country depended on you, everyone was praying for you. No fear! You did it for the excitement of the chase, seeing a Ju.88 or a ME go down in flames, while at the same time knowing there was just as good a chance it might be you. The trip home to base, the final beat-up and victory roll, and then back, for the servicing bods to do their stuff while you had a cup of tea; bit more than that later on . . . Great days. Great days. I'm not line-shooting. That's the trouble with these lads like yours. They haven't a hope of an experience like that.'

A silver birch stood weeping at the end of the garden, its

pale trunk and drooping leaves so potent an image of grief that Roy was suddenly overwhelmed. He fished out a handkerchief and blew his nose; then buried his face in it. His shoulders heaved. Reginald looked away, embarrassed.

'I say, old man . . . Hang on. Drink up.'

'Did you realize it's been a year last week?' sniffed Roy.

'What is? Oh, you mean, since they . . . That. Yes. Yes I did notice the date. Thought it best to say nothing. Rotten show.'

'Boys today don't know their luck,' said Roy, to give himself a chance to recover his composure. They sipped their drinks and looked out across the darkening lawn. 'Once,' said Roy, 'when I was in Germany just after the war, I saw a lad with a dove. Can't have been more than thirteen, fourteen, though it was hard to tell those days, when they none of them got enough to eat. I suppose that's why he didn't have a rabbit. A rabbit've been eaten. You don't eat a little white dove that easy.' He stopped, remembering Grace and the goose.

'Get on with it, then!' prompted Reggie.

'There weren't many older lads around by the end of the war. Sixteen- to twenty-year-olds you hardly ever saw. They'd have been called up; dead, probably.'

'So?' said Reggie. 'What was special about this chap?'

'Let's say fifteen.' Roy compromised. 'He was a magician. Conjuror, more like. Doing tricks, you know. That's what the dove was for. He was good, too. Pulling handkerchiefs out of hats – you couldn't see how it was done. And sometimes the dove. He was standing at the edge of a big square, on the corner of a church, and people gathered round to watch him. We passed by about ten o'clock in the morning, must've been; it was a Sunday, we were off duty, me and my mate Bill, and we stopped for a bit as well, to watch. Suddenly the dove flew away. Didn't do what it was supposed to for the trick, hiding in his pocket or whatever, it flew away. Tiny little bird. Dare say it was hungry. The boy looked ever so upset. You know how, when they do tricks conjurors keep up a bright smile and do all the patter so you get distracted and don't notice what they're doing? All that stopped straightaway, and he ran round the corner of the church after his bird. A priest stood there, all dressed in white raiment, holding the dove. Must have caught it. He handed it back to the boy who smiled again, but quite a different smile this time – soft and slow, like he was under water. And the dove preened itself on his hand.'

'Is that all?' asked Reginald crossly. The story wasn't nearly as good as the one about the goose.

'That's all that happened,' Roy admitted. 'The dove flew away, and the priest caught it and gave it back. We passed the same spot again, hours later – that evening, must've been, because it had got dark, and the boy was still there, still doing his tricks, with only a couple of people watching by then. I understood properly for the first time that the boy was starving, the dove was starving, all these people were starving. He stood there all day, twelve, thirteen hours at least, doing his tricks. The dove was all he had to keep alive with. In those days we had British Forces money to use in the Naafi, and the Germans weren't allowed that. So I couldn't give him anything. My mate had a packet of cigarettes left but I only had one or two – in the war, the RE, everyone smoked, me as well. Anyway I could only give him this couple of fags, but my mate Bill gave him a nearly full packet, and the way that lad smiled, well, it was like he'd got his bird back again.'

'No good feeling sorry for 'em,' said Reginald. 'I never did. They all voted for Hitler, didn't they? He'd have been with the Hitler Youth, sieg heiling with the rest. I never felt sorry when I shot one down. That boy did all right, don't you worry. He'd have sold your fags on the black market, lived for a week on what he made.'

It had become almost dark as they talked. Roy felt better. The Squadron Leader had not expressed a word of sympathy, offered no advice; but he had listened, one human being to another, and this alone, this companionable ear, had been a comfort. He stood up.

'If you wouldn't mind something simple, sir – sardines on toast, maybe, or scrambled egg and bacon – I could cook that up in a minute. Unless you'd rather go to the Broker's Arms.'

'I'm out for dinner tomorrow. Simple meal will do me fine. You cook whatever suits. I'll sit here and have a last Scotch. That'd better be my lot.'

Roy walked down the stairs, descending into the deep, dark well of the kitchen. What am I to do, he thought, about June and Alan and their boys, about Vera, and hers? What am I to do? *Talk* to me, Gracie, wherever you are! *O for the touch of a vanish'd hand/And the sound of a voice that is still!* The elegiac words brought him less and less solace. A man needs a wife, thought Roy Southgate; it's as simple as that.

Reginald sat on the terrace looking into the warm, sweet-smelling darkness. He lit a cigarette. The war flooded back through memory: potent, exhilarating and manly. Evenings after a successful scrap, with the boys in the mess. Plate-throwing and glass-breaking. You'd wait till someone was unprepared, and then, catching him off guard, chuck a plate across the room, at the same time shouting 'Catch!' at the top of your voice. Chap would spin round, usually too late, plate would crash to the ground in splinters. Good laugh. Then he'd bide his time and do the same to you. Kept you on your toes, ready for the unexpected. Or we'd play the rougher mess games – High Cockalorum and the other one, rum names they had, Cardinal Puff or mess rugger. These rowdy games got rid of the tension of real fighting: 28,000 feet up, when an unseen Messerschmitt would suddenly materialize out of an empty sky and red flame would spurt along the wings as cannon and machine-guns opened up, then tracer slashing viciously past the wing-tips and bang! you might be dead, spiralling downwards, waiting to hit the ground and disintegrate with your aircraft in a smashed mess of splinters, metal and bone. Hence the plate-throwing. It was childish, but it broke the tension, gave you a laugh, something to yell about.

There'd be calmer evenings with the radiogram, everyone calling for his favourite record, and games of poker. Trophies on the wall – a fragment bearing the Nazi swastika – or propped up on the mantelpiece beside a pin-up of Rita Hayworth or Dorothy Lamour; chaps sprawled over tables playing cards or chess; the newly married writing to their wives; maps, glasses, *Strand*, *Men Only*, Player's in round tins of fifty, ashtrays pinched from the Ritz or the Café de Paris – that's the way, thought Reginald, the only way for young men to live! He stubbed his cigarette hard against the square silver ashtray. It was engraved 'To Reginald Conynghame-Jervis, on his promotion to Squadron Leader, 19 September 1944, from the Boys'.

Liz was in the shop first thing every morning, in high spirits. Business had been so good for the first couple of days after her return from Italy that she had started opening at eight-thirty, on the off chance of attracting the young secretaries and shop assistants on their way to work, and had made several small sales as a result. The Italian accessories were doing so well that she was contemplating a return trip. Maybe she would consent, after all, to an assignation with Jerry's attractive friend Marco, who was surely not gay, judging from the blatant way he'd watched her breasts shift beneath her T-shirt . . .

This fantasy continued undisturbed by the automatic noises of approbation in which she enveloped her customers; but the telephone stopped it in its tracks.

'Chic to Chic!' she trilled. '*Buon giorno!* Hello?'

It was Whittington, her bank manager. Ah, she thought. Careful, Liz.

'Good morning, Mr Whittington!' she said vivaciously. 'How – ?'

He cut her short.

The news was bad. She had been spending money *abroad*, he complained in his nasal voice. Italian *lire*, he added, making it sound like the Devil's currency. Why had she not informed him of her trip? As a result, she had gone above her loan limit, above the overdraft limit arranged only last month. From now on no more cheques were to be written, at least until the overdraft was back under control. If written, they would be returned to the drawer unpaid. No exceptions.

'Look,' she said, trying to combine a confidential whisper

with her most winning voice, 'Mr Whittington, I know I've been a *very bad girl*, but I can honestly explain. I'm in the middle of the shop at this moment. Can I come and see you? . . . How soon? . . . Yes, any time tomorrow will suit me. You say. Nine o'clock? Ten? Can I give you lunch?. . . No, probably better not lunch.'

She scowled down the telephone, making exasperated faces at her customer in the intervals, and finally agreed: tomorrow at ten-forty-five. Blast it! she thought. Slap bang in the middle of the morning. Does he think I lie about all day painting my nails? Now I shall have to pay someone to come in for a whole half day.

'Annie!' she cooed. 'It looks *divine* on you! Absolutely divine! Is it for Ascot? My dear, you'll slay 'em in the aisles. Smarter than Princess Diana you'll be in that . . .'

Annie DeYong decided, in the end, *not* to buy the multicoloured crazy-paving-print two-piece for Ascot (and if she won't, thought Liz, who the hell *will?*), and, as the final straw, the girl who usually minded the shop was on holiday. By the time Reginald rang to confirm their dinner date, her early-morning optimism had abated. In consequence, she was warm and girlish on the telephone ('Sweetheart! I feel as if I haven't seen you for *months* instead of just weeks!') rather than, as she had planned, being standoffish to dampen his hopes.

By seven o'clock she was at home with a stiff drink, contemplating the transformation that would change her from a financially harassed businesswoman into Reggie's winsome companion. She had brought two outfits home from the shop and was trying to decide between them when the telephone rang. She ignored it. Minutes later it rang again. She poured scented oil into her bath and turned on the hot tap before picking up the receiver beside her bed.

'Yes?' she said shortly.

'Ma? Knew you were there! Hi. It's Lissa.'

'Alicia! Sweetheart! I'm so glad you phoned. I've been away, and I never know what number to get you on.'

'You can't. I haven't got one. I'm in a public call-box. Can you ring me back?'

She spelled out the number. Liz dialled it with sinking heart.

'Ma. Hi. Look, I've got to see you. You going to be up in London any time soon?'

'I don't plan to be. Why?'

'I'm not going to tell you down the phone. Will you send me my train fare to T. Wells?'

'*Send* it? Darling, *must* I? Can't you pay it and I'll pay you back?'

'No. I haven't got it. Send me twenty quid, Ma, first post tomorrow, and if I get it on Saturday I'll come down over the weekend.'

'Darling, you are hopeless! Why are you always so broke?' (Like mother, like daughter, she thought to herself.) 'Help! The bath'll be running over. Quick, let me scribble down your address – or is it still the Turnpike Lane one?'

'Moved since then. I'm in Leytonstone now.'

'Where the hell is . . .? Never mind. Give it to me.' Alicia dictated. 'Got it. I'll send the letter express, first thing tomorrow. Why twenty? It's only about seven quid for a day return.'

'Don't be *boring*, Ma – you know, taxis, and all that. What if I want to bring you some flowers?'

'OK, OK: twenty. See you soon, my pet. Sure you're all right?'

'Course I'm not *all right*,' said Alicia. 'I wouldn't be coming down if I was all right, would I? OK? See you Ma! Cheers!'

'Take care of yourself. Bye, darling,' said Liz forlornly.

Black to show off the tan, she'd decided hurriedly, rather than white. White was too obviously bridal. Reggie looked smart in his best summer suit, a blue silk handkerchief with red spots spilling out of its top pocket. He was disarmingly nervous. It crossed Liz's mind for the first time that he might actually love her; and this thought endeared him more than anything else could have done.

Rather than think about Alicia, she tried to concentrate on

him. This suited Reggie, who had enjoyed 'shooting a line' to Southgate about his RAF exploits, and was easily encouraged to do the same with Liz. When, therefore, she said, 'But weren't you terrified when you went out on – what were they called – missions?', he topped up her wine glass, and his own, and cast his mind pleasurably back.

'What you've got to remember,' he began, 'is that half the time you were shooting the hell out of the Hun because he was after you, or he'd just had a crack at one of your squadron and you wanted to get your blood back. You weren't fighting cold. Didn't have time to be yellow. Just got on with it. You're not on your own up there. Twelve of you, twelve Spitfires roaring off in formation, to come back in two hours' time in ones and twos. And in between you've packed in more experience than today's youngsters get in a lifetime.'

Liz was impressed. He's not absurd, she thought, for all his red face and bulging eyes. This old buffer fought and might have died in the last war, even if he did take pleasure in killing.

'What were you fighting *for*?' she asked.

'To get our own back for friends who'd been killed. Getting your blood back, it was called. To stop Hitler, of course. To serve the King – you can smile, but it mattered then. And to protect our own: families and girlfriends, young mothers pushing prams. We saw Hitler as a menace, trying to spread out all over Europe, and England too, and we had to put a stop to it. Simple as that, really.'

'And afterwards?' she persisted. 'After those mid-air battles? Did you go into shock, start to feel guilty, or what?'

'Christ, no! In fact, those times, the Battle of Britain especially, 1940, they were about the happiest of my life. The morale of our outfit was incredible. The atmosphere was more boyish high spirits than anything. We'd have colossal binges afterwards, pull each other's legs, muck about. Never felt *guilty*.'

'And when one of your comrades died? What then?'

'Life was cheap. Don't look like that, Liz. It was a great way to go – dying for your country. Better than being captured. Better than coming home to your girlfriend with two amputated legs. If a chap didn't come back, you didn't grieve. Didn't have time. In any case, you'd have gone completely nuts. Chaps'd keep a kitty in the bar so that if they bought it, the other fellows could have a last round of drinks on them. That's the only way you could get through it.'

He smiled across the table at her, and picked up his knife and fork again.

'And here I am, fifty years later, having dinner with you,' she said.

'It'd have been very different if you'd met me then,' he said, thinking, Popsies like you were two a penny in those days. None of the girls would say no to a fighter boy, young heroes patrolling the skies, risking their lives for them. You had your pick of bogle then! And of them all, I picked Mary: demure, soft-spoken, innocent Mary. It wasn't your type I was after then. So what's changed now?

Liz twisted the stem of her glass between her fingers and thought, I bet he's not kidding.

'What did you look like in those days?' she asked. 'Have you got any photographs of yourself?'

'Back at the house, yes. Come up and see my etchings . . . ! Well, let's see. About the same height but a good deal less round the middle. Hair was thicker in those days. Curly. Could never get it to lie down. Eyes blue, language to match. That's enough line-shooting. Waiter! The menu. Pudding for you, my dear, or cheese?'

He drove her back to the house to find his wartime photographs. Good: no sign of Southgate. Heads together, he inhaled the soft muskiness of her scent. She scrutinized the serious young face above the silver wings of the RAF crest emblazoned over his left breast pocket. Reginald remembered that photograph. He'd had it taken for Mary just after they married so that if they had a kid, there'd be a decent picture of his father for the lad to look at. He'd frowned slightly, so as to look mature and responsible, but the thick curls springing irrepressibly from his forehead made him look more like an ardent schoolboy.

'How young you look!' said Liz, stating the obvious. 'Touching. What do those stripes mean?'

'Flight lieutenant,' he said. 'That was '42, soon after I married. Got made Squadron Leader in '44, when I was posted to a squadron flying Typhoons over Normandy. Later on into Germany, up to the time of the surrender.'

There was a snapshot of the squadron leaning against the wing of a Spit with Rusty, their mascot. The sight of all those keen young faces – Christ! half of them, he'd even forgotten their names! – brought on a wave of sadness and regret. The wind was whipping at their hair and trouser legs as they stood, elaborately casual, distorted by the bulky Mae Wests around their shoulders. There they all were: Johnny Chilton and Lucky, Shorty and Chaggers; Thingummy; So-and-so – what the hell was his name? Alf? Wilf? No good: he'd forgotten it. Suddenly his carefully laid seduction plans seemed more trouble than they were worth. A life worth living and a death worth dying? It wasn't true that death was cheap and unheeded.

'I'll run you home,' he said.

Liz looked up in surprise.

'Oh dear,' she said. 'I *am* sorry. I've depressed you. Poor love. Christ, it just didn't occur to me. I'll get a taxi.'

'It's OK,' he insisted, 'can't have you baling out all by yourself. One for the road?'

'No,' she said, surprised and even slightly put out by his sudden melancholy. 'No thanks. Just take me home, if you're really sure.'

He drove her back, dropped her off, wouldn't come in, kissed her cheek, roared away. He was a man without artifice in the battle of the sexes, but he understood the chase, and no strategy could have been more effective as a means of recapturing her flagging attention. If I'm not careful I could lose him, thought Liz, and the way things are looking, I can't afford to let that happen.

*

On Saturday Alicia rang.

'Hi, Ma. Got the dosh. I'll come down tomorrow, then, OK?'

'Lovely, darling. I'll cook you up a nice Ma's Sunday lunch.'

'Christ, *lunch*? Don't know if I can make it that early.'

'Doesn't have to be early. We could eat at two.'

'But that'd mean I'd have to catch a train by about half-*twelve* . . .' Liz gave a silent, resigned sigh.

'Lissa, you come when it suits you, all right? I won't cook up anything special.'

'Brilliant! Hey, Ma, you still smoking?'

''Fraid so, Why?'

'Just wondered. See you tomorrow, then!'

'Are you bringing anyone, darling? You're welcome to, if you like.'

'Christ, no. I've got to *talk* to you. That's why I'm coming. Bye, Ma!'

Liz tried to prepare herself for her daughter's news. In descending order of awfulness, she decided, it would be Aids; drugs; boyfriend a drug addict; pregnancy; another abortion; job lost; broke. It had to be one of those, maybe more than one. She chose some garments from the shop which looked unlikely to sell but might fit Alicia and cheer her up. With luck she'd be out of the black-and-fringed phase by now.

Her daughter arrived at teatime on Sunday. Her hair was braided in dozens of tiny Afro plaits. She wore skin-tight multicoloured leggings and orange suede boots with pointed toes. On top was a vast holey T-shirt, adorned with beads and bits of silver necklaces. A long scarf was tied around her hips. As far as Liz could tell, Alicia wore no underwear. But she noticed, as she embraced the stiff and unresponsive young body, that at least her skin smelled clean.

'Cup of tea?' she said, leading the way to the kitchen. 'Coffee?'

'Coffee'd be great. No milk. Loads of sugar. Ta.'

'I looked out a couple of things from the shop for you,

sweetheart,' Liz began, hoping to placate her wary daughter and reduce the tension between them.

'Waste of time. (A) I wouldn't like them, I never do, and (B) I'm pregnant.'

'Oh my darling . . .' Liz heaved a sigh of relief, of apprehension, of welcome – perhaps *this* baby, finally, would be her first grandchild? – of tenderness for her daughter. Cautiously, she said, 'What are you going to do?'

'I've decided to keep this one. I'm nearly twenty-eight. It's about time I started a family, before it's too late and I've fucked up my body too much. Yeah, I can handle a baby.'

'I'm thrilled,' said Liz. 'Congratulations. Give me a hug, my darling.' They hugged.

'That coffee ready yet?' asked Alicia.

Liz loaded up a tray with coffee and biscuits, and they walked through to the sitting room.

'Am I allowed to ask about its father?' asked Liz.

'Him? Bastard! You can forget about him. He doesn't know and I'm not going to tell him.'

Thus, Liz reflected, thus, on a whim and a row, today's fathers are deprived of their children; and children of their genetic fathers and birthright, of family resemblances, characteristics, talents, history and photograph albums. So I'll be its only grandparent, Lissy its only parent. Not what you might call a big family. She sighed again. 'Lissy, my love, are you sure? He can't have been that awful. Have you known him long?'

'Yeah. Six months or so. I'm not saying I didn't fancy him, 'cos I did, he's smashing-looking, the baby'll be stunning; but he was a sexist bastard. And into drugs. And that's no good for the baby.'

'It's not good for a child to grow up without a father.'

'Didn't stop you and Dad getting divorced, did it?' Alicia flashed, and Liz was silenced.

Eventually she said, 'Have you seen anything of your father? Does he know?'

'Not for the last year or so. Last I heard, he was in the south of France. Fuck him. I don't care.'

'He might be able to help you financially.'

'Him? Give me money? You've got to be joking! Can *you* lend me a couple of hundred quid or so, Ma, just while I sort myself out? I'll pay you back.'

In the end the sum of the bad news was that, yes, Alicia was three months pregnant, yes, broke, yes, had lost her job as a waitress in a smart Soho brasserie ('The sight of all that food on people's plates made me throw up. *Not* good for business'); but no, not on drugs ('Well, only dope, and that doesn't count: *everyone* does dope'), and not HIV-positive. Oh, and could she make that two hundred five hundred while she was about it? It could have been worse, Liz told herself bleakly.

She didn't bother to show Alicia the clothes she had selected for her from the shop, which now looked pitifully inappropriate. She persuaded her daughter to eat some poached egg and fresh fruit for supper, gave her a soothing tisane and a clean cotton nightie and by ten o'clock she was tucked up in the small spare bedroom, under the Margaret W. Tarrant picture that had hung on the nursery wall of gentle Jesus surrounded by little children and baby animals. Then Liz went downstairs for a stiff drink.

Reginald surrendered the Mercedes to Roy without a murmur, without even asking him to put petrol into its insatiable tank. Roy drove to Balham and collected the boys, who had assembled a crowd of local friends to watch their departure. It was half-term; all the kids were on holiday for a week, and they made a ceremonial progress through the surrounding streets. Roy prayed that the car wouldn't be scratched, but it seemed protected by the presence of his grandsons. Beyond their own busy streets, they settled down to the purring speed of the M20. The boys squabbled about the car radio, which they tuned to one of the pop-music channels and played at top volume. Finally Roy could stand it no longer.

'Shut up, the pair of you!' he said. 'I've had quite enough of your noise, *and* that caterwauling you call music. Sounds like parrots in the jungle to me. Now settle down and keep quiet. You can have Radio 4 or nothing. Which is it to be?'

Radio 4, they said, and listened docilely to *Woman's Hour*. Before too long Joe was asleep and even Billy was lolling against him, eyelids drooping. Roy glanced through the rear-view mirror and was moved to pity at the sight of the blue-veined tracery showing through the pale skin of their throats and small, relaxed hands. My flesh and blood, he thought. I fought for you. I blundered through Germany, cold, tired, longing to be home, and what kept me going was the thought of you, my unknown future, my children's children, yet to be born. I won't let Alan hurt you! He fathered you, he's got to stick by you.

As they approached the prison, he woke them up.

'I wasn't asleep, Grandad!' said Billy.

'Nor was I,' said Joe, rubbing his eyes. They looked around.

'This'll be the last time we visit your Dad here,' said Roy. 'He's asked to be moved to another place: nearer, or at any rate, not so difficult to get to.'

It wasn't strictly true. Alan had put in a request to be removed to a prison north of London for the remaining two months of his sentence, because this would make it easier for Sheila to visit him.

'Good!' said Joe. 'I hate this bloody dump.'

'Don't use that language,' said Roy.

Billy looked at him in surprise. 'Why not?' he asked.

'Because it's bad language,' Roy answered. 'Not for children. It sounds all wrong on the lips of innocent children.'

They both began to titter.

'I mean it,' said Roy. 'I won't have you using those words in my presence. Your Nan wouldn't have stood for it, and nor will I.'

'Yes, Grandad,' they both said, obedient or mocking, it didn't matter.

'Now, have you thought what you're going to say to your

Dad? You're not just going to sit there like last time, not saying nothing, are you?'

'I dunno,' said Billy.

'I'm going to tell him I want him to come home,' said Joe. 'I miss my Nana too, but she can't ever come back. Mum told me. She's gone away for ever and now she bakes cakes for the angels in heaven.'

Roy interrupted. 'Billy? What you going to say to your Dad?'

'Tell him you got in the under-thirteens swimming team,' said Joe.

'Tell him I've took up boxing, more likely,' said Billy.

Roy, keeping an eye out for the signs to the prison, only half-heard. 'What's that?' he asked.

'Wham! Kerpow! Boxing!' said Billy. 'So I can go to football matches and smack people, support my team. Or get my own back by giving those Pakis hell what won't let us have stuff on tick.'

'Language,' said Roy. 'Don't say that. They're as good as you are.'

'They're cowards,' Billy insisted.

'Why fight them, then?' asked Roy.

Billy didn't answer, but slumped sullenly back against the rich leather of the rear seat.

In prison, despite the constraints surrounding them, the two boys were talkative. It must have been their mother's presence which had inhibited them rather than that of the warders, for after the first awkward minutes they competed, leaning eagerly across the table, to give Alan news of themselves and their neighbours.

At one point their father interrupted and said, 'Has your Mum talked to you about Sheila?'

Roy felt his heart gather itself up and stop in its tracks.

'No,' said little Joe, pausing in a headlong story. 'Who is she? Do we know her?'

'No, not yet,' said Alan. 'But I hope you'll meet her soon.'

'Who is she, Dad?' asked Billy.

He knows, thought Roy. Look at the way he's watching Alan. June's told him, and now he's testing his father, to see if he'll tell the truth. He glanced at Alan. Alan held Billy's eyes steadily for a long moment and then Joe resumed his story and Roy's heartbeat moved on. Alan did not make a second attempt to talk about Sheila. He did not mention June again, either.

At the end of the visit he fished in his pocket and brought out some carved wooden chessmen. 'Here you are,' he said. 'I made them for you. Present. Learn to play chess and I'll do you some more.'

'Honest, Dad? You made 'em yourself?' asked Billy. 'Cor, they ain't half good. You do woodworking classes, or what?'

'Yeah,' said Alan, bitterly. 'Only it's called "vocational training". But it's woodwork, all right. Ought to get your Grandpa to show you. He's the expert, aren't you, Dad?'

He remembers, thought Roy, touched almost to tears.

'That right, Grandpa? Can you make things? Could you teach us?'

'You show 'em how, Dad,' said Alan meaningfully. 'They're going to need you . . .'

'And will you teach me setch?' asked Joe.

'*Chess*, wanker!' said Billy, but it was such a relief to see them all three laughing that Roy kept quiet about the bad language. Alan hugged both his sons. First time he's done that in months, Roy thought. He touched Alan's arm, and Alan patted his father's shoulder uncertainly.

'See that warder over there?' said Alan to the boys. 'He's not a bad bloke. Go over and say hello, tell him you're my kids. Tell him your names.'

Billy took the hint, and hauled Joe off after him.

'*You* tell 'em for me, Dad,' said Alan, in a desperate undertone. 'You got to, *got to*, do you hear? I've made up my mind about Sheila, I'm not going to change it now. But I can't be the one that tells them. *You*'ve got to for me. I'm asking you, Dad. Please.'

Oh my son, my son, thought Roy.

197

'It's no good,' he said. 'I would if I could, but I can't. What you're doing is wrong, leaving 'em. They're your sons, they love you. Look how happy they were to see you. You can't do that to kids. Change your mind, son. That's all I can say. For your Mum's sake. For theirs.'

'I love her, Dad – Sheila. You haven't met her. You don't know what she's like. If you did, you'd understand. We're made for each other. I've told her I'm divorcing June. June knows as well. I've had a helluva lot of time to think and I've worked it all out. The boys can come and stay with us, Sheila and me, maybe come and live with us when they're older. Might even have a little sister for them by then. I'll have done my time by the end of the summer, with luck. I've done good behaviour, I'm going to the other place next week, more of an open prison it is, and I got my parole board coming up soon. I'm going to have Sheila meet me when I come out. You've *got* to tell the boys. I tried just then, I meant to do it, but I can't.'

'No,' said Roy. 'I won't. You hear me, Alan? Marriage is for ever and the reason is the children. Till death us do part.'

'No,' said Alan. 'No. No. No. *No!*'

As they were escorted out at the end of visiting time, Roy managed to buttonhole the warder whom Alan had indicated. Waving the boys ahead, he said in an urgent whisper, 'Keep an eye on him for the next week, won't you, until he's moved? He's a bit upset. Don't let him try anything.'

The man nodded and winked at him. He's a good bloke, thought Roy with relief, a decent man. There's good and bad in every walk of life.

Chapter Twelve

It was late June, just after summer's peak, the longest day. Week succeeded week of clear blue halcyon days. Heat hung suspended in the still air at dusk. The garden spilled over with fat perfect blooms: dark red peonies weighing down their stems, climbing roses spiralling downwards in lush abandon. Delphiniums formed up in tall columns of violet and blue with fragrant purple lavender massed in front of them, and against the red brick wall were the tall spears of foxgloves. More than a year had passed since Mary and Grace had died, the one quietly, the other fighting against death and the emergency procedures which hampered her last moments. As the anniversary had come and gone, Roy was guiltily aware that he had reached a resignation, had adjusted to her absence. Life had not stopped dead. It impelled him forward. He decided to give his own house a spring-clean and to organize a spectacular display of flowers around her shrine. That at least was something he could do for her, to show his continued love and remembrance.

He woke earlier than usual one morning. The sun was already up, the sky streaked with rose-pink pennants. It was going to be another hot day. Sooner I get going the better, thought Roy. Got all my best energies in the morning. After lunch I'm flagging, could do with a nap. He left a note on the kitchen table for Aggie, asking her to wake Reginald and take him his cup of tea, and set off as soon as he had listened to the seven o'clock news.

He caught a bus as far as St John's Church, where he got off and walked down John Street and into his own familiar road. It felt cramped after Nevill Park, the doll-sized houses jammed tightly together, but his heart tightened as he walked up his front path again. The rose bush in the tiny front garden which he had omitted to prune earlier in the year was pushing out pale pink roses. The tiny squares of grass on either side of the pathway needed trimming. Roy felt choked by its neglect. He unlocked the front door and stood for a moment inhaling the faint remembered smell of his own home. The telephone on the hall table beside him rang, making him jump.

Instinctively Roy looked at his watch. It was nearly twenty to eight. I don't want to hear, he thought. I know what it's going to say and I don't want to hear. The phone would not stop ringing. I won't answer. Don't tell me. He counted. Eight, nine, ten, eleven. On thirteen he picked it up.

Reginald woke with another headache, and in a bad temper. It was nine-thirty and Mrs Owsyerfather had knocked loudly on the door and waddled in with a pot of tea on a tray.

'Where is the name of blazes is Southgate?' he grumbled.

'And a very good morning to you, too!' she said equably. 'He left a note on the kitchen table saying I was to bring you your early-morning tea, which I'm doing, not that it's particularly early morning by my standards, but the good Lord made us all different. Unfortunately Roy didn't inform me where he was going.'

Reginald scowled.

'Now then, Squadron Leader, how can I sweeten your temper this lovely shiny morning? Is it by running you a bath or should I offer you a fine healthy breakfast? What is your pleasure?'

Reginald rubbed his eyes. 'My pleasure,' he said, still half asleep, before he could stop himself, 'would be for you to lean over so that I could give that big black bum and those huge great tits of yours a good feel.'

She stood up and folded her arms. Her face had slammed shut like a door. 'And my pleasure is to tell you, *sir*, that I'm giving notice. Not a week. On the spot. Here and now. I don't take that dirty talk from nobody. You should be ashamed of yourself.'

Christ! thought Reginald, now what have I done? He sat

up in bed and tried to look contrite. She was already walking out of the room, the offending bum moving with deliberate dignity.

'I say, Mrs um, Aggie, I'm frightfully sorry. I do apologize. I take it back. You're quite right . . .'

He heard her heavy step descending the stairs. Damn and blast the woman! he thought. Silly old Nanny. Big fat Nanny. Great big huge fat enormous Nanny. Bum. Tits. Don't care. Lying down again, he tried to go back to sleep.

A few minutes later he heard the front door being unlocked. Had she changed her mind, seen sense and come back? He swung his legs slowly out of bed, creaked to his feet and unhooked his dressing-gown from the door. He peered over the landing balustrade. It was Southgate who was shuffling about down there in the hall.

'Southgate! Where the hell have you been? Bloody nuisance!' he complained. 'Mrs Owsyerfather's given notice.'

Roy lifted his head and looked up as though he hadn't heard.

'I need the car,' he said. 'My son is dead. I have to go and tell his wife. Her phone's out of order. I must hurry. I need the car.'

Reginald grimaced at him, cupping his ear. 'What's that? Come on up here and address me properly. I can't hear a bloody word you're saying.'

Roy tipped his head up to where Reginald stood. His glasses glinted. He paused as though to gather strength, then spoke in a crescendo, 'I said, Squadron Leader, MY SON IS DEAD AND I NEED THE CAR. I have to leave at once to tell his wife. NOW CAN YOU HEAR ME?'

Reginald clutched the wooden railing tightly. His head and heart were pounding. Entire bloody world's falling to bits around my ears, he thought.

'Take it,' he said. 'Awfully sorry. Rotten luck, old chap.' He turned round and lurched back into his bedroom, climbed into bed and pulled the covers over his head.

*

Roy drove the great car as fast as he could along the winding, narrow road to East Grinstead and picked up the A22 into London. It would take him along the Brighton Road through Purley, amidst whose suburban streets his married life had begun. He tried to keep his head clear so as to concentrate on driving, but the words flew into his mind like darts. 'Deeply regret to inform you . . . your son found dead . . . every precaution taken . . . a very determined attempt . . . absolutely no hope of resuscitation . . . will of course be a post-mortem . . . no blame can be attached to prison staff . . .'

The man would divulge no details beyond confirming that Alan had not hanged himself. So what was it? thought Roy: drugs, glass, a knife? Did he slash his wrists, my strong handsome son, and watch the lifeblood ebb out while he crouched secretly over his dreadful deed, fearful of interruption and rescue? Or was it his throat he cut, to make death quicker and more certain? What strength and desperation he would have needed to slice into his own flesh. Oh my God, the agony!

Hurtling through time and place, in the swishing silence of the car, Roy howled aloud. Oh Absalom, my son, my son! I wish it was me that was dead and with my Grace; me dead and Alan alive. The car's padded interior absorbed his howls and only a few passing motorists noted that the face of the small man behind the wheel of the imposing car was clenched with tears. He hauled savagely on the wheel to overtake a dawdling caravan. As he swerved back into his lane, he saw another car approaching at speed, and the man's panic-stricken expression as he flashed by. Roy pressed harder on the accelerator.

As the thickening conurbation of south London slowed him down and traffic lights brought him to a halt, he struggled to regain self-control. How shall I break the news to June, he wondered, if she hasn't yet heard? Her phone must have been out of order, or cut off, for the governor of the new prison had read back her number correctly, but said he had been unable to get through. It was nearly noon: they wouldn't have it on the news, surely? He switched on to listen just in case; but the

202

news was all of recession and opinion polls, or events in the Soviet Union and Yugoslavia; nothing about a prison suicide.

When he drew up outside her house and rang the bell, she opened the door to him immediately with a face as stricken as his own.

'I know! I know!' she said.

She stumbled ahead of him to the kitchen, where an ashtray spilled over with acrid cigarette stubs. From an open packet she extracted and lit another. He held her free hand tightly with his own and stared at her.

'The prison rang the boys' school,' she said. 'Alan must have made sure they had the number. I tried to ring you, but you'd gone. Oh Roy, I can't believe what he done . . . He cut his throat. Drowned in his own blood.'

Her self-control had been rigid, her voice steady, but on the final words she collapsed into a wailing, gulping struggle which Roy could not bear to watch. He noticed several torn paper tissues Sellotaped across her arms.

'What's that for?' he asked. 'What happened? You burn yourself?'

She pushed up the sleeves of her shirt. Her arms were covered with wisps of Kleenex and dozens of tiny red slashes, some of them new, others fine lines of scabs, others no more than little veinlike scars. June glanced at them dismissively and knuckled the corners of her eyes. He could see no marks on her wrists.

'It's just something I do sometimes,' she said, and her weeping hiccuped to a halt. 'Don't know why. Doesn't hurt. Makes me feel better. Don't worry: none of 'em *deep*. I did a few more after the head teacher came round this morning. Tissues are just to stop them making a mess. I suppose I wanted to know how *he* felt. You don't feel a thing.'

She looked blankly at the lines and scratches. Roy felt himself being dragged into an undertow of strangeness and dislocation, of dangerous and unfamiliar currents that he did not understand, except that he knew June might at any moment lose control.

'You're out of cigarettes,' he said woodenly. 'I'll go to the end of the road, get you a couple of packs. Back in a minute.'

He walked through the hall. There was chaos everywhere. The lounge was untidy, boys' clothes scattered higgledy-piggledy over the torn and sagging furniture, the skimpy carpet curling up from the doorway for anyone to trip over. At this rate, he thought, the boys'll get taken away from her, put into a council home. With the heaviness of absolute certainty he knew that, no matter what the upheaval, they must all come and live with him in his house in Tunbridge Wells.

A week later as Roy stood in the dining-room cleaning the five multifaceted windows until they sparkled with sunshine, he noticed a small dark-haired woman standing irresolutely in the road outside his house. She walked away and moments later returned. Roy waved uncertainly, in case she was one of Alan's or Vera's old friends from school. She lifted her hand in acknowledgement, and came up the front path. He opened the door.

'I'm Sheila,' she said. 'I didn't think anyone'd be here.'

She was dressed in black. Younger than June, but not by much.

'You look like Grace, my wife,' he said. 'Alan's Mum.'

'I know. He used to tell me that as well.'

'You really do,' said Roy.

They crossed by St John's and walked along Culverdon Road to the cemetery where Alan and his mother now lay buried, side by side. Grace's grey marble tombstone was in place, shiny and new, deeply incised:

GRACE EDITH SOUTHGATE

DEARLY BELOVED WIFE OF ROY
AND MOTHER OF FREDERICK, ALAN AND VERA
1920–1990

Alan's grave was still a heap of newly turned earth. The

flowers piled above and around it were rotting already, except for one fresh vase of roses that Roy had placed there the previous day.

'I never knew he had a brother,' she said.

'Little Frederick? He died when he was a baby. What they'd call a cot death nowadays. We thought it was the Blitz, all the upsets night after night, that he was too delicate to stand it.'

'Poor little chap,' said Sheila.

'Can we go and sit down?' asked Roy after a while. 'My legs aren't too good.'

They walked over to a bench in the corner of the graveyard, from which they could hear birdsong and the rumble of nearby traffic.

'You didn't come to the funeral, then?' asked Roy.

'I didn't know if June might create a scene, or how you might feel about me turning up. It seemed best not to.'

'The boys wouldn't have known who you was.'

'June would've known. We were both at the trial. She'd recognize me.'

They sat quietly for a bit; not weeping, but not inclined to break the silence that linked them.

Eventually Sheila said, 'You were lucky. You picked right first time, you and your wife, even though you were so young. But Alan got it wrong first time. I don't say June's a bad woman, but she was wrong for him. He needs a lot of cuddles, a lot of looking after. She's highly strung, by the sound of her; tough on the outside, but inside she's all nervy. Don't tell me if I'm right or wrong; it doesn't matter now. But Alan and I, we were made for each other. We were soul mates. Made in heaven, our marriage. We knew we were going to get married, the very first week after we met. Both of us. Only trouble was, he didn't tell me he was married already. He couldn't bear his Mum to know, or you, that he wanted a divorce. He said you'd never get over it, never. He couldn't bring himself to tell June about me, either. So we went ahead and had a quiet register-office wedding, just with my Mum and a few friends. All mine, of course. They liked him; said I'd been right to wait.' She looked into the blue summer air, remembering. She even smiled.

'Poor Alan! He got involved so deep, kept so many secrets, he couldn't get untangled. I guessed after a while. Him always going away, never giving me a number where I could ring him. I asked him after six months or so: tell me honestly, have you got another woman, maybe another wife somewhere? It was a relief, I think. He said he'd tell her, ask for a divorce, but time went on and he never did. Then he said his mother was ill, and it'd finish her if she knew what he'd done. I wasn't sure whether to believe him or not.

'In the end I found out where he lived, and went to the police. Yes, me. I thought all that'd happen would be they'd tell him to make his mind up which of us he was going to divorce. I wouldn't fall pregnant till it was all sorted out, you see.'

'I see,' said Roy, thinking, She's tough, this one, and straight.

'Next thing I knew, he was arrested and charged with bigamy.'

She turned and looked at him bleakly, her face showing neither sorrow, nor guilt, nor grief, nor remorse; washed of all emotion except loneliness. She was very pale, her features small and fine. It's true, thought Roy again: she really does look like Grace.

He put his hand over hers, and she placed her other hand over his. They sat there in one another's clasp.

Finally she said, 'I'm glad I met you. I'm glad I came. Don't worry: I won't come again. It's all over now.'

'What are you going to do?' he asked.

'I don't know. Get on with life, I suppose. What else is there? I've got a job; I've got friends. Only now I haven't got Alan.' She paused.

'We really loved one another. I want you to know that. He wasn't a bad man, or thoughtless, or weak. He couldn't bear to hurt people. He couldn't bear you and his Mum to see the end of his first marriage. You'd set him such an example, he wanted the same for himself. I understood that. I loved him *better* when I knew, not less.'

She stood up. 'I'm going now. Goodbye. Thank you for talking to me. I shall remember this. I may come back, but I won't trouble you again. Goodbye, Dad.'

Roy was reflecting, as he watched her upright, narrow figure walk away from him. A year ago my beloved wife, Grace, died. It is true that time heals. I should have told her that. In time, it doesn't hurt so much.

Reginald, in his slippers and dressing-gown, was leaning over the banister rail shouting into the hall below.

'Southgate! *Southgate!* Where the devil . . .?'

The rail pressed against his chest and shot fierce little pains under his ribs, making him straighten up and rub his abdomen. Christ knows, he muttered to himself, how the blazes I'm supposed to go solo. First that perishing woman storms out over nothing, and now the little berk's disappeared. Pretty poor show . . . He heard Roy's voice calling up to him.

'Yes?'

'Where the hell's my breakfast? And the *Telegraph*? Has the post come? What have you done with my blue striped shirt? What about my bath? I've got a busy morning, I told you that last night.'

'I'm sorry, sir,' said Roy. 'I've only just got here. I spent the night in my own house. Whole place needs to be spring-cleaned, sorted out . . .'

'That's all very well, man, but . . .' Reginald was just about to ask, What do you think I'm paying you for? when he remembered that Roy was not, in fact, paid. He modified the end of his sentence to a grumble: '. . . but I have a lunch appointment in London. I have to get a move on.'

Roy glanced across the hallway at the long-case clock. 'It's not yet nine,' he said, and as he spoke the letter-box rattled and a fan of envelopes fell on to the black-and-white tiled floor. He bent stiffly to pick them up and, pushing his glasses up his nose, began to glance through them.

'Give us them, then,' said Reginald irritably. 'Bring them here.'

Roy climbed the stairs towards Reginald, handed him the letters, and went past him into the bedroom. It had a sweaty, fatty odour. He drew back all three pairs of curtains, opened the windows wide and pulled the bedclothes down to the end of the bed. For a moment the fatty odour was intensified. The smell of suppurating flesh had seemed to choke his nostrils ever since he had heard about Alan's death. His senses gagged on the abundance of summer. Flowers, fruit and vegetables left one day too long would be close to bursting, pungent with ripeness, ready to rot. Roy walked into the adjoining bathroom and turned on the taps.

'No answers to my advertisement,' Reggie was grumbling as he came back into the bedroom. 'Vicar can't suggest anyone. Hospital say they can't help. *You* must know of a charwoman? Twenty quid a week for a spot of hoovering, ironing the odd shirt? Little enough to ask. Make it twenty-five after a year.'

Roy felt an overwhelming urge to say, I'll do it, sir. Give me fifty quid a week, all found, I'll do everything, look after you and the house. He would have been happy as a butler – footman, more likely, never having grown above five feet six and skinny with it. He had never found deference a burden or an insult and he liked taking care of things, nice things, good things. He would enjoy polishing the Squadron Leader's silver, his mahogany tables, hoovering his carpets and beating his rugs on the line in the sun. He would even enjoy scrubbing the stone flags of the kitchen floor or scouring the cooker. It was satisfying, physical work and he longed to submit to its routine, to hammock himself between Monday's laundry and Friday's stocking up the pantry, to feel secure against disorder by restoring cleanliness and decorum. Above all he wanted to turn his back on the chaos of June. June, poor June, with her disfigured arms and her scrunched-up face, dragging on one cigarette after another, just like Alan.

His mind veered sharply away from the thought of his son

and he said, 'All right if I leave your breakfast tray in the dining-room?' trying to make it a statement rather than a question. 'Then I can be getting on with your shirts downstairs. You taking the car, or train?'

'Car,' said Reginald.

When Reginald finally arrived at Rules, James Tidmarsh was waiting for him at the bar. He wiped the aggrieved expression off his face as Reggie entered, though he flinched at being clapped hard on the shoulder and hailed stentoriously.

'Ah, Tidmarsh! What's your poison?'

'I'm afraid I never drink at lunchtime,' James Tidmarsh began.

Reginald interrupted, 'Nonsense, old chap! Absolute baloney! Two Glenmorangies,' he said to the barman, adding with elaborate caution, 'But you'd better make one of those a *single*.'

'If you insist,' said Tidmarsh, pained, 'I'll have a small pink gin.'

'Hold it! Scrub the single! Make that a pink gin instead!'

'Chin-chin!' said Reggie, as their drinks arrived. 'How the blazes do you cope with the air traffic round here? Lanes congested, parking impossible. Car's halfway to Tunbridge Wells.'

'I walk, on the whole,' James Tidmarsh said. Conversation was halted by the arrival of a waiter at their elbow.

'Would you care to look at the menu, gentlemen, while you wait for your table?' He looked at them uncertainly, unsure which man was the guest and thus who should be offered the menu first.

'My treat,' said Reggie. 'I insist! Mind you don't bill me for your time, though, what? Come on: what'll you have, Tidmarsh?'

James Tidmarsh would have liked a Dover sole and no starter, but Reggie overruled him. They had Arbroath Smokies with thin slices of brown bread, followed by poached fresh salmon with courgettes and sauté potatoes and a green salad.

Reggie ate Tidmarsh's potatoes, which Tidmarsh swapped him for his salad. Then they had bread-and-butter pudding, English cheese with cream crackers and Bath Olivers, and a bottle of Pouilly Fuissé, most of which Reginald drank. Midway through the meal the *maitre d'* approached their table.

'Mr Conynghame-Jervis, sir!' he said. 'It's been too long since we had the pleasure. The '83? Very good choice, a very nice year indeed. Glad we had your usual on the menu today, sir. Everything all right?'

'Excellent, thank you, Mr Last,' answered Reginald. 'Excellent. Good to be back. You still do dinner?'

'Certainly, sir. We look forward to seeing you again soon. Now, after this . . . coffee for you gentlemen? Brandy?'

'Just coffee,' said Tidmarsh firmly, wondering, What's all this leading up to? Was that performance for my benefit? What does he *want*?

Having regaled his guest with some of his riper anecdotes and staved off any specific inquiries after his welfare, Reginald forked some buttery pudding and raisins into his mouth, followed by a rich spoonful of cream, and said. 'Fact is, Tidmarsh, I'm thinking of getting married.'

'Ah,' replied his family solicitor. 'Yes. Have you, er, *proposed* marriage, Squadron Leader? Or is this marriage still hypothetical?'

'Put it this way,' said Reginald. 'I haven't proposed, but I will. And when I do, she'll accept.'

'You are not, then, I take it, asking for my advice?'

'Congratulations may be acceptable in due course,' Reggie answered sarcastically, 'but advice for the moment is not called for. It's information I am after.'

'In that case,' said Tidmarsh drily, 'I should start by saying that from now on my time is money.'

'Synchronize watches. Fourteen-twenty-two,' said Reginald. 'And counting down . . .'

In the end, what he needed to know was simple. Were he to remarry, were he to sell the house, were he to purchase a smaller one, did he have the use of Mary's share of the proceeds from The Cedars until he died, or did it go straightaway to this orphanage thing of hers?

'I will scrutinize Mrs Conynghame-Jervis's will,' said Tidmarsh, 'and let you have my opinion as soon as possible. From what I recall, the terms of the will are less than specific on this point. In any case, I am afraid it may be necessary to communicate your intention to the British Association for Adoption and Fostering, whose interpretation may differ from my own, and more particularly from your wishes.'

'Fourteen-twenty-nine,' said Reggie.

'Seventy-five pounds,' said Tidmarsh. 'It is I am afraid our minimum consultancy fee.'

'Shall we go halves on the bill?' asked Reginald.

Shortly afterwards they parted, both in a bad temper, but Reginald was planning to cheer himself up with a visit to Sabrina, whereas Tidmarsh could only look forward to an afternoon at the office.

Roy and June had finally worked out a plan and reached agreement. He would get the house in Thomas Street ready for her and the boys. Gloria would take over her mother's tenancy in Balham for the time being, so that June had the choice of going back there if things didn't work out. As soon as term ended, Billy and little Joe would go off for ten days to Cubs' summer camp, while June moved their stuff to Tunbridge Wells and settled down. By mid-August they would all be living under one roof. Meanwhile, in view of the special circumstances, both boys had been provisionally accepted at the school their father had attended.

'See how it goes,' had become Roy's motto. 'No long-term plans, no promises. See how it goes.'

He hadn't felt this tired in years. It wasn't just his age, though he was increasingly conscious of the years. Despite the warmth of July, he felt like a gnarled old tree with too many inner rings, its bark cracking, leaves loosening, sap drying up. The effort of running the Squadron Leader's house as well as preparing his own left him drained and exhausted. Take it slowly, Royston, he would try and tell himself: more haste, less speed (for that was what Grace used to say when he was rushing), but he couldn't take it slowly. Time was running out. In less than two weeks, June would be moving in. Drawers and cupboards had to be emptied of the débris of the past and the débris itself given away (if anyone would have it; thrown away in the end, more likely, though the stuff was still good, clean and darned by her dear hands). The furniture needed rearranging – he couldn't monopolize the big bedroom all on his own, wasn't fair. He'd let June have that. He'd move into Alan's old room, which was handy, being next to the bathroom and toilet, and set up the shrine on top of the chest of drawers, with her photographs on his bedside table. He'd have to ask one of his mates from the pub, or a neighbour, to help him shift the furniture. Even with another pair of hands he didn't know how he was going to manage . . . Well, leave that problem for another day. Meanwhile he had to clear out Vera's room for the boys. The floors needed scrubbing, the windows polishing, and empty drawers had to be shaken out and relined.

Roy was setting off for his own house at lunchtime, having spent the morning (it was a Monday) doing the big double wash and hanging shirts on the line, when Fred the gardener stopped the motor-mower that was carving stripes and squares around the rose-beds in the front lawn. He cocked his head twice.

'Here!' he called, 'Roy! Here a minute!'

Roy looked at him wearily, screwing up his eyes against the sharp light. 'What?' he asked.

'Over here!' said Fred again. 'Don't mind him. He's gone out ten minutes ago. Look, tell me it's none of my business, but what you killing yourself for? He don't notice and you look right knackered.'

'Now Aggie's gone,' Roy explained, 'and he can't find anyone else –'

'No wonder, from what I hear.'

'I've been doing her work. Can't let the mess pile up, can

you? Who's going to do the cleaning? Not him, that's for sure. House would be a disgrace.'

'Not your problem, mate. He upped your money?'

Roy did not feel like admitting that he was unpaid, so he simply said, 'No.'

'Nor me, neither,' replied Fred. 'Tell you the truth, if it wasn't for all the veg I takes home from out the back, and apples and that, I wouldn't stay. Four pounds an hour's all he pays, mean sod! I could get a fiver anywhere else. But it's become like my own garden; been here for over three years now, you get to care for it, don't you? Haven't had a raise since Madam died. Pity you never knew her: she was a real lady, lovely person, it's always the good ones as goes first. Take my advice: you tell him, "Squadron Leader, you got to find someone else to clean, I ain't able to do it no more, my health won't stand for it." You'll give yourself a heart attack, matey, way you're carrying on, I kid you not.'

This speech made Roy feel worse. Sitting on the bus to the shopping centre, he examined his symptoms. His legs were bad – that was nothing new, they'd been bad for a long time, but now his feet were starting to go. He had two ingrowing toenails that hurt like nobody's business; he'd go to a chiropodist if he ever got the time. Ankles were beginning to let him down, collapse on him, and his feet turned inwards so that he often tripped and had to catch on to something to save himself. One of these days he'd come a cropper.

He proffered his pensioner's bus pass.

'That's all right, Dad,' said the bus conductress, cheerful because of the fine weather. 'I didn't think you was bunking off paying!'

Then there were the noises in his head, the buzzing and fizzing and sometimes roaring sounds. He didn't know if it was his heartbeat magnified – cataracts of blood pounding up to his brain and ebbing back again before launching their next tidal wave – or whether it was just the ears that were wrong. Maybe it was nothing more than wax. He felt dizzy. His eyes would suddenly go all swimmy, like milk in a bottle tipping sideways, and when he took his glasses off to rub them a haze would come over his vision and he would feel sick. His bladder couldn't be relied on, and he'd find himself caught short without warning. He'd had to learn the location of every Gents in town.

He ought to go and see the doctor; he would, if he ever got a moment. The prospect of sitting for an hour or more in a waiting-room full of whining children and sickly people put him off. More likely to get a disease than a cure. This must be old age, I suppose, he concluded dismally. I'm glad Gracie never lived to see it.

He was going in to Woolworth's to pick up a couple of bedside rugs for the boys – they wouldn't want to put their feet on to bare lino first thing in the morning, and he'd never got round to carpeting Vera's room once she had left – when he bumped into Molly Tucker.

'Is it my old friend Roy Southgate or is it his ghost?' she hailed him cheerfully. 'Come back to haunt me, have you?'

He was so pleased to see her, he could have cried. He put a hand across his eyes.

'Hey, lovey, you all right?' she asked. 'What's up? You had your lunch yet?'

'No time,' said Roy. 'Got to get on. I'll make myself a sandwich later,'

She dodged in front of him. 'Let's have a proper look at you.'

Women are wonderful, he thought, as he sat in a wicker chair in Molly's back parlour looking out over her garden, an egg-and-ham salad inside him and a cup of tea at his elbow. They pick you up, brush you down, make a bit of a fuss, and you're back on your feet again. We should have gone together, Grace, but then, who would look after those boys? He squared his shoulders unconsciously so that Molly, coming into the room at that moment, said. 'That's more like it! You feeling better? Now, remember what I said.'

'We'll see how it goes,' said Roy. 'No long-term plans. See how it goes. You've done me a power of good and I'm ever so grateful. Let's just see how it goes.'

*

The encounter with Sabrina had been a great success, Reginald reflected several days later; the big boy had proved more than adequate to the task. Now, equally gratifying, was the news in the morning's post. Tidmarsh had been compelled to admit – reluctantly, Reggie felt sure – that the will was not specific about the necessity of his remaining in the marital home, although he, Tidmarsh, felt obliged to point out that were he, the deceased's widower, to move, BAAF, being the designated beneficiaries of the current residence and former marital home, might consider it worth the cost of challenging his legal right to half the total proceeds of the sale of The Cedars. If, of course, he were to decide to sell it. Never anything clear and simple with these legal bods, thought Reggie; always ifs and buts.

His own world had been one of instant decisions, absolute certainties, black and white. Having fought as a Pilot Officer in the last weeks of the Battle of Britain, and then flown Hurricanes on 'Rhubarb' strikes over France and with the Desert Airforce in North Africa, Reginald understood one thing: the chase. He enjoyed the chase, revelled in the chase, relished its twists and turns, and would have been disappointed in a too easy surrender. He knew that, where Liz was concerned, the chase was approaching its climax. Combat was about to be engaged. He knew she was determined to stay out of his bed until he had proposed marriage; knew that she regarded him as an honourable man, who would not retract the proposal, once made; knew that in this she was right. He for his part was equally determined to bed her first and, if all went satisfactorily, propose afterwards. Sabrina had given him the confidence to take Liz to bed. He felt more sure of himself than he had done since Mary's death. He felt randy.

Marriage, after all, was the simplest way to conduct one's life. It made a lot of sense. If Liz were around, she could deal with the little bloke, who kept muttering all of a sudden about going back to his own house. That would be thoroughly inconvenient, just when Reginald had got him trained to run the place properly, taught him how he liked his breakfast and his shirts, how much ice in his whisky. Her womanly tact would make sure Southgate stayed put.

Once she was installed she might even organize, well, perhaps not parties exactly – he was a bit long in the tooth for parties – but they'd definitely get some people round for drinks, to introduce her: this is Liz, Liz *Conynghame-Jervis*. My wife. She'd make a favourable impression, good-looking girl like her. Good old Reggie, they'd say to each other as they left, never knew he still had it in him! After that he might invite Vivian and Whatsername, dammit, – 2nd Lady Blythgowrie – and the girls down for dinner one evening, and Celia or Felicity could bring that bearded chappie along for inspection. (What was the fellow doing with a beard? When he was younger, Reggie remembered, at Oxford, you'd call out 'Beaver!' and score a point for a man with a beard; five points for a man with a ginger beard on a purple bicycle.) Well, he'd soon be back in the social swing. Been getting a bit solitary lately. Too many evenings on his own.

That shop of Liz's might be a problem. He'd persuade her to get rid of it, sell her house – tiddly little box like that wouldn't fetch much. Just as well; dangerous business letting wives have their own money. Wouldn't mind moving to somewhere a bit smaller. Five bedrooms – six, if you counted Mary's workroom – were more than the two of them needed. Unless, of course . . . No, in another year or so, when property prices had stabilized and he could walk away with enough profit on The Cedars to end his money worries, they ought to leave Tunbridge Wells and go to some sleepy Sussex village. Buy a nice old red-brick cottage beside a village pond, with a garden small enough for Mary – oops! *Liz* – to look after herself, keep her busy, give her something to do. . . . That was the sort of life he could cope with.

He looked up. The garden was folding in on itself as dusk deepened. The insects that had earlier been buzzing in the apple trees or round the roses had fallen silent. The sky was indigo, with slanting black wisps leaning towards the last strands of sunset.

He considered, and rejected, several possible locations for the coming encounter. It needn't be romantic – that was for the proposal, which was next. For this dinner, Rules was tempting. The *maître d'* would look after him, the dark red banquettes were roguishly suggestive, the food was first class; but the long drive home afterwards would tire him, as well as requiring him to stay reasonably sober. Booking a suite at the Savoy across the road was too obvious and, in any case, he wasn't sure how hotels reacted nowadays to unmarried couples arriving without luggage. He could hardly take Liz to one of those anonymous little places behind Victoria Station – half a dozen bedrooms, half a dozen double beds, half a dozen hand-basins, half a dozen curtained windows and one chain-smoking harridan on Reception – where in years gone by he had passed many an afternoon in return for a twenty-pound note.

He had no fears that alcohol might impair the big boy's performance. That had never been the problem; and in any case he hadn't been exactly stone cold the other day with Sabrina.

For this particular dinner the setting was crucial. Pick the right field of battle and you're halfway to victory. Rule one: fight in your own airspace. That was it. He would get an outside caterer to prepare a dinner for two, to be eaten here, in his own spacious dining-room. Southgate could serve it as far as the pudding and cheese, and he would arrange in advance that he should then *go home*. Fellow had spent the night away often enough lately, he couldn't remember why, but that should be no problem. He'd make it an order.

Reginald stretched his legs to unlock the tense feeling behind his knees, and scrabbled his fingers in the peanut bowl. He could picture it. They'd both be sitting out here on the terrace at the back of the house. She'd have had a few drinks, a last brandy, they'd be admiring the garden, darkness would settle, he'd steer her indoors ... Here imagination grew a little imprecise, but the next image moved to his bedroom. He'd put his arms round her, tackle the zip, dress would slip from her shoulders ... As he pictured it, the big boy responded gratifyingly to this vivid seduction scene. No problem, old boy, Reggie said to himself; she'll go down in flames!

His heart quickened at the prospect, beating so fast that it was almost painful. Extraordinary thing, he thought, this chemistry, electricity, whatever it is. Only have to think about sex and the whole system goes on red alert. Pulse races, eyes dilate, big boy stands at the ready, just because I think of Liz with her clothes off. Must be why Jane in the *Daily Mirror* was drawn wearing her undies all through the war. Making sure the lads were at the ready. And then on the day victory was declared, she took everything off – finally! He smiled to himself. He liked a joke you waited five years for. Old heart was thudding like mad. Whoa, he thought, steady on, plenty of time yet. He shifted position to relieve the constriction in his legs and chest, and thumped his ribs a couple of times. Have another cigarette, Reggie, old boy; calm down.

Imagination stumbled over the final practical aspect of the evening. Would he need johnnies? Liz, after all, could presumably still get pregnant. Well, Reggie thought indulgently, and what if she did? Plenty of men became fathers in their seventies. He rather liked the idea; indeed, he liked it better the more he thought about it. If it was a boy, they'd put his name down for Eton. Wouldn't send him to Sedbergh, no bloody chance! He'd never expose any boy of his to the crude, remorseless bullying he had endured at the hands of the stupider sons of lesser Scottish gentry or self-made Northerners. Nothing less than Eton or Harrow for his son. Have to stay on here in that case. Need space for nannies, nursemaids, whatever. He liked the idea of having a nanny in the house again. He'd sort out the money somehow. There must be a family trust that would educate his son. Decision made, he poured himself another drink. Maybe it would be a girl. No. Imagination stopped dead there. Not a girl. A son. Point was, he wouldn't need johnnies.

Aids, though. What about that? He dismissed it. Poofters got Aids, didn't they? Poofters and drug addicts. Not decent girls like Liz. Sabrina had slipped a condom on to him with cool, supple fingers, so quickly that it was there before he knew what she was up to. But that was different: they had to be careful, the paid professionals; never knew where a client had last been. Liz would be insulted.

He looked at his watch. Ten o'clock. Not too late to ring. Where the hell was Southgate? High time his dinner was on the table. Reginald walked through the French windows into the soft warmth of the drawing-room, its daytime hues harmonized to pearly grey, dark lilac and purple in the dimness of the summer evening. He snapped on a table lamp and lifted the telephone.

Chapter Thirteen

It was weeks since Liz had last seen Reginald for that oddly unsatisfactory evening together, she in her black dress and Italian tan, distracted by worry about Lissy; far too many weeks since he had dropped her off with hardly a kiss and no struggle at all. Since then, silence. Liz knew, and kept reminding herself, that a man's sense of time is quite different from that of a woman. Men can let months go by and then ring as though they had spoken to you yesterday, while women count the days and even the hours. Liz was a sophisticate in the battle of the sexes and thought she understood how the male mind worked. All the same, by the time Reginald finally telephoned, she was frantic.

Her daughter had stayed on for several days, enjoying the pampering and, in the end, graciously accepting the offer of some garments from the shop. The short, flared dresses that were in fashion that summer made ideal pregnancy-wear. Alicia surveyed her reflection and saw that she looked delicious. Liz began to think she might find herself landed with her daughter for the entire pregnancy, and wondered disloyally if this would capsize her own plans – for she did not care to be seen by Reggie in the role of prospective grandmother.

Already, this unborn baby, this foetus, was binding mother and daughter close. Lissy solemnly promised to attend the ante-natal clinic regularly, and grudgingly agreed to think about informing the baby's father. Though she didn't see why, she said, when her brother, Hugo, would make a perfectly good father-figure, if the poor bloody infant *had* to have a man in its life. Then she caught Liz's eye and acknowledged that she was being absurd, and the two of them laughed together conspiratorially: lone women, same predicament. Eventually Lissy, keen to show off her new look to her friends in London, borrowed another twenty pounds from her mother and caught the train back. Peace had been made between them.

Liz returned to worrying about Reggie. Had she said or done something wrong that last Thursday evening they had spent together? She scoured her memory but could recall only that he had talked about his wartime exploits and she – surely? – had found herself rather impressed. Had he, then, met another woman? It would not be difficult. Poor old Reggie was a walking widower in need of a wife: it stood out a mile. Maybe *that* was the problem – her refusal to go to bed with him. Perhaps he had concluded that she was prudish or frigid. Next time I will, Liz promised herself. I've made him wait long enough, poor old heffalump, and if I don't, someone else will.

Let's face it, between Lissy and the infernal bank manager, I need a cash injection fast. Whittington has been breathing down my neck like a dragon, panicking me with his talk of bankruptcy and liquidation. 'Sell the shop, Mrs Franks.' She recalled his nasal, wheedling voice. 'Sell the shop and realize your assets while you can. Pay off your creditors and take a steady, salaried job. With your experience, you could easily get a post in the – what do they call it? – women's wear section of a London department store. Money coming in regularly, you'd know where you stood. It's the recession, Mrs Franks. It's biting very hard.' 'I will *not* be a shop assistant!' Liz had said. 'I had imagined,' he said tartly, 'that was rather what you were now? Correct me if I'm wrong.' 'You're wrong,' she had retorted. 'Be that as it may . . .' His voice droned on . . . Finally, he said, 'It's up to you, Mrs Franks: the choice is yours. The bank will extend your business loan for another ninety days. After that we shall either need to see regular reducing payments, or we shall have to call in the loan. I'll confirm that in writing.'

Liz's thoughts returned to Reginald. What other solution is there? And besides, he's not too bad. At times I think he doesn't just fancy me, he actually loves me. God knows, that'd be nice. I love to be loved. Could I ever love him? He's got beautiful manners. He's overweight, yes, but I can take him in hand, get him to lose a stone or two. At least he isn't physically *repulsive*. I can face going to bed with him. He doesn't exactly drive me wild with desire, but that's not the point. He doesn't disgust me.

His house must run pretty smoothly: it's always spotless, and he's immaculately turned out. There's that manservant – time I learned his name, might be a useful ally – and presumably a housekeeper as well. Probably a cleaner comes in. Gardener. Quite a large staff. Have my hands full looking after that lot. They won't be too pleased to see me come along. Got used to having things their own way. Be like Mrs Danvers in *Rebecca* all over again, I dare say. Steady on, Liz . . . He hasn't even rung yet.

And then he did. She was watching the news. John Mc-Carthy's release was rumoured to be imminent and she didn't want to miss the sight of his face as he emerged after years in some cellar, blinking and grinning at freedom, to hug that brave, persistent girl who'd engineered it all – but it was still just speculation from various so-called Middle East experts. All the same, they had made her forget her own panic, so that when the telephone rang she was genuinely distracted.

'Yes?' she answered, abruptly, preoccupied; and then, with a glad cry that she could not disguise, '*Reggie!*'

Her voice was so womanly, so vibrant with welcome, that he could almost have said there and then, 'Marry me, Liz.' And it might have been better if he had. But Reginald over-ruled this guileless impulse and said, 'Ah! You're there. Thought you might have been away on holiday again.' (As though he'd seen her last week, instead of nearly two months ago!) 'All well with you?'

Instantly on guard, Liz answered, 'Fine. Could certainly do with a break.' (Just in case he was offering her a weekend in Venice.) 'Still here for the time being. How have you been?'

'Oh, not too bad, you know. Busy, pretty busy . . . Care to have dinner one evening? Long time no see.'

'I should think dinner would be lovely,' she said coolly. 'Do you want to fix a date now?'

Now that the moment was approaching when they must consummate or abandon their relationship, they were shy and gruff, putting off the occasion as though trying to avert it. Everyone is modest before a first encounter. Even in darkness – though wishing to make love in the dark is taken as a sign of inhibition – people must eventually bare their bodies to one another and be naked as newborns, stripped of clothing and artifice. Now that the game, the chase, was soon to culminate in this trial of their secret needs and abilities, suddenly both would have liked to postpone it. As Reggie grew older, he found the chase more fun than the capture. Perhaps he always had. Perhaps the end was too closely associated with death. Perhaps that had always been his problem. But a date had to be set.

So he said, with a touch of irritation in his voice, 'How are you placed for Saturday?'

'*This* Saturday?' asked Liz.

What's she on about, thought Reggie, *this* Saturday? This week, next week, sometime, never? Games these women play.

'Why not?' he parried.

'This Saturday would do as well as any. Had you anywhere special in mind?'

'Care to come and eat here?'

Aha, she thought. I am to be paraded for the benefit of the housekeeper, the manservant, and God knows who else!

'If you like,' she said.

'Splendid! Pick you up, what, about eight?'

'Eight on Saturday will be lovely. Look forward to it.'

They both hung up, and both glanced at the time: Reggie at an elegant, slightly tarnished brass carriage clock on the mantelpiece; Liz at a black and white digital clock in a sleek modern shape on hers. It was not quite twenty past ten. Start the countdown, thought Reggie, and his heart raced quite alarmingly at the prospect. Steady on old chap, he told himself, still got four days to go.

I'd better book a facial, thought Liz, and have my roots done; and fit in two aerobics classes between now and Saturday. Just under four days to arrange it all.

'You sure you're going to be comfy?' asked Roy, for what must have been the fifth time that day. June didn't find it annoying. It was so long since anyone had looked after her, worried about *her* comfort, that Roy's expressions of concern were a luxury.

'It's lovely, Dad,' she said. 'You've worked ever so hard. I hope you haven't done yourself an injury lugging stuff about and scrubbing the floors. Don't it all look nice, though?'

'Didn't have to do it all on my lonesome. Arthur came in from over the road to help with the heavy things and his missus took a whole lot of bits and bobs down to the church hall for the next bazaar. Molly Tucker, you don't know her, she was an old friend of Gracie's, Molly sorted out some of Grace's and Vera's and' – had to be said, you couldn't avoid it for ever – 'Alan's old clothes, and took the net curtains and your bedroom ones to the launderette and washed them. People have been good neighbours. Makes me sorry I've stayed away so long.'

'Well, now you're back,' said June firmly.

'Not for a few more days,' Roy said. 'You know how welcome you are here, but some people can make white look like black, they've got that sort of mind. Better I stay up at The Cedars till the boys get here. Then there can't be no wagging tongues.'

'Let them wag!' said June, but she was not altogether sorry to have a few nights by herself. It would give her time to settle in, get used to the feel of the place, get some idea of whether she could ever belong here, amid the classy streets, posh shops and smooth white faces of Tunbridge Wells.

'You be OK on your own?' asked Roy, again not for the first time. 'I ought to be off now, but I'll be back round about ten o'clock tomorrow morning – in time for elevenses at the latest.'

June looked at him and thought, How did this little, kind, fussy man produce the V-shaped body, strong arms, wide shoulders and broad face of my Alan? Even when he got old, Alan would never have gone like this. Roy must always have had the furrowed, anxious face of a tiny furry creature, big eyes on the alert for predators, jug ears scanning every rustle. How did this frightened little man's seed grow into the great oak of my husband? Yet Alan only looked big; he was fearful inside, always on the look-out for neglect and insult, afraid of inflicting pain, afraid of incurring it. Billy now, he takes after his Dad in looks, but he's tougher; he's got my Mum in his nature. Be good for them to live with their Grandad for a while. Too long since they had a man about the place. They'll test him, see how much he'll stand for. I must tell him not to weaken or give in to them. I wish he'd go. He looks ever so tired, and it makes me nervous, him hanging about. If I get on edge, I'll have another go at my arms and that'd make for a rotten start.

'What is it, Dad?' she asked. 'Something bugging you?'

'You *sure* you'll be OK without me? You will – you know – leave yourself alone . . .?'

Bloody hell, he can read my mind! Better watch out.

'I'll be OK, I swear it. Tell me again what you got for supper.' It comforted them both, his recitation of what was in the fridge, what was in the freezer, and what was in the cool, freshly cleaned larder. The incantation of supplies was reassuring. The hunter was home from the hill. We shall not starve this week.

'And there's lentils and a knuckle of ham,' he ended. 'So when the boys get back, if we get a cooler day, you can make ham-and-pea soup, and even a meat loaf with the rests so little Joe can learn how to use the mincer, like his Dad loved to do.'

'How'd you learn all that stuff?' June asked. 'Was it just from watching Mum?'

'Used to be a cook in my young days, before I went on the milk.'

'One day you can teach me some new recipes. Go on, off you go. Tell me next time.'

Neither was quite sure what form of parting was suitable at the end of a long day in which Roy had taken June under his roof, given her the bedroom and the very bed he had shared for over forty years with his wife – the bed in which, in all probability, Alan had been conceived. Roy feared an embrace, yet longed for physical contact, some firm touch to prove that his flesh was still solid, some momentary reminder of the scent of female softness. June wanted to know whether any echo of her dead man still clung to his father.

They'd had a dog when she was little, and after her own father had died – killed in a car accident, drunk – the dog had moped and slunk about for weeks. Eventually it seemed to forget, but two years later her uncle, her father's brother, came to visit and the dog had gone mad with joy. What did it catch that humans could not? If she inhaled deeply enough, could she catch a trace of Alan on his father?

'Don't get up,' said Roy.

'No no, I'll see you to the door,' said June.

'You'd best double-lock it from the inside. Do you want to test it?'

'OK.'

He went outside and tried the handle. It wouldn't budge, and, calling out a cheery 'That's it! You're quite safe!' he turned away and walked down the path, so that in the end they neither touched nor took any leave of one another at all.

For Roy the anti-climax was so sudden that his need for human contact, newly evoked, cried out for satisfaction. He crossed the road towards Arthur's place, but the house was in darkness, with only the hall light shining to deter passing burglars. He knocked on the door all the same and waited, but there were no answering footsteps. He rejected the pub. He was too tired for that.

On the spur of the moment, he decided to drop in on Molly before going back to The Cedars. It wasn't yet nine o'clock, still quite light, and he owed his thanks anyway for her help.

So he turned right on John's Road and set off along Woodbury Park. What would Grace have to say about the day's events? he wondered. She'd surely think he had done the right thing. Thank God she had never known about Alan's grey and bloody death! *O for the touch of a vanish'd hand* . . . But he could no longer summon up the sound of her voice that was still; he knew only that she had been his wife, that he had loved her, but now their home had been dismantled and she would no longer recognize the rooms in which she had lived and moved. The fact was, she no longer belonged there. The other night he had dreamed of finding her in the house, and, worried that the boys would be frightened by this apparent return from the dead, he had in his dream tried to hustle her away or conceal her. He had woken feeling guilty and ashamed. His own Grace, no longer welcome!

On Saturday Billy and Joe were due back from camp. June had arranged to go up to Balham, meet the Cubs' bus, and bring them back with her on the train to Tunbridge Wells, after dropping in to say hello to Gloria. Roy spent the morning at Thomas Street preparing a meal so that when Junie got home she'd only to pop it in the oven. He checked that the boys' beds were dry and aired, and nipped down the road to the newsagent to buy a comic for each of them, so they could read in bed. They'd be too excited to go to sleep straightaway, he thought, remembering the long-ago evenings when Vera and Alan used to read the *Dandy* and *Beano* in bed for hours by the dwindling light of dusk. Then he caught the bus back to The Cedars.

Going down to the kitchen to put a kettle on in case the Squadron Leader wanted a cup of something, he found a strange woman there, wearing a big white apron.

'Who are you?' she asked.

'Excuse me,' said Roy. 'I'm ever so sorry. I didn't know you was here. I came down to make a cuppa for Sir. I'll just put the kettle on. I won't be in your way.'

'He's upstairs. Outside on the terrace, I think. I'm Michaela

Simpson, by the way, Mick and Flick Catering. We're doing him a special dinner for two. You're going to be serving it, I dare say. He said he didn't need us. I must have a quick word with you later on, about the *saumon poelé*.'

'Beg your pardon?'

'The fish course,' she amended.

'Righty-ho,' said Roy. 'I'll be back in a tick. I'll just go and see what he wants.'

Reggie was sitting on the terrace with his cigarettes, an ashtray and a tall drink beside him. It looked surprisingly non-alcoholic.

'Ah!' he said. 'There you are at last. Beginning to wonder if I'd ever see hide or hair of you again.'

'I need to have a word with you, sir,' said Roy. 'I thought you might care for a coffee?'

'Mrs Mick down there mixes a bloody good Pimm's,' said Reggie. 'Have a look at the jug. Pour me another, and see if there's a drop left for yourself.'

'Not for me, thanks all the same, sir,' said Roy. 'I wondered if I might have a word . . .?'

'About tonight,' said Reginald. 'Haven't forgotten, have you?'

'You want me to serve dinner?'

'That's right. ETA latest, twenty-thirty; dinner should kick off about fifteen minutes after that. You can go after you've dished up the main course. Leave the pudding and cheese on the sideboard, clear away downstairs, and go home. I won't be needing you in the morning. Please yourself what time you come in tomorrow, as long as it's not too early.'

'Very good, sir,' said Roy. He tried again. 'Squadron Leader . . .?'

'I said go ahead. Help yourself to some Pimm's.'

Roy, seeing there was no other way to attract his attention, did so. He sipped the clear, bitter liquid. It was unexpectedly delicious.

'It's ever so nice, sir.'

'I should say it is! Perfect summer drink! Even better than

gin and It. Tell Mrs Mick downstairs to brew us up another jug, will you?'

'You wouldn't care for a coffee now, sir?'

'I said, another jug, Southgate.'

Roy returned to the terrace ten minutes later having stiffened his resolve to the point where his mouth was dry and his heart was pounding. His hands shook as he poured a fresh Pimm's into the Squadron Leader's proffered glass.

'I say, old chap, steady on.'

Roy sat down abruptly.

'The thing is, sir, I keep trying to tell you and now it's tonight. I won't be sleeping here no more. My son died . . .'

'I remember. Rotten business. Anything I can do, just let me know,' said Reggie, drawing deeply on his cigarette and averting his eyes.

'. . . and his wife couldn't cope no more on her own and the boys was running wild and the Social poking their nose in, asking questions, so I've brought them all down here, to live with me. In *my* house,' he added, as a look of horror flickered briefly across Reginald's face. 'Now I'm going to have to move back in there and look after them. She's not been that well, June, that's my daughter-in-law; it's been a great trial to her, and the boys is getting older, twelve and ten they are now.'

'You mean to tell me you're going *away?*' said Reginald. '*Leaving?*'

'Yes, sir.'

Reginald drained his Pimm's. Automatically, Roy refilled the glass. The Squadron Leader looked devastated. His colour was high, and his eyes protruded more than usual. The tiny red veins that branched like trees across his corneas appeared close to bursting. The veins on his forehead throbbed visibly, great pulsing purple ropes. Roy felt his own heart race in sympathy.

'I could always come back and clean for you, sir,' he added, although he hadn't meant to. 'For the time being, that is, until you find someone else. I could keep the kitchen and

bathroom nice, that's the main thing, and run a hoover downstairs twice a week, and if you took your shirts to the laundry
– only until – for the time being . . .'

Reggie looked at Roy in dismay. He stubbed his cigarette
out. Almost at once he lit another. Eventually he said, 'Is this
final? Suppose I offered to pay you a wage? Say we started at
twenty' – he amended it hastily – 'no, *thirty* pounds a week?'

'It's ever so good of you, sir,' Roy told him, 'but it isn't a
matter of money. It never was. I come here to give you a bit
of comfort and company, not for the wage. I'm not saying I
shan't be sorry to go sir . . .'

'Well, then?' said Reggie, clutching at a straw.

'But I have to, on account of June and the boys. I've been
happy here, sir, looking back, and I was right miserable when
I arrived. It's been like a kind of a marriage in a way, hasn't
it? You and me living together here these last, what is it, nine
months must be, sort of both looking after each other. When I
first come here, I was that cut up about my Grace I couldn't
hardly see through both eyes at once. All I done was think of
her and feel sorry for myself. But you took me out of myself,
made me see there was others besides. You done me a power of
good, sir. Vicar was right. You've looked after me, in a manner
of speaking, and I hope I've looked after you. We've been
almost like a couple.'

This was too much for Reginald, who muttered querulously,
'Hardly.' He regarded Southgate as little more than a servant,
and Roy had come to behave as though Reggie were his
master. Reginald would have been greatly surprised had
anyone told him they were equals, indeed friends; and not just
because no money had passed between them. And yet they
were equals, though only Roy had realized it.

'Blood's thicker than water, sir, and I have to put those
boys first,' Roy concluded, having at last said what he meant
to say.

'When were you thinking of leaving?' asked Reginald.

'Tonight. I thought I'd move my stuff out this afternoon,
do my packing and that, leave the spare room nice and tidy

for the next person. I'll look in next week, make sure you've got everything. But I won't be sleeping here no more. So don't you worry about your dinner. I won't be in your way. I'll serve up and go.' As a final placatory gesture he added, 'Would you like me to wear anything special, sir? I could put on a white shirt and my black trousers, make it look smarter, formal, for the occasion?'

'Thanks,' said Reginald. 'That'd be very suitable. And a plain dark tie. Black, in fact. That'll be all for now, Southgate.'

Reginald arrived sharp at eight outside Liz's Georgian doll's house in Garden Street. He wasn't feeling on top form. He'd had to park the big car a couple of hundred yards away. His head ached low down in the skull at the back, ached and thundered. Too many bloody Pimm's, he thought. Taste so innocent you think there's nothing to them, and then they deliver a kick like a mule. He cheered up at the sight of Liz. She was wearing some white thing, plain and simple, cut straight across her breasts and suspended from narrow straps, and tiny nonsensical gold sandals that teetered as she stepped forward to greet him. Something gold and chunky round her neck gleamed dully. Certainly got some decent jewellery, thought Reggie. Never marry for money, Nanny used to say; love where money is. Jolly good advice.

'*Dar*ling!' said Liz. '*Reggie! Good*ness, it seems a long time! I've missed you – bad boy.'

This was promising. Reggie felt the waist of his trousers strain, and relaxed.

'Quick drink?' asked Liz. 'Glenmorangie?' She smiled at him. 'First drink we ever had together. Remember?'

'You look very lovely,' said Reggie. 'Knock-out. No, I won't come in. Plenty of Scotch back at base, and the cook will have my guts for garters if we're late for dinner. Been cooking all day.'

'Mmm,' said Liz. 'I can't wait.'

She tottered along the pavement towards his waiting car

and slid in to the seat with a flash of burnished leg. Reggie drove along Crescent Road and down Mount Pleasant, shutting his eyes at the usual spot, then past the cricket ground into Nevill Park. He parked the car, helped her out, and, as he walked up the steps towards the front door, it swung open.

'Evening, sir,' said Southgate. 'Madam.' He took the long drift of chiffon that Liz was holding and laid it reverently across the back of a chair in the hall. As Reginald ushered Liz towards the drawing-room, Roy Southgate said, 'I've set the drinks out on the terrace, sir, seeing as it's a warm evening. Would you like me to bring them inside?'

'Liz?' Reggie turned to her. 'What do you think? Are you going to be chilly out there in that frock?'

'The terrace would be heavenly. What a lovely idea. Thank you, Southgate.' She favoured him with her Revlon-bright smile.

'Oh!' she gasped a moment later, in honest admiration. 'Your garden is *glorious*!'

'You should have seen it a few weeks ago,' Reggie replied, and Liz laughed.

'People *always* say that when you praise their garden!'

The evening started exactly according to plan. Southgate did his stuff and Mrs Mick came up trumps. The food was superb. Liz looked perfectly at home in his dining-room. Her shoulders, lips and necklace shone beguilingly. Reginald began to feel he had been over-pessimistic earlier in the day. Southgate's leaving accelerated matters but didn't really change anything. No reason to hang about. They were both adults, free and unencumbered.

Southgate cleared the plates quietly and efficiently, swept the table with a tiny dustpan and brush that he hadn't seen since Mary's day, and set out the pudding and cheese plates on the sideboard.

'Will that be all, sir?' he asked.

'Very good, Southgate. Well done. Yes, you may go now.'

'Delicious dinner,' said Liz, to no one in particular.

'Not mine, Madam,' said Roy. 'Mrs Simpson cooked.'

'Well, tell her from me it was excellent,' said Liz graciously.

'That's all, Southgate,' said Reggie, hurriedly. 'You may go now.'

'Goodbye, sir,' said Roy. 'I'll look in tomorrow. Glad you enjoyed your dinner, Madam.'

For an instant Liz frowned, but before she could ask, what does he mean, he'll 'look in' tomorrow? Reggie took charge.

'Right!' he said decisively. 'Now then! What do you fancy? Cheese first in the nasty French way, or pudding?'

'Haven't much choice, have I? Pudding would be lovely. Please.'

They had been talking, earlier, about their marriages. He described Mary: docile, unworldly, long-suffering, but with an unexpected talent for making money. 'Sounds the very opposite of my husband!' Liz had said, laughing. She told him briefly about David – impulsive, amoral, extravagant, but the sexiest man that she, at twenty-one, had ever seen. Reggie wanted to know about her children. She avoided telling him their ages. Hugo, she said, was still on his travels. Sort of Grand Tour, Reggie had offered. Yes, she had agreed (why confuse him with the facts?). He had urged her to bring Alicia down to meet him soon and Liz, thinking the sooner the better, had promised to do so.

They moved into a new phase, a sort of intimacy, a truthfulness. It was the end of games-playing, time for a mutually understood laying down of cards. Reggie lit a cigarette and exhaled slowly.

Liz felt emboldened to ask, 'Why – you don't have to answer – why did you never have children?'

'Just one of those things,' said Reginald, gruffly, swerving away. Male pride made him add, 'Not that there was anything wrong with us. Not a matter of couldn't.'

'You must have wanted them, surely? A son to carry on the family name. A daughter. I thought all men wanted a daughter. A pretty girl to wind you round her little finger.'

'Do they?' asked Reggie. His colour, thought Liz, was

233

dangerously high. His blood pressure must be appalling. She'd have him checked out.

'Or was it your wife?' she persisted.

'No . . . no . . . Mary was very keen to have kids. That's why we bought this big house in the first place.'

'Forgive me, Reggie dear. Tell me to mind my own business if you like. It just seems, you know, odd. Unlikely.'

'Another glass of wine?' he asked. 'Or would you rather have port with your cheese?'

Fluffed it, she thought. Clumsy ass. I've lost the moment.

'Port, please,' she said demurely. She sipped it in silence.

I haven't talked about this, except a few times with Mary, for forty years, thought Reginald. People must have forgotten it ever happened. Nothing was said at Mary's funeral. Vivian might remember, although why should he? Just a boy at the time. Wouldn't have meant much to him. Changed my life. Changed my marriage. Changed everything.

Mary wouldn't let me make love to her for a year afterwards and when finally she allowed me back in her bed, I couldn't do it. We lived as a non-playing couple from then on. Might have looked pukka from the outside. Never can tell what happens inside a marriage. I dare say thousands are like us. Don't tell me Chaggers still rogers his wife – or Harry, let alone Pongo and Betty. It's a very English sort of marriage, isn't it? All best behaviour and no action. From then on I could only do it with tarts. Never managed to get it up for a decent girl, not unless she acted like a whore. The surprise was the number of decent girls who liked it that way, too: who could only cope with sex as a dirty little secret. It had to be expensive and grubby and furtive for me and the bad boy. Guilty and ashamed, your Honour.

Liz was watching him, her eyes shadowy in the evening light. If I'm thinking of marrying this woman, she'll have to know. I must tell her. Now. How do I begin? His heart thundered in his chest, beat after heavy beat resounding against his ribs.

''Fifty-one,' said Reginald. 'Nineteen-fifty-one was the year

she died. Might as well tell you. Might as well come clean.'
He snorted and almost choked. Liz was alarmed. Glory be,
she said to herself, what have I started?

'She was three,' Reginald began. 'Her name was Cecily.
We called her Tush, or Tushy, for some reason. She was three
years old, three and a bit, just old enough to be out of the
harness things children wore in those days. Know what I
mean? You'd have them on the end of long straps, like a
bridle, and there would be little animals on the front, the
piece that went across the chest. Teddy bears or rabbits or
something. Tushy's used to have a white rabbit on it.'

'I know what you mean,' Liz told him.

'Anyway, she was out of the harness by then. Very proud of
herself.'

He paused again. Liz kept silent as Reginald called up his
past.

'We'd gone shopping one Saturday morning, all three of us:
me and Cecily and Mary. We lived in Tunbridge Wells by
then. We moved here just after Tush was born. Ideal house
for bringing up children. Big garden. Away from the traffic.'

He drained his port, and Liz sipped from her glass. Its
deep, peppery flavour tickled her tongue delightfully. Reggie
poured himself another glass.

'We were going along Mount Pleasant. Didn't have super-
markets in those days; couldn't get everything under one roof
like you do now. Had to go to the greengrocer for fruit and
vegetables, baker for bread, fishmonger for fish . . .'

'I know,' said Liz gently, keeping her eyes steadily on his
face.

'Mary and I were queuing in the butcher, each holding one
of Cecily's hands, had her between us. Mary said something
like, "I'll just nip into the baker and pick up a fresh Hovis,"
and I said, "Fine, you do that," and she let go of Cecily and
went out.'

'Yes?' prompted Liz.

'Moment later – few seconds, no more – Tush said, "Can I
go with Mummy?" and I said, "Course, darling," and off she

went. Not fifteen seconds had passed. Baker was one or two shops back. Mary was hardly out of the door. No distance at all.'

There was another silence, so prolonged that Liz picked up his silver lighter and lit the candles in the centre of the table. The mahogany table glowed with the reflection of their wavering, strengthening flame.

'And then,' said Reginald, in a harsh, resonant voice that came not from his throat nor his lungs but from deep in his guts, 'then I heard the squeal of a big lorry braking. I knew immediately.'

It was true. He had known. He was trained for moments like that. Only this time there was no lever to pull, no joystick, no gunsights, nothing. Just his legs, rooted to the spot, paralysed.

'After I don't know how long I ran to the door. She was in the road. Under its wheels. Dead already. You could see there was no point in calling an ambulance, though someone did. She had died instantly.'

Liz reached over the table and put her cool hand over his. His flesh was puffy and hot.

'My darling,' she breathed, hardly audible. 'I am so sorry. I am so dreadfully sorry. Darling Reggie. Poor Reggie.'

'Not poor Reggie,' he said. '*It was my fault!* No good telling me different. It was *all my fault*. I killed my daughter.'

'Reggie. You didn't. It was an accident. How could you have known?'

'I did,' he insisted. 'Yes I did. Cecily Mary, died aged three years and five months. Beloved only child. Killed by her father's carelessness.'

He had never admitted it before. In the past, to Mary, he had always blustered and evaded and denied. He had never put the truth into words before. The guilt for her death lay at his door.

Chapter Fourteen

Several hours later, Liz dozed upstairs in Reggie's large bedroom, dimly lit in the moonless summer night. He had wept the long-suppressed tears of four decades, wept for the aircrews whose names he could no longer remember, wept for his dead wife, wept above all for his child. Liz had held him, patted his hand, stroked his hair, kissed his flushed face, murmured and comforted him.

'Liz,' he had said through his tears, 'Marry me, Liz? You will marry me, won't you? You won't leave me?'

'My darling, don't be silly,' she answered. 'Of course I'll marry you.'

'I've got a ring for you. Bought it ages ago. Find it for you in the morning. Liz, you don't know how awful I've been. I was awful to Mary. It'll be different with you, I promise,' he assured her.

'You're not awful at all,' she told him. 'You're a very dear old heffalump.'

He smiled glassily at that, and repeated that he loved her, loved her and needed her, wanted her very much. At last, like a child who has cried itself out, he shuddered to a halt. Finally he had said, 'I'm so terribly tired. Forgive me, my darling – it's not at all what I had in mind. But I must sleep.'

It was not, thought Liz, exactly the seduction scene she had envisaged, either. Yet she was moved by his helplessness and honesty, by the way in which, with his long-delayed tears, the crusty old Reggie had cracked open to reveal the tender, soft Reggie within. Is it possible, she wondered, that I could come to love this man?

She sat by his bed watching over him, as she had not watched anyone since the days when her children were small and suffered from feverish childhood illnesses that kept them awake and fretful and in constant need of her reassuring presence. Whatever happened to the tender, soft Liz? she asked herself. I've developed a pretty hard shell over the years, too. Eventually she arranged herself on the little settee at the end of his bed, pushed off her sandals and let them drop on to the thick turquoise carpet, curled her feet underneath her, pillowed her head on a couple of tapestry cushions, and slept. The clock in the hall chimed three.

Some time later Reginald woke to a thumping swine of a headache and an urgently full bladder. He got up and began to grope his way to the bathroom. In the faint light he saw Liz, curled up fully dressed at the end of his bed. The sight of her stirred him to recollection, tenderness and desire. In the bathroom he dropped his dirty clothes in the laundry basket as Mrs Owsyerfather had taught him and washed his face and teeth and private parts. Wrapping the striped dressing-gown around himself, he scrutinized his face in the mirror. It was swollen and his eyes looked bloodshot, but what the hell, he thought, it was dark anyway. He tossed down a couple of aspirin for the headache, chased them with two paracetamol, patted some Trumper's cologne on to his jowls, and tiptoed back into the bedroom.

'Liz?' he whispered.

She stirred, murmured, and curled more closely into herself.

'Liz? Darling . . .'

She grumbled under her breath, rearranged her head on the cushions, and slept on. Reginald stood looking down on her. The white dress had ridden up to reveal her long thighs and the curve of her buttocks.

'Liz,' he said more loudly and, bending down, he ran his hand along the undulating lift of her thigh, as far as the line of her pants.

At this she shifted, murmured, 'Don't, please . . . no . . .' and awoke. 'Reggie!' she said. 'What time is it?'

'No idea. Does it matter?'

He bent and ruffled her hair. She lifted her head. He cupped her chin and kissed her.

'My darling,' said Liz. 'Dearest heffalump. Are you all right?'

'Mmm,' said Reggie meaningfully. 'Are you going to come to bed?'

'Get in and keep it warm for me,' said Liz. 'Is that the bathroom?'

She reappeared moments later, still dressed, as he had hoped. In the pale light preceding dawn he could see her quite clearly.

'Take your clothes off for me,' he begged.

Slowly she turned round, so that her back was to him, and lifted the dress up and over her head, dropping it to the floor in an encircling white drift. A white strapless bra bisected her back, a tiny pair of pants curved between her buttocks. She looked over her shoulder at him.

'Undo me,' she ordered.

She sat on the side of the bed and Reggie reached up with trembling fingers to unhook her bra. It fell forward on to her lap. She stood up, kicked the bra aside and took a few paces forward, still with her back turned to him.

Reggie could hardly breathe. She understands! he thought. I didn't have to tell her. She knows, she knows! Her body gleamed in the darkness, very long and slender, and he felt the bad boy becoming great and glad at the sight of her. Finally Liz hooked her thumbs in to her pants and rolled them down her legs. When she was completely naked, she turned round.

'Here I am!' she said.

She jiggled playfully to and fro and sang, in a breathy little Marilyn Monroe voice, 'I wanna be *fucked* by you . . . doo-bi-doo-doo.'

'Show me . . . show me . . .' whispered Reggie hoarsely.

Liz cupped her breasts in her hands and came towards him proffering them like a gift. But despite the aerobics classes, her body was long past its best. Her confidence was only a pretence. She could not help her voice trembling as she asked uncertainly, 'Are they all right? Am I all right? Is this what you want?'

The bad boy wavered, on the verge of subsiding, and then, as Reginald called out urgently, 'Quick! Give them to me! Liz ... hurry ... hurry,' rose up again as she thrust her breasts into his face.

When she awoke in the morning she insisted on leaving at once. 'I don't want the servants to find me here,' she said, and Reggie, whose head was now filled with an agonizing, thundering roar, had not the energy to explain.

'You've got a dreadful hangover,' she told him. 'And so have I. It's the port. Nothing like it for hangovers.'

She knelt beside his bed wearing the white dress.

'Will you be all right? Poor love – we both feel rotten. I'll give you a ring later, sweetheart. But I really *ought* to go home now.' She kissed his throbbing, darkened forehead and Reggie smiled weakly and closed his eyes and let her go.

Reginald was still in bed when Roy arrived several hours later. He clutched his chest and tried to say that it hurt, but the words came out oddly. Roy looked at him in terror. Reginald's face was twisted, his right eye drooped, and that side of his mouth was rigid. His speech was slurred.

'Are you all right, sir? Should I call an ambulance?'

Reginald shook his head and tried to sit up. Roy leaned across the bed to lever him up from the pillows, but the Squadron Leader was too heavy for him, and his limbs seemed slack. His hot, sweating body fell back against the pillows.

'I'm sorry, sir, but you're too heavy. You don't look right. I ought to call a doctor, or else the ambulance. You don't look right at all.'

'Do-er,' Reggie mumbled through twisted lips.

Roy stumbled panic-stricken from the room and half fell down the stairs. There was a telephone in the hall, but where was the local directory? He went into the study and pulled out a leather-bound book of names and addresses. With trembling fingers he turned to D for doctor and there it was, in Madam's looping handwriting: 'Doctor Duncan', and a number. Roy dialled and hurriedly explained what had happened. 'It's urgent,' he pleaded, 'it's urgent. Oh doctor, you'd best come quickly!'

'Keep him warm and the nasal passages clear,' said the doctor in a calm voice. He repeated more simply, 'Make sure he can breathe freely. Don't give him anything to eat or drink. I'll be with you in ten minutes. It's The Cedars, Nevill Park, isn't it?'

'Yes . . . His breathing's very rough, doctor —'

'Don't waste time talking,' the doctor interrupted. 'Stay by him. I'm on my way.'

When Liz rang Reginald that afternoon, there was no reply. Funny, she thought. She tried again an hour later, but there was still no reply. By eight o'clock that evening she began to be alarmed. He wouldn't have gone out without telling her, surely? Could something have happened? He hadn't looked at all well in the morning. She rang every ten minutes and then broke off to watch the news. John McCarthy had been released, but they hadn't shown any pictures of him or his girlfriend after the initial press conference. In any case she couldn't concentrate for worrying about Reginald.

In the end, remembering the name of Reginald's manservant, Southgate, she looked him up in the telephone directory and, on the off chance, rang his number.

'Oh, Madam,' said his agitated voice, 'I'm afraid Doctor says he thinks the Squadron Leader's had a stroke. I didn't know where to get hold of you. I'm ever so sorry, Madam! Oh, he did look bad. I would have rung you, Madam, but I had no idea who you was. Your surname.'

'Franks. Mrs Franks. Never mind that, Southgate,' she said crisply, thinking, Silly old fool not to know my *name*! 'Just tell me where he is now.'

'He's in the Kent & Sussex, Madam. The hospital. The same one where his wife died, and my Grace.'

'In a private ward?'

'No, Madam, he's in Men's Casualty. At least, he was.

They said they might have to move him to Cardiac or even Intensive Care. It depends how he gets on.'

'Will you be back at the house tomorrow?' she asked. 'Can I get in touch with you there?'

'Oh no, Madam,' said Roy. 'I've left Sir. I left yesterday. I'll look in and keep an eye on things, but we're not living together any more. I've gone back to my own home.'

'What about Mrs Simpson?' she asked, bewildered.

'Mrs Simpson?'

'The cook.'

'She doesn't live in, Madam. She was just outside-catering.'

'Who is there, then?' asked Liz irritably.

'There's no one, Madam. Just the Squadron Leader and me. And Fred, the gardener, he comes in a day and a half a week. But he's not due now till Wednesday. That's all there is.'

'Oh,' said Liz. 'I see. Thank you, Southgate.'

She put the receiver down and dialled the hospital.

Liz overruled the hesitation of the nurse who picked up the phone by her crisply authoritative manner, and the Sister by her genuine concern. Sister was eventually convinced that Liz was the fiancée of Mr Conynghame-Jervis in bed number four, but said she would have to talk to the doctor, and the doctor was busy. Eventually Liz learned what had happened. The patient had had a CVA, the doctor explained – a cerebrovascular accident. The circulation of blood to the brain had been interrupted. He must have had an excruciating headache immediately beforehand: hadn't he mentioned it? (And I thought he was just hungover, thought Liz, fool that I was.) There had been some degree of cerebral haemorrhage – hopefully relatively minor – and speech and movement were impaired – on his right side, as luck would have it. They would do a lumbar puncture and a CAT scan in the morning to determine the site and extent of the damage. Meanwhile the patient was reasonably comfortable.

In plain words Reggie had suffered a stroke. Not, they thought at this stage, a major stroke, though one was often followed by another. Quiet and rest and skilful nursing were crucial for the time being. It would be a few days before any long-term prognosis was possible. She was not advised to visit him yet. Excitement must be avoided at all costs.

It was close to midnight, and Liz was exhausted. It had been an exceptionally long day, but she had to know the implications of Reggie's stroke. She took out a medical dictionary. *Among the many possible effects,* it said, *are visual and speech disturbances, incontinence and weakness of the affected parts of the body. There may be severe vertigo, vomiting and double vision.* Dear God! thought Liz. Reginald was not, at least not for the foreseeable future, going to offer a bluff, cheery refuge from her financial crisis, his house a comfortable shelter in which she would be cosseted by a large staff. He was not even going to be the tender, considerate, devoted elderly husband she would have settled for. Reginald was going to be an invalid, wetting and shitting himself, mumbling and staggering, and *she* would become his unpaid nurse. Liz's hopes had been pricked one by one, like so many brightly coloured balloons, and Reggie himself had burst with the biggest pop! of all. She hadn't even, she reflected glumly, got the ring.

Roy was overcome with pity for the mumbling, frightened, sedated and stretcher-borne figure that was his last view of the Squadron Leader; but, however genuine, his pity was overlaid with relief that it was not going to be *his* job to minister to his needs. He had cared for Grace willingly, tenderly, happy to nurse her and see to her most intimate physical functions until almost the very end. But Reginald was a different kettle of fish entirely. Roy's conscience was quite clear on that score. It seemed improbable that the glamorous lady-friend would step in, either, but his first duty was to his grandsons.

June and the boys were noisy, disruptive, unpredictable, high-spirited and demanding – but, above all, *noisy*. The radio blared in the kitchen, June singing the songs she knew and commenting on the disc jockey's ineptitude when she did not. The boys' waking hours were a continuous, animated soundtrack played at top volume. It might be the stutter of simulated gunfire or the shriller whine of laser beams issuing from a starship; the shattering recreation of the last seconds of a head-on car crash or, in their quieter moments, the grunt and thump of straightforward hand-to-hand combat. They moderated their language for Roy's benefit, at least within his earshot, but he felt he should not curb what were, he assumed, the ordinary background noises of two healthy lads at play.

They ate mounds of hamburgers laced with HP sauce and chutney, followed by ice-cream embellished with sweet, sticky juices squeezed out in loops and whorls from plastic tubes. Their appetites were a source of pride to Roy, and an impetus to get back to the allotment.

'I'll have to get going before it's too late to plant,' he told June. 'I let it go this summer, had my hands full with the Squadron Leader, and never seemed to find the time to get up there. Fresh vegetables will do them a power of good: dug straight from the earth, no pesticide sprays, and none of that tasteless out-of-season produce.'

'Don't overdo it, Dad,' she said. 'Take Billy up with you. He's a big lad, he can help with the digging, and it'd be an education for him, watching you plant and weed. He don't know nothing about all that.'

It was true. They were the product of urban streets, their only controls those of threat or immediate punishment. They lacked the moral sense that had been drummed in to Roy as a child by his parents, his teachers and his Sunday school. Old-fashioned and stultifying it may have been, but he had lived his life by those early precepts: honour, decency, hard work, good manners and consideration towards those weaker than yourself. Such concepts were entirely alien to Billy and Joe. They laughed when he tried to explain. Their attitude was simple: you made the most of your advantage where you could, cheated where you could not, and lied your way out of trouble. Their contempt for authority was already evident. Teachers were wankers, policemen pigs.

The figures they admired and imitated were comic or intergalactic villains, whose vocabulary of violence, revenge and pain they copied. Their father's death seemed not to have affected their fantasies of brutality. Or had it perhaps caused them? Roy wondered. His grandsons thought themselves invincible like their screen models and, although the two brothers were close, Billy often wrestled savagely with little Joe and reduced him to tears of pain and humiliation. June, despite her efforts to control herself, would have sudden outbursts of rage. She would hit out savagely at them both, and then clutch them to her, begging forgiveness. 'You know Mum never *means* to hurt you!' she would say, and then apologize shamefacedly to Roy.

In the midst of the chaos that had transformed his orderly little house he had no time to be concerned about Reggie. Several days passed before he visited him at the hospital. He was appalled at the total change which the stroke had brought about.

Reginald recognized him, that was obvious, and struggled to express himself. His twisted mouth fought to shape words; his bulbous eyes yearned and pleaded for comprehension.

'He's doing ever so well!' a buxom physiotherapist told Roy. 'We walked four . . . five . . . *six* steps yesterday, didn't we, Mr Jervis?'

Reginald turned his head petulantly away from her.

'Is there anything I can bring you, sir?' Roy asked.

'Ith-an,' said Reggie.

'Television?' Roy tried.

'Ith-*anne*,' Reggie repeated.

'Lizanne?'

Reginald nodded and shook his head. Comprehension dawned.

'Liz!' Roy said. 'Your lady-friend! Hasn't she been to see you, sir?'

Reginald shook his head and, to Roy's horror, tears formed in the corners of his eyes and ran down the edges of his cheeks into the pillow.

'Ith-*anne*,' said Reggie again. A nurse came to Roy's rescue, beckoning him aside, out of earshot.

'He must be asking for Mrs Franks again,' she said in an undertone. 'That's his fiancée, isn't it? The lady who telephoned a few days ago. She said her name was Liz Franks. I think he'd like her to come and see him. Do you know her whereabouts?'

'No,' said Roy, 'but I'll find out. She rang me Sunday, the day he was brought in. I didn't know she was his fiancée. I'll get her number and say that he wants her to come and see him, if you think that would cheer him up.'

Reginald had closed his eyes. Roy patted his shoulder uncertainly, said he would look in again soon, and left the ward. The hospital reminded him poignantly of Grace's last weeks. He hadn't entered it since her death, and now the linoleum-covered corridors, the plastic chairs for visitors, the identical lockers beside each curtained bed, the get-well cards, the flowers – all made hope and grief surge once again, as they had done during those final weeks.

On his way out, the Sister intercepted him. 'I wonder if I might have a word?' she asked, guiding him into her small, cluttered office. A poster on the wall instructed, 'For Your Heart's Sake Get Off Your Butt.' The stout, seated character depicted, cigarette in hand, looked disconcertingly like Reggie. 'Forgive me, but you are Mr Conynghame-Jervis's first visitor. Do you know, does he have any close family? Children?'

'No, no children,' said Roy. 'He has a nephew, Lord Somebody-or-other – wait, it's coming back to me: could it be Lord Glenmorangie?'

Sister smiled and shook her head. 'Somehow I doubt it,' she said.

'Well, there was a Lord and Lady Someone who came to his wife's funeral last year; they were family. But they've never visited him at home, as far as I know. Apart from them and his lady-friend – fiancée, she says, though it's the first I've heard of it – he doesn't have any friends that I know of.'

How strange this was, Roy reflected, given that Reginald was so gregarious. He had often gone to the pub for meals and must have had drinking companions there, but he hardly ever had any telephone calls or letters, except on business. Few if any visitors had come to The Cedars. Those who did were professional people – the vicar, Mandy Hope, the doctor. Reginald had even been reduced to booking a table at the Spa Hotel for his Christmas lunch. The first Christmas after his wife died, and no one had invited him. It was worse than strange: it was disgraceful. And then of course there had been Liz.

'Does she telephone regularly, this *fiancée*?' Roy inquired.

'She rang a couple of times, shortly after he'd been admitted. Since she heard his prognosis – and I had to be honest with her and say that it will be some time before we know how much improvement to hope for – she hasn't rung again. Might *I* ask, who exactly are you?'

'I moved in with the Squadron Leader – he does hate it, by the way, being called Mr Jervis. Just thought I'd mention it – about nine, ten months ago. But now I'm not with him no more.'

'You looked after him?'

'Yes, but he looked after me, too. We was both widowed together and ever so lonely, and the vicar suggested I might care to keep him company, get him sorted out, he not being the domestic type. It worked a treat until Alan, my son, died. After that his wife and my grandsons came to live with me, so I had to move back in to my own house.'

'Well!' said Sister. She grinned at him. 'You *have* been doing your stuff. But where does that leave him? Stroke victims need a lot of TLC – tender loving care – over the first few months if they're to walk and talk reasonably normally again. That's between ourselves, of course. Don't tell *him* that. Once he's discharged he'll need full-time nursing care for a bit, but even if he makes a good recovery he oughtn't to live on his own. He could have another CVA at any time. We shall try and persuade him to stop smoking and cut down on his alcohol consumption. That would help his chances a lot.'

'What do you want me to do, Sister?' Roy asked.

247

'There doesn't seem to be a lot you *can* do. I'll get in touch with his doctor, find out from him who the nearest relatives are, wait for Mrs Franks to pay him a visit.'

'Is he going to be all right?' Roy asked.

'A lot depends on how well he's looked after and how much he wants to get better,' she answered. 'And now, Mr . . .?'

'Southgate.'

'I must be getting on. I'm most grateful for your help. Leave me your telephone number, in case of emergency.'

'He's ever such a nice old bloke,' Roy confided suddenly. 'His bark's much worse than his bite. It's a crying shame, him lying there all by himself. He doesn't deserve that. I'll try and look in again soon.'

'You've got your hands full, by the sound of it,' she said. 'Leave it to us. We'll sort something out. I'll let you know what happens if he's moved.'

Roy left, hurrying past the folding wheelchairs in the entrance with their corrugated black handgrips for frail fingers and oxygen cylinders for emergencies; past the handwritten notice saying bleakly, 'Tea, Coffee, Biscuits'; past the clock which said four-twenty-seven. Below it was a small wooden box marked 'The League of Friends. Please Help Us To Help You.' Who's going to help the Squadron Leader? he thought fiercely. He was a war hero, wasn't he? One of the Few. Fought for his country. He can't help it that he's got no children, only that posh Lord chappie and his stuck-up wife. They can blooming well get down here to see him. Blood's thicker than water. Poor old Squadron Leader: he doesn't deserve this!

Reginald lay in the narrow hospital bed, his mind like an overturned fishtank, his body suffering a dozen different kinds of discomfort. He could hear and understand everything around him but seemed unable to enunciate his words so that anyone could understand *him*. His first response to what had happened so savagely and unexpectedly had been throat-catching terror; but he had experienced terror many times before, and learned to use the adrenalin of rage to overcome it. Flat out in his hospital bed, therefore, Reggie was in an extremely bad temper and frustrated by the fact that no one seemed to recognize this. He craved a cigarette, but there was precious little chance that anybody was going to provide one, let alone allow him to smoke. His second desire was to see Liz. She obviously had no idea where he was. He kept trying to tell the nurses her name and telephone number. He tried to write, but his hand was even more unreliable than his lips. Not to worry, they said, in another day or two you'll start working with the speech therapist. Their bland and kindly reassurance was maddening. He needed Liz *now*.

His buttocks were sore from lying on the rubber undersheet, which chafed and made him too hot. The food the nurses spooned into the side of his mouth was revolting, but all appetite was killed by the nausea that welled up in him. From time to time he vomited. Worst of all, he had difficulty controlling his bladder and bowels, and if they did not bring a bedpan the instant he rang, piss and worse would dribble out of him, filling him with shame. The nurses would roll him briskly this way and that as they made up the bed with clean sheets, and never reproached him.

'You're a very *dirty* little boy, Master Reginald!' Nanny used to scold. Three years old (or was it five or seven or nine?) and still wetting the bed like a baby! 'I can't *help* it, Nanny,' he would say, 'it happens in my sleep.' Even when he had learned to control his sphincter and mistrust those insinuating dreams in which he spilled his bursting bladder with infinite relief into the lavatory bowl, only to be woken by a spreading wet warmth on the previously clean, dry sheet – even then, the prospect of going back to school could make him disgrace himself like a baby again.

Worst of all were the mornings in the dormitory. He would leap out of bed and pull up the bedclothes to conceal the evidence, but the older boys knew the signs and would rip back the sheets and mock him. 'Conynghame-Jervis has done it again! Have you been pissing, C-J?' they would ask. Or shagging – long before he knew what that word meant. When once, in an attempt to find out, he answered that he had shagged, they mocked him more than ever. 'You're filthy!' they said. 'You'll have hair growing on the palms of your hands! Show us . . . show us . . . Have you got hairy palms yet?' And they laughed at his horrified eleven-year-old face.

He had asked Nanny, when he got home, what the word meant but she had said, 'Don't let me hear such language on your lips ever again, Master Reginald,' and made him wash his mouth out with sour carbolic soap. Afterwards she had comforted him: 'Never mind. Plenty of time for that when you're grown up. You'll learn, and if you're a good boy you'll find there's more ways than one of stuffing a duck!' More mystified than ever, he had asked Gerald what it was all about, but even his brother had growled something incomprehensible and turned away. Not until he was a prefect of thirteen and about to leave prep school for Sedbergh had his house-master explained about wet dreams, and suddenly Reginald had understood what was meant by shagging. He blushed with retrospective shame.

Nobody talked about child abuse then, he thought, and none of the masters laid a finger on me; but we were abused all the same. Throughout my life I hadn't a hope of enjoying straightforward, happy sex because of those damned early accidents. Sex and peeing were one and the same thing, both equally dirty. By the time Mary and I tried to make our own fantasy world so that we could do it and not feel guilty, the confusion between sex and pissing had gone but the one between sex and death had taken over. Did everyone feel the same orgasmic excitement as they lined up the ME 109 in their sights, and let loose the tracer bullets, and watched the stream of flame issuing, spurting forth into the helpless target? Closer than brothers we were in the officers' mess, yet I could never have asked anyone that.

When the war ended we were supposed to forget about killing and being young heroes and turn into hard-working civilians in a peacetime world, settling down to desks and offices as though we had never plundered the sky. I did my best. I fathered a child, a perfect child, happy, trusting, golden . . . The forty-year-old wound, freshly reopened, made him grimace and shut his eyes and roll his head to and fro. A nurse hurried over to his bed.

'Are you all right, Mr Conynghame-Jervis? Do you need a bedpan?'

Reginald would turn into the pillow and doze during the day, exhausted by ten or fifteen minutes of strenuous physiotherapy. This meant he lay awake at night; he refused both sleeping pills and tranquillizers. He knew he had to keep what was left of his body alert and not let it slip further away from him, flabby, boneless, useless. During the long wakeful hours he listened to the other patients snoring and wheezing, groaning in pain, calling out feebly, 'Nurse! Nurse!' His mind worked, planning the future.

If I get over this, he promised himself, I shall fuck Liz with a clear conscience. But as well as that I shall *notice* her, listen to her, ask her opinion; this time I will share my life with her, not just let her exist alongside me. That lesson I have learned. We will travel together when I get my strength back, we'll visit friends, go up to London, meet her children. I want to get to know her children. What did she say they were called? The boy was Hugo, but the girl? Cecily was all that came into his mind, Cecily, Cecily, Tush, my Tushy.

Torn between the longing for Liz and distaste at the thought of her seeing him in his present state of physical incompetence, Reggie waited for her visit but stopped trying to bring it about. Meanwhile he co-operated urgently, angrily, with the physio and speech therapist, forcing his body to relearn the infantile skills of walking and talking. I *will not* be old! he thought, brimming with the uprush of deep internal furies. I have the chance to get it right this time; I refuse to be old, to disintegrate, to be tidied away and consigned to a home and collapse and mumble and fumble and stumble and smell and leak. I am going to make a complete recovery and begin life again with a wonderful young wife and *astonish them all*.

*

251

Reginald lay in bed one lunchtime, two weeks after he had first arrived, smelling the greasy, tepid smell of reheated beef, damp carrots, cabbage and burnt roast potatoes – the hospital's standard Sunday treat. Turning his head at the sound of stolid footsteps approaching, he suddenly beamed, with a beam that matched her own.

Speaking in vowels, as he had to nowadays, Reggie said, 'I-i Ow-er-ah-er!'

'How many times do I have to tell you? You can call me Mrs Odejayi or you can call me Aggie, but you will *not* call me Mrs Owsyerfather!'

'I e-y ad oo ee ou!' said Reginald.

'And I'm glad to see you, though it's more than you deserve! But the good Lord has punished you enough for the wicked words you spoke to me, so I'll forgive you. Never mind that – I'd have come to visit you long ago, if anyone had thought to tell me you was here!'

Still beaming down upon him, she leaned over to give him a kiss. The smell of bleach and carbolic and womanly sweat filled his nostrils, seeming to Reggie the sweetest, cleanest smell he had ever known.

A month ago he would have regarded her as beneath him for half a dozen reasons – black, a woman, working class, fat, middle-aged – but today he was overcome with affection towards her.

'Aggie!' he said, enunciating clearly for the first time.

She called out to all and sundry, 'There now! Did you hear that? And if that ain't this Sunday's miracle, I don't know what is. Can you do it again, Squadron Leader?'

'Aggie!' he cried joyously, 'Aggie, Aggie, Aggie!'

Chapter Fifteen

While her own future collapsed around her and even Russia seemed about to retreat from glad morning back into darkest Communism, Liz sat out the warm, wet August days in the shop. She was poised between two courses of action so finely balanced that she could not move a step towards either. Today, with not a single paying customer all morning, she had plenty of time to consider the alternatives.

One possibility was to go ahead with this suddenly preposterous marriage and become – for the foreseeable future – Reginald's wife and unpaid nurse. It seemed clear that he would be an invalid for several months to come and was heading for a doddery old age. Liz had not been able to bring herself to visit him in hospital. She hardly knew how to confront him, after their previous encounter, and was in no hurry to see for herself whether Roy's graphic description of his shambling movements, his slobbering and gibbering, was accurate.

Roy had rung her again a week after Reggie had been admitted, sounding thoroughly lugubrious. 'He can't get his words out very clear just at the minute, but they've started him on speech therapy and they say it does wonders. He's ever so determined to get better: already out of bed and practising his walking. It all depends, Sister says, on how much encouragement he gets . . .' Roy added meaningfully.

'It's awfully kind of you to have visited him, Southgate,' Liz had offered.

'*Mr* Southgate to you,' Roy muttered under his breath. Then he said, 'He's been asking for you, the nurses think, though sometimes it's a bit hard to make out what he means. They said there was a lady that rang to inquire after him and said she was his fiancée. I didn't know you was engaged.'

'Yes,' said Liz. 'Well, this is a very busy time of year for me.'

'It's up to you, Madam, of course. He's going to be there for another two weeks at least, and after that –'

· 'Very good of you to ring and let me know, *Mr* Southgate,' Liz concluded firmly, making no promises.

It would be different, she thought, if we were already married. I wouldn't have much choice then. I don't love him, and I don't suppose he actually loved me. We seemed, very briefly, to be in a convenient state of mutual need. But now all that's changed I am *not* going to put my head into the noose. I don't pretend to be a particularly nice person. I don't think I've been nice or good since David left – my erring, irresponsible, irresistible young husband, *still*, damn him, the only man I have ever really loved. After he went, I stuck it out with the kids, twelve years' hard labour on my own, but that's my lot as far as service and self-sacrifice goes.

Why should I become Reginald's unpaid nursemaid now, just because I went to bed with him once? He fancied me and I gave in. It isn't *my* fault that he had a stroke next day. He'd been looking apoplectic for months, smoking like a chimney, drinking far too much: his blood pressure must have been way over the top. Someone else can do the sweetness-and-light number for poor old Reginald. Liz knew she was being ungenerous, but her own disappointment – just when she seemed to have solved her problems – was such that she felt no sympathy towards Reggie, only indignation. She blamed him for her current predicament.

The other course of action, then, was to do what the bank insisted was unavoidable in any case, and sell the business. The bank manager had taken to asking for the shop's weekly accounts and not even a suicidal end-of-season sale brought in enough customers to cheer up the books. There was perilously little to show on the credit side and her ninety days' grace was running out. Meanwhile Lissy had rung twice asking for money. Each time, Liz had taken a couple of large notes from the till and put them quickly in to an envelope, posting it off before prudence could get the better of her; but one hundred pounds was over a third of last week's profit.

She looked up as a woman she recognized entered the shop. 'Can I help you? Are you looking for something special, or just browsing?'

'Hello,' said the woman. 'Don't I know you? Hang on, wherever from? Gosh, how rude. I am sorry: I work in the library, and I meet so many people there I can never – my name's Constance Liddell.'

'I'm Liz Franks. Don't we both go to Jenny's aerobics classes twice a week?'

'Of *course*. That's right!' the woman said. 'Though *I* don't manage to get there every week, I'm afraid. Please don't worry about me. I'm not really sure what I'm looking for. It's mainly to kill time in my lunch hour.'

'Is it something for the evening?' Liz asked. 'A wedding? Or what?'

'Oh, just something halfway decent to go out to dinner in. Suddenly everything I possess looks old and tired.'

'You couldn't've come at a better time,' Liz told her. 'All the stock is down by 50 per cent, sometimes more, and there's a huge selection. Now, let me see. You're dark with green eyes. You're what they call an autumn. All the spicy browns and reds and yellows suit you.'

'Do they?' Constance asked. 'I mainly wear beige and olive sort of colours. Sludge. Practical, washable and invisible. And red or black at night.'

'*No* one should wear red at night,' said Liz, 'unless they're very young and very blonde. It drains all the colour from the face and deposits it around the hips. No, try *this*.' She held up a long, narrow dress of rust-coloured crêpe. 'Is it for dinner in or dinner out?'

'Out,' said Constance, and she smiled. 'To tell you the truth, it's a new bloke. I've only just met him and he invited me out to dinner. Amazing that he ever spotted me. I thought my protective colouring was almost perfect. Anyway I decided something new would boost my morale, if not make me into a dazzling conversational genius. Or whatever it is he's looking for.'

'Course it will!' said Liz. 'Lucky you! *I* could do with a new bloke!'

Constance smiled sympathetically. 'Isn't it ridiculous? Here we are – well, I don't know about you, but I've got grown-up children, grandchildren as well for that matter, and yet I still get in a total tizz when some attractive male asks me out for the first time.'

'*You* don't look old enough to be a grandmother,' Liz said automatically, since every woman expected to be told that. 'Anyway, what difference does age make, in the battle of the sexes?'

'Oh dear,' said Constance. 'Do you really think it's a battle? I do *try* and tell myself it's a bit more civilized than that.'

'Don't you believe it,' Liz told her bitterly. 'Sex or war – that's all that interests men. Did you *listen* to them earlier on this year, during the Gulf War? They were revelling in it. *Loved* it.'

Constance Liddell agreed that autumn colours suited her and promised that she would bear it in mind, especially if her dinner went well. Liz tucked her cheque under the tray in the till and folded the dress carefully into a glossy Chic-to-Chic carrier bag.

'Good luck!' she said. 'Let me know how it goes.'

There's always hope, Liz reflected as the bell jangled merrily. Look at her: must be my age, hasn't even taken as good care of herself as I have, and yet *some* man, somewhere, thinks she's worth buying dinner for. Why have I been behaving as though Reginald were the last man in the world? What's to stop me selling up – shop, house, the lot – and starting again in, say, Italy or France in one of those elegant little shops in some warm provincial town catering for smart local women and their gorgeously sexy foreign husbands? Calm down, Liz, she told herself soberly. You have a daughter who is five months pregnant, which is one very good reason why you can't decamp.

I can't avoid it any longer, she concluded. I must, I shall have to, go and see Reginald. Oh God, poor old heffalump.

Poor old me. Still, I might as well know the worst. She closed the shop punctually at five-thirty, bought a small bunch of flowers and a miniature bottle of Glenmorangie, didn't bother to change, ran her hands through her hair, gave herself a blast of scent behind the ears and headed up Mount Pleasant Road towards the hospital.

Reginald's GP had taken a week to muster enough time and initiative to consult an outdated *Who's Who* and look up his patient's relatives. From it he learned that Reginald's nephew Vivian was Lord Blythgowrie (3rd Baron), a member of the Reform Club and the Ski Club of Great Britain; that his hobbies were skiing, fishing and opera; and that he was group chairman of Jervis Developments plc. Sounds pretty fly to me, thought Dr Duncan. With any luck he'll be able to lay out a few quid towards a decent private nursing home, since, unless I'm way off beam, that's where poor old Conynghame-Jervis will be spending the next few months. He picked up the telephone and dialled a City number.

Roy was standing in the kitchen peeling potatoes for a shepherd's pie. June, who was meant to be chopping onions, had put down her knife and was telling Roy alarming stories from her colourful childhood. The boys were out playing in the recreation ground up the road. Despite his efforts to maintain order and keep the place in a condition that Grace would approve, the kitchen was already showing signs of wear and tear. The lino was badly scuffed round the back door, there was mud by the sink where the boys would wash their hands (under protest) before meals, and the larder door showed the prints of grubby fingers.

'Junie . . .' said Roy. 'I hate to bother you, love, but could you get a cloth and mop up round the sink and by the door? The boys've left marks again. Don't know why. I put the doormat outside the back; they've only to wipe their feet, doesn't take a minute.'

'Oh never mind, Dad. What's the point?' June asked. 'If I

do it now, they'll only make it mucky again in ten minutes, and I hate moaning on at them. Boys will be boys.'

'They've got to learn,' Roy insisted. 'When Grace was alive she was that house-proud, the whole place shone. The Queen could have come for tea any day, needn't have given warning, we could have entertained her just as we was.'

'It was easier with just the two of you,' June said wearily. 'Kids always make a mess. Doesn't do no good to keep on at 'em.'

'Sorry I spoke,' said Roy, and wringing out the floorcloth that was kept under the sink, he bent down and swabbed the muddy footprints himself. June picked up the knife and chopped the onions vigorously into tiny transparent squares.

'I hope they'll eat it,' she said dubiously. 'Your shepherd's pie. They like hamburgers best.'

'Make a change, then, won't it?' said Roy. 'I'll just get it going in the oven, and then I thought I'd nip up the road and look in on the Squadron Leader. Must be days since I saw him. He'll have made great progress. He's got a wonderful spirit. One look at him and you can see why we won the Battle of Britain.'

'You do that, Dad,' June said.

They worked in silence. June would have preferred to get on and prepare the supper alone. She was irritated by his old-womanish ways, knew she owed him respect and gratitude, and already resented this. Roy was appalled by the slovenliness all three had revealed in their first weeks under his roof, and convinced that this was a golden opportunity to instruct the boys in good manners and proper behaviour. Start as you mean to go on, he thought. Once let them get into bad habits and it'll be too late. He mashed the potatoes, added butter and milk and pounded them to a rich smoothness.

'If you'd lay the table for four while I'm away?' he suggested.

'Not worth the bother,' June pointed out. 'They'll only take their plates next door to watch telly. Might as well let them eat it on their laps.'

'Suit yourself,' said Roy. 'You're their mother. Don't mind me.'

'Look, Dad,' said June, her voice on edge. 'You've done a wonderful thing, opening your house to us, making us welcome, and I'm really really grateful, don't think I'm not. But you can't turn two south London boys from Balham into nice Tunbridge Wells lads in a week. Give 'em time. Let them settle down, find their feet. No good nagging at 'em: you'll just make 'em fret for what they've left behind. They miss their friends as it is. They're worried about this new school. It's a lot of changes for them to digest. Give it time.'

'You know best,' said Roy. He hung up Grace's apron, put on his jacket and cap, and headed for the front door.

Roy stopped off at the newsagent to buy the *Telegraph* for the Squadron Leader and, after a moment's hesitation, a packet of Benson & Hedges. I know he's not allowed them, he thought, but I bet he's not half longing for a smoke! I remember during the war how you'd kill for a fag at times. I can slip them in his locker.

Roy was surprised, when he reached the ward, to see a visitor there already. Sister was standing beside Reginald's bed, looking both deferential and somehow defensive. The Squadron Leader lay on top of the bed, his hospital dressing-gown wrapped inadequately around his middle. Roy could see that he had lost weight. He tucked his cap into one pocket and approached tentatively.

'Ah, Souvgay!' Reginald said. 'Vair oo ah! Ow goo' ov oo-oo come! Vivian, viv iv my ma', Sou'gay. My nevew, Lor' Blyvgowie.'

'Pleased to meet you, sir,' said Roy.

'How do you do? Gather you're the one who found him,' said Vivian Blythgowrie. 'Sorry nobody got in touch with me sooner.'

'I didn't know who you were, sir,' said Roy, flustered. 'Or where you lived or who to inform. My first thought was to get the Squadron Leader into hospital.'

'Of course. But after that . . . Couldn't be helped, I dare say. Rather unfortunate, though. Fortnight passed before anyone thought to contact me. Nearest relative and so on. Pretty obvious.'

Sister intervened nervously. 'Isn't he doing *well*?' she asked Roy. '*You* must see the improvement?'

'You've done wonders,' said Roy. 'I wouldn't never have believed it, not after the way he was when he come in. Well *done*, sir!' he added to Reggie.

'Can I av a vigrett ven plea'?' Reginald asked the Sister.

'You may certainly *not*,' she replied. 'Fewer cigarettes in the first place and you probably wouldn't be here now!'

Roy caught Reginald's eye and winked heavily. 'I've brought you your *Telegraph*, sir,' he said. 'I'll just slip it into the locker. For *later*,' he added meaningfully.

'Goo' ma',' said Reginald gratefully.

'Now look here,' Vivian began. 'We ought to do some advance planning. Lot to talk about. May be a week or more before I can get down again.'

Roy was just about to take his leave when Reginald's eyes widened and a deep blush suffused his face. Roy turned to follow his gaze, and saw Liz entering the ward dressed in narrow trousers, high heels and a vivid shirt.

''Ood 'od!' said Reggie involuntarily.

'Mrs Franks!' said Roy.

'Who's *that*?' asked Vivian.

'Ith my veeanthay, Mith Fwank,' said Reginald, struggling to lever himself upright. Roy put an arm under one side, and he and Sister manoeuvred him into a sitting position. They exchanged a knowing, conspiratorial grin.

'I must be getting on,' Sister said, 'if you'll excuse me.' She walked rapidly away, her crêpe-soled shoes squeaking.

'Darling! How are you?' said Liz, bending to kiss Reginald. Retaining one of her hands in his own puffy one, Reginald explained as best as he could to his nephew that he and Liz were engaged.

'Lord Blythgowrie!' Liz said charmingly. 'I am delighted to

meet you at last. Sorry that it should be around his hospital bed, of course, poor Reggie . . . Such *rotten* luck.'

She cursed herself for not having changed or at least put lipstick on, and for what she now saw was a miserably stingy bunch of flowers, but Reginald beamed at her proudly and his eyes shone.

'Well,' said Roy, though he longed to stay and see what happened next, 'I'll be off home. Time to give the boys their tea. Supper.'

'Vanks *vair mu*' vor comin',' said Reggie significantly.

'I'll look in again soon. Honoured to have met you, my Lord. Goodbye, Mrs Franks.'

He settled his cap back on his head and left the ward.

'Reginald didn't tell me he was *engaged*,' said Vivian accusingly.

'Tol' ve girz,' said Reggie.

'It's very recent,' said Liz. 'Though we've known each other for quite a long time. It's nearly a year now, isn't it, darling?'

'Ockober,' said Reginald.

Liz released her hand, which was growing sweaty in Reginald's grasp, and, to compensate, gazed intently into his eyes. He's lost some weight, she thought. Colour's better; those awful veins on his forehead have gone. How about his speech?

'You're looking wonderful, Reggie,' she told him. '*So* much better. How do you feel?'

'Veelin' vine. Be even be'er if vey'd le' me fmoke.'

'You can't *possibly* smoke, darling,' Liz said. 'Can he, Lord Blythgowrie?'

Vivian shot her a patronizing glance and Liz thought, OK, not to be won round. Well, at least I know where I stand.

'I'm sure Reginald is well aware that he can't ever smoke again,' Vivian said crisply. 'And now, Mrs Franks, I wonder if you'd be so good as to allow me five minutes on my own with my uncle, and then perhaps if you know of anywhere decent locally, we might have a glass of wine together before I return to London.'

'*That* would be nice,' she said, riled by his adroitness in putting her down. 'Reggie, sweetheart, I'll look in again soon. Mmm . . .' She kissed his forehead, clasped one hand in both of hers for a moment, murmured 'My darling,' and left his bedside.

'Who is that?' asked Vivian, the moment she was out of earshot. 'Is she really your fiancée, Uncle Reginald? In which case, is she living with you? Or do you plan to move her in? Can she look after you? Because I rather think you're going to need a fair amount of nursing from now on. *And* someone to monitor your alcohol intake.'

Yes, Reginald explained laboriously, Liz Franks was indeed his fiancée, though they hadn't got round to deciding when they would marry. He hoped very much that she would live with him as soon as possible, since he had no desire – '*oh* i-ire' – to be transferred to a nursing home and was keen to leave this infernal hospital as quickly as possible.

'Right,' said Vivian. 'Well that gives me some idea of how matters stand for the time being. I'll have a word with Mrs Franks and see how she's placed. Meanwhile I'll come down again as soon as I can, with a bit of luck before the end of the month. Trip to Hong Kong coming up in September. Do you want me to send the girls to see you?'

'No!' said Reginald, with surprising emphasis. 'Vanks or ve same, bu' no.'

'Susan?' said Vivian, doubtfully.

No, not Susan.

'Anyone else?'

No, no one, Reggie assured him stubbornly. He was fine. Or would be, as soon as he got out of here.

'Want me to inquire about a private hospital? You must be with BUPA?'

No, neither a private hospital nor a nursing home. Reginald wanted to go back to his own home and sleep in his own bed. With Liz, he added to himself.

Vivian Blythgowrie felt he had done all that could be expected of him, and took his leave with a firm handshake and a half-formed reassurance: 'Anything you need, sure you'll . . .?

Jolly good.' Had he turned to wave as he left the ward, he would have seen Reginald ferreting in his locker for the *Telegraph*, and his hand closing gleefully upon the Benson & Hedges packet.

Liz was waiting in the corridor outside. She had applied some lipstick and tucked the shirt into her trousers, the better to display what was, Vivian conceded, an excellent figure for a woman who must be in her fifties.

'Sorry to keep you waiting,' he said brusquely. 'My car's outside.'

They descended to the ground floor and walked past the new hospital building towards the large car park at the back. A Rolls Royce detached itself from the ranks of parked cars and glided smoothly to a halt beside them. As the chauffeur slipped out to open the door and Vivian handed her in, Liz felt like a schoolgirl being taken out on Parents' Weekend.

'Where are we going?' Vivian asked.

'I thought the Spa Hotel might do,' said Liz. 'Just at the top of Reggie's road, if you know where that is. The bar isn't too bad.'

'Can you direct the driver?' he said, and she did so clearly and concisely.

He chose a table in the far corner of the Equestrian Bar, beside the window, and Liz sat down. Vivian Blythgowrie had a word with the barman and returned a moment later, followed shortly afterwards by the barman bearing a bottle of wine and two glasses. How does he do it? Liz thought to herself, this born-to-command act? Normally this place makes you buy wine by the glass.

As though answering her question, Vivian said, 'I explained that we should prefer to be left in peace. Now then . . .' He poured two glasses of wine and Liz sipped from hers. He can make the first move, she thought.

'Did you ever meet Reginald's first wife, Mary?' he asked.

'He and I only met one another in October,' Liz said. 'Mary died in . . . June, wasn't it . . . of last year.'

'She was very different from you.'

263

'Yes,' said Liz composedly, 'I imagine she must have been.'

'She was a very sweet, generous person. Immensely kind to my daughters.'

Liz nodded. 'How nice.' Bastard, she thought.

Blythgowrie took several sips of wine. Liz watched him. He is, she thought, arrogant, very much used to power, and exceedingly sexy. I can just about catch a look of Reggie in him, though he's tougher and brighter than the poor old heffalump can ever have been. Must be the same age as me.

On impulse she said, 'I wonder if you would have known my first husband? You and he might have been contemporaries.'

'Oh?' he said, sceptically.

'David Franks,' she stated. David had been a cricket Blue; they could easily both have been at Oxford at the beginning of the Sixties.

'Ah,' said Vivian. 'Yes, I believe the name rings a bell.' He sipped from his glass noncommittally as she watched him in silence.

'Mrs Franks,' he said, 'you will forgive me if I seem businesslike, but I am Reginald's nearest living relative, and I'm bound to say this engagement is news to me. He has not, as far as I know, mentioned you hitherto.'

'No,' said Liz, 'but then, I believe you haven't seen him for several months?'

'Be that as it may,' conceded Vivian, 'could you put my mind at rest on one or two points? I'm sure you'll tell me if you feel I'm being intrusive. You and David Franks were married long?'

'Over ten years. About as long as you and your first wife, I believe?'

He ignored that. 'And you're now divorced?'

'Certainly.'

'So presumably David Franks supports you and – do you have any children?'

'I have two grown-up children, yes.'

He waited for her to amplify that.

264

'My daughter, Alicia, works at the Soho Brasserie. I don't suppose you know it, but your daughters might. My son, Hugo, is currently travelling.'

'Drugs?' said Vivian.

She met his eyes steadily. 'Yes. Something, unfortunately, of which many parents nowadays have had experience.'

'Yes,' he said.

There was a long pause, during which he refilled their glasses. Liz felt her colour rising. Steady on, she told herself, you're doing well. Don't spoil it by getting reckless. She waited again for him to speak.

'My uncle,' said Vivian Blythgowrie eventually, 'is, as you must know, fairly comfortably off. He is not, however, a rich man. I don't know whether you are privy to the terms of Mary's will?'

'No.'

'Perhaps he would not object to my telling you that he has the use of the house during his lifetime, but after his death, half of it – his wife's half, so to speak – is left to a children's charity.'

Damn and blast him, thought Liz, arrogant upper-class shit.

'Ah yes,' she said. 'Because of Cecily, I imagine?'

That rocked him. '*Cecily?*' he asked, and then, recovering himself, continued, 'Of course. Their daughter. Tragic. Mary never got over that.'

'Nor,' said Liz, 'has Reggie.'

'Furthermore,' Vivian continued, 'Reginald has a small fixed income, derived from a family trust which I administer, and few if any investments. In other words, an income more than adequate for his own needs, but –'

'Not, you are thinking, sufficient for mine?' said Liz.

'I see we understand one another perfectly.'

'No,' replied Liz. 'We do not. That is to say, I understand you very well. You, however, are making a number of unjustified, and indeed insulting, assumptions about me. You have not met me or heard about me before because you and your wife have so little concern for your uncle, whose "nearest living relative" you are, that you have not seen him since his wife's funeral – over a year ago. You did not even have the decency to invite him to join you for Christmas.'

'We were skiing, in Switzerland, actually,' he said, in an attempt to regain the initiative.

'I am sure Reginald would have enjoyed that, given the chance,' she retorted. 'And now you have the nerve to pry into *my* affairs. Let me tell you that *I* am practically the only person in the last year who has had the slightest concern for Reginald's welfare. Where were you? Where were his friends? His wife's friends? You abandoned him, one and all, to *rot* in his comfortable house in Tunbridge Wells! If it weren't for that man you met earlier at his bedside, Southgate, who has looked after him devotedly, your uncle Reginald would have gone to pot. And *you* wouldn't even have known about it. I take exception, therefore, very great exception, to your inquisition. I do not propose to enlighten you as to my plans. Perhaps when you next see him, *when* you have a moment to spare, your uncle will tell you them for himself. Good evening, Lord Blythgowrie!'

She walked out thinking, Damn, damn, *damn* him!

Later that evening, swept home on a tide of such incandescent rage that she could not remember how she got there, later, sitting over a page of figures and bank statements, Elizabeth Franks thought, The truly bloody thing about that unspeakably bloody man is that he is absolutely *right*. I was of *course* interested in Reginald's money, though God knows why else anyone should want to marry him; and now that I know how he's placed it has tipped the scales conclusively against him.

An open bottle of wine stood at her right elbow. Liz had written down her major assets – house, car, shop – and what they might fetch. If she reckoned £135,000 for the house; £50,000 for the business (stock, goodwill, and eight years left on the lease); and £2,500 for the car (a lipstick-red MG, twenty years old but a 'modern classic', the garage said) – this came, at worst, to just under £190,000. Take away the mortgage of £40,000 and the bank loan of £22,000, and she had £120,000 in the world. Then there were a few tax and VAT bills to pay. But, even so, she couldn't have less than £100,000. Nothing else, of course, but still, £100,000 seemed a good round sum.

The real question was, what did she propose to do with it? France, she thought wistfully, would be idyllic. Little town in the south – not the Mediterranean, the fewer tourists the better: just the natives – with terracotta tiles and flat roofs; market day on Saturdays, long lazy afternoons . . . The perfect combination of business and pleasure. She smiled. Maybe Lissy would come as well. The baby would grow up brown and bilingual. What's to stop us? Nothing!

Emptying her wine glass, Liz realized she had eaten no supper and, thanks to Constance Liddell, no lunch either, but that, none the less (*néanmoins*, memory supplied helpfully), counting bloody Blythgowrie's two glasses, she had got through a bottle and a half of wine. That being so, she said to herself carefully and sensibly, I must be more than somewhat pissed. Which is not to say I shall change my mind in the morning, because I won't. Will I? No!

The telephone made her jump. Oof! Who's that? Blythgowrie, crawling apology? No. Reggie, hospital maunderings? Hope not. Dunno. Pick it up, then, silly cow.

'Hello?'

Lissy.

'Darling! I was just thinking about you. How *are* you? How's the bulge? Are you in a phone-box? Want me to call you back? No. Good.'

Just had a card from her father. For her birthday. Bit late.

'From Daddy? How?'

Sent it to her bank.

'I say, clever old him. Where is he?'

Somewhere in the south of France.

'Did he sign off with one name at the end of it, darling, or two?'

Just one. Just his. Why?

'Because, my treasure, I have just had the most brilliant idea. I am going to take a train to the south of France. Tomorrow, if I can fix it. Well, no, not tomorrow, but as soon as possible. I am going to find your father, and when I've found him, I shall tell him he's about to become a grandfather. Now tell me again, slowly: *what* was the postmark?'

Chapter Sixteen

'I really like that Gorby and his wife,' said June. 'What's her name? Not Rita – Raisa. Sort of Russian version of Rita, I expect. I thought it was all going to go back to the bad old days. I saw this TV programme last year, about Stalin. Terrible, what he did. Worse than Hitler.'

'Nothing changes,' said Roy. 'Human nature don't change. You think it does, but people is always the same underneath. You got to train them, civilize them, or they'll always be animals.'

'No, Dad. People is different. Takes all sorts. There'll always be bad eggs, I grant, but most people try to be decent. Love your neighbour,' she added vaguely.

'Used to,' said Roy. 'Not any more. Once it was the Ten Commandments. Now it's a comedy show on telly.'

June sighed. Gloomy old bugger, she thought. You try to change the subject, but he always brings it back to the same old thing: how much better people were in *his* young days.

'Take the youth today,' he continued, 'don't want to work, don't want to do nothing except pick up their dole money. And then it's down to the betting shop or the pub with it. When me and Grace was courting, no nice girl would be seen dead in a pub. You had Lyons tea rooms, or the Cadena, and it was your own hard-earned wages you spent. *And* there was no larking about afterwards.'

Not half, thought June. Unless human nature's changed all of a sudden.

'Me and Alan met in a pub,' she said defiantly.

'Proves my point,' said Roy.

'Met in a pub,' June continued, 'because I was working there.'

'Behind the bar, eh? Well, you see life, I suppose.'

'No,' she said, suddenly sick of his prudish, pernickety ways,

the sentimental harking back to his past, his rose-coloured innocence.

'No, *not* behind the bar. I was the lunchtime entertainment.
The stripper.'

'*June!*'

She saw that she had hurt him; also that he did not know
whether to be more shocked at the idea of her stripping, or of
his son watching.

'In my young day,' he said, tight-lipped, 'a girl'd sooner
have gone to the workhouse than show her body in front of a
load of strange men.'

'I didn't have that choice. My choice were stripping or the
streets. I had Gloria to pay for, after me Mam had told me
to go to London and get myself sorted out. But I didn't want
no abortion. I went ahead and had her. Fed her myself: that's
why me figure was big. So I stripped, to keep us both. It were
the easiest way for a girl with no exams and no references to
make money. I was nineteen, Dad, remember that.'

Roy couldn't bring himself to look at her. He was fussing
about with a dustpan and brush. It gave him an excuse to
bend down and avoid her eyes.

Right, she thought, so he's shocked. She was angry with
herself for having hurt him, yet relieved that he knew the
truth about her. Why should I be ashamed? It could have
been worse. I could have gone on the game – plenty did, and
I had a good body. Still have, as if anyone cared. All I did
was show it: look, don't touch, and three pounds ten an hour.
Bloody good money in 1971. His precious Alan couldn't keep
his eyes off me. Poor sod, with his prim and proper upbringing,
glad enough to have a chance to stare.

She'd made up her mind to go for Alan the very first time
he'd talked to her. The publican liked her to mingle with the
customers afterwards; it made them stay on for extra rounds
of drinks. She had liked Alan's strong, healthy looks; soon
found out that he had a steady job, nothing criminal; and,
most important of all, he lived on his own. There'd be no
interfering parents to put him off her, just because she was a
stripper and had an illegitimate child. So she'd set her cap at

him, twirling and gyrating just for him, and Alan knew it. He was flattered and excited and vulnerable.

Within a week they were sleeping together; within a month he'd talked her out of the job as a stripper. OK, she had said, but if I stop, how am I to earn my keep, and Gloria's? *I* will, he said; simple as that. She was nineteen, he was twenty-three, but there was no doubt which of them was more wordly-wise.

Roy was shuffling about in the larder, getting out the ingredients for God knows what: suet pudding or jam roly-poly or another of those big, heavy dishes that she could hardly persuade Billy and Joe to eat, not even to please Grandad. Oh God, she thought, he tries his best, poor sod; we all try our best, whatever he thinks.

There was a long, reproachful silence. Why the hell should I apologize, she thought, though I know that's what he's waiting for. Sorry I told you the truth, at last? Sorry I earned my keep in the only way I could? Sorry for being alive, and human, and young? She pushed her hands up inside her sleeves and clutched at her shoulders. She longed to scratch and mar the pale, freckled skin with her nails, or to watch a knife make its delicate incision – the fine parting of the flesh, the breath-holding moment until the bright line of blood sprang up.

'I'll go and get the boys from school,' she said. 'Might all muck about at the recreation ground for half an hour or so before I bring them home for their tea.' Anything to get out.

'Please yourself,' he said, his voice shaking a little. 'I'll hang their washing out on the line and get tea going; lay the table. Don't mind me.' Rather do it on my own, he thought.

She withdrew one hand from her sleeve, touched his arm and forced him to look at her. 'It were ever such a long time ago now, Dad,' she said. 'Twenty years.'

'Yes,' he said. 'And did you make him happy?' he continued unforgivably. 'Why else is my son dead?'

The front door slammed behind her and its stained-glass flower panels rattled. In the kitchen Roy stood up, his eyes opaque with tears.

*

At least once a week – perhaps more often, if he stopped to count – Roy would go and see Molly. Brisk, practical and unsentimental, she redressed the balance between his expectations of June and the disappointing reality. 'I grant you she ain't no plaster saint,' Molly told him. 'She ain't never going to be Radio One's housewife of the year; I won't even say Alan couldn't maybe have done better for himself. But she ain't a bad girl. She's had a hard life and she hasn't gone under, though plenty do. Is she on the bottle? No. Pills? No. In the nut house? No. Did she run 'ome to her Mum when that first one was born, dunno her name, the girl – no, she did not. So she took her clothes off. Is there more shame in showing or looking? And your Ally was there looking, weren't he?

'And then, later on, when they was married – and don't you kid yourself, he weren't easy – she stuck by Alan, would've waited for him and been there when he come out of prison, the which he never did, more's the pity. But she *waited*.'

'Gracie waited five years for me, all through the war,' Roy said indignantly.

'Mebbe she did,' Molly riposted, 'but there's plenty as didn't. I'm telling you that June's a good lass, when all's said and done. She done a good job with them boys. Bright as Scouts' buttons, both of 'em. Good-looking lads, too. I see trouble ahead. You listen to me, darlin': by her lights June hasn't made a bad go of things. She ain't Grace, that I grant; she ain't Molly Tucker, neither.' Molly cackled. 'Gotta praise meself, you see, 'cos no one else won't do it.'

'Am I asking too much, then?' Roy asked.

'Too much? You ain't asking enough, sonny Jim!' said Molly. 'Time you was getting back to cook those lads their tea. Now don't you be too hard on June. Give her a smile when you get in, show her you've forgotten your quarrel. Remember what the Bible says? "Let not the sun go down upon thy wrath".'

Several days later, having made a number of hard but liberating decisions, Liz Franks was buoyed up by weightless exhilaration. She had advertised the MG in a local and a specialist paper, and received a gratifying number of calls asking for more details. The house had been discussed with various estate agents. The first had pointed out that, thanks to the recession in the South-east, the bottom had fallen out of the house market. Most clients' expectations were still pitched too high, and a house was worth only what someone was willing to pay for it. 'You forget,' Liz told her witheringly, 'that I, too, am a businesswoman.'

The second was more optimistic, reassuring her about how desirable the street was, how pretty the house, and what an excellent opportunity its purchase offered, always providing it were realistically priced. But asked to dispose of the shop lease and business as well, even he jutted his lower lip and turned his gaze upwards in a parody of thoughtful misgiving.

'It's up to you,' she said. 'I don't want to deal with half a dozen different agencies. If you want to sell the house, I'd require you to dispose of the shop as well. Preferably first,' she added. 'For a number of personal reasons I am anxious to leave Tunbridge Wells as quickly as possible.'

The car sold first, at a price several hundred pounds higher than her worst estimate. Liz opened an account in Lissy's name without telling her, and put a thousand pounds into it. A red banner in the shop window, the biggest yet, proclaimed ONE WEEK ONLY! CLOSING DOWN SALE! MAKE ME AN OFFER FOR ANY GARMENT! When that's over, she thought, I'll put the best of the rest in to a large suitcase, put the very best on my own back, and set off to the south of France. In the last days of the sale she let things go for practically any price offered, refused to take credit cards, and prayed that the cheques wouldn't bounce.

Constance Liddell, the librarian, came in one evening just as she was about to close. 'You can't!' she said in dismay. 'For the first time in my life I find someone who really knows what suits me. You *can't* shut up shop! Where are you going?'

'I'm not absolutely certain,' Liz told her, 'but I'm heading first for the south of France. If that's no good I thought I might try Italy. But, tell me, how did the dinner go? It was you, wasn't it?'

Constance blushed charmingly. 'Very well,' she said, primly.

'Now don't give me that!' Liz coaxed. 'It went much better than that, judging by the look on your face.'

'Too early to tell,' said Constance, 'but he wants to see me again and he seems great. He's not married, not dirt-poor, not half-witted, and, above all, *not Polish!*'

Liz smiled. 'Well, anyway, good luck.' On impulse, she scooped a wine-red Italian dress from its hanger and thrust it into Constance's astonished grasp. 'Here!' she said. 'Take this for the next dinner. It's a present.'

'I couldn't possibly,' Constance protested.

'Go on, have it. It's your size. Wish me luck as well. God knows, I *need* it.'

'You are an angel.' Constance put her arms round Liz and kissed her on both cheeks. 'Good *luck*,' she said intensely. 'I wish we'd known each other properly before . . . and now you're going away. *Best* of luck.'

Confronting the bank manager was simplicity itself compared with her dread of telling Reggie what she had decided. Whittington was unctuous and smug, fulsome in his praise of her good sense and good timing; over-anxious to be helpful, now that she no longer needed his help. Liz commented on the change.

'Well, now you see, Mrs Franks,' he said in his nasal whine, 'banks can be very accommodating when customers take their advice.'

Stung by his pompous self-righteousness she flashed back, 'I assure you, Mr Whittington, I do *not* order my life to gain the approval of bank clerks!' Fool, she thought. Now you've made another enemy.

Reginald, after nearly a month in hospital, was evidently starting to walk about. He rang her from time to time on the ward's mobile phone. His voice was growing clearer too, and his former bark had given way to a more sibilant, liquid speech. When he rang the shop, it was easy enough to put him off. When he rang her at home in the evening, it was harder to know what to say. She was determined not to break the news over the telephone, yet she could not respond falsely to his tender murmurings and hints about their future together. She told him she was 'winding things up' and 'closing the shop', and left him to make what he could of that.

Eventually she could put off seeing him no longer. She had spent hours mentally playing through the conversation, working out what she would say, trying to anticipate his response, trying to cause the least amount of pain. These internal dialogues, in which she wrote and performed both parts, grew into a deafening cacophony. It was simpler to tell him and get it over. I never meant to hurt him, poor old heffalump, she thought. I may have been greedy and manipulative and vain, but I didn't mean to be *wicked*. But I cannot tie myself to an invalid whom I scarcely know and – let us face it – from whom there is nothing to be gained except boredom and exasperated pity on my side.

She dressed in black trousers and a tobacco-brown silk shirt, with flat black shoes, little make-up and a melancholy, dusty scent. In the ten minutes or so that it took to walk to the hospital she tried to make her mind a blank, to clear its ether of the clamorous voices that had rehearsed this conversation for so long, so that her actual words would be simple, gentle and spontaneous.

She walked into the ward. Reginald was sitting fully dressed on his bed, facing the door. He had not been forewarned of her coming, but he was alone. His rubicund face was set in lines of despondency which flamed into eagerness the moment he caught sight of her.

'Darling!' he called out. 'There she ish,' he commented in an aside to the old man in the bed next to his. 'Tol' you. Thash my fianshée.'

'Liz!' he called again. He held out both hands and drew her towards him, carrying her knuckles one by one to his lips. 'My darling,' he murmured, 'I've been longin' to shee you.'

'Reggie,' she said. 'Sweetie, is there anywhere private we can go and talk?'

'Only the day room. It's where I have to go to smoke. They try to stop me smoking. Southgate brings me them. Decent of him. The room will stink of cigarettes. But it's quiet.'

'Let's go there,' she said. He put his feet on the floor and she hooked an arm under his and supported his weight as he walked along. She knew he must be doing his best, but all the same, his shoes shuffled along the smooth polished vinyl.

She moved tattered piles of old magazines so that they could settle down side by side on a collapsing sofa. A crude ashtray shaped from silver-foil stood on a spindly occasional table. Reggie lit her cigarette and his own, and, turning her chin towards him, he said her name, its one syllable top-heavy with emotion.

'Liz . . . How are you? How have you been?'

'I'm all right,' she said. 'What about you?'

'I'm getting better. They are good here. They are teaching me to walk and talk again, just as though I'd pranged myself. It's hard work. I try and go twice round the ward every morning and afternoon, and I make myself walk right down the corridor every day. But I am getting better. They say I can probably go home in about a week.'

'Good,' she said. 'Well done. Is it very tiring?'

'Yes,' he admitted. 'I am exhausted after going down the corridor and back. I have to lie down and rest. But I *can* walk, though I still need a stick. When they first brought me in, I was almost paralysed all down here.' He indicated his right side.

'How awful,' she said. There was a silence. With an effort, he broke it.

'You said you were selling up,' he began. 'Is it because of me?'

She could not bear the unexpressed hope in his voice. 'In a way. Not really.'

'Are you going to come and live with me when I come out? We can marry straightaway, if you want. Or we could wait and see how I get on. You don't have to. I don't want to tie you down. You're still young. My darling.'

This was it. A great heaviness settled over her. She would have liked to live in deafness and dumbness rather than utter the next words. There was a rushing in her ears. She took his hand between hers and swivelled her knees towards him.

'Reginald,' she said. 'I have done wrong. I can't marry you. I should never have agreed. I am going away – almost at once. Abroad.'

'Where are you going?' he asked, pointlessly. The lips continue to move, we say the right thing, the thing that is expected of us, even at moments when the fulcrum of our lives wobbles.

Liz inhaled deeply and flicked the ash.

'I am going to the south of France, to look for my ex-husband. He's there somewhere, and I think I ought to tell him that we will soon be grandparents.'

'No!' he said in amazement. 'You? I thought *we* might have a baby. A son. You can't be a grandmother?'

'Oh Reggie,' she said. 'Oh darling. I am fifty-two. I'm past having children. I couldn't possibly have given you a son.'

'No? It seemed such a lovely idea. What would we have called him, I wonder?'

'*Not Vivian,*' she said.

'I quite agree. *Not* Vivian.' They smiled at each other. 'I never thought you were fifty-two.'

'You're so sweet,' she said. 'Oh Reggie, darling, you *are* so sweet; but I am going to leave you. There's no point in saying sorry or anything. I won't even say I'd never have made you happy. But I'm not a very nice person.'

'And I am old and fat and ill, not rich or sexually attractive,' he said. 'But it was wonderful, that night. Will I see you again?'

The cigarette was burning his fingertips. She took it from him and crushed it in the silver-foil ashtray.

'No, I don't think so,' she said. 'Though you never know.'

'I thought I was good at goodbyes. God knows, I've had plenty of practice. All my life people went away; usually because they died. You don't know how many people have died. At least you're not dying. You do look lovely. Is it some man you're going after?'

'It *is* my ex-husband,' she said. 'Honestly. I haven't seen him for several years. I don't know exactly where he is. I've only got a postmark to go by. I just somehow felt he ought to know that his daughter, our daughter, is expecting a baby.'

'Quite right. Well, now what's left for me to do? I'd better go after *my* wife. Mary.'

'Don't be bitter. Please don't say anything else, I couldn't bear it. Please don't see me out. Please don't think ill of me. Oh Reggie, please don't . . .'

The tears were misting her sight as she leaned forward and kissed him on both cheeks; they gathered in the corners of her eyes as she stood up, and ran down the side of her nose and into the lines that bracketed her mouth as she left the ward, so she could not turn round for a last wave. Not waiting for the lift, she went down the stairs into a balmy September afternoon, to find a gardener cutting the grass and buses plying the route up and down Mount Ephraim Road.

Vivian Blythgowrie had spent five demanding days on business in Hong Kong and was feeling jet-lagged and irritable. His uncle's problems could hardly have come at a more inconvenient time. Susan had promised to look into local nursing homes. Once she had found somewhere suitable, it was just a matter of making sure that Liz had been seen off. He hoped he would not have to pay her to go away but had mentally set a figure of £15,000 as his highest offer. The Blythgowrie Trust had a discreet contingencies fund. It had dealt with Celia's lamentable drugs episode under the heading of 'health problems'. It could pay off Liz.

Reginald was sitting fully dressed on the side of his bed. The expression on his face was utterly woebegone. He was not reading, not listening to the radio, not watching the nurses or the ward television. He looked like a man who has spent weeks in solitary confinement. As Vivian approached, he detected the whiff of stale cigarette smoke. He handed over *The Times*, *Country Life* and *Punch*, and a lavish bunch of flowers.

'These are from Susan,' he said. 'She sends her love.'

Reggie barely gave him time for the pleasantries before he said, his diction a good deal clearer than last time, 'Wha' did you tell her? What did you say to *Liz*?'

'Why?'

'Answer me!'

'Isn't there somewhere else we can talk?' asked Vivian, scenting trouble and unwilling to continue the conversation in a public ward. Reginald heaved himself upright and shambled down the corridor, stopping beside a large window with a railing in front of it. He leaned against the railing, rummaged in his pocket for a cigarette and lit it.

'I say, old man,' Vivian objected priggishly, 'I'm quite sure you aren't allowed to –'

'I want to know what you *said to her*?' Reginald interrupted.

'I told her about your, well, you know, your set-up.'

'What do you mean, my set-up?'

'How you were placed. That is, financially. More or less . . .'

'How dare you?' raged Reginald. His eyes blazed with fury. 'How *dare* you take it upon yourself to interfere! What gave you that right?'

'Calm down, Uncle. No need to get in such a state. You'll do yourself damage.'

'Don't patronize me, Vivian. What exactly did you say?'

'I said very little, as far as I remember. I said, I think, that you were tolerably well off but could not afford to live in great style. To ensure that she had no false expectations.'

'Thanks to you,' said Reggie, his voice flat and final, 'she's gone away. Abroad. Left me. My one hope of happiness.'

'Better off without her,' said Vivian. 'It just proves that she was only after you because she thought you were rich.'

'*Of course* she thought I was rich. I meant her to think I was rich. For God's sake, you fool, why *else* should a good-looking girl of her age marry me?'

'I would be grateful if you could avoid abusive language. That woman was no "girl". She was well into her fifties, by my reckoning,' said Vivian self-righteously.

'Liz Franks was fifty-two. She was beautiful, vivacious, and very attractive to me – yes, I mean *sexually* attractive. What is a marvellous girl like that *supposed* to love me for, you pompous, interfering prat, except money?'

It was many years since anyone had used such ephithets to Vivian Blythgowrie. He contrived, as always, to conceal his emotions behind a mask of self-control, but inwardly he was seething. First there had been that calculating tart with her outrageous allegations; and now Reginald, a clapped-out old fogey, was making remarks that were simply inexcusable. An idle parasite who had depended throughout his life on his, Vivian's generosity: how dared he call him names? Come along, he told himself, calm down. Remember that the man is your uncle; he is elderly and he has been very ill. It must have affected his mind.

'Let us say no more about it. I assumed you wouldn't wish to marry a gold-digger,' Vivian said icily, 'and on that basis – '

'I wanted to marry *Liz*,' Reggie retorted. 'I'm not such an idiot as to imagine that she loved me for my character or my good looks. But she wanted a comfortable life and I wanted *her*. You would rather I had found some dry, upper-crust widow – that *would* have met with your approval. Come off your high horse, Vivian. You don't think Susan, ten years younger than you, and, if I remember rightly, a top model girl at the time, married you for your *character*? She married you because she liked the idea of having a title, and you married her because you wanted an heir. It's what the upper classes have always married for. So out went poor Geraldine, you hung on to the girls (never understood how you got away with that), and in came a younger, better-looking wife. As it happens, *she* hasn't given you an heir, either. Time for a change of model soon, eh, Vivian?'

'There is no need to be offensive,' Vivian said, still containing his anger, although Reginald's analysis was spot on. Much as he resented having his marriage exposed, he had never seen his normally affable, easy-going uncle so enraged. One more outburst might bring on another stroke.

Reginald stamped out his cigarette on the grey-and-white vinyl floor and turned to his nephew. 'You haven't yet answered my question. What made you think you were entitled to poke your nose in my business?'

'Because I am the head of the family and, as such, the guardian of its interests.'

'Did it never cross your mind,' said Reginald, 'as you sprang to the defence of the family money – of which, incidentally, there is more, *much* more than enough – that I might *love* Liz Franks? That I wanted to marry her whatever her reasons? And that I have no chance, now, of finding anyone else? That thanks to you, damn you, I have had my *last fuck?*'

Vivian saw his opportunity and seized the initiative. 'Spare me,' he said with distaste, 'the details of your erotic activities. I intervened in this preposterous so-called engagement in your own best interests. Events have proved me absolutely right. If that woman had felt any real affection for you, she would not have decamped as soon as she found out how you stood financially. I was perfectly justified in doing what I did, and I take great exception to your remarks. I am now returning to London. If you want to see any other member of the family, you have only to ask. Susan is making inquiries as to a suitable local nursing home, since you are clearly unfit to live alone. The Trust will cover its costs, until your house is sold. That's it. Nothing else. Goodbye, Uncle Reginald.'

The sound of their argument had penetrated to Sister's office. As Vivian's footsteps strode purposefully away down the corridor, she emerged.

'What the dickens is going on?' she asked '*Mr* Conynghame-Jervis! You know very well that smoking is not permitted, above all not to you; and the doctor has warned you about getting over-excited. You really *must* . . .' Her voice trailed off as she took his wrist between a cool, professional finger and thumb and glanced down at her watch. 'Go and lie on your bed,' she ordered. 'I will ask a nurse to come and give you something to calm you down. That pulse-rate is far too high. If this is the effect of visitors, we shall have to ban them.'

Then she smiled. 'With the possible exception of that good-looking fiancée of yours! When is *she* coming again?'

'Never,' said Reginald, with finality. 'Never.'

He shuffled laboriously back to the ward muttering under his breath, 'Never again, never again. I am old and I shall never fuck again.'

Chapter Seventeen

Once or twice a week Roy went up to The Cedars to collect the Squadron Leader's post (if any) and make sure all was well. He would run a duster over the dining table and sideboard, slip a freshly heated hot-water bottle between the clean sheets with which he had made up the beds, and throw open the windows so that fresh autumnal air billowed the curtains and stirred up the motionless rooms. It was something he could do to help the poor chap and it gave him a much-needed break from the clatter and rumpus of his own house.

June made efforts to please him, although within a day or two she usually reverted to her own slapdash ways. She had no routine, but wandered through each day doing the chores at different times, and sometimes not doing them at all. Why doesn't she make the beds as soon as the boys have gone off to school? Roy thought in exasperation. Then tidy up the kitchen, put their dirty clothes in the machine, go to the shops while that's doing ... Behind his impatience lay the real question: why isn't she more like Grace?

He couldn't see why June took so much trouble over her looks, putting her hair in curlers each night and making up her face for half an hour each morning, although she hadn't a man to primp for. He wondered, he admitted guiltily to himself, how she felt without a man in her bed. But she left her arms alone; the cuts had healed to faint brown lines, and though she was often short with the boys, she had managed to govern her tongue with him since their last upset.

Billy and Joe were clever boys who thrived in the new school and, although at first they grumbled about their homework, they were soon getting good marks.

'Look what my teacher put, Grandad,' little Joe said, showing him an arithmetic book with '7/10 – well done, Joe! A very good start!' written at the end of some exercise. Roy peered at the complicated rows of figures.

'It's not a bit like the sums we did when I was a lad,' he said, feigning stupidity so that Joe would have to explain. 'How do you work out these difficult figures?'

'It's *easy* with a calculator,' Joe told him, and he demonstrated patiently how it was done, his stubby fingers and bitten nails darting confidently over the numbered rubber squares.

'Isn't that cheating?' Roy asked. 'Aren't you meant to work it out in your head? Mental arithmetic, *we* used to call it.'

'*No*, Grandad!' Joe scoffed. 'You do it on the calculator. Everyone does. It still doesn't mean it's a doddle 'cos you have to get the working method right else it doesn't come out.'

Such moments made up for the loss of his peace and privacy. He hankered for an afternoon nap that was not punctuated by the background roar of TV laughter rising to a crescendo and dying down to shrill yappings of hysteria. On other days the theme tune from one of June's favourite programmes would nag insistently in his head, interrupting his thoughts, imposing itself until he eased his legs off the bed and abandoned all hope of sleep.

As September presaged October, the weather became raw. Roy found himself acutely aware of the progress of the seasons. The days shortened, the street lights came on earlier, people's windows turned to golden squares suddenly obliterated by drawn curtains. Up at the allotment his plants grew brown and died. Trees took on the fading bronze of autumn. All flesh is grass, he remembered from the funeral service, and his own wrinkled, laborious flesh seemed out of place next to the vigour and tautness of the boys' limbs. Roy felt sure they must find him physically repulsive and tried not to upset them by contact with his skin or his smell. He got up early to use the bathroom before anyone else was about, shuffling through his ablutions with a new disgust for his own bodily decay.

Grace and her lingering, pervasive presence had almost vanished. She had come to represent all the lost sweetness of his life; the happy, haloed times. Those days had ended with

Alan's trial, his prison sentence and his death – images which still cut like scissors through the tissue paper in which Roy's imagination tried to swathe them. He had apologized to June for his cruel accusation, and after that neither of them ever mentioned Alan's name. Occasionally Roy found himself thinking wistfully about Sheila.

One afternoon, well over a month since the day when Reginald had been taken away by ambulance, Roy arrived at The Cedars to find a number of large brown envelopes lying on the doormat. Might as well drop them off at the hospital, he thought. It was on his way home and he hadn't seen the Squadron Leader since that dramatic afternoon when they had all been gathered round his bed – Mrs Franks and His Lordship and Sister.

He took the lift to the third floor and walked into the ward. The bed was empty. He stopped one of the bustling nurses in mid-stride. 'Where's the Squadron Leader?'

'Who? Bed number four? He was moved to another ward, couple of days ago. I wasn't on shift. You'd better find Sister: she'll know.'

Roy found Sister, pen to her lips, scrutinizing a patient's chart, and waited meekly until she had finished.

She looked up. 'Oh, it's you. You're Mr C-J's friend, if I remember? I'm very sorry to have to tell you he's had another stroke. It often happens that one follows another, especially if the patient hasn't had complete peace and quiet. We don't think this one is as serious as the first; but it's not a good sign. Just when he was doing so well! We can't keep him here much longer: we're desperately short of beds. You'll find him in ward number three – second on the left. He could do with cheering up – he's not had many visitors. But don't stay long and, whatever you do, don't excite him.'

Roy was shocked by the blank expression on the Squadron Leader's face. All his fighting spirit seemed to have gone. His mouth sagged open like that of a dead man, his hands lay slackly uncurled on top of the bedcover. Roy approached gingerly, half hoping to be able to leave the envelopes and go.

As he came close, Reginald's eyes opened.

'Hey-o,' he said. 'Ishyou.'

'Hello, sir. I was up at your house just now, making sure everything was all right, and I thought I'd pop in with your letters, case any was urgent. How are you?'

The liquid sound Reggie uttered could have meant 'lousy' or 'drowsy'. 'I won't stay long, sir. Sister said you mustn't be excited. I'm ever so sorry you had another attack. You was doing so well.'

Reggie made another wetly explosive noise: 'passed out', perhaps; or more likely 'bastard'. He held out his left hand for the letters, but hardly glanced at them before letting them fall on to the bed.

'Is there any you'd like me to read out to you?' Roy inquired, but Reginald shook his head.

'Keep your pecker up, Squadron Leader,' Roy urged. 'You're not the sort to give in. I was saying to June, that's my daughter-in-law, the one who lives with me now, you remember? – her and the boys? – well, I was saying to June, he's got such spirit, one look at him and you can see why we won the Battle of Britain.'

Reginald ignored this. Without even attempting a smile he pulled at Roy's sleeve. Roy bent closer. Reggie tried to whisper something, but try as he might, Roy could not get his meaning.

'It's warm?' he guessed. 'Undone?'

Reginald made sketching gestures.

'You want to write it down?'

Reggie nodded. Roy found an old envelope in his jacket pocket and a pencil on the bedside table. He propped Reggie up in bed, noticing how much lighter he was. In big wavy capitals, using his left hand, Reggie wrote: LIZ GONE. As though worn out by the effort, he fell back against the pillows and closed his eyes again.

Roy stayed beside the bed, trying to gather his thoughts.

'*You* remember that night we danced together, sir: New Year's Eve? That must have been a lonely sight, you and me, two blokes dancing. But it wasn't too bad, was it? All the old songs. That was only six months after your wife died, and my Grace. We was getting better already. Or there was the evening we sat over dinner – terrific storm that night, unless I'm mistaken – and I told you the story of Grace and the goose? We forgot our troubles that night, didn't we, sir? There was other times, too, out on the back terrace. You'll see: things pass, no matter how bad it looks at first. They say time heals and it's true, honest to God. It'll be the same with Mrs Franks. Main thing now is for you to get *better*. Buck up, sir. You got to make up your mind to it, eh?'

Roy looked into Reginald's face for some flicker of acknowledgement, but there was none. He stood irresolutely beside the bed for another moment or two, then gripped the Squadron Leader's shoulder, patted his arm and said, 'Chin up, sir!' Then he walked away.

The sight of the Squadron Leader brought so low, all the fight gone out of him, troubled Roy. His own heart had been bothering him lately. There was a roaring in his ears sometimes, a rhythmical thunder like the sound of the sea in a shell. Who would look after him if he had a stroke? Not June, that was certain. He booked an appointment with his doctor and spent an anxious hour in the waiting room amid the débris of winter colds and flu. Whining children were getting under people's feet, trying to play with broken plastic toys and being snapped at by their weary mothers. Why didn't they wipe their noses and tell them to *sit still*? he wondered. He picked up a copy of *Waterways World* but could not concentrate.

Finally it was his turn. He described his symptoms. The doctor took his blood pressure and said, 'Nothing much wrong with that! Let's shine some light in your ears.' A chill, pointed tube was inserted into Roy's obediently inclined ears, first one side and then the other. He felt his heartbeat accelerate.

'Problem solved!' said the doctor. 'Cerumen, that's all it is. Build-up of wax in the ears. I'll give you some oil to dislodge it. You'll be surprised how much better you can hear afterwards, too.'

'But my heart, doctor?' asked Roy.

'Going like a metronome. Heart of man fifteen years younger. No worries there. You're in very good shape for your age. What are you? Seventy?'

'Seventy-two – nearly seventy-three,' said Roy.

'What did I tell you? Fit as a fiddle! Good for you.'

The doctor warmed some oil in a tiny phial, poured it into Roy's ears and plugged them with cotton wool.

'Wait outside for ten minutes or so,' he said, 'and that will melt the cerumen. Come back in between patients – I'll tell the nurse – and I'll syringe them for you. OK?'

'Yes, doctor,' Roy said, docile and trusting.

When his ears had been syringed, wiped, inspected, shaken and tested – and it was true: he *could* hear better – the doctor scribbled something on to a prescription pad and tore it off.

'Here you are. In case it builds up again. As an OAP you won't have anything to pay. Very good day to you, Mr Southgate.'

As he left the surgery, Roy felt light-hearted and proud of himself. He stopped at the chemist on his way home and picked up his prescription. He told June what the doctor had said. 'Heart of a man fifteen years younger . . .' When the boys got home, he told them, too. 'Your old Grandad's got the heart of a man fifteen years younger!'

Finally, June said, 'Oh put a sock in it, Dad! We've all heard it by now.'

He was hurt, and retreated upstairs to write a letter to Vera. *She* would be glad to hear his news.

From his bedroom he could hear the television blaring more loudly than ever. The boys ought to be doing their homework, not watching rubbish. June was obviously in there with them, laughing away. Nobody takes responsibility round here except me, he thought querulously. She's almost as much of a child as they are! He heard the telephone ring, and opened his bedroom door.

'I'll go!' June sang up the stairs, and called out to the boys, 'Turn the blasted telly down, will you?'

He shut the door again, but with his newly cleaned ears he could hear what she was saying and it was evident that she was talking to a man.

'All right, love,' Roy heard, 'I'm impatient too, but it's not *easy* . . .' Then she lowered her voice, so that Roy couldn't catch her words. He went to his door and opened it a wedge.

'I'll be down the pub later on, then,' she was saying, in a hoarse whisper. 'I'll be there before closing time. He'll be asleep by then. Poor old sod: early to bed, early to rise – I don't know why he bothers. Kept saying all day long he's got the heart of a man fifteen years younger. What the hell *for*? I wanted to say. Might as well be dead as live like him. Still, if it weren't for him I'd never have met you, would I, eh? Think of that!'

There was a pause, and then she laughed. 'He can babysit – not that he'll know it! Don't matter, so long as they're not alone. Wouldn't be the first time.' There was another pause, and then Roy, straining his ears, heard June say, 'Me too, darling, me too. Well, see how it goes. I'm not promising. And I can't stay the whole night.'

Roy shut the door silently before the conversation ended. His face burned, partly from shame for having eavesdropped, partly from outrage at what he had heard. Alan was scarcely three months dead and already she was making secret assignations! It isn't right, he thought – and using me as their baby-sitter, too. He was tempted to go down and confront her, to reveal what he had heard, but he knew he was in the wrong. Least said, soonest mended: no good creating a fuss now. 'Eavesdroppers never hear good of themselves,' Grace would have said, and she'd have been right.

Hastily he finished off his letter to Vera:

So there it is, Vera, love: your old Dad's got the heart of a 55-year old! What do you think of that, not bad, eh? Well, that's all for now. June and the boys send their love. Next week I'll start Christmas shopping so you get the parcel in good time. Any ideas, better let me know quickly.

Ever your loving Dad

He licked the three sides of the airletter and stuck it down, addressed it and walked downstairs. June was in the kitchen ironing a blouse.

'Just nipping out to post this,' he said.

'When will you be back?' she asked.

'Won't be long. Might look in at the pub for a Guinness.'

'But you'll be back to say goodnight to the boys?' she persisted.

'Bound to be.'

He took his cap and jacket from the hallstand and walked out into the foggy October evening, banging the door on the hullabaloo that had taken over his quiet refuge, the home that he and Grace had built. We come a long way, he thought, me and her. I started off in a seaside boarding house, and Lord knows how many nights I had to sleep in the same bed with my Grandma, her snoring like a train letting off steam, and when I got too big for that, sleeping under the kitchen table to make room for any latecomer who could pay a bob or two for my bed. Grace came from respectable people; not church-goers – Quakers, they were, but hard-working folk. No luxuries for *us* as kiddies. From that early hardship we built our own comfort; from blunt words and no nonsense we taught each other tenderness; from uncertainty we created security, for each other and for the children. June is trampling over all that, undoing the effort of years with her slovenly ways.

It's not working, he thought, all four of us living together. He corrected himself: it's working for them but not for me. The boys are happier and healthier, cleaner and better behaved; even their language has improved. June's a long way from the chain-smoking slut she was that day when I broke the news about Alan and found her with her arms cut to pieces, blood oozing through the tissues she'd stuck all over herself. Face it, Roy: it's three against one. You can't throw them out. But oh, he thought, my peace is gone – how all my peace is gone!

He dropped his letter disconsolately into the box outside

the post office, waited for the sound of its rustle, but instead of heading towards the Downs Tavern, he set off briskly, or as briskly as his legs could manage in the damp evening air, down Woodbury Park Road. He knew that all day he had been resisting the temptation to go and share his troubles with Molly. He could resist no longer.

Her curtains were drawn, but light shone behind the front door. Roy rang the bell, heard shuffling feet, and the door opened a couple of inches, stopped by the safety-chain. Molly peered shortsightedly into the darkness.

'Who's there?'

'It's me. Roy.'

'Speak up. Who is it?'

This time Roy heard the undertone of fear in her voice. Much more loudly, he said, 'Roy Southgate. It's me, Molly. Can I come in?'

'What you doing at this hour? Another ten minutes and I'd have been getting ready to turn in. Come on, I'll make you some hot chocolate.'

In Molly's kitchen the table was already laid for breakfast. A blue-and-white-striped egg cup, one side-plate, one teacup and saucer, a knife, teaspoon, salt cellar and a jar of marmalade with a jam spoon on a dish were arranged ready for the next morning. She stood with her back to him heating milk at the stove. Roy told her about the telephone conversation he had overheard.

'Serves you right!' she scolded. 'Eavesdroppers never hear good of themselves!'

'I never thought to see the day . . . under my own roof, she was arranging to meet some fellow she can't hardly know, since she's only been here seven or eight weeks . . . and Alan dead three months! Makes you think, don't it? I'm that ashamed.'

'Ashamed of yourself, I hope.'

'I were so full of myself earlier on – what with the doctor saying I had the heart of a man fifteen years younger –'

'*Did* he?' she exclaimed. 'Well that's good news!'

'Yes, he did, not that June cared.'

'No reason why she should. But *I* care. Look here, Roy Southgate, I'll wait no longer to say what's staring you in the face. You ought to ask me to marry you, then you can give up what ain't right or proper and ain't never going to work – which is trying to live under one roof with that young woman and two young lads. You can move in with me.'

Roy looked at her. He was flattered, shocked, amazed.

'Well!' he said. 'You take the biscuit! Well! Bless me if I don't know what to say!'

'I told you what you got to say. You got to ask me to marry you.'

'Do you want to?'

'Course I do!'

'Will you?'

'Yes.'

'Look out – the milk's boiling over.'

'Are you going to give me a kiss?' she said. 'Or do I have to do everything for you?'

He put his arms round her, felt the soft loops of her flesh under his hands, smelled the dry, crisp smell of her dyed blonde curls, saw the grey springing through at their roots, touched the pale wrinkles of her lips, looked into the curving folds around her eyes. He bent his head towards her, smelled the soap on her skin, and had just time to see her smile before he closed his eyes and kissed her.

'Will you marry me, Molly?'

'I told you, yes. We don't have to . . . you know . . . *do* anything if you don't want – if you can't manage, it won't matter.'

'I expect it'll take a bit of time,' Roy said. He felt foolish because he couldn't stop himself smiling and he felt she wanted to be serious.

'What you grinning about?' asked Molly.

'We'll have to get used to each other.' He smiled again.

'You know something, Roy Southgate?'

'What's that?'

'You look happy. You look really and truly happy, for the first time in a year.'

He had nearly forgotten what his own laugh sounded like. It was hoarse and squeaky, both at once.

Just before Christmas, Roy set out to visit the Squadron Leader in the Three Pines Nursing Home, only a few doors down from The Cedars in Nevill Park. He went to the house first to pick up the post. There was a For Sale board up outside. He let himself in and picked up a handful of square white envelopes from the doormat, to which he added the Christmas card from himself and Molly. The radiators hadn't been turned on all autumn and the rooms were cold and silent. There were dust-sheets covering the furniture in the drawing-room. The mantelpiece had a fine layer of powdery dust and the little carriage clock with the sweet high chime had stopped.

Roy rubbed the dining table with the back of his sleeve, but the broad shining sweep of darker mahogany only emphasized the unloved look of everything else. Downstairs in the kitchen the stone-flagged floors were clammy and chill. Crockery stood in piles on the kitchen table; a couple of crates filled with newspaper waited on the floor. The refrigerator door was open; nothing inside. In the pantry, a few bags of flour and breakfast cereal and some old coronation cake tins were all that remained. He took a couple of dusters from the drawer at the end of the kitchen table and went back upstairs.

Roy dusted the dining table and the sideboard, checking the drawers where the silver cutlery was kept. It had all gone. He flicked the duster over the mantelpiece in the drawing-room and, on his way past it, the pretty semicircular table with marquetry inlay that stood to one side of the hall. Then he went back to the basement. No point in airing the bedrooms or checking the beds. If I start I'll never stop, he thought. Time to get over to the nursing home.

He put on his hat and coat and new fur-lined gloves and

tucked the Squadron Leader's post into his pocket. Double-locking the front door, he stepped down into the gravelled drive. The leafless roses were dripping and one branch of the big cedar by the front gate was hanging down as though broken by the wind. Roy headed down the road. It was already dusk and Molly would worry if he were late home for his tea.

A harassed young foreign woman – Filipino, perhaps, like some of the cleaners at the hospital – answered the door.

'I've come to see the Squadron Leader,' Roy stated clearly. She looked blank. 'Mr Conynghame-Jervis.' he added.

'Oh, him,' she said. 'Mr Reginald. I think he's in the television room.'

She led the way towards the sound of a raucous children's programme. Seven or eight residents were grouped in a semicircle around the set, some in wheelchairs, others in dressing-gowns. One had a large long-haired cat on his lap, which he was stroking rhythmically. The cat focused its huge orange eyes upon Roy as he stood in the doorway.

He recognized the Squadron Leader more by his dressing-gown than anything else. Dark red and navy stripes separated by a narrow yellow line: Roy had often held it out for him first thing in the morning, after running his bath. He walked towards the dressing-gown.

'Sir!' he said.

Reggie looked up.

'Oh, hello, it's you,' he said, in a single monotonous note.

'How are you, sir?' Roy asked. 'I've brought you your Christmas post.'

'Not too bad,' said Reggie. His gaze returned to the television set.

'Is there a visitor's room?' Roy asked. 'Or can we go to yours?'

'Not now,' said Reginald. 'Soon be suppertime. Not allowed till after supper.'

He put his hands down to the wheels of his chair and began laboriously to propel himself forward.

'Let me push you, sir,' Roy said. 'You just show me the way.'

Reggie waved an arm down the corridor. 'Doesn't matter. Anywhere. It's all the same,' he said.

Roy found that the Squadron Leader's speech was fairly easy to follow once you got used to it, but his mind wandered off. His concentration would falter and, as though he were aware of this, he would quickly ask a question, but one with no apparent point to it.

'When can you come out of here?' Roy asked eventually.

'Don't know,' said Reginald. 'Ask Susan. She found it. Her idea. Do you know where my hat is? If you would find my hat I could go home.'

Alarmed, Roy said, 'No, sir, don't do that.'

'He giving you trouble?' said a nurse, her fixed smile belying the severity of her voice. 'Come on now, Mr Reginald. None of your nonsense. Have you been a bad lad? He probably needs the toilet,' she added in an undertone.

'Shall I take him?' Roy asked.

'He can't manage by himself. It takes two of us. *Do you need the toilet?*' she asked emphatically. 'You haven't been dirty, have you?'

Reggie shook his head.

'He won't do it while you're here,' she said, 'case he's made a mess of himself and we have to clean him up. He doesn't like that. Tries to get cross with us.'

'I must be off now, sir,' said Roy, taking the hint. He swivelled the wheelchair away from the intrusive nurse and wheeled Reginald towards the front door. 'I'll try to visit you once more before Christmas.'

'If you would be kind enough to look out my hat, I could go home,' Reginald said again. 'Don't remember where I put it.'

'I'm afraid it's not as simple as that, sir,' Roy said. 'I'm awfully sorry.' He buttoned his coat, rummaged for his gloves, and settled the cap on his head. He bent towards the Squadron Leader and tried to smile. 'I'll be back soon, see how you're getting on. Not to worry.' As he opened the heavy front door, a nurse came towards them down the corridor.

'Take me with you,' said Reginald urgently. 'Take me with you. I want to go home. Why doesn't someone find Mary and tell her I want to go home?'

'Your wife is dead, sir, you know that, and *I* can't take you with me,' Roy said, gulping. 'I *can't*, sir. I'm married. Me and Molly have got married, that's why I can't. Otherwise, God knows, sir, I would.'

He opened the door.

'Take me home with you,' Reginald implored. 'I want to go home. Don't leave me. Look after me. I will behave myself.'

'*Course* you'll be good, Mr Reginald,' was the last Roy heard as he stepped out into the winter evening.

2203S